COYOTE RISING

COYOTE RISING

A Novel of Interstellar Revolution

ALLEN M. STEELE

ACE BOOKS, NEW YORK

THE BERKLEY PUBLISHING GROUP
Published by the Penguin Group
Penguin Group (USA) Inc.
375 Hudson Street, New York, New York 10014, USA
Penguin Group (Canada), 10 Alcorn Avenue, Toronto, Ontario M4V 3B2, Canada
(a division of Pearson Penguin Canada Inc.)
Penguin Books Ltd., 80 Strand, London WC2R 0RL, England
Penguin Group Ireland, 25 St. Stephen's Green, Dublin 2, Ireland (a division of Penguin Books Ltd.)
Penguin Group (Australia), 250 Camberwell Road, Camberwell, Victoria 3124, Australia
(a division of Pearson Australia Group Pty. Ltd.)
Penguin Books India Pvt. Ltd., 11 Community Centre, Panchsheel Park, New Delhi—110 017, India
Penguin Group (NZ), Cnr. Airborne and Rosedale Roads, Albany, Auckland 1310, New Zealand
(a division of Pearson New Zealand Ltd.)
Penguin Books (South Africa) (Pty.) Ltd., 24 Sturdee Avenue, Rosebank, Johannesburg 2196, South Africa

Penguin Books Ltd., Registered Offices: 80 Strand, London WC2R 0RL, England

This is a work of fiction. Names, characters, places, and incidents either are the product of the author's imagination or are used fictitiously, and any resemblance to actual persons, living or dead, business establishments, events, or locales is entirely coincidental.

The material in this book has been previously published, in versions that are either slightly or substantially different.
"The Madwoman of Shuttlefield"—May 2003, *Asimov's Science Fiction*
"Benjamin the Unbeliever"—August 2003, *Asimov's Science Fiction*
"The Garcia Narrows Bridge"—January 2004, *Asimov's Science Fiction*
"Thompson's Ferry"—March 2004, *Asimov's Science Fiction*
"Incident at Goat Kill Creek"—April/May 2004, *Asimov's Science Fiction*
"Shady Grove"—July 2004, *Asimov's Science Fiction*
"Liberation Day"—October/November 2004, *Asimov's Science Fiction*
"Home of the Brave"—December 2004, *Asimov's Science Fiction*
Text design by Kristin del Rosario.

ACE is an imprint of The Berkley Publishing Group.
ACE and the "A" design are trademarks belonging to Penguin Group (USA) Inc.

First edition: December 2004

Library of Congress Cataloging-in-Publication Data

Steele, Allen M.
    Coyote rising : Allen Steele.— 1st ed.
      p. cm.
    ISBN 0-441-01205-1
    1. Hijacking of aircraft—Fiction.   2. Space colonies—Fiction.   3. Space flight—Fiction.
  4. Space ships—Fiction.   I. Title

    PS3569.T338425C694   2004
    813'.54—dc22

                                                                                    2004048834

PRINTED IN THE UNITED STATES OF AMERICA

10   9   8   7   6   5   4   3   2   1

CONTENTS

DRAMATIS PERSONAE

New Florida Colonists

Matriarch Luisa Hernandez—colonial governor
Savant Manuel Castro—lieutenant governor
Allegra DiSilvio—composer
Benjamin Harlan—drifter
James Alonzo Garcia—architect
LEVIN FAMILY
    Cecelia "Sissy" Levin—chicken farmer, original colonist
    Chris Levin—Chief Proctor, Cecelia's son
THOMPSON FAMILY
    Clark Thompson—mayor, Thompson's Landing
    Molly Thompson—wife
    Lars Thompson—nephew (older)
    Garth Thompson—nephew (younger)
CHURCH OF UNIVERSAL TRANSFORMATION
    Rev. Zoltan Shirow—founder and pastor
    Greer, Renaldo, Doria, Ian, Byron, Clarice, Ernst, Angela, Boris,
        Jim, Dex, and others—church members
Klon Newall—construction foreman
Frederic LaRoux–geologist
Enrique Constanza—electronics engineer
Jaime Hodge—field worker
Lonnie Dielman—Thompson's Ferry militia
Juanita Morales—Thompson's Ferry militia
Tomas Conseco—child

Midland colonists

Robert E. Lee—Mayor of Defiance; former commanding officer, URSS *Alabama*

Dana Monroe—Lee's partner; former *Alabama* chief engineer

MONTERO FAMILY:

   Carlos Montero (aka "Rigil Kent")—resistance leader

   Wendy Gunther—Carlos's wife

   Susan Gunther—Wendy and Carlos's daughter

   Maria Montero—Carlos's sister, resistance fighter

DREYFUS FAMILY:

   Jack Dreyfus—former *Alabama* engineer

   Lisa Dreyfus—wife

   Barry Dreyfus—son; resistance fighter

Ted LeMare—former *Alabama* ensign

Jean Swenson—former *Alabama* communications officer

Tom Shapiro—former *Alabama* first officer

Kim Newell—former *Alabama* shuttle pilot

Kuniko Okada—chief physician

Henry Johnson—astrophysicist

Union Guard/Union Astronautica

Capt. Fernando Baptiste—commanding officer, WHSS *Spirit of Social Collectivism Carried to the Stars*

Savant Gregor Hull—member, Council of Savants

Patriarch Leonardo Samoza—chief of operations, Copernicus Centre

Capt. Ramon Lopez—squad leader

Lt. Bon Cortez—expedition member

Warrant Officer Giselle Acosta

Sgt. Arthur Cartman

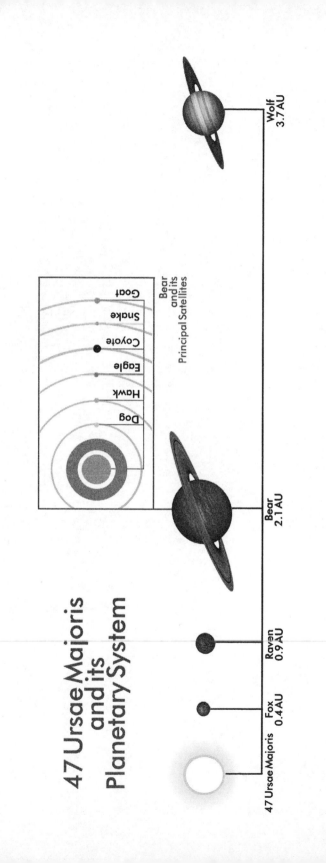

47 Ursae Majoris and its Planetary System

47 Ursae Majoris

Fox
0.4 AU

Raven
0.9 AU

Bear
2.1 AU

Wolf
3.7 AU

Bear and its Principal Satellites

Dog Hawk Eagle Coyote Snake Goat

PROLOGUE

"Have you ever been to Earth?"

At first, Fernando Baptiste didn't realize he was being spoken to; his attention was on the lunar landscape passing by the maglev. Mare Imbrium was a grey, flat wasteland pitted here and there by ancient impact craters. Far away, he could make out the hulking forms of He_3 combines, massive crawlers that scooped up powdery regolith and seined it for volatiles. It was the middle of the Moon's two-week day; stark sunlight, polarized by the train windows, cast long shadows from the high peaks of the Apienne Mountains.

Every seat was taken, but it was late, and nearly everyone was asleep; the lights were turned down low, and only the steward moved down the narrow aisle. The young boy sitting next to Fernando, though, was awake. He had the straight black hair and angular features of someone of Hispanic ancestry, but his face had the sallow complexion of a child born and raised on the Moon. No more than twelve or thirteen, Baptiste guessed. A book lay open in his lap, a luminescent holo of a dinosaur displayed on its screen. He wasn't looking at it, but rather at Baptiste himself.

"Sure," he said, quietly so as not to disturb anyone dozing around them. "Not recently, but I was born there. In a small town in Belize."

The boy nodded once, then stared down at his book. Baptiste watched as he idly touched the upper right corner of the page; the tyrannosaur took a couple of steps forward, raised its head, and bellowed silently. Unimpressed, the boy touched the side of the book; the screen changed, and another Jurassic animal appeared. Baptiste didn't know much about dinosaurs, so he couldn't identify this one.

"Have you ever been there?" he asked. "To Earth, I mean."

The boy shook his head. He didn't say anything, yet Baptiste noticed the way his eyes shifted to the insignia on his charcoal black uniform. Most Selenians were reticent in the presence of a Union Astronautica officer, but this child wasn't quite old enough to be intimidated. He was curious about the spacer sitting beside him, yet he had probably been taught not to bother strangers.

Baptiste gazed again out the window. For the first time, he noticed Earth hovering above the horizon. Perhaps that was what had prompted the boy's question: the sight of the cloudy blue-green orb, juxtaposed with the UA officer next to him. He had satisfied the boy's curiosity, and perhaps he should let it go at that, yet it had been a long ride from Archimedes, where he'd boarded the train, and it was probably another half hour or so until they pulled into Copernicus Centre, his final destination. He'd slept for most of the trip, and he wasn't ready to pull out his own book and study the material he'd been sent. Perhaps a little light conversation might take the edge off things. Besides, what harm could come from talking to a child . . . ?

"I haven't been to Earth lately," he said, "but I know of a place that's very much like it."

The boy had just turned another page in his book; this seemingly off-hand remark caught his attention. "What do you mean? There's nowhere like . . ." Then he frowned. "Oh . . . Tranquillity Centre. My father once took me there on holiday. It's not the same."

"You're right." Baptiste smiled. "It's not the same. The domes are just giant gardens, with manicured trees and tame animals no more threatening than a teb . . . and a young man like you has outgrown tebs, haven't you." The boy grinned; he was past the age of needing a teddy bear as a playmate, even if he wasn't old enough to appreciate the miracle of forests growing beneath vast domes on the Moon. Baptiste crossed his arms and lowered his voice. "No, I'm talking about something entirely different . . . a world far away from here, so far away that, if you were to leave for it today, by the time you arrived, everyone you left behind would be very old, perhaps even dead."

The boy stared at him for a long moment, not realizing what he was saying, then his dark brown eyes widened. "You mean . . . ?"

"Yes. I'm talking about Coyote."

Once again, the boy seemed self-conscious about whom he was speaking to: a spacer, one of those who voyaged into the outer system. The lunar colonies boasted a population of over 7 million, with a couple of million more living on orbitals scattered across cislunar space, yet Mars was still a frontier of only a few hundred thousand residents, and even fewer lived on the Jovian moons. It was rare to encounter a uniformed Union Astronautica officer, and Baptiste knew without asking that the boy recognized the gold braid on his shoulders, the silver bangle dangling from his left ear. This man wasn't just an officer, but a ship's captain.

"I'm . . ." The boy hesitated. "I'm joining my family at Copernicus. We're supposed to be going there. Coyote, I mean."

"Really?" Baptiste raised an eyebrow; now it was his turn to be surprised. "A future colonist, eh?" The boy nodded. "And which ship are you taking?"

"This one." The boy touched the side of his book. The dinosaur vanished; he closed the book, ran his finger down the index bar, then opened it again and touched the upper corner of the page. A hologram of a starship appeared. "The *Spirit of* . . . um . . ."

"The *Spirit of Social Collectivism Carried to the Stars.*" Baptiste hid a smile behind his hand; no sense in telling the lad the truth. Or at least not all of it . . . "I've heard of it. The newest colony ship. A fine vessel. Are you nervous? About leaving home, I mean."

"A little." The boy idly rotated the image; the *Spirit* turned on its axis, displaying the unfolded flanges of its diametric-drive engine along its cylindrical aft section, the enormous dish of its telemetry antenna raised from the blunt prow of the forward section. "The Moon's always been home. Never even been to Earth. And now . . ."

"And now you're going all the way to 47 Ursae Majoris." Baptiste tapped his lip with his forefinger. "And that frightens you, doesn't it?" The boy said nothing; he stared fixedly at the image in his book. "So tell me, what's your name?"

"Tomas. Tomas Conseco . . . Tom."

"Pleased to make your acquaintance, Señor Conseco. I'm Captain

Baptiste." He gave Tom a sly wink. "For the time being, you can call me
Fernando . . . but that's just between you and me, eh? If there's anyone
else around, you just call me Captain, or Captain Baptiste." The boy nodded. "Here. Let me show you something."

Baptiste reached into the pocket of the seat back in front of him and
pulled out his own book. He pressed his thumb against the verification
plate on the cover; the book beeped twice, and he selected a coded prefix on the index table, pressed it, and spread the book open in his lap.
The holographic image of a planetary system appeared: a tiny star, or-
bited by four planets. A tap of his fingertip and the tiny system rose from
the book, the planets slowly revolving around the star.

"That's 47 Ursae Majoris," Baptiste said, pointing to the miniature
sun. "It's a GO-class star, about forty-six light-years from Earth. A little
less luminescent than our own sun, which means it's—"

"I know." Tomas squirmed impatiently. "We were taught all that in
Basic Astronomy. I got an E," he added proudly.

"Really. So you're an expert." Baptiste touched the upper margin of
the right page, and the third planet of the system expanded, becoming a
ringed jovian surrounded by six major satellites. "That's Bear, its primary," he said, pointing to the gas giant. "It's the third planet of 47 Ursae
Majoris. Now, tell me . . . which one is Coyote?" Tom peered at the
satellites, then pointed to the fourth one. "Very good. Now then, tell me
about the *Alabama*."

"That was the first starship. It left Earth in 2070."

"Excellent. I'm impressed. And who was aboard?"

"Some people from the United Republic of America. They were led by
Captain Robert E. Lee. . . ."

"Umm . . . almost right, but not quite." Baptiste closed the page,
opened another one. A flat image of the URSS *Alabama* appeared within
the book: a smaller vessel, less than half the size of a *Destiny*-class starship and not nearly as elegant in design, the conical scoop of its Bussard
ramscoop protruding from the spherical main fuel tank at its bow. "R.E.
Lee was the commanding officer, and about half of his crew were loyal
to the URA, but the other half were political dissidents whom Captain
Lee led in a successful effort to steal his own ship. The theft of the *Al-*

abama was the first major event in the downfall of the Republic. You haven't been taught this in history class?"

Tomas looked embarrassed. "I didn't do so well in history," he admitted. "I got a U."

"Well, now . . . we'll have to make up for that, won't we?" Baptiste opened another page; an ancient photograph appeared, flat and unenhanced by holographics: Lee standing at the lowered gangway of one of the *Alabama*'s shuttles, shaking hands with an older gentleman. "That's Captain Lee with Roland Shaw, the Republic's Director of Internal Security. This picture was taken on Merritt Island, the old Gingrich Space Center in Florida, just before Lee escaped with the forty-seven dissidents he managed to smuggle aboard the *Alabama* . . . quite a story in itself. No one knew it at the time, but Shaw was part of the conspiracy. He secretly worked behind the scenes to help Lee get all those people aboard the *Alabama*."

"What happened to him?"

"Shaw? He was arrested for high treason and was executed. . . ."

"No, I mean Captain Lee."

"You're getting ahead of yourself." But the boy was clearly fascinated, and so Baptiste obliged his interest. "The *Alabama* managed to escape with only minutes to spare, and no one's heard from Captain Lee or his crew since then. Whether they're dead or alive, no one knows. They're still on their way to 47 Uma, and won't arrive until 2300 . . . by our reckoning at least. It'll seem a little shorter for them."

"That's the part I don't understand."

"Well, when you approach the speed of light, time passes more slowly. Since *Alabama* has a cruise velocity of twenty percent lightspeed, this means that, even though two hundred and thirty years will have passed by the time it reaches Coyote, for everyone aboard it'll seem as if only two hundred and twenty-six years have passed. A difference of a little more than four years."

Tomas looked unsettled by this knowledge, and Baptiste smiled. "But since the *Spirit* has a cruise velocity of ninety-five percent light-speed, it means that it will take only a little more than forty-eight years to get there. For everyone aboard it'll seem as if only about fifteen and a half years have passed. By Earth reckoning, you'll arrive in 2308, about eight years after the *Alabama*."

Tomas's eyes widened. "You mean I'll be able to meet Captain Lee?"

"Maybe." Baptiste shrugged. "His ship still hasn't arrived, and neither have the four colony ships that have been launched since then. Remember, radio waves travel at the speed of light. Since nothing travels faster than light, no one here will hear anything from Coyote for quite some time to come. So we won't know until we . . . that is, until you . . ."

"You're the captain, aren't you?" Tom didn't look away as he said this. "The captain of the *Spirit*, I mean."

No point in hiding the truth any longer. Baptiste closed the book and put it away. "You're quite intuitive."

"I figured it out when I saw your uniform." Tomas looked straight ahead. "That's why I wanted to talk to you . . . sir, I mean. Captain Baptiste."

Across the aisle, a woman opened her eyes. Baptiste met her curious gaze, and she quickly looked out the window, feigning disinterest; her companion continued to snore softly. "Well, for the short time we've got left together, let's keep on being friends, shall we? I'm still Fernando, and you're still Tom. Okay?"

"Okay. Sure." The boy's voice was very soft; now that he'd admitted knowing who his traveling companion was, he seemed more nervous than before. "Can I ask you one more thing?"

"You may ask anything you like."

"Is it . . . ?" Tom hesitated. "Is it very dangerous, where we're going? Coyote, I mean?"

"It'll be difficult, yes," he replied, carefully gauging his words. "Like I said, there are things you've taken for granted before that you'll have to do without. And you'll have to work hard to make yourself at home. Coyote is a whole new world, so it'll be like starting over on Earth back when hardly anyone lived there. You'll have blue skies and fresh water, and you won't have to worry about airlocks or radiation or . . ."

"I know. That's what my father tells me. But . . ." He stopped, still refusing to look at Baptiste. "That's not what I meant. Could I . . . could I be killed?"

How could he give an honest answer? All available information indicated that Coyote was habitable. The *Alabama* had a hundred and four passengers aboard when it departed from Earth, and four more ships had gone out since then, each carrying a thousand passengers. By the time they arrived in forty-eight years, the colony on Coyote should be well established. Indeed, toward the end of its flight, the *Spirit* would probably pass the first Union Astronautica ship, the *Glorious Destiny*, on its return trip to Earth.

Nonetheless, no one knew exactly what was out there.

"You won't die there," Baptiste said flatly. "You'll be safe. You have my word."

He took the boy's hand, gave it a reassuring squeeze. Tomas smiled and nodded slightly. In that instant a bond was formed between them.

And then the train bumped and began to decelerate, and a few seconds later the ceiling lights brightened. Around them, passengers stirred from their sleep, yawning and stretching their cramped legs. Glancing out the window, Baptiste could make out a silver-blue aura upon the distant horizon, still many miles away but coming closer: Copernicus Centre, the largest spaceport on the Moon. A luminescent speck rose from within the crater wall, a shuttle lifting off for rendezvous with some vessel in lunar orbit.

"My family will be waiting for me when I get in," Tomas said. "Can I . . . would you like to meet them?"

"That may not be such a good idea." Baptiste shook his head. "I think this should be our secret." Then he forced a smile. "Can we keep this between us, Senor Conseco? What we've talked about tonight?"

"Sure." The boy nodded, understanding the situation. "I can keep a secret, Fernando . . . Captain Baptiste, I mean."

"Thank you." Baptiste looked away, yet he kept an eye on his traveling companion. And in the last few moments before the train trundled to a halt, he saw Tom's hand steal toward the book Baptiste had placed in the seat pocket before him. Without making any fuss about it, Baptiste pulled out the book and put it in his own lap.

Coyote still had its secrets. And he had one or two of his own.

* * *

The lunar headquarters of the Union Astronautica was located within the north wall of Copernicus, with the office of the Patriarch occupying a suite high on the crater rim. The south wall was too far away to be seen, yet through the floor-to-ceiling windows of the suite Baptiste could nonetheless gaze out upon the vast spaceport spread out across the crater floor: hangars, dry docks, warehouses, fuel depots, the network of roads leading from one launchpad to another where moonships awaited liftoff.

The Patriarch's senior aide—a young lieutenant in silver-braided waistcoat, polite yet perfunctory—had greeted him, then requested that he wait there while he informed the chief of his arrival before vanishing through the door leading to the inner sanctum. That had been nearly twenty minutes ago, but Baptiste wasn't impatient. This was only the second time he'd been there, and the view was spectacular. So he sat on a couch facing the windows and watched as a shuttle to Highgate silently rose into the black sky. Too bad he couldn't have brought the boy he met on the train—Tomas, was it?—up here; he probably would have loved it.

The door whisked open; the aide told him that the Patriarch would see him. Baptiste picked up his valise, stood up, and followed the lieutenant to the inner office. The aide stepped aside as Baptiste crossed the threshold, then turned and left, allowing the door to shut quietly behind him. Obviously, the chief wanted to see Baptiste alone.

"Captain Fernando Baptiste, at your service, sir." He snapped to rigid attention—spine straight, arms at his side, legs together—and locked his gaze upon the luminescent emblem of the Union Astronautica above the Patriarch's desk. Indeed, it was one of the few things in the Patriarch's office he could see; with ceiling lights dimmed, the office was illuminated by earthlight streaming in thin bars through the window slats.

"Oh, come now, Captain. You're behaving like an actor in some third-rate skiffy." A dry chuckle from the other side of the room. "I hate those things, don't you? Cheap melodrama, usually written by someone who's only been a tourist . . . if that, even."

"I wouldn't know, sir. I don't watch skiffies very often." Baptiste maintained his stiff posture.

"Hmm . . . probably just as well. Still, entertaining enough, for what they are." A figure glided from the darkness. "If you keep that up, though, you're going to get a crick in the neck . . . and I'll tell you right now, I'm not impressed."

Baptiste relaxed, assuming an at-ease posture. He could see the Patriarch more clearly: a short, stocky man, his scalp shaved clean, a narrow goatee framing a broad mouth, stark black eyes buried deep within his skull. Patriarch Leonardo Somoza, former member of the Union Proletariate, highest-ranking UA officer on the Moon . . . and, regardless of a cultivated air of affability, a man widely regarded to be merciless with anyone who roused his ire. *Be careful when you see him,* others had privately warned Baptiste. *Leo would just as soon cut off your balls as offer you a drink.*

"Would you like a drink?" The Patriarch now stood only a few inches away, peering up at Baptiste's face. "I'm going to have one, and I don't like drinking alone."

Baptiste forced a smile. "Thank you, sir. Whatever you're having."

"Uh-huh." Somoza studied him for another moment, then turned away. "We haven't met till now," he said as he walked toward a cabinet on the other side of the room, "but you've come highly recommended for this mission. Twelve years deep-space experience, commanding officer of the second Titan expedition . . . impressive. Very impressive."

"Thank you, sir. I'm glad you approve."

"Uh-huh." Somoza opened the cabinet, regarded a small collection of cut-glass decanters, finally selected one. He said nothing as he poured a measure of pale brown liquid into two glasses, then added ice and water to each one. "Of course, this is . . . well, somewhat tame compared to Titan, don't you think?"

Titan had been a nightmare. The first lander sent down from his ship had been caught in a storm while making atmospheric entry and crashed on the moon's uncharted surface, killing half the crewmen aboard. Baptiste dispatched the second lander to recover the survivors,

and the rescue mission had nearly failed as well, with his first officer losing his life in the effort. The review board had absolved Captain Baptiste
of any blame, though, and three months later the Proletariate ceremoni-
ally presented him with the Prix de Coeur, the Western Hemisphere
Union's highest military medal of honor. And two years after that, the
Union Astronautica offered him the command of the *Spirit*.

"Not at all, sir." Baptiste accepted the drink, took a sip. Bourbon. He
hated bourbon. "Coyote may not be Titan, but I'm sure it must present
its own challenges."

"I'm sure it will." The Patriarch gestured to a couple of chairs positioned in front of the windows. "In fact, that's why I wished to meet
with you. Have you had a chance to review the material we sent you?"

Baptiste hesitated. "Not in depth, sir. I didn't receive it until shortly
before I boarded the train. I've been rather busy."

"Of course." Somoza smiled as he sat down. "There are always last-
minute details. I trust that you managed to read the summary, at the
very least."

"An assessment by the Savants Council of possible social conditions
on Coyote." Through the window slats, Baptiste saw another shuttle
coming in for touchdown. There was a lot of traffic coming and going
out in the spaceport. "My apologies, sir. I didn't get very far into it."

"Uh-huh." Somoza frowned as he jiggled the ice in his glass. "Normally I wouldn't accept failure by a senior officer to read a classified report. Yet I anticipated that you might be involved with other tasks, so
I've invited someone to bring you up to date." He looked over his shoulder. "Gregor? If you'll join us, please?"

Baptiste glanced behind him to see a form step out from the deep
shadows of the office, a tall figure cloaked in a black robe. As he stepped
closer, ruby eyes lit within the cowl pulled over his head; there was the
subtle mechanical whir from inside the robe.

"An honor to meet you, Captain Baptiste." The voice was a smooth
buzz, inflective of its vowels yet oddly without accent. "My colleagues
and I have followed your career with great interest."

A Savant. Like almost everyone else he knew, Baptiste found himself
nervous in the company of these creatures: persons who'd chosen to

have their minds downloaded into mechanical forms, eschewing their human bodies for virtual immortality as cyborgs. Baptiste believed them to be closet sociopaths, people who would rather interface with an AI than look another person straight in the eye. The fact that they all looked very much alike didn't help much either: the same black robes, the same skeletal forms. Yet once WHU granted them legal status as citizens, many had gone to work for the Union Astronautica, where they served as a legion of posthuman intellects. For some reason, space attracted them.

The *Spirit*'s complement included five Savants. Having no need to breathe, eat, or indulge any of the other biological functions they had forsaken, they would remain awake during the half century it took for the starship to travel to 47 Ursae Majoris, standing watch while he and everyone else slept the dreamless sleep of biostasis. What they'd do during that time, what they would think about, God only knew; their intellects were as alien to unaltered humans as that of ants. Or perhaps ghosts, although Baptiste didn't believe in such things.

"Captain, allow me to introduce you to Savant Gregor Hull." Somoza gestured lazily toward the Savant. "Savant Hull is the senior member of a group that's been studying the social dynamics of small founding populations." He glanced at Hull. "If you'll continue?"

"Thank you, sir." The Savant glided across the office until he stopped next to Somoza. Although there was another chair nearby, Hull didn't take a seat. Indeed, Baptiste reflected, one thing that made the Savants seem so otherworldly was the fact that they seldom sat down; they didn't need to rest, or at least not as flesh-and-blood humans did. "As Patriarch Somoza says, my team has done considerable historical research into colonies, both in space and on Earth. Our major finding is that, once a population grows to a certain size, there's a strong tendency for it to sever ties to home."

Baptiste shrugged. "Makes sense . . . especially if you're referring to Coyote. Establishing a self-sufficient colony out there was the principal reason the URA built the *Alabama* in the first place."

"Yes, it was, Captain." The Savant's voice was a monotonous purr. "But remember, the *Alabama* was hijacked by renegades . . . 'dissident intellectuals' as they were known back then. They were committed to achieving political independence the moment they left Earth, and so there's every reason to believe that, if their colony survives, they'll be even more committed toward maintaining their independence."

"The Union Astronautica anticipated this when it launched the *Glorious Destiny* four years ago." The Patriarch crossed his legs. "That is why we put a large company of Union Guard aboard that ship, to make sure that there would be . . . well, little resistance from the original settlers." He chuckled, shook his head. " 'Will be,' I should say. One of the drawbacks of thinking in interstellar terms . . . *Alabama* is still en route to 47 Ursae Majoris, and, regardless of its greater velocity, *Glorious Destiny* is still a considerable distance behind it. So we're discussing future events as if they've already happened."

Baptiste nodded. The colony established by the crew of the *Alabama* would be almost four years old by the time *Glorious Destiny* arrived . . . and once the *Spirit* reached the 47 Ursae Majoris system almost eight years after the *Alabama*, three more ships from the Western Hemisphere Union would have followed the *Glorious Destiny*. So they were, in fact, engaging in a protracted form of time travel.

"If that's so," he said, "then *Glorious Destiny* . . . shouldn't have . . . won't have . . . much difficulty asserting control over the original colonists."

"That would appear to be the case," Hull said. "However, my group has projected a very strong likelihood that the original colonists may revolt against the newcomers. Indeed, we believe that recent immigrants may even take sides with the original colonists."

"You're sure?" Baptiste raised an eyebrow. "No offense, but it sounds like so much guesswork. There are quite a number of factors we simply don't know. . . ."

"History shows this to be a pattern that has repeated itself many times in the past. Those who come to a frontier first believe that the land belongs to them. They resent those who follow them, particularly if they represent some strong authority." Hull paused. "An admirable tendency, true, but one that doesn't bode well for our purposes."

"Savant Hull's report has been studied at the highest level. His findings have been very persuasive." Somoza's tone was no longer cordial; realizing that the Patriarch was deadly serious, Baptiste wiped the smile from his face. "Regardless of the time factor involved, we cannot allow even the slightest chance for Coyote to slip from Union control. It's absolutely vital for us to establish a viable colony out there."

Again, Baptiste nodded. Earth's natural resources had been exhausted; long-term effects of global warming had rendered entire countries uninhabitable, while the shorelines of others had disappeared beneath the rising oceans. It was only the development of space resources—the extraction of helium-3 from the lunar regolith, the mining of the Moon and nearby asteroids—that kept the human race from extinction, even then, just barely; the populations of the orbital colonies and the settlements on the Moon and Mars represented only a fraction of the human race, and the attempt to terraform Mars had met with disaster. Unless humankind found another home, it was doomed to a slow and miserable death.

The Western Hemisphere Union wasn't the only government to be aware of that fact. Baptiste had seen the intelligence reports: the European Alliance had recently initiated a program to build starships of its own. Although the diametric drive was a classified secret, it was only a matter of time before the European Space Administration figured out how to duplicate it. Either that, or their spies would unearth the secret. One way or another, it wouldn't be very much longer until the EA would be capable of sending a vessel of its own into interstellar space.

Yet even after centuries of search by orbital observatories, the only world within fifty light-years of Earth that appeared capable of supporting human life was Coyote. That was why the Union had resorted to assembling and launching a small fleet of starships even before the *Alabama* made it to the 47 Ursae Majoris system. No one had the luxury of waiting to receive the first radio transmissions; Coyote had to be settled now.

"I doubt the earlier ships will have much trouble," the Patriarch continued. "Nearly a hundred Guardsmen have already been sent to Coyote, and with any luck our precautions will be unnecessary . . . no offense, Gregor." The Savant made no sound, but his metallic head tilted slightly forward, emulating a nod. "However, having more forces on the ground may be warranted if there is an uprising under way by the time you arrive."

"So what do you want me do, sir?"

"We're changing your mission parameters." Somoza absently drummed his fingers on the glass in his hand. "We need you to stabilize the colony. Prop up the colonial government under Matriarch Hernandez, make sure that Union control remains intact. To this end, we're increasing the military detachment—three hundred more soldiers, replacing the same number of civilians that you were originally carrying—along with gyros, skimmers, and long-range artillery. You're still going to be carrying civilians of course, but your primary objective will now be military."

Baptiste didn't say anything, though he felt something freeze within his chest. Until a few minutes ago, he'd believed that he was doing little more than transporting another thousand colonists to Coyote. Nine hundred and thirty-five civilians, most of whom had won their berths aboard the *Spirit* by participating in public lotteries, plus fifty Union Guard soldiers and officers, whose main purpose for being aboard was to protect them from whatever threats might have been discovered on the new world. Once they were there, he and his flight crew, along with the five Savants who'd accompanied them, would return to Earth, where comfortable retirement awaited them. A long voyage, to be sure, but one with benefits: a good home wherever he wanted, a generous stipend, perhaps even a position as a Patriarch . . .

That had changed. Instead he was being asked—ordered, really—to lead a military expedition to Coyote and assist in quelling an uprising that the Savants believed might occur. This wasn't the mission he'd been asked to perform.

"I realize that this is a major change of plan, nor the one for which you were selected." Somoza looked sympathetic, like a father who'd asked a favorite son to do something particularly odious. "Believe me, though, we wouldn't be asking you to do this if we didn't think that you were capable of carrying it out. You've shown that you can make hard decisions, Fernando. We hope . . . we believe . . . that you're capable of doing this."

Damn him! There was no way he could back out. Not without losing not only face, but also everything he'd worked all his life to achieve. If he refused, the Patriarch would probably nod, shrug, tell him that he understood . . . and his next job would be running freighters to Mars. And that would be all he'd do for the rest of his life.

"I understand, sir," he said. "I'll do my best."

"Thank you, Captain." Somoza smiled. "That's all I ask. And believe me, you won't be alone. I'm sending one of my best people with you."

Before he could inquire who that might be, Hull took a step forward. "I'm looking forward to working with you, Captain Baptiste," he said, extending a clawlike hand from beneath his robe. "I trust we'll have an interesting voyage together."

Baptist forced a smile. "I'm sure we will," he said, surrendering warm flesh to the Savant's cold grasp. "To Coyote."

"To Coyote."

Book 3

Saints and Strangers

The *Mayflower* was packed to the gunwales, for 102 passengers had been crammed on board with their goods and supplies. No impression is more deeply imbedded in the popular mind, nothing is more firmly woven into the American *mythos* than the notion that these first Pilgrims were a homogeneous and united group. . . . It is a pleasing fancy, but the Pilgrims would have exploded it in the name of "ye truth."

—GEORGE F. WILLISON,
Saints and Strangers

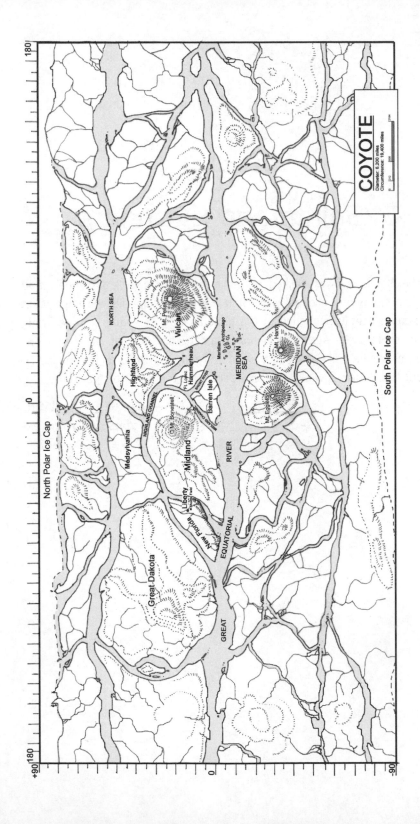

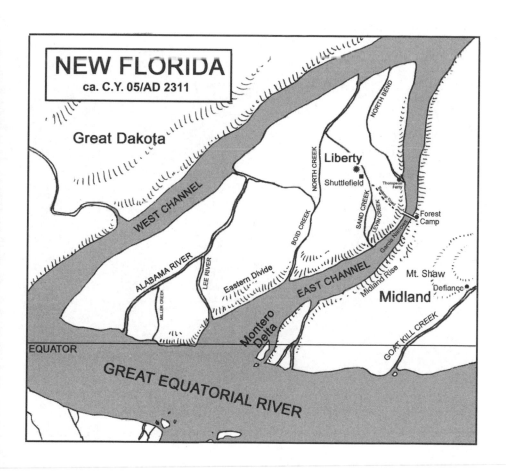

NEW FLORIDA
ca. C.Y. 05/AD 2311

Great Dakota

WEST CHANNEL

NORTH BEND

NORTH CREEK

Liberty

Shuttlefield

Thompson Ferry

Forest Camp

SAND CREEK

LEVIN CREEK

Garcia Narrows

BOID CREEK

ALABAMA RIVER

LEE RIVER

MILLER CREEK

Eastern Divide

EAST CHANNEL

Midland Rise

Mt. Shaw

Defiance

Midland

Montero Delta

GOAT KILL CREEK

EQUATOR

GREAT EQUATORIAL RIVER

Part 1

THE MADWOMAN OF SHUTTLEFIELD

The first night Allegra DiSilvio spent on Coyote, she met the mad-woman of Shuttlefield. It seemed like an accident at the time, but in the weeks and months to follow she'd come to realize that it was much more, that their fates were linked by forces beyond their control.

The shuttle from the *Long Journey* touched down in a broad meadow just outside the town of Liberty. The high grass had been cleared from the landing pad, burned by controlled fires to create a flat expanse nearly a half mile in diameter, upon which the gull-winged spacecraft settled after making its long fall from orbit. As she descended the gang-way ramp and walked out from beneath the hull, Allegra looked up to catch her first sight of Bear: a giant blue planet encircled by silver rings, hovering in an azure sky. The air was fresh, scented with midsummer sourgrass; a warm breeze caressed the dark stubble of her shaved scalp, and it was in that moment she knew she'd made it. The journey was over; she was on Coyote.

Dropping the single bag she had been allowed to bring with her from Earth, Allegra fell to her hands and knees and wept.

Eight months of waiting to hear whether she'd won the lottery, two more months of nervous anticipation before she was assigned a berth aboard the next starship to 47 Ursae Majoris, a week of sitting in Quito before boarding the Union Astronautica space elevator in the Andes Mountains of Ecuador, three days spent traveling to lunar orbit, where she boarded the *Long Journey* . . . then, forty-eight years in dreamless biostasis, to wake up cold, naked, and bald, forty-six light-years from everything familiar, with everyone she had ever known either long dead or irrevocably out of her reach.

She was so happy, she could cry. *Thank you, God,* she thought. *Thank you, thank you . . . I'm here, and I'm free, and the worst is over.*

She had no idea just how wrong she was. And it wasn't until after she'd made friends with a crazy old lady that she'd thank anyone again.

Liberty was the first colony on Coyote, established by the crew of the URSS *Alabama* in A.D. 2300, or C.Y. 01 by the Lemarean calendar. It was now 2306 by Gregorian reckoning, though, and the original colonists had long since abandoned their settlement, disappearing into the wilderness just days after the arrival of WHSS *Seeking Glorious Destiny Among the Stars for the Greater Good of Social Collectivism*, the next ship from Earth. No one knew why they'd fled—or at least those who knew weren't saying—but the fact remained that Liberty had been built to house only a hundred people. *Glorious Destiny* brought a thousand people to the new world, and the third ship—*Traveling Forth to Spread Social Collectivism to New Frontiers*—had brought a thousand more, and so by the time the *Long Journey to the Galaxy in the Spirit of Social Collectivism* reached Coyote, the population of New Florida had swelled to drastic proportions.

The log cabins erected by the first settlers were currently occupied by Union Astronautica officers from *Glorious Destiny* and *New Frontiers*. It hadn't been long before every tree within ten miles had been cut down for the construction of new houses, with roads expanding outward into what had once been marshes. Once the last stands of blackwood and faux birch were gone, most of the wildlife moved away. The swoops and creek cats that once preyed upon livestock were seldom seen anymore, and with automatic guns placed around the colony's perimeter only rarely did anyone hear the nocturnal screams of boids. Still there wasn't enough timber to build homes for everyone.

Newcomers were expected to fend for themselves. In the spirit of social collectivism, aid was given in the form of temporary shelter and two meals a day, but beyond that it was every man and woman for himself. The Union Astronautica guaranteed free passage to Coyote for those who won the public lottery, but stopped short of promising anything once they'd arrived. Collectivist theory held that a sane society was one in which everyone reaped the rewards of individual efforts; but Liberty was still very much a frontier town, and anyone asking for room and board in the homes owned by those who'd come earlier was likely to receive a cold stare in return. All men were created equal, yet some were clearly more equal than others.

And so, once she'd picked herself up from the ground, Allegra found herself taking up residence not in Liberty, where she thought she'd be living, but in Shuttlefield, the sprawling encampment surrounding the landing pad. She made her way to a small bamboo hut with a cloverweed-thatched roof where she stood in line for an hour before she was issued a small tent that had been patched many times by those who'd used it earlier, a soiled sleeping bag that smelled of mildew, and a ration card that entitled her to eat in what had once been Liberty's grange hall before it was made into the community center. The bored Union Guard soldier behind the counter told her that she could pitch her tent wherever she wanted, then hinted that he'd be happy to share his cabin if she'd sleep with him. She refused, and he impatiently cocked his thumb toward the door before turning to the next person in line.

Shuttlefield was a slum; there was no other way to describe it. Row upon row of tents, arranged in untidy ranks along muddy footpaths trampled by countless feet, littered with trash and cratered by potholes. The industrious had erected shelter from bamboo grown from seeds brought from Earth; others lived out of old cargo containers into which they had cut doors and windows. Dirty children chased starving dogs between clotheslines draped with what looked like rags until Allegra realized that they were garments; the smoke from cook fires was rank with the odor of compost. Two faux birch shacks, side by side, had handwritten signs for MEN and WOMEN above their doors; the stench of urine and feces lay thick around them, yet it didn't stop people from pitching tents nearby. The voices she heard were mostly Anglo, but her ears also picked up other tongues—Spanish, Russian, German, various Arab and Asian dialects—all mixed together in a constant background hum.

And everywhere, everyone seemed to be selling something, from kiosks in front of their shelters. Plucked carcasses of chickens dangled upside down from twine suspended between poles. Shirts, jackets, and trousers stitched from some hide she'd never seen before—she'd later learn that it was swamper fur—were laid out on rickety tables. Jars of spices and preserved vegetables stood next to the pickled remains of creatures she didn't recognize. Obsolete pads containing data and entertainment from Earth, their sellers promising that their power cells were still fresh, their memories virus-clean. A captive creek cat in a wooden cage, lying on its side and nursing a half dozen babies; raise the kits until they're half-grown, their owner said, then kill the mother and inbreed her offspring for their pelts: a great business opportunity.

A small man with a furtive look in his eyes sidled up to Allegra, glanced both ways, then offered her a small plastic vial half-filled with an oily clear liquid. Sting, he confided. Pseudowasp venom. Just put a drop or two on your tongue, and you'll think you're back home. . . .

Allegra shook her head and kept walking, her back aching from the duffel bag carried over her shoulder and the folded tent beneath her arm. Home? This was home now. There was nothing on Earth for her to go back to, even if she could return.

She found a bare spot of ground amid several shanties, yet no sooner had she put down her belongings when a man emerged from the nearest shack. He asked if she was a member of the Cutters Guild; when she professed ignorance, he gruffly told her that this was Guild territory. Reluctant to get in a quarrel, Allegra obediently picked up her stuff and went farther down the street until she spotted another vacant place, this time among a cluster of tents much like her own. She was beginning to erect the poles when two older women came over to her site; without explanation, one knocked over her poles while the other grabbed her bag and threw it in the street. When Allegra resisted, the first woman angrily knocked her to the ground. This was New Frontiers turf; who did she think she was, trying to squat here? A small crowd had gathered to watch; seeing that no one was going to take her side, Allegra quickly gathered her things and hurried away.

For the next several hours, she wandered the streets of Shuttlefield, searching for some place to put up her tent. Every time she found a likely-looking spot—and after the second incident, she was careful to

ask permission from the nearest neighbor—she discovered that it had already been claimed by one group or another. It soon became clear that
Shuttlefield was dominated by a hierarchy of guilds, groups, and clubs,
ranging from societies that had originated among the passengers of earlier ships to gangs of hard-eyed men who guarded their territory with
machetes. A couple of times Allegra was informed that she was welcome
to stay, but only so long as she agreed to pay a weekly tax, usually one-
third of what she earned from whatever job she eventually found or,
failing that, one meal out of three from her ration card. A large,
comfortable-looking shack occupied by single women of various ages
turned out to be the local brothel; if she stayed there, the madam told
her, she'd be expected to pay the rent on her back. At least she was polite about it; Allegra replied that she'd keep her offer in mind, but they
both knew that it was an option only if she were desperate.

By dusk, she was footsore, hungry, and on the verge of giving up,
when Allegra found herself at the edge of town. It was close to a
swamp—the sourgrass grew chest high there, and not far away were a
cluster of the ball plants she'd been warned to avoid—and there was
only one other dwelling, a slope-roofed and windowless shack nailed together from discarded pieces of faux birch. Potted plants hung from the
roof eaves above the front door, and smoke rose from a chimney hole,
yet there was no one in sight. Walking closer, Allegra heard the clucking
of chickens from a wire-fenced pen out back; it also seemed as if she
heard singing, a low and discordant voice from within the shack.

Allegra hesitated. This lonesome hovel away from all the others, so
close to the swamp where who-knew-what might lurk, made her nervous. Yet darkness was settling upon the town, and she knew she
couldn't go any farther. So she picked a spot of ground about ten yards
from the shack and quietly went about pitching her tent. If someone
protested, she'd just have to negotiate a temporary arrangement; she'd
gladly trade a couple of meals for a night of sleep.

No one bothered her as she erected her shelter, and although the
voice stopped singing and even the chickens went quiet after a while, no
one objected to her presence. The sun was down by the time she was
finished, and dark clouds shrouded the giant planet high above her. It

looked like rain, so she crawled into the tent, dragging her belongings behind her.

Once she had laid out her sleeping bag, Allegra unzipped her duffel bag and dug through it until she found the lightstick she'd been given before she left the *Long Journey*. The night was cool, so she found a sweater and pulled it on. There were a couple of food bars in the bottom of the bag; she unwrapped one. Although she was tempted to eat the other as well, she knew she'd want it in the morning. The way things were going, there was no telling what she'd have to suffer through before she got a decent meal. It was already evident that Shuttlefield had its own way of doing things, and the system was rigged to prevent newcomers from taking advantage of it.

Yet she was free. That counted for something. She had escaped Earth, and now she was . . .

A shuffling sound from outside.

Allegra froze, then slowly raised her eyes.

She had left the tent flap partially unzipped at the top. In the sallow glow of her lightstick, she saw someone peering in through the insect netting: a woman's face, deeply lined, framed by lank hair that might once have been blond before it turned ash grey.

They silently regarded each other as the first drops of night rain began tapping at the tent's plastic roof. The woman's eyes were blue, Allegra observed, yet they seemed much darker, as if something had leached all the color from her irises, leaving only an afterimage of blue.

"Why are you here?" the woman asked.

"I'm . . . I'm sorry," Allegra said. "I didn't mean to . . ."

"Sorry for what?" The eyes grew sharper, yet the voice was hollow. Like her face, it was neither young nor old. She spoke English rather than Anglo; that caught Allegra by surprise, and she had to take a moment to translate mentally the older dialect.

"Sorry for trespassing," she replied, carefully speaking the English she'd learned in school. "I was—"

"Trespassing where?" Not a question. A demand.

"Here . . . your place. I know it's probably not . . ."

"My place?" A hint of a smile that quickly disappeared, replaced by the dark scowl. "Yes, this is my place. The Eastern Divide, the Great Equatorial River, Midland, the Meridian Sea, all the places he sailed . . . those are Rigil Kent's places. My son lives in Liberty, but he never comes to see me. No one in Shuttlefield but thieves and scum. But here . . ." Again, the fleeting smile. "Everything is mine. The chickens, the stars, and everything in between. Who are you? And why are you here?"

The rush of words caught her unprepared; Allegra understood only the last part. "Allegra DiSilvio," she said. "I've just arrived from the . . ."

"Did Rigil Kent send you?" More insistently now.

In a flash of insight that she'd come to realize was fortunate, Allegra didn't ask whom she meant. What was important was her response. "No," she said, "he didn't send me. I'm on my own."

The woman stared at her. The rain was falling harder; somewhere in the distance, she heard the rumble of thunder. Water spilled through a leak in the tent, spattered across her sleeping bag. Still the woman's eyes didn't stray from her own, even though the rain was matting her grey hair. Finally, she spoke:

"You may stay."

Allegra let out her breath. "Thank you. I promise I won't . . ."

The face vanished. Allegra heard footsteps receding. A door creaked open, slammed shut. Chickens cackled briefly, then abruptly went quiet, as if cowed into silence.

Allegra waited a few seconds, then hastily closed the tent flap. She used the discarded food wrapper to plug the leak, then removed her boots and pushed herself into her sleeping bag, reluctant to take off her clothes even though they were filthy. She fell asleep while the summer storm raged around her. She hadn't turned off the light even though common sense dictated that she needed to preserve its chemical battery.

She was safe. But for the first time since she'd arrived, she was truly frightened.

The next morning, Allegra saw her neighbor just once, and only briefly. She awoke to hear the chickens clucking, and crawled out of her tent to see the woman standing in the pen behind her house, throwing corn from an apron tied around her waist. When Allegra called to her, though, she turned and walked back into her house, slamming the door shut behind her. Allegra considered going over and knocking, but decided against it; the old woman clearly wanted to be left alone, and Allegra might be pushing her luck by intruding on her privacy.

So she changed clothes, wrapped a scarf around her bare scalp, and left to make the long hike into Liberty. She did so reluctantly; although there were no other tents nearby, she didn't know for certain that she wasn't camped on some group's turf. Nonetheless, her stomach was growling, and she didn't want to consume her last food bar unless necessary. And somehow, she had a feeling that people tended to leave her strange neighbor alone.

The road to Liberty was littered with trash: discarded wrappers, broken bottles, empty cans, bits and pieces of this and that. If Shuttlefield's residents made any effort to landfill or recycle their garbage, it wasn't evident. She passed farm fields where men and women worked on their hands and knees, pulling cloverweed from between rows of crops planted earlier in the summer. Coyote's seasons were three times as long as they were on Earth—ninety-one or ninety-two days in each month, twelve months in a year by the LeMarean calendar—still, it was near the end of Hamaliel, the second month of summer; the farmers would be working hard to pull in the midseason harvest so that they could plant again before autumn. The original colonists had struggled to keep themselves fed through the first long winter they faced on Coyote, and they only had a hundred or so mouths to feed.

The distant roar of engines drew her attention; looking up, she saw a shuttle descending to the landing pad. More passengers from the *Long Journey* being ferried down to Coyote; with the arrival of a new ship from Earth, the population of New Florida would increase by another thousand people. Social collectivism might have worked well in the Western Hemisphere Union, built upon the smoldering remains of the United Republic of America, but there it benefited from established cities and high-tech infrastructure. Coyote was still largely unexplored; what little technology had been brought from Earth was irreplaceable, unavailable to the average person, so the colonists had to live off the land as best they could. Judging from what she'd already seen in Shuttlefield, utopian political theory had broken down; too many people had come there too quickly, forcing the newcomers to fend for themselves in a feudal hierarchy in which the weak were at the mercy of the strong, and everyone was under the iron heel of the colonial government. Unless she wanted to become a prostitute or live out the rest of her life as a serf, she'd better find a way to survive.

Allegra came upon a marsh where Japanese bamboo was grown. The most recent crop had already been harvested, its stumps extending for a hundred acres or so, the ground littered with broken shoots. On impulse, she left the path and waded out into the marsh, where she searched the ground until she found a foot-long stalk that was relatively undamaged. Tucking it beneath her arm, she returned to the road.

It would do for a start. All she needed was a sharp knife.

Liberty was much different than Shuttlefield. The streets were wide and clean, recently paved with gravel, lined on either side by log cabins. There were no hustlers, no kiosks; near the town center, she found small shops, their wares displayed behind glass windows. Yet everyone she passed refused to look her way, save for Proctors in blue uniforms who eyed her with suspicion. When she paused before the open half door of the glassblower's shop to watch the men inside thrust white-hot rods into the furnace, a blueshirt walked over to tap her on the shoulder, shake his head, and point the way to the community hall. Few words were spoken, yet the message was clear; she was only allowed to pass through on her way to the community hall, and not linger where she didn't belong.

Breakfast was a lukewarm porridge containing potatoes and chunks of fish meat; it resembled clam chowder, but tasted like sour milk. The old man who ladled it out in the serving line told her that it was creek crab stew, and she should eat up—it was only a day old. When Allegra asked what was on the menu for dinner, he grinned as he added a slice of stale bread to her plate. More of the same . . . and by then it'd be a day and a half old.

She found a place at one of the long wooden tables that ran down the length of the community hall and tried not to meet the gaze of any of the others seated nearby, even though she recognized several from the *Long Journey*. She'd made friends with no one during her passage from Earth, and wasn't in a hurry to do so now, so she distracted herself by studying an old mural painted on the wall. Rendered in native dyes by an untrained yet talented hand, it depicted the URSS *Alabama* in orbit above Coyote. Apparently an artifact left behind by Liberty's original residents before they'd fled. No one knew where they'd gone, although it was believed that they had started another colony somewhere on Midland, across the East Channel from New Florida.

Allegra was wondering how hard it might be to seek them out when she heard a mechanical sound behind her: servomotors shifting gears, the thin whine of an electrical power source. Then a filtered burr of a voice, addressing her in Anglo:

"Pardon me, but are you Allegra DiSilvio?"

She looked up to see a silver skull peering at her from within a black cowl, her face dully reflected in its ruby eyes. A Savant: a posthuman who had once been flesh and blood until he'd relinquished his humanity to have his mind downloaded into cyborg form, becoming an immortal intellect. Allegra detested them. Savants operated the starships, but it was surprising to find one here and now. And worse, it had come looking for her.

"That's me." She put down her spoon. "Who're you?"

"Manuel Castro. Lieutenant governor of the New Florida Colony." A clawlike hand rose from the folds of its dark cloak. "Please don't get up. I only meant to introduce myself."

Allegra made no effort to rise. "Pleased to meet you, Savant Castro. Now if you'll excuse me . . ."

"Oh, now . . . no reason to be rude. I merely wish to welcome you to Coyote, make sure that all your needs are being met."

"Really? Well, then, you could start by giving me a place to stay. A house here in town would be fine . . . one room will do. And some fresh clothing . . . I've only got one other change."

"Unfortunately, there are no vacancies in Liberty. If you'd like, I can add your name to the waiting list and notify you if something opens up. As for clothing, I'm afraid you'll have to continue wearing what you've brought until you've tallied enough hours in public service to exchange them for new clothes. However, I have a list of work details that are looking for new employees."

"Thanks, but I'll . . ." A new thought occurred to her. "Are there any openings here? I think I could give a hand in the kitchen, if they need some assistance."

"Just a moment." Castro paused for a moment, his quantum-comp brain accessing data from a central AI. "Ah, yes . . . you're in luck. The community kitchen needs a new dishwasher for the morning-to-midday shift. Eight hours per day, starting at 0600 and ending at 1400. No previous experience required. One and a half hours credit per hour served."

"When does it start?"

"Tomorrow morning."

"Thank you. I'll take it." She turned back to her meal, yet the Savant made no move to leave. It patiently stood behind her, its body making quiet machine noises. Allegra dipped her spoon into the foul stew, waited for Castro to go away. All around her, the table had gone silent; she felt eyes upon her as others watched and listened.

"From your records, I understand you had a reputation back on Earth," Castro said. "You were known as a musician."

"Not exactly. I was a composer. I didn't perform." Looking straight ahead, she refused to meet his fathomless glass eyes.

Another pause. "Ah, yes . . . so I see. You wrote music for the Connecticut River Ensemble. In fact, I think I have one of your works. . . ."

From its mouth grille, a familiar melody emerged: "Sunrise on Holyoke," a minuet for string quartet. She'd written it early one winter morning when she'd lived in the foothills of the Berkshires, trying to capture the feeling of the dawnlight over the Holyoke range. A delicate and ethereal piece, reconstructed in electronic tonalities by something that had given up all pretense of humanity.

"Yes, that's mine. Thank you very much for reminding me." She glanced over her shoulder. "My stew's getting cold. If you don't mind . . ."

The music abruptly ended. "I'm sorry. I'm afraid I can't do it justice." A moment passed. "If you're ever inclined to compose again, we would be glad to have you do so. We sadly lack for culture here."

"Thank you. I'll consider it."

She waited, staring determinedly into her soup bowl. After a few moments, she heard the rustle of its cloak, the subdued whir and click of its legs as it walked away. There was quiet around her, like the brief silence that falls between movements of a symphony, then murmuring voices slowly returned.

For an instant they seemed to fill a void within her, one that she'd fought so long and hard to conquer . . . but then, once more, the music failed to reach her. She heard nothing, saw nothing.

"Hey, lady," someone seated nearby whispered. "You know who that was?"

"Yeah, jeez!" another person murmured. "Manny Castro! No one ever stood up to him like that. . . ."

"Who did you say you were? I didn't catch . . ."

"Excuse me." The plate and bowl rattled softly in her hands as she stood up. She carried it to a wooden cart, where she placed it with a clatter that sounded all too loud to her ears. Remembering the bamboo stalk she'd left on the table, she went back to retrieve it. Then, ignoring the questioning faces around her, she quickly strode out of the dining hall.

All this distance, only to have the past catch up to her. She began to make the long walk back to Shuttlefield.

When she returned to her tent, she found that it was still there. However, it hadn't gone unnoticed. A Proctor knelt before the tent, holding the flap open as he peered inside.

"Pardon me," she asked as she came up behind him, "but is there something I can help you with?"

Hearing her, the Proctor turned to look around. A young man with short-cropped blond hair, handsome yet overweight; he couldn't have been much older than twenty Earth-years, almost half Allegra's age. He dropped the tent flap and stood up, brushing dirt from his knees.

"Is this yours?" Less a question than a statement. His face seemed oddly familiar, although she was certain she'd never met him before.

"Yes, it's mine. Do you have a problem with that?"

Her attitude took him by surprise; he blinked, stepping back before he caught himself. Perhaps he'd never been challenged in this way. "It wasn't here the last time I stopped by," he said, businesslike but not unkind. "I wanted to know who was setting up here."

"I arrived last night." Allegra glanced toward the nearby shack; her neighbor was nowhere to be seen, yet she observed that the front door was ajar. "Came in yesterday from the *Long Journey*," she continued, softening her own tone. "I couldn't find another place to stay, so . . ."

"Everyone from the *Journey* is being put over there." The young blueshirt turned to point toward the other side of Shuttlefield; as he did, she noticed the chevrons on the right sleeve of his uniform. "Didn't anyone tell you?"

"No one told me anything . . . and now I suppose you want me to move." She didn't relish the thought of packing up again and relocating across town. At least here she was closer to Liberty; it would cut her morning hike to work. "I spoke with the lady who lives next door, and she didn't seem to mind if I . . ."

"I know. I've just talked to her." He cast a wary eye upon the shack, and for an instant it seemed like the door moved a few inches, as if someone behind it was eavesdropping. The Proctor raised a hand to his face. "Can I speak with you in private?" he whispered. "You're not in trouble, I promise. It's just . . . we need to talk."

Mystified, Allegra nodded, and the blueshirt led her around to the other side of the tent. He crouched once more, and she settled down upon her knees. From there they could only see the shack roof; even the chicken pen was hidden from sight.

"My name's Chris," he said quietly as he offered his hand. "Chris Levin . . . I'm the Chief Proctor."

A lot of authority for someone nearly young enough to be her son. "Allegra DiSilvio," she replied, shaking hands with him. "Look, I'm sorry I was so . . ."

"Don't worry about it." Chris displayed a smile that didn't quite reach his eyes. "I'm sure you've noticed by now, but the lady over there . . . well, she keeps to herself. Doesn't leave the house much."

"I picked up on that."

Chris idly plucked at some grass between his knees. "Her name's Cecelia . . . Cecelia Levin, although everyone calls her Sissy. She's my mother."

Allegra felt the blood rush from her face. She suddenly recalled the old woman having mentioned that she had a son in Liberty. "I'm sorry. I didn't know."

"You couldn't have. You've just arrived." He shook his head. "Look, my mother is . . . truth is, she's not well. She's very sick, in fact . . . as you may have noticed."

Allegra nodded. His mother had stood out in the pouring rain the night before and raved about how she owned both her chickens and the stars; yes, that qualified as unusual behavior. "I'm sorry to hear that."

"Can't be helped. Mom's been through a lot in the last few years. She—" He broke off. "Long story. In any case, that's why no one has set up camp out here. People are afraid of her . . . and to tell the truth, she chases them away. Which is why you're unusual."

"How come?"

Chris raised his eyes, and she could see that they were much the same as his mother's: blue yet somehow hollow, although not with quite the same degree of darkness. "She let you stay. Believe me, if she didn't like you, your tent wouldn't still be standing. Oh, she might have let you spend the night, but as soon as you left she would have set fire to it. That's what she's done to everyone else who's tried to camp next to her."

Allegra felt a cold chill. She started to rise, but Chris clasped her wrist. "No, no . . . calm down. She's not going to do that. She likes you. She told me so herself."

"She . . . likes me?"

"Uh-huh . . . or at least as much as she likes anyone these days. She believes you're a nice woman who's come to keep her company."

"She wouldn't even speak to me this morning!"

"She's shy."

"Oh, for the love of . . . !"

"Look," he said, an edge in his voice, "she wants you to stay, and I want you to stay. No one will bother you out here, and she needs someone to look out for her."

"I . . . I can't do that," Allegra said. "I've just taken a job in Liberty . . . washing dishes at the community hall. I can't afford to . . ."

"Great. I'm glad you've found work." He paused, and smiled meaningfully. "That won't pay much, though, and by winter this tent of yours will be pretty cold. But I can fix that. Stay here and take care of Mom when you're not working, and you'll have your own cabin . . . with a woodstove and even your own privy. That's better than anyone else from your ship will get. And you'll never have to deal with gangs or turf-tax. Anyone who bothers you spends six months in the stockade, doing hard time on the public works crew. Got me?"

Allegra understood. She was being given the responsibility of looking out for the demented mother of the Chief Proctor. So long as Sissy Levin had company, Allegra DiSilvio would never have to worry about freezing to death in the dark, being shaken down by the local stooges, or being raped in her tent. She would have shelter, protection, and the solitude she craved.

"Got you," she said. "It's a deal."

They shook on it, then Chris heaved himself to his feet, extending a hand to help her up. "I'll talk to Mom, tell her that you're staying," he said. "Don't rush things. She'll introduce herself to you when she feels like it. But I think you'll make great friends."

"Thanks. We'll work things out." Allegra watched as he turned toward the shack. The door was cracked open; for an instant, she caught a glimpse of Sissy's face. "Just one more thing . . ."

"Yes?" The Chief stopped, looked back at her.

"How long have you been here? I mean . . . which ship did you come in on?"

Chris hesitated. "We've been here three Coyote years," he said. "We came aboard the *Alabama*."

Allegra gaped at him. "I thought all the first-timers had left."

He nodded solemnly. "They did. We're the ones who stayed behind."

"So why . . . ?"

But he was already walking away. Obviously, that was a question he didn't want to answer.

Time was measured by the length of her hair. A week after Allegra started work at the community kitchen, she had little more than fuzz on top of her head; that was the day she palmed a small paring knife from the sink and took it home. Its absence wasn't noticed, and it gave her the first tool she needed to do her work. By the time her shack was built, she no longer needed to wear a head scarf, and she used a few credits to purchase a brush from the general store in Liberty (where she was allowed to enter, so long as she bought something). She had to push back her hair from her face while she finished carving her first flute. A short blade of sourgrass inserted within the bamboo shaft below the mouthpiece served as its reed, and with a little practice she was able to play simple tunes, although not well. It wasn't until late summer, when her chestnut hair had finally returned to the neck length she'd worn it on Earth, that she finally had her first real conversation with Sissy Levin.

For many weeks, her reclusive neighbor continued to avoid her; their brief encounter the first night Allegra spent on Coyote was the only time she'd spoken with her. Every morning, just after sunrise when Allegra left to go into Liberty, she spotted Sissy feeding her chickens. She'd wave and call her name—"Good morning, Ms. Levin, how are you?"—and she had little doubt that her voice carried across the short distance between their shacks, but Sissy never acknowledged her except for the briefest of nods. So Allegra would go to work, and early in the afternoon she'd return to find her neighbor nowhere in sight. Every now and then, Allegra would venture over to knock on her door, yet no matter how long or patiently she'd wait outside, Sissy never greeted her.

Nonetheless, there were signs that Sissy was coming to accept her. About half a month after a group of men from the Carpenters Guild arrived with a cartful of lumber and spent the afternoon building a one-room shack for Allegra, complete with a woodstove fashioned from a discarded fuel cell, some basic furniture, and a small privy out back ("No charge, lady," the foreman said, "this one's on the Chief") she came home to find a wicker basket of fresh eggs on the front porch. Allegra carefully placed the eggs in the cabinet above the stove, then carried the basket over to Sissy's house. Again, there was no response to her knocks, and finally Allegra gave up and went home, leaving the basket next to her door. A few days later, though, the basket reappeared . . . this time, though just after sunrise, even before Allegra had woken up.

This pattern continued for a while. Then one afternoon, Allegra returned home to open the door and discover a dead chicken hanging upside down from the ceiling. The bird hadn't been plucked or cleaned; it was simply a carcass, its neck broken, its feet tied together with the rough twine from which it had been suspended from a crossbeam. Allegra shrieked when she saw it, and for a moment she thought she heard mad laughter from next door. She didn't know whether it was a gift or a threat, but she wasn't about to ask; she didn't know how to clean the bird, so she took it to the community hall the next morning, and a cook with whom she'd become friendly did it for her. The chicken made a good lunch, and Allegra kept the feathers as stuffing for a pillow. Nevertheless, she stayed away from Sissy for a while, and three weeks passed before she found any more eggs on her doorstep.

The first flute Allegra made didn't have a very good sound, so she gathered some more bamboo and started over again, this time experimenting with different kinds of reeds: faux birch bark, chicken feathers, cloverleaf, whatever else she could find. She'd never fashioned her own instruments before—what little she knew, she'd learned from observing craftsmen back in New England—so it was mainly a matter of trial and error. Eventually, she discovered that swamper skin, cured and tightly stretched, produced the best results. She got it from a glovemaker in Shuttlefield; when Sissy began leaving eggs on her doorstep again, Allegra bartered a few for a square foot of skin, with the promise that she wouldn't go into the clothing business herself.

Early one evening she sat out on her front porch, playing the flute she'd most recently fashioned. The sun had gone down, and Bear was rising to the east; she'd carried a fish-oil lamp out onto the porch, and its warm glow cast her shadow across the rough planks of the porch. The night was cool, the air redolent with the scent of approaching autumn. Not far away, she could see bonfires within Shuttlefield. It was the fourth week of Uriel, the last month of Coyote summer; next Zaphael would be First Landing Day, the colony's biggest holiday. Already the inhabitants were gearing up for the celebration, yet she wanted nothing to do with it. Her only desire was to be left alone, to practice her art in solitude.

The new flute had a nice sound: neither too shrill nor too low, and she was able to run up and down the scales without any effort. Now that she knew how to make one, it shouldn't be hard to duplicate others like it. On impulse, she shifted to a piece she'd written for the Connecticut River Ensemble. She was about halfway through the first stanza when a nearby voice began humming the melody, and she turned to see Sissy Levin standing next to her.

Allegra was so startled, she nearly dropped the flute. Sissy didn't notice. She leaned against the awning post, her eyes closed, a soft smile upon her face. In the wan lamplight, Allegra could clearly see the deep wrinkles around her mouth, the crow's-feet at the corners of her eyes; as always, her hair was an uncombed mass that formed a ragged halo around her head. Even so, at that moment she seemed at peace.

Her fingers trembling upon the flute, Allegra managed to finish the composition, with Sissy humming along with it. When she followed a melody, Allegra realized, Sissy had a beautiful voice; she repeated the first stanza just so she could hear more of it. When she was done, she lowered her instrument, but was careful not to speak. Let the moment take its own course. . . .

"That's a nice song," Sissy said quietly, not opening her eyes. "What's it called?"

" 'Deerfield River,' " Allegra replied. "Do you like it?"

A nod, ever so slight. "I think I remember it. Wasn't it once in a movie?"

"No . . . no, not that I know of." Although there were probably other pieces that sounded a bit like it; Allegra's style had been influenced by earlier composers. "It's my own. I wrote it for—"

"I think I once heard it in a movie. The one where there's a man who meets this woman in Vienna, and they fall in love even though she's dying, and then they—" She stopped abruptly, and opened her eyes to gaze off into some private memory. "It's a great movie. I really liked it. Jim and I saw it . . . oh, I don't know how many times. I'm sorry about the chicken. It was meant to be a joke, but I don't think you thought it was very funny."

The abrupt change of subject caught Allegra off guard. For a moment, she didn't know what Sissy was talking about. "Well . . . no, it wasn't, but . . ."

"That was Beatrice. She was very old and couldn't lay eggs anymore, and she'd bully the other hens, so I had to . . ." Her hands came together, made a throttling motion. "Very sad, very sad . . . I hope at least that you did something good with her."

"I took her to work," Allegra said. "At the community kitchen. We . . ."

"The grange."

"Yes, the grange hall. A friend of mine cleaned her and we had it—I mean, we had her—for lunch." She wondered if she should be saying this; Beatrice had apparently meant something to Sissy.

"Good. At least you didn't throw her away. That would've been . . . cruel. She laid good eggs, and it would have been disrespectful. You haven't thrown those away, I hope."

"Oh, no!" Allegra shook her head. "I've eaten every one. They're delicious. Thank you very much for—"

"Did you make this?" Sissy darted forward, snatched the flute from her hands. Afraid that she'd damage it, Allegra started to reach for her instrument, but stopped herself when she saw how carefully Sissy handled it. She closely studied the patterns carved along the shaft, then before Allegra could object she blew into the mouthpiece. A harsh piping note came out, and she winced. "You do this much better. Can you make me one?"

"I . . . I'd be happy to." Allegra thought of the half dozen inferior flutes in her shack, and briefly considered giving one to her neighbor. But no . . . she'd want one that sounded just like Allegra's. "I'm already planning to make more, so I'll give you the first one I . . ."

"You're going to make more? Why?"

"Well, I was thinking about selling them. To earn a little more . . ."

"No." Sissy didn't raise her voice, yet her tone was uncompromising. "No no no no. I won't allow you to sell anything out here. It'll bring the others, the . . ." She glanced in the direction of the ale-soaked laughter that brayed from the bonfires. "I don't want them around. If they come, they'll bring Rigil Kent."

"Oh, no. I don't intend to sell them here." Allegra had recently struck up tentative friendships with various kiosk owners in Shuttlefield, and there was even a shop owner in Liberty who'd expressed interest in her work. Like Sissy, she had no wish to have strangers appearing at her front door. Yet something else she said raised her attention. "Who . . . who's Rigil Kent?"

Sissy's face darkened, and for a moment Allegra was afraid that she'd said the wrong thing. But Sissy simply handed the flute back to her, then thrust her hands into the pocket of her threadbare apron.

"If he comes back," she said quietly, "you'll know."

She started to turn away, heading back toward her shack. Then she stopped and looked back at Allegra. "I'll give you more eggs if you teach me how to play. Can you do that?"

"I'd be delighted, Sissy."

Her brow raised in astonishment. "How do you know my name?"

"Chris told me."

"Chris." She scowled. "My son. Fat worthless . . ." She stopped herself, rubbed her eyes. "What did you say your name was?"

"Allegra. Allegra DiSilvio."

She considered this. "Nice name. Sounds like music. The movie I saw, it was called . . ." She shook her head. "Never mind. I'm Cecelia . . . my friends call me Sissy."

"Pleased to meet you, Sissy," Allegra said. "Drop by anytime."

"No more chickens. I promise." And then she walked away. Allegra watched until she disappeared inside her shack, and only then she let out her breath.

At least Sissy was speaking to her.

* * *

Three nights later, she met Rigil Kent.

Allegra had no desire to participate in the First Landing Day festivities, but it was hard to avoid them; when she reported to work that morning, the kitchen staff was already busy preparing for the evening fiesta. Several hogs had been slaughtered the night before and were being slow-roasted in the smokehouse behind the hall, while huge cauldrons of potatoes and beans simmered on the kitchen stoves; out back, kegs of sourgrass ale were being unloaded from a cart. After breakfast was over, while the cooks began baking bread and strawberry pie, she helped cover the table with fresh white linen, upon which were placed center-pieces of fresh-cut wildflowers.

Matriarch Luisa Hernandez stopped by shortly after noon. A thickset woman with short auburn hair beneath the raised hood of her blue robe, the colonial governor was seldom seen in public; this was only the third time Allegra had laid eyes upon her. She hovered near the door, silently observing the preparations, Savant Castro at her side speaking to her in a low voice. At one point, Allegra glanced over to see the Matriarch studying her from across the room. Their eyes met, and a faint smile touched the other woman's lips. She briefly nodded to Allegra. Feeling a chill, Allegra went back to setting tables; when she looked again, the Matriarch had disappeared, as had Manuel Castro.

Did the Matriarch know who she was? She had to assume that she did. With any luck, though, she would leave her alone.

What surprised her the most, though, was one of the decorations: a flag of the United Republic of America, carefully unwrapped from a plastic bag and suspended from the rafters high above the hall. When Allegra asked where it had come from, one of the cooks told her that it had been presented to Captain Robert E. Lee shortly before the *Alabama* escaped from Earth. The original settlers had left it behind, and now it was kept by Matriarch Hernandez in trust for the colony, to be publicly displayed only on this day.

Only on this day. For most of the Coyote year—1,096 days, or three Earth-years—the colony carefully doled out its meager resources in only dribs and drabs. There were few other holidays, and none as important or elaborate as this; on this day, the residents of Shuttlefield gathered together at the community hall for a great feast commemorating the arrival of the *Alabama*. Yet as she headed home, she saw shopkeepers closing storm shutters and nailing boards across their doors, noted the absence of children, the increased visibility of Proctors and Union Guard soldiers.

Suddenly she understood. This was the day the proletariat would be allowed to gorge themselves on rich food, get drunk on ale, celebrate a ghastly replication of freedom under the indulgent yet watchful eye of Union authority. A brief loosening of the leash to keep the commoners happy and content, while tactfully reminding them that it was only a temporary condition. Walking through Shuttlefield, though, she saw that the subtlety had been lost on everyone. No one was working, and by early afternoon the First Landing celebration was already in full swing. Out in the streets, the various guilds and groups that ruled Shuttlefield were carousing beneath the autumn sun: handmade banners flew above tents and shacks, while drunks staggered about with beads around their necks and wildness in their eyes, proclaiming everyone they saw to be their best friend. The paths between the camps were jagged with broken ale jugs, the air rank with smoke, alcohol, and piss. She came upon crowd cheering at something in their midst; stepping closer, Allegra saw two naked men, their bodies caked with mud, wrestling in the middle of a drainage ditch.

Disgusted, she quickly moved away, only to have her arm grabbed by someone who thought she needed a kiss. She managed to pull herself free, but he wasn't giving up so easily. "C'mon, sweets, y'know you wan' it," he slurred as he followed her down the street. "Jus' a lil' sugar, tha's all I . . ."

"Get lost, Will," a familiar voice said. "Leave her alone, or you'll spend the night in the stockade."

Allegra looked around, found Chris Levin behind her. Two other Proctors were with him; one had already twisted the drunk's arm behind his back, and the other booted him in the ass. He fell facedown into the mud, muttered an obscenity, then hauled himself to his feet and wandered away.

"Sorry about that." Chris paid little attention to what was going on behind them. "You're not hurt, are you?"

An odd question, considering what his men had just done to the drunk. "You didn't need to . . ."

"Sorry, but I think I did." He turned to his officers. "You guys continue patrol. I'll walk her home." They nodded and headed away. "And keep an eye on the creek," he called after them. "If you see anything, let me know."

That piqued her curiosity; he obviously meant Sand Creek, the narrow river that bordered the two settlements to the east. Chris saw the puzzled look on her face. "Nothing for you to worry about," he said quietly. "Look, if you don't mind, I'd like for you to stay with my mother tonight. You may have to skip the fiesta, but . . ."

"That's all right. I wasn't planning to attend anyway." From what she'd already seen, the last place she wanted to be was at the community hall.

"I was hoping you'd say that." He seemed genuinely relieved. "If you want, I can have dinner brought over to you. . . ."

"I'd appreciate that." They sidestepped a couple of more drunks swaggering down the street, their arms around each other. One of them bumped shoulders with Chris; he turned and started to swear at the Chief Proctor, then realized who he was and thought better of it. Chris stared them down, then ushered Allegra away. "One more thing," he murmured, reaching beneath his jacket. "I think you should keep this with you."

She stared at the small pistol he offered her. A Peacekeeper Mark III flechette gun, the type carried by the Union Guard. "No, sorry . . . that's where I draw the line."

Chris hesitated, then saw that arguing with her was pointless. "Suit yourself," he said. He reholstered the pistol, then unclipped a com unit from his belt. "But carry this, at least. If you run into any trouble, give us a call. We'll have someone out there as quick as we can."

Allegra accepted the com, slipped it in a pocket of her catskin vest. "Are you really expecting much trouble tonight?"

"Not really. Things might get a little out of control once people start drinking hard, but . . ." He shrugged. "Nothing we can't handle." Then he paused. "But there's a small chance that Mama might . . . well, someone might come to see her that she doesn't want to see."

"Rigil Kent?"

She smiled when she said that, meaning it as a joke, yet Chris gave her a sharp look. "What has she told you?" he asked, his voice low.

His question surprised her, although she was quick enough to hide her expression. Until that moment, she'd assumed that "Rigil Kent" was a manifestation of Sissy's madness, an imaginary person she'd created as a stand-in for everyone she distrusted. Certainly there was no one in the colony who went by that name; she'd already checked the roll to make sure. But Chris apparently accepted him as being real.

"A little." Which wasn't entirely untruthful. "Enough to know that she hates him."

Chris was quiet for a moment. "He may come into town tonight," he said. "This time last year, he led a small raiding party up Sand Creek. They broke into the armory in Liberty and made off with some guns, then left a note on the door signed as Rigil Kent." He shook his head. "You don't need to know what it said. But before they did all that, he stopped by to see Mama. He wanted her to come with them. She refused, of course . . . she despises him almost as much as I do."

"Of course. Can't blame her."

That caused him to raise an eyebrow. "Then you know what he did."

She shrugged. "Like I said, not very much. She hasn't told me everything."

"Probably not." He looked down at the ground as they walked along. "He used to be my best friend, back when we were kids. But then he killed my brother and . . . anyway, there's things you just don't forgive."

Apparently not. And now she had a better idea whom he was talking about. "If he shows up, I'll let you know."

"I'd appreciate it." By then they were on the outskirts of town; her shack was only a few hundred feet away. "You know, she's really come to like you," he said. "That's a major accomplishment . . . for her, I mean. She used to live in Liberty, in the cabin my dad built for us. I still live there, but she moved all the way out here because she didn't want to see anyone anymore . . . not even me. But you've managed to get through to her somehow."

"We've got much in common," Allegra said. And that, at least, wasn't a lie.

Allegra took a nap, then changed into a long skirt and a sweater. Through her window, she could see Uma setting to the west, Bear rising to the east. She usually began making dinner about that time, but this night she'd get a break from that chore if Chris kept his word about sending over food from the community hall. So she picked up her flute, along with the one she'd finished the previous evening, and went out to sit on the porch and watch the sun go down.

As twilight set in, Shuttlefield went quiet. No doubt everyone had gone into Liberty for the fiesta. She waited until she heard the chickens clucking in her neighbor's backyard, then she picked up her flute and began to play. Not one of her own pieces this time, but a traditional English hymn she'd learned while studying music at Berklee. For some reason, it seemed appropriate for the moment.

After a while, she heard the door of Sissy's shack creak open. Allegra didn't look up but continued playing, and a minute later there was the faint rustle of an apron next to her. "That's very nice," Sissy said quietly. "What's it called?"

" 'Jerusalem.' " Allegra smiled. "It's really easy to play. Would you like to try?"

Sissy quickly shook her head. "Oh, no . . . I can't. . . ."

"No, really. It's simple. Here . . ." She picked up the new flute. "I made this for you. Try it out."

Sissy stared at it. "I . . . but I have to start dinner. . . ."

"No, you don't. It's being brought to us tonight. Roast pork, potatoes, fresh greens, pie . . . the works." She grinned. "Believe me, it's good. Helped make it myself."

Sissy stared at her, and Allegra realized that it was probably the first time in many years that she had been offered a meal. For a few seconds she was afraid that her neighbor would flee back to her windowless hovel, slam the door shut, and not emerge again for several days. Yet a look of wary acceptance came upon her face. Taking the flute, Sissy sat down on the porch.

"Show me how you do this," she said. ˙

It didn't take long for her to learn how to work the finger holes; teaching her how to master the first notes, though, took a little more effort. Yet Sissy didn't give up; she seemed determined to learn how to play, and she gave Allegra her undivided attention as the younger woman patiently demonstrated the basic fingering techniques.

They took a break when someone arrived with two covered baskets. Allegra carried them inside; Sissy was reluctant to follow her until Allegra pointed out that it would be much less messy if they ate indoors. The older woman stood quietly, her hands folded in front of her, and watched as she lit the oil lamp and set the table for two. Allegra only had one chair; she was about to sit on the bed when Sissy abruptly disappeared, returning a few moments later with a rickety chair of her own. She placed it at the table, then sat down and watched as Allegra served her a plate.

They ate in silence; through the open door, they could hear the distant sounds of the First Landing festivities. The night was becoming cool, so Allegra shut the door, then put some wood in the stove and started a fire. Sissy never looked up from her meal; she ate with total concentration, never speaking while she cleaned her plate and beckoned for seconds. Allegra wondered how long it had been since she had eaten anything except chicken and eggs. She made a note to herself to start bringing home leftovers from the kitchen; malnutrition might have something to do with Sissy's mental condition. . . .

"Why are you here?" Sissy asked.

The question was abrupt, without preamble . . . and, Allegra realized, it was the very same one she'd posed the night they first met. But they were no longer strangers, rather two friends enjoying a quiet dinner together. How much had changed since then.

"You mean, why did I come here?" Allegra shrugged. "Like I told you . . . I couldn't find anywhere else in town, so I pitched my . . ."

"That's not what I mean."

Allegra didn't say anything for a moment. She put her knife and fork together on her plate, folded her hands, to and turned her gaze toward the window. Far away across the fields, she could see the house lights of Liberty; in that instant, they resembled the lights of cities she had left behind, the places she had visited. Atlanta, Dallas, Brasilia, Mexico City . . .

"A long time ago," she began, "I was . . . well, I wasn't rich, nor was I famous, but I had a lot of money and I was quite well known. For what I do, I mean."

"For making music."

"For making music, yes." She absently played with her fork, stirring some gravy left on her plate. "I traveled a great deal and was constantly in demand as a composer. All the people I knew were artists who were also rich and famous." As rich as social collectivism would allow, at least; she'd learned how to stash her overseas royalties quietly in trust funds maintained by European banks, as many people did to avoid the domestic salary caps imposed by the Union. But it was complicated, and there was no reason why Sissy should have to know that. "And for a while I was satisfied with my life, but then . . . I don't know. At some point, I stopped enjoying life. It seemed as if everyone I knew was a stranger, that the only things they wanted were more fame, more money, and all I wanted was to practice my art. And then one day, I found that I couldn't even do that anymore. . . ."

"You couldn't make music?"

Allegra didn't look up. "No. Oh, I could still play"—she picked up her flute from where she had placed it on the table—"but nothing new came to me, just variations of things I'd done before. And when it became obvious to everyone that I was blocked, all the people I thought were my friends went away, and I was alone."

"What about your family?"

She felt wetness at the corners of her eyes. "No family. I never made time for that. Too busy. There was once someone I loved, but . . ." She took a deep breath that rattled in her throat. "Well, it wasn't long before he was gone, too."

Allegra picked up the napkin from her lap, daubed her eyes. "So I decided to leave everything behind, go as far away as I could. The Union Astronautica had started the public lottery for people who wanted to come here. The selection was supposed to be totally random, but I met someone who knew how to rig the system. I gave him everything I owned so that I'd get a winning number, then took only what I could carry in my bag. And . . . well, anyway, here I am."

"So why are you here?"

Allegra gazed across the table at Sissy. Hadn't she heard anything she had just said? Just as on Earth, everything she did was pointless—another exercise in self-indulgence. Yet she couldn't bring herself to scold her neighbor. It wasn't Sissy's fault that she was disturbed. Someone had hurt her a long time ago, and now . . .

"Excuse me. I think I need to visit the privy." Allegra pushed back her chair, stood up. "If you'd gather the dishes and put 'em over there, I'll wash them tomorrow."

"Okay." Sissy continued to stare at her. "If there's any food left, can I give it to my chickens?"

"Sure. Why not?" She tried not to laugh. Her best friend was a lunatic who cared more about her damn birds than anything else. "I'll be back," she said, then opened the door and stepped outside.

The night was darker than she'd expected; a thick blanket of clouds had moved across the sky, obscuring the wan light cast by Bear. She regretted not having carried a lamp with her, yet the privy was located only a couple of dozen feet behind her house, and she knew the way even in the dark.

She was halfway across the backyard, though, when she heard the soft crackle of a foot stepping upon dry grass, somewhere close behind her.

Allegra stopped, slowly turned . . . and a rod was thrust against her chest. "Hold it," a voice said, very quietly. "Don't move."

Against the darkness, she detected a vague form. The rod was a rifle barrel; of that she was certain, although she couldn't see anything else. "Sure, all right," she whispered, even as she realized that the voice had spoken in English. "Please don't hurt me."

"We won't, if you cooperate." *We* won't? That meant there were others nearby. "Where's Cecelia?"

"I don't . . ." It took Allegra a moment to realize that he meant Sissy. "She's gone. I don't know where she is . . . maybe at the fiesta."

By then her eyes had become dark-adapted, and she could make out the figure a little better: a bearded young man, probably in his early twenties, wearing a catskin serape, his eyes shaded by a broad hat. She carefully kept her hands in sight, and although he didn't turn it away from her, at least he stepped back a little when he saw that she wasn't armed.

"I rather doubt that," he murmured. "She doesn't go into town much."

"How would you know?"

A pause. "Then you know who I am."

"I've got a good idea. . . ."

"Get this over, man," a voice whispered from behind her. "We're running out of—"

"Calm down." The intruder hesitated, his head briefly turning toward her cabin. "Is she in there?" She didn't answer. "Call her out."

"No. Sorry, but I won't."

He let out his breath. "Look, I'm not going to hurt her, or you either. I just want to talk to—"

"She doesn't want to talk to you." Allegra remembered the com Chris had given her. It was on her bedside table, where she had put it before she had taken her afternoon nap. Even if she could get to it, she wasn't sure how much difference it would make. The Proctors were a long way off, and these men sounded as if they were anxious to leave. "If you want to speak to her, you're going to have to go in there yourself."

He took a step toward the cabin. "Carlos, damn it!" the one behind her snapped. "We don't have time for this! Let's go!"

Carlos. Now she knew who he was, even if she had only suspected it before: Carlos Montero, one of the original settlers. The teenager who had sailed alone down the Great Equatorial River, charting the southern coast of Midland the year after the *Alabama* arrived. Like the other colonists, he'd vanished into the wilderness when the *Glorious Destiny* showed up. Now he was back.

"So you're Rigil Kent," she whispered. "Glad to make your acquaintance."

"Guess they found my note." He chuckled softly. "I imagine Chris doesn't have much good to say about me."

"Neither does his mother. Please, just leave her alone."

"Look, I don't want to push this." He lowered his gun. "Would you just deliver a message . . . ?"

"Damn it!" Now the second figure came in sight; Allegra wasn't surprised to see that he wasn't much older than Carlos, also wearing a poncho and carrying a rifle. He grasped his friend's arm, pulling him away. "Time's up, man! Move or lose it!"

"Cut it out, Barry." Carlos shook off his hand, looked at Allegra again. "Tell her Susan's all right, that she's doing well, and so's Wendy. Tell her that we miss her, and if she ever changes her mind, all she has to do is . . ."

A brilliant flash from the direction of the landing field. For a moment Allegra thought someone was shooting off fireworks, then the hollow thud of an explosion rippled across the Shuttlefield as a ball of fire rose above the settlement. She suddenly knew what it was: one of the *Long Journey* shuttles blowing up.

"That's it! We're out of here!" Barry turned to run, sprinting away into the dark marshland behind the shacks. "Go!"

Yet Carlos lingered for another moment. Now Allegra could see him clearly; there was a ruthless grin on his face as he looked at her one last time. "And one more thing," he said, no longer bothering to keep his voice low, "and you can pass this along to Chris or whoever else . . . Coyote belongs to us!" He jabbed a finger toward the explosion. "Rigil Kent was here!"

And then he was gone, loping off into the swamp. In another moment he had vanished, leaving behind the shouts of angry and frightened men, the rank odor of burning fuel.

Wrapping her arms around herself, Allegra walked back to the cabin. As she turned the corner, she was surprised to find Sissy standing outside the door. She watched the distant conflagration, her face without emotion. Allegra saw that she clutched her flute.

"He returned." Her voice was a hoarse whisper. "I knew he would."

"I . . . I saw him." Allegra came closer, intending to comfort her. "He was outside. He told me to tell you . . ."

"I know. I heard everything . . . every word."

And then she raised the flute, put it to her mouth, and began to play the opening bars of "Jerusalem." Flawlessly, without a single missed note.

The shuttle burned all night; by morning it was a blackened skeleton that lay in the center of the landing field. Fortunately, the blaze didn't spread to the rest of Shuttlefield; Allegra would later learn that the townspeople, upon realizing that their homes weren't in danger, abandoned all efforts at forming a bucket brigade and spent the rest of the night dancing around the burning spacecraft, throwing empty ale jugs into the pyre. It was the highlight of First Landing Day, one people would talk about for a long time to come.

Later that day, Chris Levin came out to check on his mother. She was through feeding the chickens, though, and didn't want to talk to him. The door of her shack remained shut even after he pounded on it, and after a while he gave up and walked over to visit Allegra. She told him that they'd spent a quiet evening in her house and were unaware of any trouble until they heard the explosion. No, they hadn't seen anyone; did he know who was responsible? Chris didn't seem entirely satisfied by her answer, but he didn't challenge it, either. Allegra returned the com he'd lent her, and he left once again.

In the months to come, as the last warm days faded away and the long autumn set in, she continued to make flutes. Once she had enough, she began selling them to shops and kiosks. Most of those who purchased them didn't know how to play them, so she began giving lessons, at first in Shuttlefield, then in Liberty. By midwinter she was holding weekly seminars in the community center, and earning enough that she was eventually able to quit her job as a dishwasher. Some of her students turned out to have talent, and it wasn't long before she had trained enough musicians to form the Coyote Wood Ensemble.

One morning, she awoke to see the first flakes of snow falling upon the marshes. Winter was coming, and yet she didn't feel the cold. Instead, for the first time in many years, she perceived a muse whose voice she hadn't heard in many years. She picked up her flute, put it to her lips, and without thinking about what she was doing, began to play an unfamiliar melody; for her, it sounded like a song of redemption. When she was done, there were tears in her eyes. Two days later, she taught it to her students. She called the piece "Cecelia."

Despite invitations to move to Liberty, she remained in Shuttlefield, living in the small one-room cabin on the outskirts of town. Every morning, just after sunrise, she sat outside and waited for her neighbor to finish feeding the chickens. Then, regardless of whether the days were warm or if there was snow on the ground, they would practice together. Two women, playing the flute, watching the sun come up over Shuttlefield.

And waiting. Waiting for the return of Rigil Kent.

Part 2

BENJAMIN THE UNBELIEVER
(from the memoirs of Benjamin Harlan)

Three days after I betrayed the prophet, the hunting party from Defiance found me at the base of Mt. Shaw: starving, barely conscious, more dead than alive. At least so I'm told; that part of my memory is a blank spot. The hunters fashioned a litter from tree branches, then tied me to it and dragged me back to their hidden settlement. I slept for the next two days, waking up only now and then, often screaming from nightmares that I don't remember.

I went into the wilderness of Midland along with thirty-one people, including their leader, the Reverend Zoltan Shirow. I was the only one who came back out. So far as I know, the rest are dead, including the woman I loved. I tried to save them, but I couldn't. Indeed, perhaps only God could have saved them . . . and if Zoltan is to be believed, then God had His own plans for him.

I begin my story here so you'll know, from the beginning, that it ends in tragedy. This is a dark tale, no two ways about it. Zoltan's disciples were in search of spiritual transformation; I wish I could believe that they achieved their goal, yet there's no way of knowing, for when the time came for me to stand with them, I fled for my life. Though my motives were base and self-serving, I'm the only one who survived.

A lot of time has passed since then, but I've never spoken about what happened until now. Not just because what I endured has been too painful to recall, but also because I've had to give myself time to understand what happened. Guilt is a terrible burden, and no one who considers himself to be a decent person should ever have to shoulder the blame for abandoning someone he loved.

This is my testament: the final days of Zoltan Shirow, God's messenger to Coyote, as told by Ben Harlan, his last remaining follower. Or, as Zoltan liked to call me, Benjamin the Unbeliever.

The prophet fell from the sun on a cold winter morning, his coming heralded not by the trumpets of angels but by the sonic boom of an orbital shuttle. I was standing at the edge of the snow-covered landing field as the spacecraft gently touched down, waiting to unload freight from the starship that had arrived a couple of days earlier. I like to think that, if I had known who was aboard, I might have called in sick, but the truth is that it wouldn't have mattered, because Zoltan probably would have found me anyway. Just as Jesus needed Judas to fulfill his destiny, Zoltan needed me . . . and I needed the job.

Good-paying jobs were tough to find in Shuttlefield. I'd been on Coyote for nearly seven months, a little more than a year and a half by Earth reckoning. My ship, the *Long Journey*—full name, the WHSS *Long Journey to the Galaxy in the Spirit of Social Collectivism*—was the third Union Astronautica ship to reach 47 Ursae Majoris. On the strength of a winning number on a lottery ticket and promises of a better life on the new world, I'd spent forty-eight years in biostasis to get away from the Western Hemisphere Union, only to find that the same people who ran the show back there were also in charge out here. And that's how I found myself huddled in a leaky tent, eating creek crab stew and wondering how a smart guy like me had been rooked so badly, when the fact of the matter is that I'm not very smart and the system is rigged to take advantage of losers. So screw social collectivism and the horse it rode in on. On second thought, let's eat the horse—if we had one to eat, that is—and let the guys who came up with collectivist theory go screw themselves.

When it was announced, in the first week of Barchiel, c.y. 05, that the fourth Union ship from Earth—the WHSS *Magnificent Voyage to the Stars in Search of Social Collectivism*, or the *Magnificent Voyage* for short—had entered the system and would soon be making orbit around Coyote, I was the first person in line at the community hall in Liberty for the job of unloading freight from its shuttles. Literally the first; there were nearly three hundred guys behind me, waiting for a Union Guard soldier to open the door and let us in. During the warm seasons, we would have been working on the collective farms, but it was the middle of Coyote's 274-day winter and jobs were scarce, so I was willing to stand in the cold for three hours just for the chance to schlep cargo containers.

And that's why I was at the landing field in Shuttlefield that morning, stamping my feet in the snow and blowing in my hands as I watched the gangway come down from the shuttle's belly. The first people off were the pilot and copilot; perhaps they were expecting a brass band, because they stopped and stared at the dozen or so guys in patched-up parkas who looked as if they hadn't eaten a decent meal in six months. A Guard officer emerged from the crowd, saluted them, murmured a few words, then led them away. Poor bastards—nearly a half century in space, only to find starving peasants. I felt sorry for them, but envied them even more. As members of *Magnificent Voyage*'s flight crew, they'd have the benefit of warm houses and good food before they reboarded the starship to make the long return flight to Earth. They were just passing through; the rest of us were stuck here.

The passengers came next, a steady parade of men, women, and children, every one of them with the shaved heads and shuffling gait of those who've recently emerged from the dreamless coma of biostasis. Their duffel bags were stuffed with the few belongings they'd been allowed to bring from Earth, their parkas and caps were clean and new, and not one of them had any clue as to where they were or what they'd gotten themselves into. One by one, they stepped off the ramp, squinted against the bright sunlight, looked around in confusion, then followed the person in front of them, who didn't have a clue as to where he or she was going either. Fresh meat for Coyote. I found myself wondering how many of them would make it through their first year. We'd already lost more than forty colonists to hunger, cold, disease, and predators. The cemetery outside Liberty had room for plenty more.

About thirty people had come down the gangway when there was a pause in the procession. At first I thought everyone had disembarked, until I remembered that the shuttles had a passenger load of sixty. There had to be more; the shuttles wouldn't fly down half-full. I had just turned to the guy next to me—Jaime Hodge, one of my camp buddies—

and was about to say something like *What's the holdup?* when his eyes widened.

"Holy crap," Jaime murmured. "Would you look at that?"

I looked around to see a figure in a hooded white robe step through the hatch. At first I thought it was a Savant—just what we needed, another goddamn posthuman—but quickly realized I was wrong. For one thing, Savants wore black; for another, there was also a huge bulge on his back, as if he was carrying an oversize pack beneath his robe. He kept his head lowered, so I couldn't see his face.

And right behind him, a long line of men and women, each wearing identical robes. A few had their cowls pulled up, but most had let them fall back on their shoulders; unlike the other passengers, they weren't carrying bags. What really set them apart, though, was an air of implacable calm. No hesitation, no uncertainty; they followed their leader as if they knew exactly where they were going. Some actually smiled. I'd seen all kinds come off the shuttles, but never anything like this.

The first guy stepped off the ramp, stopped, turned around. Everyone behind him halted; they silently watched as he bent over. The shuttle's thrusters had melted away the snow, exposing charred grass and baked mud; he scooped up a fistful of dirt, then he rose and looked at the people behind him. He said something I didn't quite catch—"the promised land" was all I heard—before everyone on the ramp began to yell:

"Amen!"

"Thank you, Reverend!"

"Hallelujah!"

"Praise the Lord!"

"Oh, yeah. Go tell it on the mountain." Jaime glanced at me. "All we need now, a bunch of . . ."

Then his mouth sagged open, and so did mine, for at that instant the leader opened his robe and let it drop to his feet, and everyone got their first good look at who—or what—had just come to Coyote.

Two great wings the color of brown suede unfolded from his back. They expanded to full length, revealing serrated tips and delicate ribbing beneath the thin skin. Then he turned, and his face was revealed. Narrow eyes were sunk deep within a skull whose jaw had been enlarged to provide room for a pair of sharp fangs; above his broad mouth, a nose shortened to become a snout. His ears were oversize, slightly pointed at the tips. Like everyone else's, his body had been shaved before he had entered biostasis, yet dark stubble was growing back on his barrel chest. His arms were thick and muscular, his hands deformed claws with talons for fingers.

A murmur swept through the crowd as everyone shrank back; only the gargoyle remained calm. Indeed, it almost seemed as if he was relishing the moment. Then he smiled—benignly, like he was forgiving us—and bowed from the waist, folding his hands together as if in supplication.

"Sorry," he said, his voice oddly mild. "Didn't mean to shock you."

A couple of nervous laughs. He responded with a grin that exposed his fangs once more. "If you think *I'm* weird," he added, cocking a thumb toward the hatch behind him, "wait'll you get a load of the *next* guy."

Revulsion gave way to laughter. "Hey, man!" Jaime yelled. "Can you fly with those things?"

Irritation crossed his face, quickly replaced by a self-deprecating smile. "I don't know," he said. "Let me try."

Motioning for everyone to give him room, he stepped away from his entourage. He bent slightly forward, and the batlike wings spread outward to their full span—nearly eight feet, impressive enough to raise a few gasps.

"He's never going to make it," someone murmured. "Air's too thin." And he was right, of course. Coyote's atmospheric pressure at sea level was about the same as that of Denver or Albuquerque back on Earth. Oh, swoops had no trouble flying here, nor did skeeters, or any of the other birds and bugs that had evolved on this world. But a winged man? No way.

If the gargoyle heard this, though, he didn't pay attention. He shut his eyes, scrunched up his face, took a deep breath, held it . . . and the wings flapped feebly, not giving him so much as an inch of lift.

He opened one eye, peered at Jaime. "Am I there yet?" Then he looked down at his feet, saw that they hadn't left the ground. "Aw, shucks . . . all this way for nothing."

By then everyone was whooping it up. It was the funniest thing we'd seen in months . . . and believe me, there wasn't much to laugh about on Coyote. The batman's followers joined in; they could take a joke. He let the laughter run its course, then he folded his wings and stood erect.

"Now that we've met," he said, speaking loudly enough for all to hear, "let me introduce myself. I'm Zoltan Shirow . . . the Reverend Zoltan Shirow . . . founding pastor of the Church of Universal Transformation. Don't be scared, though . . . we're not looking for donations." That earned a couple of guffaws. "This is my congregation," he continued, gesturing to the people behind him. "We refer to ourselves as Universalists, but if you want, you can call us the guys in the white robes."

A few chuckles. "We're a small, nondenominational sect, and we've come here in search of religious freedom. Like I said, we're not looking for money, nor are we trying to make converts. All we want to do is be able to practice our beliefs in peace."

"What do you mean, universal transformation?" someone from the back of the crowd called out.

"You're pretty much looking at it." That brought some more laughs. "Seriously, though, once we've set up camp, you're all welcome to drop by for a visit. Tell your friends, too. And we'd likewise appreciate any hospitality you could show us . . . this is all new to us, and Lord knows we could use all the help we can get."

He stopped, looked around. "For starters, is there anyone here who could show us where we can put ourselves? No need for anyone to haul anything . . . we can carry our own belongings. Just someone to show us around."

To this day, I don't know why I raised my hand. Perhaps it was because I was charmed by a dude who looked like a bat and spoke like a stand-up comedian. Maybe I was just interested in finding out who these people were. I may have even wanted to see if they had anything I could beg, borrow, or steal. A few others volunteered, too, but Shirow saw me first. Almost at random, he pointed my way.

And that's how it all began. As simple as that.

The Universalists had brought a lot of stuff with them, much more than they would have normally been allowed under Union Astronautica regulations. Their belongings were clearly marked by the stenciled emblem of their sect—a red circle enclosing a white Gaelic cross—along with their individual names. As I watched, each church member claimed at least two bags, and they still left several large containers behind in the shuttle's cargo bay. True to Shirow's word, though, they politely declined assistance from anyone who offered to help carry their stuff; two members stayed behind to safeguard the containers until someone came back for them. And so I fell in with the Universalists, and together we walked into town.

It's hard to describe just how awful Shuttlefield was in those days. Adjectives like *stinking, impoverished,* or *filthy* don't quite cut it; *slum* and *hellhole* are good approximations, but they don't get close enough. Zoltan didn't seem to notice any of this. He strode through Shuttlefield as if he was a papal envoy, ignoring the hard-eyed stares of hucksters selling handmade clothes from their kiosks, artfully stepping past whores who tried to offer their services. At first I marched with him, pointing out the location of bathhouses and garbage pits, but he said little or nothing; his dark gaze roved across the town, taking in everything yet never stopping. After a while I found myself unable to keep up with him. Falling back into the ranks of his congregation, I found myself walking alongside a small figure whose hood was still raised.

"Doesn't speak much, does he?" I murmured.

"Oh, no," she replied. "Zoltan likes to talk. He just waits until he has something to say."

Glancing down at her, I found myself gazing into the most beautiful pair of blue-green eyes I'd ever seen. The girl wasn't more than nineteen or twenty, only half my age, and so petite that it seemed as if she would wilt in the cold; yet she carried about her an air of calm that seemed to make her invulnerable to the winter chill. She met my eye, favored me with a delicate smile.

"Just wait," she added. "You'll see."

"That's assuming I hang around long enough." I didn't mean it to sound insulting, but it came out that way.

She let it pass. "You're with us now, aren't you?"

"Well, yeah, but I'm trying to find a place for you to camp." We were near the middle of town. "We're not going to find anything if we keep going this way."

"What about over there?" This from a man walking along behind us; like the girl, his hooded cloak lent him a monkish appearance. He pointed to a small bare spot of ground between two camps. "We could put . . ."

"Oh, no, you don't." I shook my head. "That belongs to the Cutters Guild. And next to them is New Frontiers turf, the people who came on the second ship. Set up here, and you're in for a fight."

The girl shook her head. "We don't wish to quarrel with anyone." Then she looked at me again. "What do you mean by 'turf'?"

That led me to try to explain how things worked in Shuttlefield. "And what do the authorities have to say about this?" she asked. "We were told that there was a local government in place."

"Government?" I couldn't help but laugh out loud. "It's a joke. Shuttlefield's run by the Central Committee . . . Matriarch Hernandez and her crew, Union Astronautica officers from *Glorious Destiny*. We rarely see them down here . . . they're all in Liberty. So far as they're concerned, everyone here is just a supply of cheap labor. As long as we don't riot or burn the place down, they don't give a shit how we live."

The girl blanched. "What about the Guard?" she asked. "Aren't they supposed to protect the colony?"

"Look around." I waved a hand across the shantytown surrounding us. "You think there's law here? I've known guys who've had their throats cut just because they didn't pay their rent on time, and the Guard didn't do . . . um, squat about it. Same for the Proctors . . . the blueshirts, we call 'em. They work for the Committee, and their main job is making sure the status quo is maintained."

"So why don't you leave?" This from the man walking behind us. "Why stay here if it's so bad?"

I shrugged. "Where would we go?" Before he could answer that, I went on. "Oh, sure, New Florida's big enough for another colony, and there's a whole planet that hasn't been explored . . . but once you get outside the perimeter defense system, you're on your own, and there are things out there that'll kill you before you can bat an eye."

"So no one has left?"

"The original colonists did. That was a long time ago, though, and no one has seen 'em since. Generally speaking, people who come here stay put. Safety in numbers. It ain't much, but at least it's something." I shook my head. "All hail the glories of social collectivism and all that crap."

A look passed between them. "I take it you don't believe in collectivist theory," the girl said, very quietly.

Back on Earth, publicly criticizing social collectivism could earn you a six-week stay in a rehab clinic and temporary loss of citizenship. But Earth was forty-six light-years away; so as far as most people in Shuttlefield were concerned, I could have stood on an outhouse roof to proclaim that Karl Marx enjoyed sex with farm animals, and no one would have cared. "I'm not a believer, no."

"So what *do* you believe?"

Zoltan Shirow had stopped, turned to look back at me. I'd later learn that there was little that his ears couldn't pick up. For the moment, though, there was this simple question. Everyone came to a halt; they wanted to hear my answer.

"I . . . I don't believe in anything," I replied, embarrassed by the sudden attention.

"Ah . . . I see." His eyes bore into mine. "Not even God?"

Silence. Even in the frigid cold, I felt an uncomfortable warmth. "I . . . I . . . I don't know."

"So you believe in nothing." Shirow nodded almost sadly. "Pity." Then he turned to look around. "So tell me . . . where should we pitch our tents?"

So far as I could see, there was nowhere these people could set up camp. All the available, turf had already been claimed. "There's a few acres just south of here," I said, pointing in the direction I'd been leading them. "That's where everyone from your ship is being put."

"Thank you, but we'd rather have some privacy. Is there anyplace else?"

The only vacant area left was out near the swamps where the tall grass hadn't yet been cut down. Sissy Levin and Allegra DiSilvio lived out there; but Sissy was insane, and Allegra was a hermit, so people tended to leave them alone. I figured that was as good a place as any for the Church of Universal Transformation.

"Over there," I said. "There's only a couple of people out that way."

Shirow nodded. "Very well, then. That's where we'll go."

"You're going to have a hard time. It hasn't been cleared yet."

"We'll manage. You know why?" I didn't answer, and he smiled. "Because *I* believe in *you*." Then he turned to his followers. "Come on . . . that's where we're going."

As one, without so much as a single word or question, they turned and began to follow Shirow as he marched off in the direction I'd indicated. Astonished, I watched as one white-robed acolyte after another walked past me, heading toward a place I'd picked almost at random. So far as they knew, I could have sent them toward a boid nest, yet they trusted me. . . .

No. They trusted *him*. With absolute, unquestioning faith that what he said was right. I was still staring after them when the girl stopped. She turned, and came back to me. Once again I found myself attracted by those bright green eyes, that air of invulnerability.

"Do you want a better life?" she asked. I nodded dumbly. "Then come along."

"Why?"

"Because I believe in you, too." Then she took my hand and led me away.

The Church of Universal Transformation had come to Coyote well prepared for life in the wild: thirty-one dome tents complete with their own solar heaters, with room for three in each; brand-new sleeping bags; hand and power tools of all kinds, along with a couple of portable RTF generators to run the electric lamps they strung up around the campsite; a ninety-day supply of freeze-dried vegetarian food; adequate clothing for both winter and summer; pads loaded with a small library of books about wilderness survival, homesteading, and craft-making; medical supplies for nearly every contingency.

All these riches were carefully packed inside the cargo containers; once I showed them the unclaimed marshland outside town, fifteen men went back to the landing field and unloaded the crates from the shuttle, lugging the crates across Shuttlefield past townspeople who watched with curiosity and envy. When I asked how they'd managed to get around the strict weight limitations imposed by the Union Astronautica, they merely smiled and gave noncommittal answers. After a while I gave up, figuring that the church had greased a few palms here and there. Compared to the miserable living conditions endured by everyone else in Shuttlefield, the Universalists were ready to live like kings.

Yet they weren't lazy. Far from it; as soon as they had all their gear, they took off their robes, put on parkas, unpacked their tools, and went to work. A half dozen men used scythes and hand axes to clear away the spider bush and sourgrass, while several more picked up shovels and began digging a fire pit and the women erected tents and foraged for wood. Although they weren't yet acclimated to Coyote's thin air, they seldom rested and they never complained; they smiled and laughed as they went about their labors. When one person needed to take a breather, another person simply picked up where he or she had left off.

During all this, the Reverend Shirow walked among them, wearing a wool tunic with long slits on its back through which his wings protruded. Now and then he'd take a few whacks with an ax or lend a hand with a shovel, yet he didn't do much work himself; instead he supervised everyone, instructing them where and how to do their jobs, sometimes pausing to share a few quiet words with one church member or another. Zoltan's private tent was the first to go up, though, and once it was ready for occupancy it wasn't long before he vanished into it. No one seemed to mind; it was as if he had the right to excuse himself while his followers busted their asses.

After a little while I found myself joining in. I told myself that I had nothing else worth doing that day, that I'd get paid for helping unload their stuff from the shuttle. The truth of the matter was that these people fascinated me, and I wanted to be with them. . . .

Well, no. Not quite. *One* of them fascinated me: the girl I had met earlier. Her name was Greer—no one used their last names, and I never learned hers—and when she shed her shapeless robe, I saw that she was one of the most beautiful women I had ever seen. So, yeah, sex was on my mind, but if getting laid was my only consideration, I could have just as easily bargained an hour or two with one of the ladies at the Sugar Shack. Greer was different; she had accepted me without reservation, despite the fact that I was stranger in dirty clothes, and had told me that she believed in me even though I'd already told her leader that I didn't believe in God or, by extension, he himself.

When you meet someone like Greer, all you want to do is become part of her world. So I put aside my reluctance, picked up a shovel, and spent the better part of the day helping a few guys dig a couple of deep-pit latrines. It didn't put me any closer to Greer, since she was one of the women erecting the tents, but I figured that I had to take this slowly, show her that I wasn't just a creek cat on the prowl.

And it seemed to work. Every now and then, when I paused to rest, I'd spot her nearby; she'd look in my direction, favor me with a shy smile, then go back to what she was doing. I considered crawling out of the pit and going over to chat with her, but none of the men with whom I was working—Boris, Jim, Renaldo, Dex—showed any sign of slacking off, so I decided that it would send the wrong signal. I dug and I dug and I dug, and got blisters on my hands and dirt in my teeth, and told myself that I was just helping out some newcomers, when all I really wanted to do was look into those lovely eyes once more.

They didn't stop working until Uma went down and twilight was setting in. By then most of the land had been cleared; the tents were all up, and a bonfire was crackling in the stone-ringed pit in the middle of camp. That time of evening, most of the colonists would trudge down the road to Liberty, where they'd stand in line outside the community hall to be doled out some leftover creek crab stew. The Universalists were serving stew, too, but it wasn't sour crap made from native crustaceans; it was a thick curry of rice and red beans. No one made a big deal of inviting me to join them for dinner; one of the women just handed me a bowl and spoon, and a couple of men moved aside to let me join the circle around the fire. Much to my surprise, a bottle of dry red wine made its way around the circle; everyone took a sip before passing it on, but no one seemed intent on getting drunk. Instead, it was done in a ritualistic sort of way, like taking communion in church.

Conversation was light, mostly about the trouble everyone had breathing the rarefied air, how hard it was to break ground in midwinter. Soon the stars began to come out, and they all stopped to admire the sight of Bear rising above the horizon. Greer sat across the fire from me; she looked up now and then, smiling when she caught my eye, but no words were spoken between us. I was in no hurry to rush the matter. Indeed, it felt as if I were among friends.

Through all this, Zoltan sat cross-legged at the edge of the fire, surrounded by his followers and yet aloof, involved in the small talk but somehow disengaged, a batlike form whose shadowed features were made eldritch by the dancing flames. After everyone had eaten, and the bottle had made its way around, he gently cleared his throat. Conversation stopped as all eyes turned toward him.

"I think," he said, "the time has come to offer prayer."

His congregation put down their plates and spoons, bowed their heads, and shut their eyes. I ducked my head a little, but didn't close my eyes; I haven't prayed since I was little kid, and didn't see much reason to start again.

"Lord," Zoltan began, "thank you for bringing us safely to this world, and for allowing us to find a new home here. We thank you for this first day on Coyote, and for the blessing of our fellowship. We pray that you'll let us continue in the spirit of the vision revealed during the Holy Transformation, and that our mission here will be successful."

Thinking that he was done, I looked up, only to find that everyone was still looking down. Embarrassed, my first impulse was to bow my head again . . . yet then I saw that Shirow's eyes were open and he was gazing at me from across the fire pit.

In that moment, there were simply the two of us: the preacher and the atheist, the chimera and the human, separated by flames yet bound together by silence. No one else was watching; no one else could see into the place where we had met.

"We thank you for your gift," Zoltan said, never taking his eyes from mine. "Benjamin Harlan, who claims to be an unbeliever, yet who has labored with us and now shares our company. We welcome him as a friend, and hope that he will remain with us through the days to come." My expression must have amused him, for he smiled ever so slightly. "For all these blessings," he finished, "we offer our devotion in your name. Amen."

"Amen," the Universalists murmured, then they opened their eyes and raised their heads. Many looked toward me, smiling as they did so. Uneasy by this attention, I hastily looked away . . . and found Greer gazing at me, her face solemn, her eyes questioning.

"Umm . . . amen," I mumbled. "Thanks. I appreciate it." I picked up my plate, started to rise. "Where should I take this? I mean, for it to . . . y'know, be cleaned."

"You mean no one told you?" Dex asked. "You're doing the dishes to-night."

Everyone laughed, and that broke the moment. "Oh, c'mon," Zoltan said. "Don't worry about it. You're our guest. Stay with us a while."

"No, really . . . I've got to get back to camp."

"Why? Is there something else you need to do tonight?"

How did he know that? How had he come to the realization that there was nothing that required my urgent attention? I had been a drifter before I had come to Coyote, and little had changed since then. Home was a tent in the *Long Journey* camp; no one would break into it because I had little, other than a filthy sleeping bag, some extra clothes, and a dead flashlight, that anyone would want to steal. My place in life was on the lowest rung of the ladder; I got by through doing odd jobs when I could find them and living off the dole when I couldn't. If I froze to death that night, no one would miss me; my body would be buried in the cemetery, my few belongings claimed by anyone who might want them.

"Well . . ." I sat down again. "If you insist."

"I insist on nothing. Anything you do should be of your own free will. But we're new here, and we need a guide, someone who's been on Coy-ote for a while. You've already demonstrated a willingness to help us." He grinned. "Why not join us? We have enough to share with one more."

Indeed, they did. I'd seen their supplies and caught myself wondering now and then how I might be able to sneak something out of there without them noticing. Now that Zoltan was practically inviting me to move in with them, such larceny was unnecessary. All I had to do was play the friendly native, and I'd never have to cut bamboo or dig pota-toes ever again.

Still, there was no question that this was a religious cult. Not only that, but they followed someone who looked like a bat. The whole thing was spooky, and I wasn't ready to start wearing a white robe.

"And it doesn't bother you that I'm not . . . I mean, one of you?" Sev-eral people frowned at this. "No offense," I quickly added, "but I've al-ready told you that I'm not a believer. Hell—I mean, heck—I don't even know what you guys believe *in*."

That eased things a bit. Frowns turned to smiles, and a few people chuckled. "Most of us weren't believers when we joined," Renaldo began. "We soon learned that—"

"Your sharing our beliefs isn't necessary," Shirow said, interrupting Renaldo with an upraised hand. "No one here will proselytize or try to convert you, so long as you neither say or do anything intended to diminish our faith. In fact, I enjoy the fact that we have an atheist in our midst." His face stretched into a broad grin that exposed his fangs. "Benjamin the Unbeliever . . . you know, I rather like the sound of that."

More laughter, but not unkind. I found myself laughing with them. I was beginning to like Zoltan; appearances notwithstanding, he seemed like an easygoing sort of guy. And his people weren't all that weird, once you got to know them. Another glance at Greer, and I realized again that I'd like to get to know her most of all.

"Well, if it's Gunga Din you're looking for, I'm your man." I stood up, brushed off the back of my trousers. "I'll come back tomorrow and bring my stuff with me."

"Just like that?" Zoltan looked at me askance. "Don't you have any questions?"

Once again, I was being put on the spot. Everyone gazed at me, awaiting my response. It seemed as if Zoltan was testing me in some way, trying to find out where I was coming from. Oh, I had plenty of questions, all right, but I didn't want to screw the deal. So I picked the most obvious one.

"Sure, I do," I said. "How come you look the way you do?"

The smiles vanished, replaced by expressions of reverence. Some turned their eyes toward the fire; others folded their hands together, looked down at the ground. For a moment I thought I'd blown it. Greer didn't look away, though, nor did Zoltan.

"A good question," he said quietly, "and one that deserves an answer." Then he shook his head. "But not tonight. Come back tomorrow, and perhaps we'll tell you . . . if and when you're ready for the truth."

He fell silent once more. My audience with him was over; I was being excused. I mumbled a clumsy good-bye, then left the warmth of the campfire and began trudging back through the cold to my squalid little tent. Yet I didn't feel humiliated. The opposite, in fact. I had just stumbled upon the best scam since Abraham, and all I had to do was go along for the ride.

Or at least so I thought. What I didn't know was where the ride would eventually take one.

Next morning, I packed up my gear, folded my tent, and bid a not-so-fond farewell to *Long Journey* turf. The camp chief was surprised to see me go, but hardly choked up about it; he'd never liked me very much, and the feeling was mutual. He'd lose rent for a while, but a new ship had just arrived and eventually he'd find some poor bastard who'd want my space. The few friends I had there were surprised as well, and a couple of them tried to get me to tell them where I was headed, but I kept my mouth shut; I didn't want anyone else horning in on the act. Jaime tried to follow me, but I sidetracked him by cutting through Trappers Guild turf. By the time he finished apologizing to them, I was on the dirt road leading to the edge of town.

The Universalists weren't shocked when I reappeared; in fact, they were expecting me. Renaldo and Ernst took one look at the ragged tent I tried to pitch near their own and pronounced it to be uninhabitable; for then, I'd share quarters with them. Clarice wrinkled her nose when she saw my clothes; burn them, she said, they had plenty to spare. They didn't have an extra sleeping bag, unfortunately, but Arthur relieved me of mine and took it away to be washed. And then everyone agreed that I smelled nearly as bad as the stuff I'd brought with me; before I had a chance to object, water had been boiled, tarps had been erected around a collapsible washtub, and I was being treated to my first hot bath in so long that I'd forgotten what it was like. Nor did I have to do it alone; while Angela washed my feet, Doria rinsed my hair, and neither of them took offense at the embarrassing development that soon occurred between my legs.

I emerged from my bath feeling as clean as the day I was born, wearing clothes so fresh that they crinkled as I walked. And the treatment wasn't over yet; while I was washing up, Greer made breakfast for me. It was light fare—a bowl of hot oatmeal, a couple of slices of fresh-baked bread, a cup of vegetable juice—but it was much better than what I had been eating for the last year. I ate sitting cross-legged on the ground in front of the fire pit; Greer sat at my side, silently watching as I wolfed everything down. I had to restrain myself from licking the bowl, and when I was done, I turned to her.

"That was the best"—I covered my mouth to stifle a belch—"breakfast I've had in years. Thanks."

"You're welcome. And thank you for coming back. We're glad to have you with us." She paused, and added, "And so is Zoltan. He asked me to tell you that."

"Uh-huh." Although church members were hard at work all around us, continuing to put the camp together, Zoltan was nowhere to be seen. "Where is he, anyway?"

"In communion with Byron." Greer nodded toward his tent, a couple of dozen feet away. It occupied the center of the campsite; I noticed that its door flap was closed. "He spends time alone with one of us each day, in meditation. We try to respect their privacy."

I remembered how he had made himself absent the day before, while everyone else was working. "And who decides who gets to, um, meditate with him?"

"He does, of course. He picks someone with whom to share communion, takes him or her into his tent." She pointed to her left forearm. "You know who it is because they'll wear a black sash around their arm. That means they're excused from their chores for the rest of the day, so that they may contemplate the lesson Zoltan has given them." She gave me a sly wink. "So of course we're very happy about it when Zoltan summons one of us," she quietly added, as if letting me in on a secret. "It means we get a day off."

Communion, my ass. I knew a freeloader when I saw one. I had to admit, though, that extending the same privilege each day to one of his followers was a smart move; it kept the troops in line. But I kept my opinion to myself. "I'm sure he's busy. I'll just have to catch up with him some other time."

"Umm . . ." She hesitated. "One thing you should know is that you don't approach him first. When he's ready to speak to you, he will . . . but you'll have to wait for that moment. Then you can talk to him."

I nodded, trying to keep a poker face. "Still, there's a lot I'd like to ask him. After all, he left me hanging last night."

"Such as?"

"Well, for starters, why he looks like a . . ."

Greer's hand darted forth to cover my mouth. Ian happened to be walking past at that moment; he cast a dark look in my direction, then hastened away, carrying an armload of fresh-cut sourgrass to a bonfire burning nearby. Greer watched him go, then removed her hand from my face. "We found something queer earlier this morning," she said, her voice a little more loud than usual. "A plant of some sort. We were hoping you could tell us what it is."

I glanced again at Zoltan's tent. He'd already demonstrated a keen sense of hearing. "Sure," I said, picking myself off the ground. "That's why I'm here."

Greer showed me where I could wash my plate and bowl, then led me through the camp, taking me toward the uncleared marshland. We walked slowly, avoiding the people working around us. "You must never speak of this in public," she said, keeping her voice low. "It's a sacred thing, the very root of our faith. In fact, I shouldn't be telling you even this much . . . Zoltan will, when he feels that you're ready."

I shrugged. "Maybe so, but yesterday you guys got off a shuttle in full view of several dozen people. They all saw him . . . and believe me, word travels fast in Shuttlefield. Even if I don't ask, someone else will."

"I know. The same questions we faced back on Earth." She shook her head. "Outsiders have a difficult time understanding the Transformation, how it's central to our beliefs. That's why we're reluctant to speak of it."

"Sure . . . but Zoltan invited me to join you, right? Even though he knows I'm not a believer." She nodded. "So if he did, and your people have accepted me, wouldn't it make sense for me to know?" She frowned, her eyes narrowing as she considered my question. "I promise, it's just between you and me. Besides, I've already brought my stuff over here. Take my word for it, I'm not going back anytime soon."

"Well . . ." She glanced around. "But only if you won't tell anyone I told you."

I promised her that I wouldn't. By then we were away from the center of the camp; no one else was around. Greer knelt down behind a vacant tent, and in a hushed voice she told me about the Holy Transformation of Zoltan Shirow.

It happened during the Dixie Rebellion, back in 2241 when a small group of Southern nationalists, nostalgic for the United Republic of America—and before that, the Civil War of the 1860s—attempted to stage an insurrection against the Western Hemisphere Union. For several months, the Army of Dixie committed terrorist acts across the South, planting bombs in government offices in Memphis and Atlanta and assassinating government officials in Birmingham, until the Agencia Security succeeded in breaking up the network. With most of their leaders arrested, the surviving Dixies retreated to the hill country of eastern Tennessee, where they battled Union Guard troops dispatched to arrest them.

One of the Guard soldiers sent in for the mop-up operation was one Corporal Zoltan Shirow, a young recruit who had never seen combat duty before. His patrol was searching for a Dixie hideout near the town of McMinnville when they were caught in an ambush that killed the rest of his team. Critically wounded, Corporal Shirow managed to escape in a maxvee, only to crash his vehicle in a patch of woods just outside town.

"This is the First Station," Greer said. "Zoltan the warrior, the sinner without knowledge of God."

"All right," I said. "I got that part. . . ."

She held up a hand. "It was then that he was discovered by the Redeemer, and brought to the Room of Pain and Understanding."

The Redeemer went by the name of Dr. Owen Dunn. The Universalists held a special place for him in their mythology roughly analogous to John the Baptist and Satan rolled into one, but the truth was much more prosaic, as I later learned. Dr. Dunn had moved from Nashville to McMinnville some years earlier, when he set up a small private practice. On the surface, he appeared to be little more than a country doctor, mending broken bones and delivering babies. What no one knew was that he had secretly continued the research that had caused him to be dismissed from the faculty of the Vanderbilt University School of Medicine.

Dunn was interested in the creation of *homo superior*. Unlike scientists engaged in genengineering, though, he believed that it was possible to refashion a full-grown adult into a posthuman, using nanoplastiosurgical techniques he had developed while at Vanderbilt. The medical school considered his research to be unethical, though, and rightly so; Dunn could be charitably described as a quack, yet it's more accurate to say that he was a biomedical researcher who had gone insane. To put it in blunt—albeit clichéd—terms, he was a mad doctor.

Before leaving Vanderbilt, he stole some experimental nanites from the med school laboratory, and while living in McMinnville he had quietly continued his research, hoping eventually to produce a breakthrough that would restore his standing in the scientific community. To that end, Dunn had invested his earnings in the surreptitious purchase of commercial medical equipment—including a cell regenerator of the type used in hospitals for the cloning of new tissue—which he set up in the basement of his house. When that wasn't sufficient, his experiments took on a gothic air. He resorted to disinterring freshly buried bodies from nearby cemeteries. As Dunn himself would later admit, once he had been arrested and brought to trial, his methods were reminiscent of

Frankenstein, even though they yielded positive results. Over time, he learned how to restructure flesh and bone from deceased donors into whatever form he desired.

The major drawback, of course, was that he needed a living person to complete his studies . . . and for what he intended to do, it was unlikely that he'd find any volunteers. So when Dunn found the wounded Corporal Shirow in the woods near his house, he was presented with an opportunity he couldn't pass up.

Zoltan was unconscious and close to death, but it was a relatively simple matter to remove the bullet from his left shoulder, perform emergency surgery, and let him heal. During this time, the doctor kept the soldier unconscious. Strapped down on an operating table in Dunn's basement, there was little chance of anyone finding him; conveniently, the Union Guard assumed that Corporal Shirow had become a deserter. Dunn cloned samples of Shirow's tissue until he had sufficient living flesh and cartilage for his purposes. Once he was sure that the soldier was healthy enough to undergo further operations, Dunn went to work.

"This was the Second Station," Greer told me. "The Redeemer transformed Zoltan into a figure he had seen in his dreams, an avatar of what he considered to be a perfectly adapted form."

"A bat?" I stared at her.

"If that's how you see him, then yes, that's what he looks like. We believe that the Redeemer, however misguided he may have been, was working under divine influence . . . that God instructed him to make a man who would resemble Lucifer, in order to test the will of those who would meet him."

"Who came up with this?"

Greer smiled. "Zoltan did. During the Holy Transformation."

Those who later investigated the incident found that Dunn had drawn inspiration from the Gustav Dore illustrations of *The Inferno*, the demons Dante described as occupying the inner circles of Hell. Yet the worst thing that Dunn did to Zoltan was to keep the soldier conscious; because he wanted to study his reactions, Dunn used local anesthesia whenever possible. As a result, Shirow was aware of everything that was going on, even as he lay facedown on the operating table while the doctor meticulously grafted new cartilage and muscle to his shoulder blades, patiently building blood vessels and splicing nerves, eventually cutting fatty tissue from Zoltan's thighs and midriff when Dunn's supply of cloned flesh ran low. In his own sick way, Dunn was brilliant; not only were the new wings not rejected, but Zoltan was gradually able to manipulate them.

Once that phase was successful, Dunn went to work on the soldier's face and hands. And for that, too, Zoltan was the sole witness. The cinder-block basement had no windows, and the nearest neighbor lived a half mile away. By the time Zoltan's screams were heard by a former patient who happened to drop by one afternoon to deliver a gift to the good doctor, there was little left of the lost soldier's mind.

"It was during his ordeal," Greer went on, "that Zoltan arrived at the Third Station, for while he suffered, he heard the voice of God, telling him that there was a purpose to this."

"Which was . . . ?"

"God gave Zoltan a mission." Although she spoke in hushed tones, she looked me straight in the eye, making sure that I understood everything she said. "He was to spread His word to all who would look past his new form, telling them that humanity was about to undergo a universal transformation . . . not of the body, but of the soul." She smiled then. "Through the Redeemer's actions, God chose Zoltan to be His prophet."

Another way of looking at it was that Zoltan Shirow went mad. That much was clear to me, even if it wasn't to her. During the endless hours, days, and weeks he'd spent in Dunn's basement lab, held immobile while the doctor carefully reshaped his body, the patient gradually slipped over the edge of sanity. And no wonder; if I'd experienced what he had been through, I probably would have been talking to God myself. The mind finds ways of dealing with pain.

"You know," I said, as gently as I could, "it's possible that Zoltan may be . . ."

"Crazy?"

"I didn't say that."

"But that's what you were about to say." Greer gave me a condescending look. "We've all heard it before. I thought the same thing myself, when I first met him. But, Ben, you have to listen to him. You need to open up your heart, let him . . ."

The tent behind us rustled; another church member had come home, probably to get something from his or her belongings. Reminded that she shouldn't be speaking to me this way, Greer went silent. Touching my arm, she stood up, took a few steps away from the tent.

"Let me show you what we found," she said aloud. "Maybe you know what it is."

I nodded and followed her to past the edge of the cleared area. A few yards away from camp, the sourgrass grew chest high, bowed by the winter snow. We pushed through it until Greer stopped and pointed to several spherical plants growing above ground. Resembling gigantic onions, their thick brown leaves were layered with frost.

"Ball plants," I said. "You should stay clear of them."

"Are they dangerous?"

"Not now, no, but by spring they'll start to flower." I pointed to the wilted stalks protruding from the tops of the balls. "When that happens, they'll attract pseudowasps . . . and believe me, you don't want to get stung by them."

"Thank you. I'll tell the others." Greer stared at the plants. "Why are they so big? Are they fruit or something?"

"Uh-uh. They're carnivorous." I stepped closer to one of the balls. "In late autumn, just before the first snow, swampers take shelter in them. To hibernate, y'know? They curl up together inside to get out of the cold. But one or two always die during winter, and so the plant feeds off their bodies as they decay. It's sort of like . . ." I searched for the right word. "Symbiosis, I think they call it."

She shuddered. "Horrible."

"Just nature." I shrugged. "That's the way things work around here."

It was also much the same way Zoltan worked. Through temptation, he'd managed to attract her and the other followers to take shelter within the folds of his wings; it wasn't until later, once they were held captive, that he fed off them.

Unfortunately, that simile didn't occur to me until sometime after. By then, it was much too late. I had become something of a swamper myself.

Winter went by the way winter does on Coyote: slowly, with every day a little colder than the day before. For anyone who hasn't lived here, it's hard to realize just how long winter lasts on this world; three times longer than on Earth, it sometimes seems as if spring will never come. People rose early in Shuttlefield: knocking fresh snow off their shacks and checking to see if anyone had died during the night before trudging over to the community hall in Liberty to receive another bowl of gruel. And then you'd have the rest of the day to kill. Try to stay warm. Try not to do anything that would draw the attention of the Proctors or the Union Guard. Try to stay alive. Try to stay sane.

It was a little less difficult for me to get by since I'd taken up with the Universalists. Or at least for a while. They'd brought plenty of food with them, and their heated tents were a luxury no one else in Shuttlefield had. They went about their business quietly, a small group of pilgrims in monkish robes who kept to themselves except when they went into town to barter spare items for whatever they might need. In the first few weeks after their arrival, visitors were welcomed to their camp. No effort was spared to make them feel at home, until it soon become apparent that many of those who dropped by were merely looking for handouts. Seeing their rations running low, the Universalists reluctantly stopped being quite so generous, and that's when the trouble began.

The first sign of friction came when Caitlin, one of the younger church members, was harassed by a couple of Cutters as she tried to trade a power cell for a pair of catskin gloves at one of the kiosks. The craftsman tested the cell and claimed that it was depleted by 10 percent;

when Caitlin insisted that the cell was fully charged, two Cutters who happened to be loitering nearby—or, more likely, following the girl—stepped in. At some point in the argument, one of them made a grab for Caitlin, saying that he wanted to see what she was hiding beneath her robe. Caitlin managed to get away; she rushed back and told everyone what had happened, and that evening during dinner Zoltan forbade anyone from going out alone.

A few days later, some New Frontiers guys sauntered into our camp, demanding to see "the freak"—meaning Zoltan—and be fed, in no particular order. When Ernst informed them that the Reverend Shirow was in meditation and that we had no food to spare, they got ugly about it; one of them shoved Ernst to the ground while two more tried take off with a generator. That was when I first saw how capable the Universalists were of defending themselves; within moments, the intruders were surrounded by church members wielding quarterstaves they'd fashioned from bamboo stalks. A few bruises later, the gang was sent running; but that evening, for the first time, Zoltan declared that we would begin posting overnight watches, with everyone taking turns guarding the camp.

Yet I can't honestly say that the Universalists were without blame. By early Machidiel, the third month of winter, their food supply was running short, and so the church members were forced to go into Liberty every morning to eat breakfast at the community hall. It wouldn't have been so bad if they had stuck together as a group, but some of them took it upon themselves to take the opportunity to sit with other colonists . . . and once they'd made their acquaintance, they couldn't resist the urge to tell them that the Reverend Zoltan Shirow was God's chosen messenger to Coyote.

By then, I'd been allowed to know the details of the holy mission. According to Zoltan, God had told him to seek out a group of disciples and take them to a place where no one had gone before, where they would spread the word of universal transformation. That was why he had brought his followers to Coyote; they'd done so by taking everything they owned—bank accounts, real estate, personal property, the works—and surrendering it all to the church, which in turn sold or exchanged them for berths aboard the *Magnificent Voyage*, along with all the supplies they could bribe Union Astronautica officials at Highgate into letting them carry to the new world. So it was no wonder that they had come well stocked; some of these people had exchanged houses for tents, family fortunes for a diet of rice and beans.

And, indeed, the people who joined the Church of Universal Transformation had come from all walks of life. Ian had been an AI systems engineer, Renaldo a schoolteacher, Clarice an award-winning dramatist, Dex an attorney; many came from wealthy families, and I was surprised to find that Doria's husband—her former husband, rather; they'd separated when she joined the church—was a member of the Union Proletariate. Greer had been a student of historical linguistics at the University of Colorado when she, like the others, had heard about the former Union Guard soldier who'd undergone hideous torture at the hands of a madman and survived to proclaim that the human race was on the verge of becoming something new and better. None of them had been poor or ignorant; but they had all been searching for greater meaning in their lives, something in which they could believe: a revival of the soul, far beyond the false promises of social collectivism. And while countless thousands who'd heard Zoltan's message had turned away, this small handful had chosen to cast aside everything else and follow him. They'd found contentment in the church, a purpose for existence; no wonder they wanted to share this revelation with those they met, forgetting Zoltan's early promise that they wouldn't try to convert anyone to their beliefs.

Yet they found no new disciples on Coyote. The people who'd come here had made sacrifices of their own; their lives were hard, and most didn't like the way they were being treated by the Matriarch Hernandez and her cronies. Some of them weren't going to take it anymore; during the long winter, rumors circulated through Shuttlefield about various individuals who'd suddenly vanished, packing up their gear and heading off into the wilderness before the Guard and the Proctors knew they were gone. But the vast majority who'd remained behind weren't ready to surrender themselves to a cult operated by a guy who looked like a demon and claimed to be a prophet. The Universalists had been virtually unknown when they left Earth, but by the end of winter every person in New Florida knew of their beliefs . . . and no one wanted anything to do with them.

Although I lived in their camp, I wasn't a member of their church. Zoltan and I remained on friendly terms, but he never called me into his tent, as he often did with everyone else. This distinction, though, was lost on everyone I knew in Shuttlefield. I'd had few friends before I'd moved out of the *Long Journey* camp. The attitude, however, of those few I did have, changed toward me; they no longer greeted me when I saw them in town, but walked past as quickly as they could, refusing to make eye contact. At first I thought it was jealousy—after all, I was living in comfort, with no other responsibilities than to tell a bunch of greenhorns what plants or animals to avoid—but it wasn't until I saw Jaime Hodge that I learned the real reason.

He was in line outside the community hall late one afternoon, waiting to be let in for dinner, when I walked up behind him. I usually ate dinner at camp, but I happened to be running an errand in Liberty, so I decided to eat at the hall instead of waiting until I got home. Jaime glanced back when I joined the chow line, saw me standing there, then turned away.

"How's it going, dude?" I asked. "Keeping warm?"

"Yeah. Sure." He looked straight ahead.

"Days are getting a little longer." The sun wasn't down yet, and it was almost 1900. "Think spring is almost sprung."

"Could be."

I tried to think of something to say. The left shoulder of his parka was becoming frayed; I could see tufts of fiber peeking through the seam. "Y'know, I could help you with this," I said, touching his jacket. "I know a girl back at my camp who's good at patching. . . ."

"I can take care of it myself." Jaime shook off my hand. "And if I want religion, I'll get it my own way."

"Huh? Hey, whoa . . . just trying to be helpful. I know someone who's good at patching up clothes. . . ."

"You know what I'm talking about."

I did, but I wasn't about to let it slide. "Jaime," I said quietly, "let me tell you something. I may be staying with them, but I'm not *with* them. Y'know what I mean?"

He seemed to think about that. Finally, he turned around, looked me in the eye. "If you're not one of them," he said, "then why did you park your tent over there?"

"Free food. No rent. No hassle." I shrugged. "I'm tellin' you, running into these guys is the best thing that's ever happened to me."

I was trying to make it light, but it didn't work. His face darkened, his lip curling into an ugly smirk. "Right. All the food you can eat, and all you have to do is suck up to the bat."

My face grew warm. "Now, wait a minute," I said, taking a step closer. "If you think . . ."

"No, *you* wait a minute." Jaime planted a hand against my chest, shoved me back. "Maybe I'm hungry, but at least no one's trying to brainwash my ass. So far as I can tell, that's what's going to happen to you . . . if it hasn't already."

There was nothing guys in Shuttlefield liked more than watching a fight. From the corner of my eye, I saw people beginning to close in, forming a circle around us. Beyond the edge of the crowd, I caught a glimpse of a Proctor hovering nearby. He was doing nothing to stop this, though; from the look on his face, he was anticipating a good brawl before dinner. No one was on my side; they knew who I was, and they were hoping that Jaime would smear my face in the mud.

I caught myself wishing that a couple of the Universalists were with me just then. Two of the larger members, like Boris and Jim, and armed with quarterstaves. But they weren't there, and I knew that Zoltan's order that no one should leave camp alone applied to me as well.

"Ease down, buddy." Carefully keeping my hands in my pockets, I lowered my voice. "I'm not trying to start nothing with you."

"Yeah? Well, then go tell your pals not to start nothing with us." Jaime wasn't backing down, but he wasn't pushing it either. Whatever friendship still remained between us was staying his hand. "I don't want to know about God, I don't want to turn into a bat, and if they don't find someplace else to carry on with their weird shit, we're coming over and having ourselves a little Easter egg hunt."

Ugly murmurs from all around us—*you tell 'em, guy* and *we'll bust their asses* and so forth—and that was when I realized, for the first time, just how much danger we were in. The fact that a big, mean smile was plastered on the face of the nearby Proctor only confirmed my suspicion; if a mob descended upon the Universalist camp, nothing would stop them. Not the Proctors, not the Union Guard. Zoltan and his followers had become pariahs.

"I hear you," I said. "Is that it?"

Jaime said nothing for a moment. "Yeah, that's it." He stepped back, cocked his head away from the hall. "Go on, beat it. Get out of here."

Disappointed that they weren't going to see a fight, the crowd began to dissolve. Watching them shoulder each other as they sought to resume their former places in line, I couldn't help but feel sorry for them. Caught like rats in a maze, all they could worry about was whether a small band of pilgrims would try to show them a way out. Until that moment, I hadn't realized just how much the Universalists had come to mean to me. They weren't just two hots and a cot, but something more.

I'd lost my appetite, though, so I started to head toward the road leading back to Shuttlefield. Feeling a hand on my arm, I looked around, saw that Jaime had stepped out of line. Thinking he intended to restart our quarrel, I stiffened up, but he quickly shook his head.

"Relax. I don't mean nothing." Behind him, a few people glanced in our direction, but no one did anything. The front door had just opened, and the line was shuffling toward it. "Look, I'm sorry," he continued, his voice a near whisper. "My fault. I shouldn't have started it."

"Yeah, sure. Okay . . ."

"Look, can I give you some advice? Between you and me?" I nodded. "Get out of there. Fold your tent, pack up your gear, and scram. We'll take you back."

"Who will?"

"Your friends, man. The people who care for you . . ."

"I know who they are," I said. And then I turned my back on him and walked away.

*   *   *

Later that evening, after dinner was over and everyone was still seated around the fire, I told them what had happened. Several weeks earlier, when they had still believed that no one would do them any harm, they might have been willing to turn the other cheek. The incident with the New Frontiers gang had put them on their guard, though, and when I got to the part about the not-so-veiled threat Jaime had made, they weren't so complacent.

Greer was sitting next to me. As I spoke, she put an arm around my shoulder; after a few minutes, it traveled down to my waist. She might have only meant to offer comfort, but somehow it didn't seem that way. Greer and I had become close after I'd moved in with the Universalists, but I'd come to accept the fact that, while she clearly liked me, there was little chance that our relationship would ever become more than friendship. While sex wasn't absolutely forbidden among his disciples, abstinence was one of the virtues Zoltan preached, and after a while I'd given up on the idea of sleeping with her. Yet she was snuggling up with me, and it was hard not to become aroused by her touch.

If Zoltan noticed, though, he was too distracted to care. He sat quietly while I spoke, hunched forward with his hands clasped together between his knees, wings folded against his back, gazing into the fire. When I was done, an uneasy silence fell upon the circle. Everyone waited for him to respond, but he remained silent for a few moments.

"Thank you, Ben," he said at last. "I'm glad that you've brought this to our attention . . . and I'm pleased that you were able to escape without harm. It must have been difficult, standing up to a friend like that."

"He's not my friend." My throat felt dry as I spoke. "I thought he was, but . . . well, that's changed."

Zoltan nodded sadly. "Much has changed now." He raised his eyes to look at the others. "Make no mistake . . . if Ben's warning is correct, and I believe it is, then we're no longer safe here. We can post more guards at night, and try to keep everyone out of town unless it's absolutely necessary, but in the long run it will be pointless."

"I don't agree, Reverend." Standing behind Zoltan, Ian leaned against his staff, the hood of his robe pulled up against the cold wind that snapped at the fire. "If someone tries to attack us, I'm sure we can defend ourselves. We've got thirty men and women. . . ."

"Against how many?" This from Boris; sitting on the other side of the fire, his face pensive. "There are almost three thousand people in Shuttlefield. If even a small fraction of them decided to come down on us, we'd be overrun. And if Ben's right, we can't expect any help from the Proctors or the Union."

"But they're supposed to be protecting us." Clarice was usually the quietest member of the group, but that day she wore the black sash of someone who had taken communion with Zoltan; perhaps that status gave her the courage to speak her mind. "Why wouldn't they step in if they saw . . . ?"

"You weren't here for the last First Landing Day." When I spoke up again, everyone went quiet. "That's the annual holiday to commemorate the arrival of the *Alabama* . . . happens on Uriel 47, at the end of summer. Last year, while the big feast was going on at the community hall, some Rigil Kent guerrillas snuck into Shuttlefield and blew up a shuttle."

"I don't understand." Ian looked confused. "Who—I mean, what—is Rigil Kent? And why would they want to blow up a shuttle?"

"A group from the *Alabama*. They've staged sneak attacks on Liberty. They come across the East Channel from Midland, mainly to steal guns. The last time they were here, someone named Rigil Kent left a note on the boathouse door, claiming responsibility for the bombing and saying that they would continue until the WHU returned Liberty to its rightful owners. There was a small riot when that happened . . . everyone was dancing around the shuttle, watching it burn. The Guard couldn't do a thing about it, neither could the Proctors. So if they can't stop something like that, how could . . . ?"

"Interesting." Zoltan was intrigued. "And you say they're coming over from Midland?"

"That's where they went after *Glorious Destiny* arrived." I shrugged. "From what I've heard, though, no one's been able to figure out exactly where they are. It's a big island, four times larger than New Florida. Plenty of places for people to hide. So the Guard hasn't been able to—"

"That's good to know," Renaldo said, "but it doesn't get us any closer to fighting off—"

"You're missing the point." Zoltan raised a hand. "First, there's no way we can defend ourselves . . . not against a lynch mob, at least, and that's the inevitable outcome if we stay here much longer. And second, even if we managed to remain here, it would only be because we've decided to lie low."

He gazed at the others. "But that's not our mission. The Lord has ordained us to spread the word of universal transformation. This is why we're here. It's clear to me, though, that our efforts have become futile."

Several people gasped. Others stared in disbelief at their leader. Feeling Greer tremble, I wrapped my arm around her; she sank closer against me, and I could tell that she was afraid.

"Yes . . . futile." Zoltan's voice became solemn. "Liberty and Shuttlefield are lost to God's word, just as Sodom and Gomorrah once were. Destruction awaits this place, and there's nothing we can do. Therefore, like Lot and his family, we must move on."

"Where?" Renaldo demanded.

"You need ask?" Zoltan looked up at him. "You haven't been listening to our brother Benjamin. He has shown us the way."

At this moment, I saw what was coming. "Oh, no, wait a minute. . . ."

"Be quiet!" he snapped.

It was the first time I'd heard him raise his voice; like the others, I was stunned into silence. Zoltan rose from his seat, his wings unfurling like great brown sails that caught the night wind. In that instant, he became a bat-winged messiah, standing tall against the giant planet looming behind him. If anything else remains with me, it's this single moment.

"The path is evident," he said. "Our destiny is clear. We shall go to Midland."

A range of expressions passed across the faces of his congregation: disbelief, uncertainty, dread. Then, as if a switch had been thrown, acceptance descended upon them. The prophet had spoken. He had received a vision, one that would lead them from peril to the destiny he'd foretold. They had followed him across forty-six light-years to this world; they would happily let him lead them just a few miles more.

Only it wasn't just a few miles, or even a few hundred. And they had no idea what they were getting themselves into. "You don't . . ." My voice faltered. "I'm sorry, but . . . Reverend, but I don't think you understand. . . ."

"Understand what?"

"You don't . . . I mean, Midland is uncharted territory. The only maps we have of it were made from orbit. The only people who've explored the interior are the *Alabama* colonists who've gone there. . . ."

"Then we'll find them."

"How? No one knows where they are."

He sadly shook his head, as if that were only a minor detail, and I was a child asking foolish questions. "Always the unbeliever. You've been among us for all this time, and still you haven't learned the truth." Knowing chuckles rose from around the fire as he regarded me with fondness. "God will show us the way, Benjamin. He will lead us, and He will protect us."

Then he turned to the rest of his flock. "Rest tonight. We'll begin making our preparations tomorrow. Be discreet, though . . . don't let anyone outside this camp know of our plans. With luck, we'll make our exodus within the next few days, before anyone knows we're gone."

He looked back at me again. "Benjamin, you're welcome to come with us. In fact, we would appreciate your guidance. But you're under no obligation." He paused. "Will you join us?"

"I . . . I'm going to have to think about this."

"By all means, please do."

He bowed his head and led his followers in a brief prayer. Then the meeting broke up; people got up, began going about the usual chores they did before bed. There was nothing for me to do, so I headed for the tent I shared with Ernst and Renaldo when Greer caught me by the arm.

"Where do you think you're going?" she asked.

"Well, it's not my turn to do the dishes or stand watch, so I . . ."

"How lucky. It's not my turn either." She leaned a little closer. "And you know what else? Juanita and Mary have decided that they'd rather spend the night with Clarice and Bethany. So guess what that gives me?"

"Umm . . . a tent by yourself, I think."

Her eyes were bright as she shook her head. "No. A tent with you."

Then she led me away, taking me to a place where, for a few long and memorable hours, we were alone together. By the time the sun rose the next morning, my decision was made. There was no going back.

We left Shuttlefield three days later, in the early morning just before sunrise. No one saw us as we set out on foot, a procession of men and women quietly walking through the silent town, duffel bags strapped to our backs. We took as much as we could carry, but there was much we had to leave behind; once our campsite was found abandoned, no doubt the townspeople would fight over discarded tent heaters, electrical tools, and generators. As it was, we were happy just to leave Shuttlefield in peace.

We took the road into Liberty, then cut across a potato field toward Sand Creek. The creek was still frozen over, so we didn't anticipate any trouble crossing it. A thick ice-fog lay over the field, making it seem as if we were walking through a mist of pearl; we couldn't see more than ten feet ahead, so it came as a surprise when, just before we reached the creek, we came upon a lone figure standing near its banks, wearing a dark cloak with its hood raised.

"Good morning," he said, his voice an electronic purr from the grilled mouth of his metallic head. "I take it you're leaving."

In all the time that I'd been on Coyote, I'd seen Manuel Castro only a few times, and then only from a distance. One of the Savants who'd been aboard the *Glorious Destiny*, he was the colony's lieutenant governor, Matriarch Hernandez's right-hand man . . . if one could consider a mechanistic posthuman still a man.

Zoltan was at the head of the line. He wore his robe over his folded wings, and as the rest of us came to a halt, he stepped forward, pulling down his hood so that Castro could see him face-to-face. They made an odd pair: black and white, the cyborg and the gargoyle. "With all due respect, yes, we are. I hope you don't take it as an insult."

A strange rattle from the Savant: an approximation of a laugh. "I should, but I won't. The Reverend Zoltan Shirow, isn't it? I'm sorry we haven't met until now. I've been told that your presence in Shuttlefield has been . . . troublesome, shall we say?"

"If there's been any trouble, it hasn't been our fault." Zoltan paused. "I hope you're not here to stop us."

"Not at all. I'm only here to enjoy the sunrise." Castro raised a claw-like hand from beneath his cloak, gestured toward the wan yellow sun burning through the mist. "Beautiful, isn't it? This is the time of day I enjoy the most."

I glanced around, half-expecting to see Guard soldiers emerging from the fog. If Castro had brought any soldiers with him, our exodus would have been short-lived; we were unarmed save for the quarterstaves a few of us carried. But the Savant was alone.

"Then you don't mind?" Zoltan asked.

"Not at all." Castro shook his head. "From time to time, various individuals make an effort to leave the colony. If they're people whose talents we value, then we endeavor to keep them here. More often than not we allow potential subversives the option of going away. We let them think that they've escaped, but believe me, there's little that happens that the Central Committee doesn't know about."

Greer and I gave each other an uncertain look. How could they have known what we were planning? There were rumors that the Proctors had informants among the colonists, yet we had taken pains not to speak to anyone about our plans. On the other hand, perhaps the Savant was merely pretending to know something that he really didn't.

"We aren't subversives." Zoltan's voice took on a defensive edge. "All we ever wanted to do was settle here in peace."

"I won't argue your intentions. Nonetheless, if you'd decided to stay, there would have been trouble, and we would have been forced to take

measures against those who might have harmed you, or even you yourselves. So it's just as well that you leave before it comes to that. No one
will stop you, Reverend. You're free to do as you will."

"Thank you." Zoltan bowed slightly. "You're quite generous."

"Only looking out for the colony's best interests." Again, the strange
laugh. "I assume you're heading to Midland. That's where most people
go when they leave here."

The Universalists stirred uneasily, glancing at one another. We'd already decided that, if we were stopped by the Guard, we would claim
that we were going to establish a small settlement on the northern tip of
New Florida. Yet Zoltan decided to be truthful. "That's our intent, yes.
After we're across the creek, we plan to hike downstream until we reach
the Shapiro Pass. There we'll build rafts and use them to cross the Eastern Divide until we reach the East Channel."

"Oh, no . . . no. That's the worst way possible. The Shapiro Pass is
treacherous. Believe me, your rafts will be destroyed in the rapids."

"You know another way?" I asked, stepping forward so that the Savant could see me.

Castro briefly regarded me with his glass eyes, then he looked at
Zoltan once more. "Your guide?" he asked. Zoltan nodded, and the Savant shook his head again. "Once you've crossed Sand Creek, go due
east until you reach North Bend. Follow it southeast until you reach the
Divide. You should be able to reach it by tomorrow afternoon. There
you'll find the Monroe Pass. It's marked on your map, if you're carrying
one. That's where you'll find another way to cross the East Channel."

He was right. The Monroe Pass was much closer; I'd decided to use
the Shapiro Pass because that was how the Montero Expedition had left
New Florida three years ago. "What do you mean, we'll find another
way to cross?"

"As I said, others have gone before you. You'll find them. Trust me."

I wasn't quite ready to trust Savant Castro, but if what he said was true,
it would cut a couple of days off our journey. And I had to admit, any way
off New Florida that didn't entail braving the Shapiro Pass sounded good
to me. I looked at Zoltan and reluctantly nodded; he said nothing to me,
but turned to Castro once more. "Thank you. We're in your debt."

"Not at all. But tell me one thing . . . what do you expect to find out there? Surely not the original colonists. They've made it clear that they don't want anything to do with us . . . except for whatever they can steal in the middle of the night."

"We're hoping we may be able to change their minds." Zoltan smiled. "Since you're being helpful, perhaps you can tell us where we might find them."

If the Savant could have grinned, he probably would have. "If I knew that . . . well, things would be different. I'm sorry, but you'll have to seek them out yourselves. In any event, good luck to you. Farewell."

And with that, he stepped back into the mist, drifting away like a black wraith. We heard the crunch of his metal feet against the icy ground, then he was gone.

Zoltan waited a few moments, before turning to the rest of us. "If Pharaoh had let the Children of Israel leave Egypt so easily, then a lot of trouble could have been avoided. I take this as a good sign."

Or an omen, I thought. Moses and his people spent forty years in the wilderness not because of anything the Egyptians did to them, but because of what they did to themselves . . . including the worship of false idols.

But I didn't voice my thoughts, and perhaps that was the first act of my betrayal.

We crossed Sand Creek without incident; the ice was still strong, and we safely made it to the other side. Instead of going downstream, though, we took the Savant's advice and went due east, following the orbital map and electronic compass Ian had bartered from a kiosk for one of our generators. As the group's guide, I was the one entrusted with the map and compass, but it wasn't long before we found that they were unnecessary; a trail had already been cut through the high grass and spider bush on the other side of the creek, marked here and there with strips of blue cloth tied around trunks of faux birch. As Castro said, someone else had gone before us.

We marched all day, stopping now and then to rest. By early evening we'd reached North Bend, a broad stream that ran parallel to Sand Creek. Beyond it we could make out the great limestone wall of the Eastern Divide, only about fifteen miles to the southeast. It was tempting to press onward, but we were footsore and tired, so Zoltan called a halt. We pitched our tents and gathered wood, and by the time Uma went down and Bear was rising to the east, we were gathered around a warm campfire, eating beans and gazing up at the stars. After dinner Zoltan led his followers in prayer, asking for His help in the long journey ahead.

I prayed for something else: a few more weeks of cold weather. There was another reason why we'd left the colony on short notice. The grasslands of New Florida were haunted by boids: huge, carnivorous avians, known to lurk in the tall grass and attack anything unwise enough to pass through their territory . . . and beyond Shuttlefield and Liberty, guarded by a broad circle of motion-activated particle-beam guns, all of New Florida was their domain. But the boids migrated south during winter, so for a few months it was possible to hike across the northern part of the island without worrying about them. And just as well; boids had no fear of humans, and our bamboo staffs would have been useless against them.

Still, I volunteered for the overnight watch and didn't return to the tent I shared with Greer and Clarice until Michael relieved me shortly after midnight. Greer's body kept me warm, as she had ever since our first night together, but it was a long time before I was able to go to sleep. I couldn't help but remember the exchange between Zoltan and Castro.

The Savant asked the Reverend what he expected to find out there. Why had Zoltan evaded his question? What *was* he expecting to find out here?

I didn't know, and it would be a long time before I learned the truth.

* * *

Daybreak came cold and bleak, with a new layer of frost on the ground. Even though we were only about twenty-five miles from the colony, it seemed as if Shuttlefield was a comfortable place we'd left far behind. A breakfast of lukewarm porridge heated over the dying cinders of our campfire, another prayer by Zoltan, then we hefted our bags onto our aching backs and continued down the trail, following the creek toward the Eastern Divide.

The day was bright and clear, and by the time Uma had risen high in the cloudless blue sky, it seemed as if the world had thawed a bit. Everyone's spirits began to rise; the Universalists sang traditional hymns as they marched along—"Onward, Christian Soldiers," "The Old Rugged Cross," "Faith of Our Fathers"—while the Eastern Divide grew steadily closer, no longer a thin purple line across the horizon but now a massive buttress through which West Bend had carved a narrow gorge.

We were within the shadows of the Eastern Divide, close enough to the Monroe Pass that we could hear the low rumble of rapids, when we came upon a sign: a wooden plank, nailed to the burned stump of a blackwood tree that had been felled by lightning. I was at the front of the line, so I walked closer to read what was painted on it:

WELCOME TO THOMPSON'S FERRY
PASSAGE NEGOTIABLE—TRADE & BARTER
STOP HERE—LAY DOWN GUNS—YELL LOUD & WAIT
TRESPASSERS SHOT ON SIGHT!

Shading my eyes with my hand, I peered up at the limestone bluffs. No movement save for the breeze wafting through the bare branches of some scraggly trees that clung to the rock. The sign looked old, the paint faded and peeling. No telling how long it had been there.

"Hello!" I yelled. "Anyone there?" My voice echoed off the bluffs; I waited another few moments, then stepped past the sign.

A high-pitched *zeee!* passed my right ear, then a bullet chipped a splinter off the top of the sign. A half second later, the hollow bang of the gunshot reverberated from somewhere up in the rocks. I instinctively ducked, raising my hands above my head.

"Hey, cut it out!" I shouted. "I'm unarmed!"

"Can't you read?" a voice yelled down.

"I can read . . . can't you hear?" I straightened up, keeping my hands in sight. From the corner of my eye, I could hear the Universalists ducking their heads or diving for cover behind spider bushes. All except Zoltan, who calmly stood his ground, a little annoyed but otherwise unperturbed.

"We're not carrying!" I couldn't see where the shot had come from, but whoever had opened fire on me was a crack shot; otherwise, I would have been missing part of my skull. "We're just trying to . . . !"

"We come in peace." Zoltan barely raised his voice, yet he spoke loud enough to be heard up on the bluffs. "We mean no harm. We only want passage across the channel." Then he turned to the others. "Come out," he said quietly. "Let them see you."

His followers reluctantly emerged from hiding, leaving their packs where they'd dropped them. Everyone looked scared, and some seemed ready to run back the way we'd come, but as always, their faith in their leader was greater than their fear. Soon they were all out in the open once more, their hands in plain view.

A minute passed, then a figure emerged from hiding among the boulders near the entrance to the pass: a long-haired boy, wearing a catskin coat a size too large, his trousers tucked into old Union Guard boots. He ambled toward us, a carbine cradled in his arms. He couldn't have been more than twelve, yet his distrustful eyes were those of a man twice his age.

"Who are you?" he demanded, looking first at me, then at Zoltan.

"The Reverend Zoltan Shirow, of the Church of Universal Transformation." Zoltan spoke before I could answer. "These people are my congregation, and this is our guide, Benjamin Harlan. I apologize for our lack of manners. We didn't think anyone was here."

"Huh . . . yeah, well, you got fooled, didn't you?" His gaze swept across everyone, taking us in. "You have anything to trade, or are you just . . . ?

Then he stopped, cocking his head slightly as if listening to something we couldn't hear. I recognized the motion; the boy had a subcutaneous implant. He murmured something beneath his breath, then looked at us again. "Okay, c'mon. Pick up your stuff and follow me." He grinned. "Mind yourself, though. My brother's up there, and he hasn't shot anyone since last week."

It sounded like teenage braggadocio, but I wasn't ready to push it. "After you," I said, then hefted my bag and let him lead the way.

The trail took us into the Monroe Pass, where it became a narrow shelf that had gradually eroded into the limestone. We went slowly, picking our way across slick rocks as icy water sprayed us; one false step meant falling into the rapids churning just a few feet below. The kid stopped every now and then to look back, making sure that he hadn't lost anyone; it occurred to me that he and his brother didn't really need to stand guard duty, because the gorge itself was its own natural fortification. Whatever they were protecting, it must be valuable. Either that, or they simply didn't like people dropping in unannounced.

We emerged from the gorge to find ourselves on the other side of the Eastern Divide. A stony beach lay beneath the towering white wall; West Bend emptied into the East Channel, and only a couple of miles across the water lay the rocky coast of Midland.

Thompson's Ferry was a small village of faux birch–shingled cabins elevated on stilts, with smoke rising from their stone chimneys. Goats and pigs sulked within small pens matted with cut sourgrass, and from somewhere nearby I heard the barking of a small dog. Jutting out into the channel was a small pier, against which was tied a large raft; skin kayaks lay upside down on the beach, and fishing nets were draped across wooden racks. I smelled salt and fish and woodsmoke, and in the half-light of the late-afternoon sun, the whole scene looked as gentle as a painting.

But then I heard pebbles crunch underfoot behind us, and I looked around to see a young man standing on a footpath leading up to the top of the bluffs, holding a rifle in his hands. Seeing me gazing at him, he gave me a tip of his cap. This was the sentry who'd fired the warning shot; he'd been tailing us ever since we'd entered the pass. I nodded back to him: no hard feelings, mate, just don't use me for target practice again.

The kid led us to a lodge in the center of town, a large blackwood cabin with a sat dish fastened to its chimney. "Hang on," he said. "I'll go get the boss." But he was only halfway up the back porch steps when its door swung open and the chief appeared.

Six feet and a few inches tall, with a lot of muscle packed into skin that looked as weatherbeaten as his clothes and a greying beard that reached halfway down his chest, he looked as if he had been molded by the world in which he lived: stone and sand, tidewater and salt. "Thank you, Garth," he murmured. "I'll take it from here." He stepped to the railing. "Let's get down to the basics. Name's Clark Thompson, and this is my place. You've already met my nephew Garth, and that's Lars, my other nephew . . . they're sort of the reception committee."

"Pleased to meet you, Mr. Thompson." Zoltan walked forward. "I'm the Reverend Zoltan. . . ."

"Already know who you are, Rev. We're a long way from Shuttlefield, but word gets around." Thompson grinned; he was missing a couple of teeth. "Even if you hadn't split town a couple of days ago, it's hard not to hear about someone who looks the way you do."

Laughter from around us. I turned my head, saw that about twenty people had appeared, emerging from the adjacent cabins: several men, a few women, three or four kids, each of them as tough as Clark Thompson and his kin. A couple of men carried guns; they weren't aiming them at us, but it was the second time that day I'd been welcomed by men with loaded weapons, and I still wasn't quite over the first time.

Zoltan remained unruffled. "If you know who we are, then you know why we're here." Thompson nodded, but said nothing. "All we want is a way across the channel. We're willing to trade whatever we can for—"

"Happy to hear it. My boys wouldn't have led you here if you weren't. But only a few people know about this place, and most of them are here right now. So who told you how to get here?"

"Savant Castro." Thompson scowled as I said this; behind me, I could hear whispers through the crowd. "He told us they sometimes let people leave, if he thinks keeping 'em around is more trouble than it's worth. I guess we qualify."

"Maybe so . . . but Manny Castro doesn't strike me as any sort of humanitarian." Thompson shook his head. "Damned if I know what it is, but he's got his own agenda." He absently gazed up at the Divide as if trying to make up his mind. If he refused to give us a ride across the channel, we'd have little choice but to turn back; given the size of the settlement, it was obvious we couldn't remain there. "All right," he said at last, "we'll get you across the channel. We've never said no to anyone, and I'm not about to start now."

"Thank you." I tried not to let my relief show.

"It's my business. Just one more question . . . where do you think you'll go, once you reach Midland?"

"We want to find the original colonists," Zoltan began, and everyone standing around broke out in laughter. He waited until it subsided, then went on. "Any help you may be able to give us would be appreciated."

"Can't help you much there, preacher," Thompson said. "We've only seen them a few times ourselves, and when we do they're not very sociable."

That had to be a lie. Thompson's Ferry was the only settlement on New Florida besides Liberty and Shuttlefield; if the *Alabama* colonists came there at all, then it must be to trade. And when people get together to trade, they usually swap more than material goods. But we were on the chief's good side, so I kept my mouth shut.

Thompson pointed to a spot on the beach a few yards away. "You can camp out over there. Dinner's on the house . . . hope you like chowder, because that's the only thing on the menu. We'll dicker over the fare later." He turned to his younger nephew. "C'mon, Garth. Let's tell your aunt we've got guests."

That was the end of it. Garth followed his uncle into the lodge; the crowd began to melt away, and the Universalists carried their gear to the place where Thompson said we could pitch our tents. Exhausted, I slumped down on the steps. The sun was beginning to set behind the

Eastern Divide, with a stiff wind coming off the channel, but for the moment we'd found a place of refuge, and some semblance of hospitality.

And yet, I couldn't help but wonder whether I should have taken Jaime's advice.

Dinner was served in the lodge, within a main room illuminated by fish-oil lamps hung from the rafters and warmed by a driftwood fire blazing in the stone hearth. Apparently the residents of Thompson's Ferry gathered there every night, for when we trooped in through the door, we found the locals already seated at a long blackwood table that ran down the center of the room. Space was made for us at the table, and soon an enormous pot of redfish chowder was brought out from the kitchen by a pleasant older lady whom everyone called Aunt Molly. Talking nonstop, she ladled out bowls of chowder, added a thick slice of homemade bread to each plate, then handed them to the nearest person, who passed them down the line. No one began eating until everyone was served, though, and after Aunt Molly had bowed her head and said grace.

The only persons missing from the table were Zoltan and Renaldo. Zoltan had vanished into his tent as soon as it was erected, and hadn't reappeared by the time his followers had finished setting up camp. Once more, I was mystified by his reclusiveness, even if it didn't seem to bother anyone else. It was Renaldo's turn to wear the black sash around his left forearm; he'd begged another bowl of chowder from Aunt Molly, then quietly went out the door with it, apparently taking it to Zoltan's tent. Clark Thompson watched him go, but said nothing. After dinner he tapped me on the shoulder and gestured for me to follow him into an adjacent room.

"Pretty rude of the Reverend, skipping out like that," he said once he'd shut the door. "Can't say I appreciate it very much."

"He's like that. Sorry." The walls were crowded with stacked barrels, with boxes and crates and coiled rope scattered here and there, surrounding a table and two chairs beneath an oil lamp. "Has to have his private time once a day. To meditate with his followers."

"Yeah, well . . ." Thompson turned up the lamp a little higher, then sat down behind the table. "Next time he decides to meditate when my wife's cooked a meal for him, I'm going to feed him fish-head soup instead."

"Knowing him, he'd probably thank her for it."

A quizzical smile. "You're not with them? Oh, I can see you're traveling with 'em . . . but you're not a true believer?"

"Is it that obvious?"

"Like the nose on your face. Knew it the moment you walked into town. Everyone else kept quiet, like a herd of sheep following the Judas ram. You're the only one who spoke up."

"I'm their guide. Sort of a job, y'know. I don't . . ."

"That's your business, friend." Thompson held up a hand. "I don't care why you've fallen in with these characters. What I want to know is, why did Castro send you my way?"

"I've told you everything I know." I sat down in the other chair. "If it makes any difference, it was a surprise to me, too."

"Oh, it makes a difference." He pulled out a penknife, flicked it open, and idly began to trim his fingernails. "We've got about thirty people living here, and every one of them came from Shuttlefield. My wife and I, along with the boys, were aboard the *Glorious Destiny*. When we saw what that bitch Hernandez had in mind, we grabbed what we could and took off. Started out with just one cabin, but it wasn't long before others followed us."

"From other ships?"

"Uh-huh. The ones who managed to get away, that is. We've built this place from scratch and put in the ferry late last summer. At first it was just so we could going hunting on the other side of the channel, but every so often someone shows up who wants to get over to Midland . . . usually folks like you, fed up with Shuttlefield. Until now, though, we thought the Union was unaware of our existence." He let out his breath. "And now you tell us that Manny Castro not only knows we're here, but he's even willing to provide exact directions."

"Maybe he doesn't consider you a threat."

"Maybe." Thompson silently regarded me for a few moments, as if trying to decide whether to trust me. Then he leaned back in his chair to open a crate behind him, pulling out a ceramic jug. Pulling out the cork, he passed it me. "Bearshine," he murmured. "Sort of like whiskey, but distilled from corn mash. Be careful, it's got a kick. Don't worry, you won't go blind."

He was right about the kick. I could have started a fire with the stuff. The booze scorched my throat but made a nice warm place in my stomach. "Like it?" he asked. "Now ask yourself, how would we be able to make corn liquor when we can't grow corn here?"

I thought about it for a moment. "You're getting it in trade."

"Sure we are. And they grow corn in Liberty. That's not where this comes from, though." He nodded in the general direction of the channel. "We're getting it from over there, from people who sometimes come back across. But I haven't carried any corn on my ferry."

"And you just said you've been running the ferry since only late last summer."

"Uh-huh. That's right." He tapped the jug with the blade of his knife. "So where do you think this stuff is coming from?"

I realized what he was getting at. "The original colonists."

"Yup." He nodded. "You say you're their guide. I take it that means you have a map. Are you carrying it now?"

I reached into my parka, pulled out the map we had been using. Thompson moved the jug aside as I spread it across the table. "Okay," he said, pointing to our location on the east coast of New Florida, "here's where we are, and over there is where we'll put you off tomorrow morning." His finger traced down the rocky western coast of Midland.

"There's a place about a mile south where you can climb up the bluffs . . . don't worry, you can't miss it. At the top of the ridge, you'll find a path leading southwest."

"Where does it go?"

"When my boys and I hacked it out, it went back about thirty miles. Haven't been down it lately, so I don't know if it's been expanded since then. But here's the important part." He pointed farther inland to a highland region that covered most of the subcontinent. "That's the Gillis Range, with Mt. Shaw down here. From what I've been told . . . and believe me, it ain't much . . . somewhere on the other side of Mt. Shaw is where the *Alabama* crew is holed up."

Like most maps of Coyote, mine wasn't very detailed; it had been made from high-orbit photos, and 95 percent of the planet hadn't been explored, let alone named. It appeared, though, that the Gillis Range split in half at its southern end, with a waterway forming a broad river valley between Mt. Shaw and another mountain to the southeast. It would make sense that the original colonists would settle in there: a source of fresh water and plenty of land, but protected on three sides by high terrain.

"I see." I traced my finger around the southern edge of the range. "So all we'd have to do is hike around Mt. Shaw. . . ."

"Uh-uh. Think again." Thompson pointed from the East Channel to the base of the mountain. "That's about a hundred and fifty miles. It's flat country, more or less, so you can make it in about a week, maybe two. But if you decide to go all the way around the range, then come up the valley, that's going to be . . . what? Another two hundred, maybe three hundred miles?"

"I guess. We can make it."

"You guess?" Thompson raised his eyes from the map. "Let me remind you of something . . . we're halfway through Machidiel, which means we're coming into spring. The boids will start migrating north pretty soon, and the lowlands are their stomping grounds. And I notice your people aren't carrying any firearms."

He was right. Almost four hundred miles across uncharted terrain, with nothing more than quarterstaves for protection . . . useless against a creature capable of ripping your head off with one swipe of its beak. Not only that, but we carried precious little food. We might be able to forage for a while, but the longer we stayed out in the open, the less chance we'd have of survival.

"Someone must have made it. How else would you be getting this?"

Thompson smiled. "That's what I figure." He pointed to Mt. Shaw. "If there's a new trail, then it must lead straight over the mountain. And even if there isn't one, it's the most direct route, and it'll cut a couple hundred miles off your trip."

I stared at the map. There was no indication of how tall the mountain was or how steep its incline might be. Yet Clark Thompson had a good point; if we could make it across Mt. Shaw, then we'd come down into the valley where the *Alabama* colonists were likely to be hiding. It was a risk, to be sure, but it was the best shot we had.

"Thanks." I picked up the jug, took another slug of bearshine. "What do I owe you for this?"

Thompson sat back in his chair, thought about it for a moment. "If you make it, come back sometime and tell me."

"So you'll know where you're getting your booze from?"

"No," he said quietly. "So I'll know that there is indeed a God, and that She looks out for holy fools."

The ferry was a raft comprised of several blackwood logs lashed together, with a rotary winch from a rover mounted in its center. A thick cable made of coiled tree vine was stretched all the way across the East Channel, anchored to boulders on both sides of the river; it fed through the winch, and when Lars and Garth stood on either side of the raft and turned the crank hand over hand, the raft was slowly pulled across the channel. It might not have been the quickest or easiest way of getting across the East Channel, but it was the safest; the ferry was located about fifteen miles north of the shoals at the channel's most narrow point, and the swift current could easily have swept small boats downstream.

Clark Thompson might have been sympathetic to us, but he was also a businessman. It took three round-trips to get everyone to Midland, and it cost us six of our tents and three data pads; he already had enough lanterns and warm clothes. Yet he was generous enough to supply us with some dried fish, and he slipped me a jug of bearshine when no one was looking. I shook hands with him, and he wished me good luck; the last I saw of him, he was standing on the wharf, watching us go.

By the time the Universalists were all on the far side of the channel, the day was more than half over. Following Clark's instructions, I led them down the stony beach until we reached a place where a landslide had occurred long before, opening a narrow ravine in the limestone bluffs. A long, steep climb upward through the breach, and we came out on top of a high ridge. Behind and below us lay the East Channel . . . and before us stretched Midland, a vast savanna leading to forest, the Gillis Range visible in the distance as a ragged purple line across the horizon.

Once I found the trailhead Clark had told me about, I sat down on a boulder, spread the map across my lap, and pulled out the compass. When I had my bearings, I put everything back in my pocket, shouldered my pack once more, and began to lead the others down the hillside.

Everyone was happy; I remember that clearly. We'd made our escape from New Florida; the day was bright and warm, the road ahead clear and easy to follow. The Universalists began singing "God of Our Fathers" almost as soon as we reached the bottom of the ridge; I joined in even though I didn't know the words. And most of all, I remember Greer. She walked a few steps behind Zoltan, but whenever I looked back at her it was as if she were right beside me; the smile never left her face, and her eyes were as bright as the day we'd first met. After a while, Zoltan permitted her to join me; together we marched into the wilderness, two lovers with nothing before us save the brightest of futures.

It was a wonderful moment, one I'll never forget or regret. And like all wonderful moments, it didn't last very long. A pleasant dream, with the nightmare soon to follow.

New Florida, for the most part, was flat terrain, wide-open grasslands laced by streams, interspersed by swamps and occasional woods. During winter, when the ground was frozen and the swamps were dry, you could walk across it with relatively little effort.

Midland wasn't like that. By the end of the third day, we'd left the savanna and entered a vast rain forest that gradually became more dense, with faux birch and spider bush disappearing beneath a canopy of trees of a kind we'd never seen before, somewhat resembling elms except with thicker trunks and broader leaves, from which rough-barked vines dangled like serpents. Even in midday, sunlight seeped through only in sparse patches; it was cold down on the forest floor, the overgrowth brittle with frost.

We could no longer see the mountains; it wasn't long before we could no longer see the sun either, and on the fourth day we lost the trail itself. I don't know whether we'd taken a wrong turn or if the trail simply ended; I only know that, in a moment of clarity, I came to the realization that the path had simply vanished. We doubled back, losing an hour in our effort to retrace our steps, but the trail was no longer there. All we had left was the map and the compass I carried in my pocket; without them, we would have been completely lost.

Day in and day out, we fought our way through the forest, using our staffs to hack our way through dense foliage. At night, we huddled together against the cold; the dead branches we found were either frozen or too rotted to be burned, so what little warmth we got was from setting fire to small piles of twigs and leaves. No longer having as many tents as we once had, we were forced to double up in our sleeping arrangements, with four or five people crammed together into tents meant for three. At least it helped keep us warm; Greer and I learned how to zip our bags together, and we went to sleep with our arms around each other, jostled by others sharing our tent.

Yet Zoltan always claimed a tent for himself, in order for him to continue his daily communion with God. He may have had some interesting chats with the Lord during that time, but if he had, he wasn't sharing what he'd learned with us. He became silent, rarely speaking, and although he still invited others to join him in meditation, he ceased leading us in prayer in the morning, and after a week or so he neglected to offer prayer in the evening as well. By then the hymns had stopped. Ian and Renaldo got into a fistfight one morning over whose turn it was to carry a tent, and Clarice and Ana stopped talking to one another over something that occurred when no one else was watching.

But the gradual disintegration of morale wasn't the worst, nor were the endless days of making our way through the rain forest, or even the cold. All those miseries we might have been able to endure, had it not been for one more thing.

Hunger.

When we'd set out from Shuttlefield, we'd packed as much food as we could carry on our backs, along with our tents, clothes and sleeping bags. There were thirty-two of us—thirty-one, rather; as always, Zoltan never carried anything—so we were able to bring quite a lot of food, and we'd stocked up on more at Thompson's Ferry. I figured that, by the time we began to run low, we would be only a few days away from wherever the original colonists had settled, and all we'd have to do was go on short rations for a while. If worse came to worst, we could live off the land; a few of the native plants were edible, and I knew which ones they were.

What I didn't take into account was the fact that we were traveling through unknown territory in the dead of winter. First, we burned up a lot of calories, not just hiking but also keeping warm. We filled up at breakfast, then ate again at night: two meals a day for thirty people, not counting all the times when someone would nibble a biscuit or open a can of beans while we were taking rest breaks, and we used up our supplies very quickly. I didn't notice our rate of consumption at first because my mind was focused on getting us through the forest, and I was also half-expecting Zoltan to do his part by keeping his people in line. But Zoltan said nothing, and almost two weeks went by before it hit me that our packs were getting lighter and we were leaving behind a trail of plastic wrappers and cans.

Second, none of the plants I'd learned how to eat on New Florida grew in the forests of Midland. Sourgrass, cloverweed, Johnson's thistle . . . all were crowded out by the dense shrub that made up the undergrowth, and even those plants had gone into long-term dormancy. The streams and creeks where we might have found fish were frozen over, and any animals that we might have been able to trap were either in hibernation or had gone south for the winter. It was all we could do just to find dry tinder for firewood.

Most of the Universalists were city people before they'd left Earth. They'd done pretty well so far, making their way through an alien jungle carrying forty or fifty pounds on their backs; their faith had supplied motivation where experience had failed. But by the time we'd stopped eating breakfast and were skimping on the evening meal, the base of Mt. Shaw was still a day away. Spirits were running low, and Zoltan was almost totally incommunicado.

Unless you've been there, you don't know what it's like to face slow starvation. I'm not talking about skipping a meal or two, or even fasting; I mean the desperation that comes with the realization that you're running out of food, and the knowledge that when it's gone, it may be a long time before you eat again. There was a hollow ache in the pit of my stomach where there should have been weight, and an invisible band had formed on either side of my skull, pressing in on my temples. We had to find something to eat, and soon.

Just before we reached Mt. Shaw, we came upon a low swamp. The ice was thin, so we had to detour around it, but then I noticed a small cluster of ball plants growing on a tiny island in its center. I'd sooner throw a dead rat in a cook pot than a swamper. Nonetheless, they could be eaten, and they hibernated within ball plants, so I drafted a couple of guys, and we waded across the swamp, each footstep breaking through the ice and filling our boots with frigid slush, until we reached the island.

While the others waited behind me, I pulled out my knife and used it to cut open the thick leaves of the nearest plant. I intended to pull out a few sleeping swampers, then have the other guys club them to death. Skin 'em, stew 'em, eat 'em up . . . that was the plan.

What I'd neglected was the fact that pseudowasps sometimes also hibernated inside the balls. It was one of the more interesting symbiotic systems that had evolved on Coyote: pseudowasps protected the ball plants during summer, during which time they pollinated their flower tops; in late autumn, swampers curled up within the balls, and the pseudowasps retreated into their underground nests. Yet now and then, the odd pseudowasp or two would seek refuge within the ball plants themselves, perhaps to ward off any predators who might try to get at the swampers.

That's what happened to me. No sooner had I begun cutting my way into the nearest ball plant when a pseudowasp, awakened by my knife, burrowed out of the incision I'd made. Before I could react, it alighted on the back of my left hand and stung me.

My hand swelled up, but that wasn't the worst of it. Pseudowasp venom contains a toxin somewhat similar to lysergic acid; it causes paralysis in other insects, but in humans it produces hallucinations. In Shuttlefield, there was even an underground trade in what was known as "sting"—venom extracted from pseudowasps that had been captured, then sold as a cheap high.

I've never been a doper, so I wasn't prepared for what happened next. Within a half hour, colors began to get brighter as everything seemed to slow down; it seemed as if there was a subtle electric hum in the air, and nothing anyone said to me made sense. By the time my companions helped me stagger out of the swamp, I was raving like a lunatic. I vaguely recall trying to take my clothes off, insisting that the perfect way to enjoy this lovely winter day was for everyone to get naked and have an orgy, swigging the bearshine Clark had given me and telling Zoltan that he should use those wings of his to fly back to Thompson's Ferry and grab us a couple more jugs. Everything was happy and wonderful and exquisitely beautiful; these people were all my friends, and it mattered little that we were lost and close to starvation.

At some point, though, my vision began to tunnel. Suddenly feeling very tired, I sat down on a log, saying that I needed to take a rest. Go ahead with the party, gang, I'll be along in just a moment. And then I passed out.

When I came to, I found myself in a tent. Night had fallen; I could smell the smoke of a campfire. From somewhere outside I could hear low voices. And I wasn't alone; in the soft glow of a lantern, Zoltan was seated cross-legged on the other side of the tent.

"Welcome back," he said. He'd removed his robe, and his wings furled about his bare shoulders. "We were worried about you. Feeling better?"

"A little." Not much. My head pounded, and my throat was parched. Without asking, he handed me a water bottle. I unscrewed the cap and drank. "Where are we? How far have we . . . ?"

"Where we were before you fainted." His face was hideous in the half-light; it had been a long time since I'd noticed just how ugly he was. "We couldn't go any farther, not with you in this condition, so we stopped for the night."

"Oh, God . . . I'm sorry, I didn't mean to . . ."

"Don't be. It wasn't your fault." Zoltan took the bottle from me, replaced the cap. "In fact, I rather envy you. Seems to me that you've had a moment of revelation."

My mind was too fogged for me to realize what he was saying. "Yeah, well . . . getting stung will do that to you." My left hand was sore; it had been bandaged, and the swelling had gone down. There were antibiotics in the first-aid kit we were carrying; if this had happened to someone else, I might have been able to administer them in time to prevent the venom from taking effect. Unfortunately, these people didn't know much about pseudowasps. "My fault. I should have warned you."

"Why? How can you warn someone about God?" Zoltan shook his head. "He does what He chooses to do, speaks to you when you least expect it."

"I don't understand."

"You know about the Holy Transformation. I must assume you do, because you've never asked me about it, not since the first night you spent with us. One of my followers must have told you . . . probably Greer, since you two have become close." I said nothing, and he went on. "When God came to me, while I was in the Room of Pain and Understanding, He told me that I had a mission in life. Gather as many as I could find who would believe His word and take them to another place, where we would spread the word that the universal transformation was forthcoming."

He shifted a little, stretching his legs. "I thought we'd receive that sign in Shuttlefield, but when it didn't happen and it became apparent that we were surrounded by those who'd eventually try to kill us, I realized that our mission would be fulfilled elsewhere. And so, like Moses and the Israelites, we've set forth into the wilderness . . . and now it's become clear to me what our purpose truly is, for through you, God has spoken."

"Zoltan . . . Reverend Shirow . . . I was stung by a pseudowasp. It makes people freak out, do weird things. That's all. I didn't hear God. I was just hallucinating."

"Perhaps you think you were suffering hallucinations. Yet during that time, you told us that you loved us all, that we should freely share our love with one another." I started to protest, but he held up a hand. "You say you were under the influence of the pseudowasp, and perhaps you were . . . but I think God was speaking through you."

"But I'm not a believer. I've told you. You've said it yourself."

"You've led us to this place, and God has spoken through you." He gazed at me with great tenderness, as if I were a lost child whom he had found. "I know now what He has planned for us," he said very quietly. "We are going to die here."

"No, we're not." I shook my head. "We're going to make it through this. We're going to get over that mountain, then . . ."

"You can't refuse. It's God's will that we perish together. Perhaps not now, but soon, very soon." Zoltan took a deep breath, let it out as a sigh. "Benjamin, you're one of us now. The time has come for you to join us, body and soul."

Reaching around behind him, he pulled out a soft leather bag. He unzipped it and reached inside; when his hand came out, it held the black sash I'd seen the others wear so many times before. With great rever-ence, he laid it on the ground between us.

"Remove your coat," he said quietly, "and roll up the left sleeve of your shirt."

I fumbled at the zipper of my parka. My head still felt as if it were stuffed full of cotton, my mind not ready to cooperate with me. So this was going to be my initiation. Well, why not? I'd come this far with these people; regardless of what I'd just told Zoltan, we'd probably per-ish together. Might as well go the distance.

"Wrap it around your elbow," Zoltan said, handing the sash to me, "and pull it as tight as you can." He slid his hand into the bag once more. "This will take only a minute, then we'll be done."

I'd already wrapped the sash around my arm, but the last thing he said made me hesitate. I watched as he produced a small gold chalice. He carefully placed it on the ground; in the glow of the lantern, its rim held faint crimson stain, like something that he hadn't been able to wash out. It looked like . . .

"What . . . what are you doing?" By then I'd seen the other things in his hand: the silver hypodermic needle; the small coil of surgical tubing; the deflated rubber valve. Yet even then, it hadn't quite sunk in. I needed to have him tell me.

Perhaps he knew that he didn't need to. His eyes slowly rose from the chalice, met my own. "Will you share yourself with me?" he whispered.

It was then that everything became clear. Why his followers wore the sash, why they were excused from their chores for the day. The black cloth concealed the puncture marks in their arms; a day's rest helped them recover from their blood loss.

In church, communion is celebrated in a symbolic manner. A chalice of wine for the blood of the savior, a wafer of bread for his flesh. Whether or not one believes in the miracle of transubstantiation is al-most beside the point; it's the act of worship that counts. Yet Zoltan had twisted this ritual, turning it around so that it fit his own self-image. He wasn't interested in symbolic deeds, nor was he willing to share himself with his followers. What he demanded was fealty, utter obedience; he wanted to be a god. So he brought them into his tent, told them what-ever they wanted to hear, then . . .

"Benjamin." He crawled closer, the needle raised in his right hand. "Will you share yourself with me? Will you give your blood to . . . ?"

"Get away!"

I kicked him as hard as I could, swinging my right foot into his stom-ach. Zoltan grunted and toppled over backward, and I scrambled across the tent and unzipped the flap. I was almost halfway out of the tent when I felt his hand close around my left ankle. I blindly kicked back, felt the sole of my foot connect with something fleshy. Zoltan cried out in pain, and the people seated around the campfire looked around as I pitched forward on hands and knees from his tent.

I rose to my feet, wavered unsteadily. Someone said my name, and I saw Greer coming toward me. I didn't want her to touch me—I didn't want anyone to touch me—so I lurched away, escaping the fire and the tents, until I fell to my knees beneath a tree.

I tried to vomit, but there was nothing in my stomach for me to throw up; all I could do was dry-heave. When my guts stopped convulsing, I fell into a pile of dry leaves at the base. Darkness closed in, and I was gone.

I awoke to find that someone had unrolled my sleeping bag and covered me with it. Probably Greer; she was the only person who ac-knowledged my presence that morning, and even she kept her distance. No one would speak to me; they quietly took down the tents and packed up their gear, treating me as if I was a guest who'd overstayed his welcome.

And perhaps I was. The map and compass were missing from my parka. Thinking they might have been taken from me while I was asleep, I asked the others who had them, only to receive stares and headshakes as nonverbal responses. Although it was clear that Zoltan was leading us through the forest, he didn't appear to have them either. It's possible that I might have lost them in the swamp, but when I attempted to go back to search for them, Zoltan beckoned for the others to come with him. So not only had I been ostracized, but the Universalists were willing to leave me behind. I had no choice but to follow them; shouldering my pack, I brought up the rear.

Even without the benefit of map and compass, Zoltan knew where he was going. At that point, it would have been difficult to miss finding the eastern slope of Mt. Shaw. By the end of the day, when we finally emerged from the forest, the mountain loomed before us, three thousand feet high, its summit still covered with snow. We made camp at its base, but no one invited me to share a tent with them. The only food left was some rice, but I wasn't offered any, and when I attempted to join the Universalists by the fire they'd built, Boris stepped in front of me, blocking my way with his staff. I retreated to where I had unrolled my sleeping bag and sat there alone, shivering in the cold, my stomach growling.

Shortly after everyone turned in for the night, though, Greer came to me. Glancing over her shoulder to see if anyone was watching, she knelt beside my sleeping bag, then reached beneath her robe and produced a bowl. "Eat fast," she whispered. "I can't let anyone see me doing this."

There was only a handful of rice in the bowl, but it was better than nothing. "Thanks," I mumbled, my teeth chattering as I took it from her. "You're . . ."

"Zoltan says you're no longer one of us. You refused to share communion with him. That makes you a heretic. We're not allowed to associate with you."

"That's what he says, huh?" I stuffed cold rice into my mouth. "And how many times have you let him drink your blood? Or have you lost count?"

She let out her breath. "It's not like that, Ben. You might think it's just about drinking blood, but it's a form of sacred worship. The prophet partakes of our essence, and in that way we become closer not only to him but also God. . . ."

"Oh, come off it. There's nothing sacred about what he's doing. Zoltan wants to play vampire, that's fine, but leave God out of it. He's just using you for . . ."

"No! God has sent him to us to fulfill His mission. . . ."

"And you know what Zoltan told me last night? He says he wants us all to die!" I was no longer bothering to keep my voice low. "This isn't communion. This isn't worship. You've been brainwashed, kid. He's going to . . ."

"Greer. Come away from him."

I looked up, saw Zoltan emerge from the shadows. How long he'd been standing there, I had no idea. His wings were hidden under his robe, and I couldn't see his face beneath his upraised hood, yet in that moment, backlit against the dying campfire, he looked as demonic as anything Dr. Owen Dunn might have imagined in the depths of his insanity.

Greer started to rise, but I grabbed her wrist. "Don't listen to him," I said. "He's crazy, out of his mind. There's nothing he can do to you if you don't . . ."

"Greer, leave him." Zoltan remained calm. "We've known all along that's he's an unbeliever. Now he's revealed himself to be more."

"What? A heretic? Just because I won't grovel?" I struggled to my feet, dropping the empty bowl but keeping my grip on Greer's wrist. "You're a lousy excuse for a prophet, Shirow. Jesus would have been sick if he'd ever met you. . . ."

"Enough!" Zoltan leveled a taloned finger at me. "Thou art damned! Thou art excommunicated! Thou art no longer of the body of the church!"

"Yeah. Right." From behind him, the other Universalists were emerging from their tents, drawn by the sound of our voices. "So I'm damned and excommunicated, and you'll never get me to . . ." I stopped, shook my head. "But I'm one thing you're not, Shirow, and the one thing you can't do without just now."

"And what's that?"

"I'm the only guy who knows how to get over that mountain."

He stared at me. "God will show us the way."

"Maybe I don't have the map and compass anymore, but I don't think you do either, and I was the only one who was paying attention to where we were going while y'all were singing church hymns. Not only that, but Clark Thompson told *me* how to find the *Alabama* colonists, and not *you*. So unless God gives out travel plans, buddy, you're screwed."

I was bluffing, of course; Thompson's directions hadn't been specific. Not only that, but I was gambling that Zoltan hadn't stolen the map and compass from me. I hadn't seen him or anyone else produce them all day, which led me to believe that they had been lost.

"You say you want to die out here." Desperate, I kept talking, trying to get through to them. "Great . . . so what's that going to prove? If no one knows why, then it'll all be for nothing . . . nothing! What sort of a holy mission is that, pal?"

Greer trembled against me; I released her wrist, but she didn't move away. No one said anything; they waited in silence for their prophet to denounce the heretic, the unbeliever, the damned soul who'd dared challenge God's chosen messenger to Coyote.

Zoltan said nothing for a few moments. He was stuck, and he knew it. "The Lord works in mysterious ways," he said at last. "You may lead us across the mountain, Benjamin."

"Thank you." I let out my breath, hesitated. "And in exchange for my services as your guide, there's one more thing I want from you."

"And this is . . . ?"

"Your tent, please. And without you in it." I bent down, gathered my bag and pack. "It's freezing out here, and I'm sure no one will object if you share space with them."

Zoltan didn't reply. He simply stepped aside. My arms full, I walked past him, ignoring his followers as I headed over to his tent.

Yet when I looked back, Greer wasn't with me. She had moved against his side, and he'd put his arms around her. That was when I knew she was lost to me.

It took two days for us to climb Mt. Shaw. It should have taken only one, but the mountainside was steep. With no trail to follow, we had to pick our way around granite ledges and across landslides, taking a zigzag course up the eastern slope. The higher we went, the colder the air became, and soon every breath we took was painful. Once we passed the tree line about three-quarters of the way up the mountain we found ourselves plodding, sometimes crawling, through knee-deep drifts.

Everyone was weak from hunger and cold. When we stopped to make camp, there was no level place for us to pitch our tents, nor any dry wood to gather for a fire. We managed to half cook the remaining rice in snow melted in a pan over a portable stove—at that altitude, it was impossible to bring the water to a boil—but several people had come down with altitude sickness and couldn't eat. No one's clothes were dry, and some of us were showing the first signs of acute hypothermia. We spent a chilly night on the mountain, huddled together in our bags as the wind kicked up snow around us, Bear glaring down upon us like the eye of an angry god.

When morning finally came, we discovered that Clarice was no longer among us. Renaldo found her ten feet away; sometime during the night, she had rolled down the slope in her sleeping bag until she landed in a deep snowdrift. She was still alive, but only barely; her face was pale, her lips blue, and she never regained consciousness despite our attempts to keep her warm. Clarice died as Uma was rising over the summit; with the ground too hard for us to dig a grave and no one strong enough to carry her body, the only thing we could do was zip her corpse inside her bag and stack some rocks on top of it. Zoltan muttered a brief prayer, then we continued our ascent, leaving her behind.

We reached the top of the mountain late in the afternoon the second day. The view was magnificent—a great valley several thousand feet below, surrounded by the Gillis Range with the mammoth volcanic cone of Mt. Bonestell far away to the northwest—but no one was in any condition to appreciate it. By then several people were leaning heavily upon their staffs or each other, their feet numb from frostbite; Ian was snow-blind, relying on Dex to lead him, and most of the others were listless and mumbling incoherently.

To make matters worse, thick clouds coming in from the northeast warned that a storm was approaching. We had to get off the summit as soon as we could. Still pretending that I knew the way, I made the best guess I could, then began leading the group down the western slope.

We made it to the tree line shortly after dusk, but still we couldn't find anyplace for us to set up our tents. The stronger members of the group erected a couple of lean-to shelters from fallen branches, then covered them with unfolded tents. Unable to build a fire, with nothing left to eat, we crowded together beneath the shelters as the first flakes of snow began to fall upon us. That night, even Bear had forsaken us; the sky was dark, the stars invisible behind the storm sweeping down the mountain.

No one spoke to me except when they had to. I was necessary, but that was all; any sense of brotherhood had long since vanished. Greer stayed away from me. That hurt the most, because although I had stopped caring very much about the rest of the group, I still loved her. But during that last, long night, even though she slept only a few feet away, she was as distant as if we were separated by miles.

By daybreak, though, the snow was still falling and the shelters were covered with nearly a foot of fresh powder. Three more people had died during the night: Boris, and two others whose names I can't recall today. Yet there was no way we could continue our descent; visibility had been reduced to less than five feet, and most of the group were suffering from frostbite and hypothermia.

That was when the true horror began.

* * *

"We have to eat," Zoltan said, as I was helping Renaldo drag the bodies from beneath the shelter. "If we don't eat, we'll die."

"Yeah, sure. No problem." I could barely see him through the snow; he was sitting on a log, staring at me. "Know just the place. Nice little cafe at the bottom of the mountain. Just a few miles away. Great prime rib. C'mon, let's go."

A bad joke. I couldn't help it. Four people dead already, and doubtless more to come. Ian most likely, or perhaps Doria; both were comatose, and there was nothing we could do to save them. Even another handful of raw rice sounded like a feast just then. But when I looked at him, I saw that he was gazing at the corpses in a way that made me feel uncomfortable.

"Put them over there," he said, pointing to a place nearby. "Get some knives." He looked at Renaldo. "See if you can find some dry wood. We need to make a fire."

"What are you saying?" I whispered.

For several long moments, Zoltan didn't reply. "We need to eat," he said. "If we don't, we'll die."

"You told me God wants us to die," I said. "Isn't that your . . . ?"

And then he lifted his gaze, and in that instant I saw something in his eyes I'd never seen before. . . .

No. That's not right. It had been there all along; I had just refused to acknowledge it, even though I knew it to be true. Zoltan Shirow was insane. He had always been insane. From the moment wings had been grafted to his back, he had been mad; nevertheless, he had concealed it behind the veneer of presumed prophecy.

Cannibalism can be accepted if you're desperate to survive. Many have done it before in order to continue living, and more often than not they weren't crazy. As repulsive as it may be, it's a pragmatic choice; eat the dead and remain alive, or die yourself. Yet in that instant, looking into Zoltan's eyes, I realized that this was what he'd had in mind all along. Given a choice, though, he would have preferred to taste my flesh than that of any of his followers. He wasn't going to wait until I died of cold or starvation. That was why he'd let me remain with the group. I wouldn't give him my blood, so he'd consume my body instead. Don't ask me how I knew what he intended; I just did.

"Okay," I said. "You're right. It's gotta be done." I turned to Renaldo. "You go get the knives . . . I think they're in Boris's bag. I'll get some wood."

Renaldo nodded dumbly. His mind was gone. He began trudging back through the snow toward the nearest lean-to. I watched him go, then I turned and started hobbling down the slope.

After the first few steps, I broke into a run. I had nothing with me except the clothes on my back and the boots I was wearing; no pack, no bag, no lantern, no stove. But if I returned to the shelter where I'd left my things, I had little doubt that I'd never come out again.

And I didn't have Greer. I tried to forget that as I ran for my life.

I had almost made a clean getaway when I heard Zoltan call my name. I wanted to keep going, but something made me stop, look back around. Zoltan was still where I'd left him; he hadn't moved at all, making no effort to pursue me. A gargoyle crouching in the snow. He knew what I was doing.

"Benjamin," he said, his voice almost lost to me, "do you believe?"

I started to say something, but I didn't. Instead, I started running again.

How I survived, I'll never know. By all rights, I should have perished on Mt. Shaw. I ate snow and the bark off trees, and slept covered by piles of dead leaves, and kept going downhill until I found my way to the bottom of the mountain, where a hunting party found me three days later. If Zoltan had been around, he might have said that what saved me was divine providence. Personally, I think it was fear, and the knowledge of what I'd left behind.

A doctor named Kuniko Okada nursed me back to health. Two toes on my left foot had rotted with gangrene from frostbite, so she was forced to amputate them, but other than that and severe malnutrition I'd come through in relatively good shape. I remained in her care for the next week, until I was strong enough to get out of bed and hobble across her cabin with the aid of a walking stick. It wasn't until Dr. Okada helped me out onto the porch that I discovered that the place was suspended fifteen feet above the ground.

The original colonists had built their new settlement within the boughs of an ancient stand of blackwood trees, not far from a wide creek that flowed down from the Gillis Range. Looking out from Dr. Okada's porch, I saw a village of tree houses, connected to one another by rope bridges, with livestock pens, brick kilns, and grain sheds scattered across the forest floor. I even saw the still where they made their bearshine. No wonder the Union hadn't been able to discover its location; the blackwoods not only provided protection against boids, but also camouflage from the cameras and infrared sensors of the spacecraft orbiting high above.

Once I was well, I agreed to meet with the Defiance Town Council. I recognized their leader as soon as I walked into the room: Robert E. Lee, former captain of the URSS *Alabama*, the man who'd stolen Earth's first starship and brought a group of political dissidents to the new world. His beard had gone white, lending him a strong resemblance to his famous ancestor, but he was clearly the same man whose face I'd seen in history texts when I was growing up. Lee was almost as surprised to see me as I was to meet him, as were the other members of the Council. Although I wasn't the first Shuttlefield refugee who'd managed to find their way to Defiance, I was the only man who'd ever crossed Mt. Shaw during winter. Not only that, but apparently I'd done it on my own, with only the clothes on my back.

I had a little trouble telling them my story; the form of English they spoke was over two hundred years old, and only recently had they learned Anglo. Once we were past the language barrier, I informed them that they were only half-right; I hadn't been alone, but so far as I knew there were no other survivors. Lee and the others listened to my story, and when I was done they excused me in order to hold an executive session. It didn't last long; when I was brought back into the meeting room, Lee told me that the Council had voted unanimously to accept me as a new member of their town. I accepted the invitation, of course.

A month later, I was able to walk on my own. By then it was early spring; the snow had melted, and it was possible to climb Mt. Shaw safely once more. I took a few days off from my new job as goatherd to escort a small group of men up the western slope. It was a slow ascent— I had to stop often to rest my left foot, and also try to remember the way I'd come—but after a couple of days of searching we managed to find the place just below the tree line where I'd last seen the members of the Church of Universal Transformation.

Two lean-to shelters, already on the verge of collapse, lay near a ring of stones where a fire had been built. Within them, we discovered rotting sleeping bags and backpacks, tattered robes and dead lanterns, a couple of Bibles whose brown pages fluttered in the cool wind. Charred and broken bones lay in and around the fire pit; not far away, we found a pile of mutilated skeletons, some missing their arms and legs, others with skulls fractured as if struck from behind by one of the staffs that lay here and there.

There was no way to identify anyone. Weather, animals, and insects had done their work on the bodies, and I couldn't look for myself. After a few minutes, I knelt on the ground and wept until one of my companions picked me up and led me away.

I'm sure none of them survived. There's no way anyone else could have made it off the mountain. Not even Greer. Even today, her fate is something I can't bear to contemplate.

And yet . . .

Before my partners buried them, they carefully counted the corpses. They came up with twenty-seven bodies. Not counting Clarice, whose body was left on the other side of Mt. Shaw, or me, that was two short of the thirty-one Universalists who left Shuttlefield, including Zoltan Shirow. We never found anything that looked like a wing, or a skull with fangs among its teeth, or a hand whose fingers had been reshaped as talons.

To this day, though, people who've ventured into the Gillis Range have come back with stories of shadowy forms half-seen through the trees. Sometimes they've caught a glimpse of a figure with batlike wings, and sometimes they've spotted what appears to be a young woman. These could only be stories; the mountains are haunted, and lonely as only the wilderness can be.

I don't know the answer. But every night, before I go to bed, I pray to God that I never will.

Part 3

THE GARCIA NARROWS BRIDGE

The day is Anael, Adnachiel 66, c.y. 05: a perfect morning in early autumn. The place is the Eastern Divide, the great row of limestone bluffs running along the eastern coast of New Florida, separating its flat marshlands from the East Channel. On the other side of the channel is Midland, the equatorial continent that straddles the northern half of Coyote's meridian; like most of the planet, it's largely unexplored, but this is about to change. For where there was once only an expanse of water, there's now an alien object, something never before seen on this world.

A bridge.

Almost two miles long, with a midlength clearance of 110 feet, the bridge is built almost entirely of native wood and stone; indeed, the only metal used in its construction are the thick steel bolts that hold together the post-and-beam structure of the six blackwood arches holding up the concrete roadway. The arches and the towers that support them rest upon massive limestone piers, and suspended between each arch is a hinged span that seems to float in midair above the channel. The bridge appears fragile, but appearances are deceiving: designed to withstand the harshest winter storm or the highest spring flood, it can hold the weight of pedestrians, carts, rovers . . . even an army, if need be.

At the moment, though, the bridge is vacant. For the first time since last Machidiel, when construction began, no one stands upon it. The scaffolds have been dismantled, along with the temporary caissons that once surrounded the piers at the base of the towers; the bamboo basket that transported workmen along a long cable strung between the towers is still in place, but soon it'll be taken down. The bridge is finished. The only thing left to be done is the dedication ceremony.

Almost eight hundred people have gathered beneath the river bluffs. During the course of the last year, a small town has grown up within the shadows of the Eastern Divide: dormitories, commissaries, warehouses, and sheds, sprawling across acres of savanna near the limestone quarries where workers chipped out the blocks used to build the towers. Today, though, Bridgeton is empty; everyone has hiked up the new road blasted through the Divide, where they now gaze across the Narrows at a slightly smaller group standing atop the Midland Rise: Forest Camp, whose workmen chopped down the blackwoods and milled them for the massive beams used for the arches and support towers.

More than fourteen hundred men and women have labored long and hard for nearly seven months, almost two years by Gregorian reckoning. They paid for the bridge not only with sweat and muscle, but also blood: seven people perished in construction accidents ranging from falling from the towers to drowning in the channel. But this day is not for mourning, but for celebration. Red and blue pennants dangle from the trusses, and garlands of wildflowers are woven around the handrails. In the Bridgeton mess hall, the long tables have been laid out, and dozens of chickens and pigs have been butchered, in preparation for a midday fiesta, while casks of sourgrass ale carted in from Shuttlefield wait to be tapped. Outside the hall, a small stage has been set up—the Coyote Wood Ensemble will perform a symphony written especially for this occasion by Allegra DiSilvio—and a nearby field has been cleared for a softball game. The crowd shuffles restlessly, impatient to get through the dedication ceremonies so they can begin the long-awaited party.

Standing at the bridge entrance is a small group of dignitaries. The colonial governor, the Matriarch Luisa Hernandez, a stocky woman in a purple brocade cape, her hood pulled back. The lieutenant governor, the Savant Manuel Castro, his black robe concealing his skull-like face and metallic form. Chris Levin, the Chief Proctor, one of the original colonists from the URSS *Alabama*, the first starship to reach the 47 Ursae Majoris system; his eyes constantly shift back and forth, as if searching for trouble. Leaders of the various guilds whose members were recruited for the construction effort; many of them are mildly inebriated, having already sampled the ale before coming up to the bridge.

And in their midst, a quiet figure, slight of build and stooped at the shoulders, his thin face framed by a beard peppered with grey. He wears a threadbare frock coat despite the warmth of the day, and his soft brown eyes peer owlishly from behind wire-rim glasses.

James Alonzo Garcia, architect and chief engineer of the Garcia Narrows Bridge. Not the sort of person one would expect to lead such a monumental task. Indeed, he sees himself not so much as an engineer but rather as a poet. Instead of words, though, physics is his form, mathematics his meter; for him, the bridge that bears his name is a poem of gravity and resistance, tension and compression, an elegant sonnet whose couplets are expressed in equations. Others may see the bridge as an edifice, yet for him it is a song that only he can hear.

It is his masterpiece. And he hates it.

A red ribbon has been stretched across the entrance, tied together in a thick bow. James Garcia—formerly known, a lifetime ago back on Earth, as "Crazy Jimmy"—looks down, gently squeezes his left thumb. Digits appear on the fingernail: 1329:47:03. Almost noon. He's supposed to deliver a speech at this time; a few public words, expressing his thoughts upon the grand occasion. This sort of thing isn't in his character—he's shy, reticent when it comes to things like this—yet a mike dangles from his left ear, wired to a sound system set up so that what he says can be heard by all. Everyone is waiting for him, but he holds off, delaying the ceremony.

Across the channel, just for a moment, he catches a flash of light. Once, twice, three times, from a rocky outcrop on the Midland Rise just below the east side of the bridge. As if to shade his eyes from the sun, Garcia briefly raises a hand. The light winks twice more, then is no longer seen.

He turns to the woman standing next to him, nods briefly. The Matriarch smiles, then turns to Savant Castro. Ruby-colored eyes stare into his own, then a metallic claw comes from beneath the cloak, offering a pair of shears painted gold to resemble ceremonial scissors.

Garcia accepts the shears, steps forward to the ribbon. Seeing this, a cheer rises from the nearby onlookers, reciprocated a few moments later by those on the other side of the channel. Garcia lets the applause wash over him. For better or worse, this is his moment; none of it would have been possible were it not for him.

He raises the shears, his hands trembling as he opens the blades. So tempting just to cut the ribbon, get it over and done. But, no, there are things that must be said; this is an historic event, after all, and history must be served.

And so he speaks . . .

In order to properly understand what James Alonzo Garcia said that day, and why he did what he did, one must go back. Not to the beginnings of the colonization of Coyote—that story has already been told elsewhere—but to the events after the disappearance of the original settlers and the arrival of the next wave of colonists from Earth. It explains why a bridge was constructed across the Eastern Channel, and why Crazy Jimmy was the man who built it.

When the *Alabama* party abandoned their original settlement and fled New Florida, following the unexpected arrival of the WHSS *Glorious Destiny*, they did so in longboats, kayaks, and sea canoes they had fashioned from native materials. Using a route discovered by the Montero Expedition of c.y. 02, they traveled down Sand Creek until they reached the Shapiro Pass, which allowed them access through the Eastern Divide to the East Channel. By the time a squad of Union Guard soldiers led by Luisa Hernandez set foot in Liberty, the settlers had already crossed the channel and vanished into the wilds of Midland, never to be seen again.

Once the Western Hemisphere Union assumed control of New Florida, the Matriarch turned her attention to tracking down the *Alabama* party. Despite her efforts, though, their whereabouts remained a mystery; although every square mile of Coyote was surveyed from orbit, no signs of human habitation were found anywhere on the planet. No radio signals were detected by long-range sensors, and low-altitude sorties by shuttles were likewise unsuccessful.

Suspecting that the colonists had established a new settlement somewhere on Midland, Savant Castro proposed sending a military expedition into the adjacent continent. However, the Matriarch declined. Her primary objective had already been fulfilled, so there was no real reason to pursue them. Her major concern now was assuring the survival of the one thousand people aboard the *Glorious Destiny*; since Liberty was much too small to house all of them, a second town was established near the landing field. During their first long winter on Coyote, most of the immigrants were forced to live in tents, subsisting on meager rations brought from Earth; morale was low, and only a relative handful of Union Guard soldiers were available to keep them in line. So Hernandez was unwilling to spare any of her troops; the location of the vanished colonists would have to remain a mystery, at least for the time being.

As time went on, though, the Matriarch came to realize that her troubles had only begun. Over the course of the next year and a half, by LeMarean reckoning, three more ships arrived—the *New Frontiers*, the *Long Journey*, and the *Magnificent Voyage*—each depositing a thousand more colonists on New Florida before turning around for the trip back to Earth. The majority were unsuited for frontier life; although most had won their berths through public lotteries, many had bribed their way aboard; nor was it a secret that some were political exiles or furloughed criminals. Shuttlefield swelled in size, soon becoming a shantytown ruled by various guilds, groups, and gangs. The newcomers were put to work on collective farms, yet after a while even the Matriarch was forced to admit—albeit only to Manuel Castro, her closest aide—that social collectivism was inadequate for settling a new world.

Making the situation worse was the fact that New Florida was a savanna, a vast expanse of grasslands and swamp, with few forests to supply wood for building new houses. Within a year, all the nearby stands of blackwood and faux birch had been leveled; although Japanese bamboo had been successfully introduced, it wasn't suitable for dwellings able to withstand Coyote's long winters. Clearly, they had to look elsewhere for native resources.

And so the Matriarch cast her gaze upon Midland. Not only was it closer and more accessible than Great Dakota to the west, but its lowlands were also covered by dense rain forests. Geological surveys along the Gillis Range indicated that the mountains held sizable deposits of iron, titanium, copper, even silver and gold—metals scarce on New Florida. Midland was virgin territory, just waiting to be conquered.

All they needed was a way to get there.

The East Channel was the obstacle. From high orbit, it only looked like a river, until one realized that, at the Montero Delta, where the channel flowed into the Great Equatorial River, it was nearly fifty miles wide. Furthermore, there were only four major passes through the Eastern Divide, none of which was easily navigable except during late winter and early spring, when the streams that had carved them through solid limestone were flooded by melting snow . . . and even then, it was only a one-way trip, because the currents were too swift to make a return crossing.

A group of malcontents, fed up with life in Shuttlefield, had built a tiny settlement near the Monroe Pass, establishing a ferry able to carry people over to Midland, including a religious cult whom the Matriarch was only too glad to let go. However, Thompson's Ferry was inadequate for her purposes; she needed reliable access across the channel, one that was firmly under Union control, so she would be able to send timber and mining crews into Midland and bring back wood and ore. As things stood boats were dependent upon weather and the seasons, aircraft limited by low payloads and inability to land in difficult terrain.

Clearly, she needed a bridge. And that was when she turned to James Alonzo Garcia.

In the year 2246, the sea-mining industry had grown to the extent that OceanSpace LLC determined that it was more cost-efficient to build a permanent colony on the continental shelf off the Atlantic coast of Florida. Until then, the only successful deep-ocean habs had been small installations capable of supporting no more than fifty people at a time; OceanSpace wanted a small city, located more than three hundred feet beneath the surface, able to support more than a thousand people in a shirtsleeve environment. Not only that, but it also would have to sustain a one-atmosphere internal pressure of oxygen-nitrogen instead of oxygen-helium, and be totally self-sufficient. And it had to be comfortable; no bunks or crowded compartments, but rather individual living quarters, spacious pedestrian malls, even holotheaters and miniature golf courses.

Quite a few people thought it was impossible. Many predicted that the colony was a disaster waiting to happen, and they produced graphs, simulations, and pie charts to make the point. Yet six years later, Aquarius opened its airlocks to submersibles bringing aboard its first residents. Despite dire forecasts, the buckydomes never collapsed under pressure, nor did its hydrothermal power systems or open-loop life-support systems ever fail.

The architect responsible for this miracle was James Alonzo Garcia. He was thirty-one years old when Aquarius was finished, yet he never visited his creation; he was prone to seasickness.

In 2253, the Mars colonies needed an efficient means of traversing the Valles Marineris. Until then, the only way to travel from one side of the vast canyon system to the other was by means of airship. Semirigid dirigibles could only carry a handful of people, though, and had limited cargo capacity, and were also vulnerable to Martian weather conditions. A solution had to be found.

On Ares Day, 2258, the Alice B. Stanley Bridge across the Noctis Labyrinthis was officially dedicated. Over ten miles in length, with twin five-hundred-foot towers supporting a stayed-cable roadway above a chasm nearly a mile deep, the bridge was so enormous that it could be seen by the naked eye from low orbit. Again, there were predictions that it would be destroyed by the first major dust storm or marsquake, yet the Stanley Bridge survived everything that nature threw at it.

Its designer, the thirty-nine-year-old engineer James Alonzo Garcia, attended the opening ceremonies via holotransmission from his home in Athens, Georgia. He claimed that the flu prevented him from making the trip to Mars, yet everyone who worked on the project knew that he was mortified by the prospect of setting foot aboard anything that left the ground.

Crazy Jimmy didn't earn his nickname by accident. The stereotypical image of the civil engineer is one of a broad-shouldered, barrel-chested man with a blueprint in one hand and a protractor in the other. Garcia didn't fit the profile: ascetic and thin-faced, he looked more like Robert Browning than Robert Moses. Those who knew him personally—there weren't many, outside a small circle of associates—often described him in two terms: genius and mad. He graduated from the University of Georgia at age twenty-one with a doctorate in physics, and after that he seldom left home, and only then if he could travel by maglev train. He wore black at all times, and his favorite article of clothing was a frock coat he'd found in his grandfather's attic. He slept no more than four or five hours a night. He had no apparent interest in women; his only love affair was with a seventeen-year-old second cousin he met at a family reunion when he was twenty-three, and he was shattered when she spurned his marriage proposal. Though he claimed to be an atheist, those closest to him knew that he believed in reincarnation and that in a past life he had once been a dog.

Nevertheless, no one denied the fact that Garcia was brilliant, albeit otherworldly. He perceived complex engineering problems in poetic terms; for him, an equation was a couplet, an algorithm a rhyme. Aquarius was a homage to Edgar Allan Poe's "The City Under the Sea" expressed in mathematical terms, the Stanley Bridge a contemplation on the value of *pi* as a material object. In these things, and others—elaborate homes he designed for friends, skyscrapers that seemed to defy gravity, the occasional public monument as a diversion—he displayed his gifts.

Although he was a perfectionist by nature, he was far from perfect himself. Garcia had little patience for those who couldn't keep up with him. He fired assistants for as little reason as showing up for work a couple of minutes late, and once walked off project in which he had been involved for several years only because the client failed to appreciate the awning he'd designed for the front entrance. Many of his colleagues perceived him as arrogant, and few realized that his erratic behavior stemmed from a deep sense of insecurity. For all his talent, James Garcia was a lonely man, unable to communicate with the world in any meaningful way except through the things he built.

Even today, historians disagree over what compelled James Garcia to migrate to Coyote. Certainly it wasn't to find adventure; for all intents and purposes, he was a recluse. Some speculate that he was seeking another off-world challenge after the Stanley Bridge. If that was so, then why travel forty-six light-years, leaving behind everything he knew? Jonas NcNair, the architecture critic, believes that he may have lost favor with the Proletariate after he refused to design a new Government Centre for the Western Hemisphere Union in Havana, an allegation supported by Garcia's well-documented dislike for social collectivism, a system that wouldn't allow him to earn as much as he did when he worked on projects in Europe and the Pacific Coalition. Or perhaps, as some have theorized, like so many others who went to Coyote before him, Garcia simply reached a point in life when he wanted to make a fresh start.

The truth is very simple: he had no choice. The Proletariate realized that, sooner or later, Coyote would require the services of a master architect, someone able to tackle the most difficult engineering problems. Only one person fit that description, and so he was drafted. Had he been given advance warning, Garcia might have been able to flee the Union; like so many other rich people in the WHU, he kept his private earnings in Swiss banks, and the Union was willing to look the other way so long as he paid his taxes and didn't flaunt his wealth in public. One of the tenets of collectivist theory was that individuals should be willing to make sacrifices for the greater good of society, so when the Proletariate decided that Coyote needed the talents of James Alonzo Garcia, he awoke one morning to find all his lines of credit frozen, his travel permits denied, his contacts no longer willing to answer the phone, and a Patriarch and two Proctors waiting in his office with an offer that he could not refuse.

And so, on Barchiel 6, c.y. 05, James Alonzo Garcia walked down the ramp of a Union shuttle. Unlike the hundreds of other immigrants who'd spent the last forty-eight years in biostasis aboard the *Magnificent Voyage*, though, Garcia never had to endure a cold night in Shuttlefield. The moment he set foot on Coyote, proctors ushered him to a waiting maxvee, which spirited him away to Liberty, where he was assigned to a three-room log cabin in the center of town. And that evening, while he was unpacking his bags, Garcia received his first visitors: Luisa Hernandez and Manuel Castro. They personally brought him dinner, and while a Union Guard soldier stood watch outside the three of them had a meeting. It lasted only an hour, and after they left Garcia stood on the front porch of his new home, silently gazing up at Bear as it rose into the night sky.

Garcia was treated with far more dignity than the average immigrant. Since all the usual weight limits had been waived in his favor, his comps, books, and even his antique drafting board had all been freighted from Earth. When it was apparent that he needed a warmer jacket than his frock coat, he was given a fur-lined parka (which he wore only on the coldest days). He didn't eat in the community hall, but instead took his meals in the privacy of his home. Whenever he needed anything—pads, fresh sheets and blankets for his bed, a coffeepot, a new pair of boots—it was available simply for the asking. Compared to the thousands living in squalor in Shuttlefield, James Garcia lived like a prince . . . and all he was expected to do in return was to lend his talents to the colony.

His circumstances weren't unbearable. He hadn't left behind anyone he couldn't live without, and while his quarters were relatively primitive, they weren't uncomfortable. So he went to work on the first task given to him by the Matriarch, designing a master plan for Shuttlefield that would ease the settlement's overpopulation problems. It took only six weeks for him to come up with a wheel-shaped layout for streets and neighborhoods, complete with a sewage system, a zoned business district, schools and a public commons, with roads leading to Liberty, the nearby farms, and the landing field. Although it was something a first-year student could have done, when he showed it to the Matriarch she praised him as a genius.

And that's when she told him she needed a bridge.

From the outset, Garcia knew that building a bridge across the East Channel would be more difficult than it might seem. No two bridges are exactly alike, no matter how similar they may appear; each poses its own unique challenges, and while the Stanley Bridge was one of the largest ever built, Garcia quickly realized that this new one would stretch the limits of his ingenuity.

Midway through Machadiel, the last month of winter, Garcia joined a four-man expedition down Sand Creek to survey the channel and the Eastern Divide. Never much of a traveler, the architect made the trip only with great reluctance; however, he knew that he had to see the channel with his own eyes and not simply rely on reports made by others.

Another expedition member was Chris Levin, the Chief Proctor. Levin was the natural choice to lead the survey team; not only had he designed and built the single-mast keelboat, the *Lady of Huntsville*, which the team used for the trip, but he had also been on the ill-fated Montero Expedition that crossed the Eastern Divide three years earlier.

Sand Creek was still running high, so the boat made it through the Shapiro Pass without any difficulties. Once they reached the East Channel, the expedition turned north, spending the next several days exploring the seventy-mile stretch between the Shapiro Pass and Thompson's Ferry. It was a slow and arduous voyage; the current was against them, making the ride anything but smooth, and Garcia was frequently seasick, trying the patience of the other men aboard. After the first two days on the channel, Garcia elected not to remain aboard any longer. While Levin and his first mate, Union Guard lieutenant Bon Cortez, went ahead in the keelboat, Garcia and Frederic LaRoux, a geologist, hiked the rocky beach beneath the towering bluffs of the Eastern Divide, catching up with the *Lady of Huntsville* when it came ashore for the evening.

This turned out to be a wise decision, for it gave Garcia and LaRoux a chance to inspect the bluffs more closely. As Garcia suspected, much of the Eastern Divide was comprised of porous limestone, unsuitable for supporting a large structure. However, here and there the limestone had been eroded away, exposing impermeable shale beneath it. And midway between the Shapiro Pass and Thompson's Ferry, fortuitously located at the most narrow point of the Eastern Channel, rested a granite bluff suitable for their needs.

The Narrows, as Levin labeled the straits on his map, were a little less than two miles across; the Midland Rise could easily be seen from the beach. The expedition made camp on the western side, and spent the next several days surveying the site from both sides of the channel, using deep-core drills to extract rock samples and sonar to gauge the depth of the waters. At midpoint, the Narrows were nearly a hundred feet deep, but at several places the floor rose to within forty feet of the surface. Soundings revealed the existence of solid bedrock several feet beneath the muddy river bottom. Garcia climbed to the top of the Eastern Divide and set up his theodolite, then spent a day examining the eastern side of the channel through its scope, repeating this the following day from the top of the Rise, while Bon Cortez stood two miles away with a meter stick in hand.

Eight days after it set sail upon the East Channel, the *Lady of Huntsville* arrived at Thompson's Ferry, thirty-eight miles upstream from the Narrows. Levin, Cortez, and LaRoux took advantage of Clark Thompson's hospitality, luxuriating in hot baths and devouring everything Aunt Molly put before them; they spoke enthusiastically about what they'd found, and Thompson listened with interest as they told him about the plans to build a bridge across the Narrows. The loner Garcia shared none of this. Locking himself inside a storeroom of the town lodge, he spread his maps, charts, and notebooks across a table and went straight to work, sleeping on the bare wooden floor and eating only when Molly Thompson insisted that he needed food.

Two days after the *Lady of Huntsville* showed up at the ferry, Clark Thompson and his nephew Garth went fishing. Cortez and LaRoux took little note of this, but Levin watched from the deck of the lodge while their kayak made its way toward Midland. It returned many hours later, just before sundown; apparently it had been a bad day for fishing, for neither of the men brought home anything. The Chief Proctor took note of the fact that their bait box apparently remained untouched, but he carefully said nothing.

The following morning, Garcia emerged from the storeroom, haggard and red-eyed, with several scrolls beneath his arms and a hoarse-throated request to return to Liberty at once. His bridge existed, if only on paper and within his mind's eye.

All he needed to do was build it.

James Garcia was under no delusions. Since there were no iron deposits on New Florida, and the ones on Midland weren't ready to be mined, the bridge would have to be built almost entirely out of wood and stone. With no iron for cables, he ruled out any sort of suspension bridge. While the channel was relatively shallow, its current was swift; the support towers would therefore have to be erected while the waters were at their lowest mark, during late spring and summer. And because none of the heavy machinery available to him on Earth or Mars—tower cranes, dredges, earthmovers—existed on Coyote, they would have to rely upon hand-built derricks, high explosives, portable generators, and sheer muscle. In short, a two-mile bridge would have to be built within a short period of time, using only native materials, under primitive conditions.

A Crazy Jimmy project, to be sure. And he couldn't have been happier; it was the sort of challenge he thrived upon.

When Garcia showed his plans to Luisa Hernandez, the Matriarch quickly gave her approval to the project. Indeed, he was surprised at her sanguine acceptance of the difficulties; it didn't seem to matter very much to her that the bridge would tax the colony's resources in terms of both material and human effort. *Whatever you need*, she said, *you'll get it*.

Such carte blanche should have been an engineer's dream, but Garcia would soon learn otherwise. A few days later, the Matriarch held a public meeting in Liberty. The community hall was filled to capacity, with hundreds of colonists standing outside; flanked by her staff, with Chris Levin on one side and Manuel Castro on the other, Hernandez announced plans to build a bridge across the East Channel to Midland, with work beginning immediately. She went on to state that the bridge would be the colony's first priority for the coming year, and that, in the spirit of social collectivism, she expected every able-bodied person to contribute to the effort.

It soon became clear what the Matriarch meant; she wasn't seeking volunteers so much as she was issuing a draft notice. Over the course of the next two weeks, Proctors combed Shuttlefield, locating every man and woman above the age of eighteen and checking their employment status against their records. Everyone who wasn't already working on the farms or serving some other vital function was conscripted to the construction project. No exceptions, no deferrals. When someone tried to refuse, they were informed that their ration cards would be voided, meaning that they wouldn't be allowed to eat in the community hall. When the Cutters Guild attempted to go on strike, the Matriarch responded by having their leaders arrested and their camp torn down by the Union Guard, their belongings confiscated and impounded. Upon seeing what happened to the largest and most powerful group in Shuttlefield, the other guilds hastily fell into line.

Garcia was outraged, yet when he told the Matriarch that he needed skilled workmen, not slave laborers, she replied by saying that wasn't true; everyone would be paid, in credits good for purchasing goods at shops in Liberty (which, it went without saying, were co-opted by the colonial government, meaning that a large percentage of workers' payments would go straight back to the Union). She then pointed out that most of Shuttlefield was unemployed, with little to do except sit around and wait for a job to open up. The bridge would shake them out of their indolence, give them a purpose for their lives. This was the genius of collectivist theory: the efforts of individuals applied to the greater good of society as a whole. Why, didn't he believe in social collectivism?

Garcia grumbled and returned to his drafting board.

Since the Narrows lay sixty miles from Liberty, one of the first tasks was the establishment of a road to the Eastern Divide. Thirty men spent two weeks marching through the grasslands, burning all the swampgrass and spider bush in their way and building footbridges across the swamps. There were several stands of blackwood and faux birch along the way, the last few remaining in that part of New Florida. They were cut down, the logs hauled on carts down what came to be known as Swamp Road to the construction site. A new settlement began to take form beneath the Eastern Divide—barracks, latrines, a mess hall, warehouses, craft shops—and it wasn't long before Shuttlefield began to empty out, as men and women were relocated to the coast. Every day, Bridgeton grew a little more, while Shuttlefield gradually shrank.

While that was going on, a new ferry was established on the channel. Chris Levin, temporarily released from his duties as Chief Proctor, was put in charge of building a fleet of construction barges. Yet another crew under Bon Cortez was given the task of setting up a logging camp and lumber mill on the other side of Midland Rise, with roads leading to the rain forests a few miles away. Forest Camp was smaller than Bridgeton, but no less active. Only the toughest men and women lived there, the ones who didn't mind getting splinters in their hands or enduring the long nights spent huddled around smoky fires. Indeed, many preferred the hardship; at least they were away from Shuttlefield, and more or less free so long as they ignored the armed soldiers loitering nearby.

Garcia remained in Liberty during that period. He worked out of his cabin, revising his blueprints, receiving daily reports via satphone from his foremen. Every few days, he'd warily climb aboard a gyro piloted by a Guardsman and pay a visit to the construction site; he still disliked flying, but it was the only way he was able to get to the Narrows on short notice. Those who saw him then remember a small figure in a frock coat, his hands clasped behind his back, silently walking past stacks of cut timber as he listened to crew chiefs whose names he often forgot, occasionally stopping to jot down notes in his pad.

He rarely spoke, though, so no one knew what was on his mind.

Garcia wasn't the only one quietly observing what was going on. The activity at Forest Camp had drawn the attention of others who had a vested interest in the Narrows.

When Clark Thompson and his nephew went fishing that day in Machadiel, they weren't out to hook a few channelmouth. After they rowed across the channel, the elder Thompson left Garth behind with the boat while he hiked up a narrow path leading to top of the Midland Rise. A young man whom he knew only as Rigil Kent was waiting for him, summoned two days earlier by a brief satphone call Clark had made when no one was watching. The two men had a short conversation, then once again Rigil Kent vanished into the woods.

Rigil Kent was the alias adopted by Carlos Montero, the *Alabama* colonist who, on and off over the course of the last two years, had waged guerrilla war against the Union. Twice already he'd led small raiding parties across the channel—the first time to steal firearms from Liberty, the second to blow up a shuttle. Although his efforts were still sporadic, Carlos's objective was to force the Union off New Florida; even if he couldn't get the newcomers to return to Earth, at least he might be able to make them surrender Liberty, which he and his followers considered to be stolen property.

After his rendezvous with Clark Thompson, Carlos returned to Defiance, the settlement hidden within a river valley on the other side of Mt. Shaw that the Matriarch had been unable to find. That evening, he made his report to the Town Council. Like everyone else, Robert Lee—once the former commanding officer of the *Alabama*, by then the elected mayor of Defiance—was disturbed to learn that Luisa Hernandez intended to erect a bridge across the East Channel. Thus far, Lee had supported the resistance efforts only reluctantly; he believed that, if his people lay low on Midland, the Union would leave them alone. Yet it had become clear that the Matriarch wanted Midland as well as New Florida. Once the bridge was built, it would only be a matter of time before Union troops invaded Midland.

Several Council members favored destroying the bridge before it could be completed, yet Lee had no desire to do anything that might kill or injure any civilians working on the project. Several newcomers had already made their way across the Gillis Range to Defiance; from them, he'd learned that the Union had misled immigrants as to how they'd be living on Coyote. If Rigil Kent attacked the bridge, then innocent lives would doubtless be lost, and Lee knew that would only cause colonists who might otherwise be sympathetic to their cause to turn against them. There's a fine line between being a freedom fighter and being a terrorist, and Lee was reluctant to cross it.

However, Carlos had another idea. According to what Clark Thompson had told him, it appeared that the bridge's architect might not be marching in lockstep with the Matriarch. If that was true, then they might be able to reach him somehow, perhaps convince him of the error of his ways. If they could do so, perhaps there might be a way to make the bridge work *for* them . . .

The Council listened to him, and Lee gave his approval. *See if you can contact Garcia,* Lee told Carlos. *Maybe we can work something out with him.*

And that's what Rigil Kent set forth to do.

By the middle of Ambriel, the second month of spring, the first phase was well under way. The spring floods had subsided by then, allowing for the construction of eight watertight caissons, made of thick, rough-barked logs harvested on Midland that had been hauled by barges from Forest Camp into the Narrows, where they were vertically sunk in a straight line across the channel, a quarter mile from one another. Once the water was pumped out, masons descended into the shafts to build permanent caissons for the support towers; from the New Florida side, limestone blocks were excavated from quarries near Bridgeton and transported by barges to the caissons, where they were slowly lowered by hand-cranked derricks into the empty shafts. Once the permanent caissons were finished, they would be filled with concrete brought over from Bridgeton, forming the piers for the support towers.

In the meantime, mill workers at Forest Camp were busy stockpiling wooden beams for the trusses. Care was taken to keep the beams individually cut to precise specifications; once finished, they were covered with canvas tarps to prevent sun and rain from warping them. While that was going on, a demolition crew was using plastic explosives to blast road cuts through the Eastern Divide and the Midland Rise, providing easy access to the Narrows from either side of the channel.

By then, it had become impractical for James Garcia to remain in Liberty. Although he'd found a reliable chief foreman—Klon Newall, a civil engineer who, by coincidence, had overseen construction of the Stanley Bridge before deciding to immigrate to Coyote—there were too many details that he had to look after himself. So once a one-room cabin was built for him in Bridgeton, he packed up his belongings and moved there.

Garcia soon discovered that he no longer had the same degree of solitude he'd enjoyed in Liberty. Since there was no one to bring his meals to him, he had to eat in the mess hall, sitting alongside sweaty, dirt-caked workmen. The air was thick was limestone dust from the quarries, forcing him to put a wet handkerchief against his face whenever he went outside; at night, as he hunched over his drafting board, his thoughts were frequently interrupted by the sounds of men and women carousing in the nearby dormitories. With the exception of Klon, there was no one in Bridgeton with whom he felt comfortable. The workers remained unfriendly toward him, treating him with resentment as if he was the source of their hardships.

And hardships there were aplenty. Because the Matriarch trusted no one working, she posted Union Guard soldiers in Bridgeton and Forest Camp, to prevent anyone from taking off into the wilderness. Naturally it wasn't long before some of those soldiers began to assume roles as straw bosses. Workers caught resting at any time other than designated breaks were subject to spending the night in the stockade, deprived of food and water. One evening, in the privacy of Garcia's cabin, Klon told him that earlier that day he'd found three Guardsmen surrounding a young woman in the mess hall kitchen; only his timely arrival prevented her from being gang-raped. A few days later, a workman on Tower Two fell from the top of the temporary caisson; if someone had dived into the water after him, his life might have been saved, but the Guardsman standing watch on the nearby barge thought that he should swim back by himself and demanded that everyone stay on the job. The current was too swift, and the workman was pulled under; he drowned in the channel. Later, his body washed up several miles downstream.

These incidents, and others like them, began to open Garcia's eyes. In the past, he'd always been able to maintain a certain distance from his work, his hands remaining clean, his mind focused entirely upon the discrete poetry of physics, the hidden music of mathematics. Yet on Coyote, there was no room for such luxuries; there was only one brutal day after another, of watching men and women being slowly ground down beneath the burden of his dreams. There was beauty in what they were building, yes, but it was tainted with their suffering . . . and with each passing day, James Garcia perceived the monstrosity that his masterpiece was gradually becoming.

Although he protested to Luisa Hernandez that his people were being mistreated, she turned a deaf ear, saying that discipline needed to be maintained if the bridge was to be finished before the winter. He tried to talk to Manuel Castro, but the Savant was detached from all human feeling, and in his glass eyes Garcia saw only a disturbing reflection of himself. Chris Levin was a little more understanding, yet he insisted that there was little he could do; his job was making sure that the barges he built didn't sink. What it all came down to was the fact that Garcia himself was in charge . . . even though, beyond a certain point, his authority was nonexistent. The Matriarch wanted nothing more from him than what he'd always done before, and yet he'd found that he was no longer able to do even that.

In desperation, Garcia decided to relocate to the other side of the channel. There was no private cabin for him in Forest Camp, but that didn't matter; he requisitioned a tent and had it erected as far from the mill and the barracks as possible. And so, on Ambriel 91, the last day of the second month of spring, a keelboat transported his drafting board, comp, and books across the East Channel.

Forest Camp offered a little more solitude than Bridgeton. There weren't as many people over there, consequently there were fewer soldiers, most of whom tended to be less overbearing. With the absence of quarries, the air was cleaner; demolition work on the Rise had already been completed, so there were no more sudden explosions. Garcia came to know a few of the lumberjacks and mill workers, but otherwise he kept to himself. He spent his days making sure that the truss beams had the proper dimensions, and received regular reports from Klon via his comp. When he grew tired of watching tower construction from the Rise, he went off by himself to meditate, taking short hikes along the timber paths that meandered through the nearby rain forest, quickly being reduced to vast acres of stumps.

And then, on the afternoon of Muriel 15, he went for a walk and didn't return.

When Garcia failed to show up for dinner, several men took lanterns and went off to look for him. Failing to find him, they alerted Bridgeton; within the hour, gyros were making low-level passes above Midland, their searchlights lancing down into the forest, and by daybreak a squad of soldiers had been ferried across the channel to continue the manhunt. Yet no trace of him was found, nor was there any indication that he'd been attacked by a predator. He had simply vanished.

The search went on for two days, during which soldiers fanned out across a semicircle with a twenty-mile radius inland and to either side of Forest Camp. They even paddled kayaks down the channel, checking the riverbanks just in case he'd fallen off the Midland Rise and drowned. Nothing, not so much as a shred of clothing or a footprint.

By nightfall of the second day, the search parties had returned to Forest Camp. Proctors were once again questioning those few who had last seen him when someone happened to walk past Garcia's tent and noticed that the light was on. Looking inside, he was startled to find the architect sitting at his comp, calmly sorting through the reports that had piled up in his absence, as if nothing had happened.

When Luisa Hernandez received word that Garcia had reappeared, she insisted that he be brought to her at once. Garcia had barely finished a late dinner when he was bustled aboard a gyro and flown to Liberty, where Hernandez, Manny Castro, and Chris Levin were waiting for him. With two Guardsmen posted outside her cabin, the Matriarch, the Savant, and the Chief Proctor began interrogating the architect as to where he'd been for the last sixty-two hours.

They were surprised when he informed them that he'd been kidnapped.

He'd been wandering along a timber trail, he said, when three men he'd never seen before emerged from the undergrowth. Before he could resist, they'd pulled his arms behind his back, yanked a bag over his head, and injected him with something that knocked him out. To prove his story, Garcia loosened his shirt collar and showed them a bruise on the right side of his neck where the needle had gone in.

When he woke up many hours later, he found that he was in a deep cave, apparently somewhere in the hills some distance from the East Channel. The cave entrance was covered with a thick blanket, so he had no idea whether it was day or night. There was a fire, with the smoke rising through a chimney vent high above. And he wasn't alone; the three men who had taken him were there, along with a fourth, a young man who identified himself as Rigil Kent.

Levin wanted to learn more about Rigil Kent, but there was little that Garcia could tell him; all four wore bandannas across the lower parts of their faces and never took off their wide-brimmed hats (although Garcia mentioned that Kent wore an old-style ball cap embroidered with the words URSS ALABAMA). They carried rifles, and it was made clear to him that he wouldn't leave until they were ready for him to go. Nonetheless he was treated well; he was never roughed up or beaten, and he was given food and water. When he needed to relieve himself, he was led to the back of the cave, where a chamber pot had been placed. When he got tired they gave him a bedroll and let him stretch out next to the fire. But he was never left unguarded; nor did he ever get a good look at his captors' faces.

"So why were you there?" Castro asked, and Garcia shrugged. They only wanted to know the details of the bridge project: how it was going to be built, what form it would take, when he anticipated that it would be finished. *"You didn't tell them, did you?"* Of course he did . . . why not? It wasn't as if it was classified information; even the lowliest quarryman knew how the bridge was going to be built. In fact, he was under the impression that they'd been quietly observing the construction effort for quite some time; they'd addressed him by name, and knew that he was the architect and chief engineer. Since there was no point in being stubborn, he told them everything they wished to learn, even tracing sketches in the dirt on the cave floor. *"And what happened then?"* They knocked him out again. When he came to, he found himself back in the same place where he'd been taken. Indeed, the worst part of his ordeal was retracing his steps in the dark; he had gotten lost a couple of times before he managed to find his tent.

Hernandez, Castro, and Levin made him repeat his story again, with Castro asking him to reiterate various parts of it. They were suspicious, of course—how could Garcia have been taken so far, then back again, while search parties were looking for him?

Despite their doubts, there was nothing to disprove his story, and enough physical evidence to support it: his clothes were dirty and rumpled, as if he'd slept in them for a couple of days, and he was obviously exhausted. So they told him that they were glad to have him back, then had a soldier walk him to his cabin.

After that Garcia wasn't allowed to return to Forest Camp. Luisa Hernandez decided that he needed to be kept on a leash, so he continued to work out of his cabin in Bridgeton. The few times he crossed the channel to Midland, it was with a Proctor constantly at his side.

By then, though, it didn't matter. A plan had been set in motion.

* * *

As spring became summer, the bridge grew a little more with each passing day. The piers for the eight support towers were completed in the first month of Verchiel, when the last layers of concrete were poured into the caissons, and attention shifted to building the towers themselves. By then, there were almost as many men working on the river at any given time as there were on the shore, with boats moving back and forth across the Narrows, hauling construction material out to the barges anchored next to the piers. It was hard, backbreaking labor for the carpenters on the towers; exhaustion took its toll as accidents began to occur more frequently, causing men to be rushed to the first-aid tent set up on the Midland side.

Every day, James Garcia stood on the Eastern Divide, watching the activity through binoculars as he listened to radio reports from Klon and the other foremen. As the accident rate began to rise, he voiced his concerns to Luisa Hernandez, yet she remained adamant in her refusal to let work stop for even a single hour. The Matriarch was determined to see the bridge finished by autumn and would allow nothing to stand in her way. So Garcia quietly decided to take the matter into his own hands.

He began by instituting a regular schedule of job rotation, reassigning men who'd been on the towers to Bridgeton and Forest Camp, and bringing those who'd been onshore to the river. The changes slowed things a bit, at least at first, while foremen retrained people to handle different jobs; but it also meant that the workmen were given breaks from the repetitive tasks that caused them to become sloppy and careless.

Garcia also had the soldiers removed from the construction site. That took a little more doing, since the Matriarch continued to believe that anyone working on the bridge would try to escape if not watched every moment. The architect persisted, pointing out that it was better for morale if the men were able to work without having guns pointed at their backs. Besides, boids had recently been sighted lurking near Bridgeton and Forest Camp; now that it was the warm season again, the carnivorous avians had returned from the southern regions where they migrated for the winter, so Union Guard were needed to protect the settlements from the man-eaters. Reluctantly, Hernandez agreed, and the soldiers were replaced by Proctors.

Garcia himself started spending more time with the workers. No longer as aloof as he'd once been, he began by going out to the towers, ostensibly to check on their progress but also to see how the guys working on them were doing. He made an effort to memorize their names; very often, at the end of the day, he'd join them for dinner. No longer preferring to sit by himself, he'd carry his plate over from the serving line and take a seat at the long tables between men and women who'd been hauling beams or hammering nails for the last ten hours. They didn't know what to make of this at first, and many remained hostile or suspicious, but gradually he began to make friends among them. Soon he began to learn who they were, the individual circumstances that led them to come to Coyote.

His attention to the workers was good for morale, too, but that wasn't the sole reason why Garcia courted them. Through short encounters on the bridge and dinnertime chats, he slowly determined who among them was loyal to the Union and who was not.

By midsummer, the bridge was beginning to take form. Upon each tower base, two A-frame structures were built, cross-braced to provide stability. The towers gradually rose in height from both ends of the bridge, with Towers One and Eight eighty feet tall, Towers Two and Seven ninety feet, Towers Three and Six a hundred feet, and Towers Four and Five rising a hundred and ten feet above the Narrows. Once finished, the bridge would be shaped like a longbow, thus allowing for compression at the center span.

The towers were completed on Hamaliel 37, a week ahead of schedule. For the occasion, Luisa Hernandez made a surprise visit. Escorted by a pair of Guardsmen, with Savant Castro walking just a few steps behind her and Garcia, the Matriarch strode up the packed-earth path leading through the road cut recently blasted through the Eastern Divide until she reached the end of the unfinished ramp leading to the bridge, and silently gazed out upon the long row of towers that loomed above the East Channel. Derricks bolted to platforms on top of the towers hauled truss beams up from barges; the humid air was filled with the sound of hammers and saws as carpenters worked on temporary scaffolds suspended from the towers.

The Matriarch silently observed the activity before her, making a face as she batted at the skeeters that tormented her. Garcia tried to explain what was being done, yet it was clear that the details bored her; she only seemed to take interest when she noticed a couple of nearby workmen fastening safety lines around their stomachs and thighs, mountaineering-style.

"Seems like a lot of wasted effort," she said, and Garcia informed her that he had mandated the practice as a safety precaution after a couple of men had fallen to their deaths from the towers. She shrugged as she swatted another skeeter. "Very well. If you think it's important." Then she turned to smile at him. "Have you given any thought as to what we should call this? Whom we should name it after?"

"No, ma'am." Garcia watched the men attaching safety lines to themselves. "I have more important things to think about just now."

She regarded him coldly. "Perhaps you should take this into consideration," she replied, then she turned to march away.

Before work commenced on the arches, Garcia had cable cars in-stalled between the towers. Made of tightly coiled rough-barked vine harvested from the Midland forests and greased with creek cat fat, the cables were stretched from one tower to the next, with sturdy baskets woven from sourgrass hanging from pulleys running along the cables. Although riding the cable was hair-raising, it was the quickest way to transport workers from one end of the bridge to another, and once they got used to racing along a hundred feet above the channel, many said the commute was the best part of the day.

Providing cheap thrills, though, was the farthest thing from Garcia's mind; he also had a quick means of getting people over to Midland. By First Landing Day, Uriel 47, Garcia and Klon had recruited nearly three hundred men and women they knew they could trust; two and three at a time, they were transferred across the channel to Forest Camp, where they switched jobs with people who had been working on the timber crews and at the mill. Since it was all part of the job-rotation system Garcia had set up, the Proctors took little notice; only a few foremen were keeping track of who was where at any one time, and most of them had already been enlisted by Garcia.

The arches weren't long enough to support the roadway by themselves; to make up for the distance, and also to relieve the bridge from stress in the event of high winds, Garcia designed bolt-hinged suspension spans that would be laid between them. The hundred-foot spans—four in all, practically small bridges in themselves—were built as single-piece units on the wharves beneath the Midland Rise; once completed, they would be floated on barges out into the channel, then carefully hoisted into place by the tower derricks.

No one noticed the extra care that was being taken, by mill workers in the Forest Camp, to carve small cavities within the cross braces of the suspension spans. Each cavity was large enough to contain a one-pound plastique charge, and was hidden by a thin panel through which a tiny hole had been drilled.

The suspension spans were raised during mid-Adnachiel, two weeks after the trusswork for the arches was completed. All that was left to be done was the laying of rough-barked planks for the roadway and rigging solar-powered lights on lampposts. For all intents and purposes, the bridge was nearly finished.

Even while preparations were being made for the dedication ceremony, Chris Levin kept a wary eye upon the construction site. Although there had been no further sign of Rigil Kent, the Chief Proctor was unconvinced that his nemesis had lost interest in the bridge. He pulled the guards out of Forest Camp and posted a twenty-seven-hour watch on the bridge itself, with Proctors stationed on the roadway and at the entrances and more patrolling the channel itself. Because they were alert for trouble onshore or on the water, they weren't closely observing the workmen wiring the electrical fixtures, and thus failed to notice where some of the wires were leading.

On the evening of Raphael, Adnachiel 65, in the cool twilight as the sun setting behind the Eastern Divide, James Alonzo Garcia inspected the bridge one last time. Although there were soldiers every few hundred feet, for the first time in months he walked alone. Hands clasped behind his back, wearing the frock coat that had become increasingly frayed and dirty over the past several months, the architect strolled down the entire length of the bridge, taking the moment to admire his work. Of all the things he'd built, this was his greatest achievement. Aquarius might have been more revolutionary in design, the Stanley Bridge taller and more ambitious, yet this edifice—as yet unchristened, or at least nameless until the next day—was the thing of which he was the most proud.

But he heard no poetry in its arches, felt no music in its towers. He had long since stopped thinking in abstract terms; too many lives had been lost, too many injustices had been committed, for him to find any beauty in his accomplishment. The symphony was almost finished; all that remained for him to do was to write the coda.

When he reached the Midland end of the bridge, he found Klon Newall waiting for him. He shook hands with his chief foreman, exchanged a few pleasantries. A meaningful look passed between them, and Klon nodded once. Everything was ready.

Garcia nodded in return. Then he began to walk back toward New Florida, as alone as he ever had been.

So now it's the following morning, and he stands before the red ribbon stretched across the entrance, the gold shears in his hands poised before the bow. On either side of him, there's an expectant silence. The architect hesitates, then he begins to speak:

"This bridge . . ." Garcia coughs, clearing his dry throat. His voice, picked up by the mike under his left ear, is carried to the crowd behind him by the loudspeakers and reverberates ten seconds later off the Midland Rise. "Pardon me . . . this bridge is the result of months of effort by hundreds of men and women. They've suffered long and hard to bring it into existence. Some of them sacrificed their lives. Nothing I can say will ever make up for this. I just . . . I just . . ."

Uncertain of what to say next, he hesitates. From the corner of his eye, he sees Luisa Hernandez staring at him. This isn't what she expected: a few words extolling the virtues of social collectivism, perhaps, or promises of the riches to be found in the mountains of Midland.

"Others would like to claim this bridge for themselves," he continues, steadfastly refusing to meet the Matriarch's angry gaze. "They would claim credit for the work of others, but they must be told that all this wasn't done in their name. We didn't build this for them . . . we built it for ourselves, for our own future." He hesitates. "What we'll call this is not for me to decide, but for you. Let history give it a name. My work is done."

Then he turns to look at the Matriarch. "But this . . . *this* is for you, ma'am." And then he cuts the ribbon.

A thin wire was concealed within the fabric of the ribbon, which led to a detonator hidden beneath Tower One. When Garcia severed it, he tripped the detonator, which in turn caused an electrical charge to be sent to charges concealed within the crossbeams of the suspension spans. A quick succession of thunderous explosions echoed off the limestone walls of the Eastern Divide and the Midland Rise, and the spans toppled into the channel.

On the New Florida side of the Narrows, there is a collective gasp of horror from the officials standing nearby. On the Midland side, though, a loud cheer rises from the hundreds of people whose freedom Garcia had secretly arranged over the past few months as they watch the spans crash into the channel, leaving behind only a series of towers and arches unconnected to one another. The few Proctors and Union Guard soldiers remaining on the eastern side of the channel are caught unprepared for the mob that descends upon them; a couple of them try to resist, but they are quickly brought down, with the rest forced to flee for boats anchored beneath the bluffs.

The bridge could be repaired, of course . . . but not until the following spring, when it would become possible to replace the suspension spans. The seasonal currents within East Channel would not permit restoration work before next year. New beams would have to be harvested from the few remaining stands of blackwood on the western side of New Florida. By then, the men and women of Forest Camp had escaped into the Midland wilderness, where they were met by Rigil Kent's compatriots, eager to enlist those ready to defy the Western Hemisphere Union.

Garcia was not among them.

To this day, no one knows why he didn't take the chance to escape. The cable car had been left intact for that very purpose; the moment he severed the ribbon, the plan called for him to run over to it, jump aboard, and race across the Narrows, going from tower to tower until he made his way to Midland.

Instead, Garcia kept his back turned toward the bridge even as it was being ruined by his own hand and calmly waited for a couple of soldiers to put him under arrest and take him away. Perhaps he realized that any attempt to escape was futile, that he would have been shot before he made it to the first tower. Or perhaps, as others have speculated, there was only one way this particular poem could end.

Whatever the reason, Garcia spent the next two days in the Liberty stockade, a windowless log cabin built by the original settlers. He was doubtless interrogated, and equally without doubt he told his interrogators everything that he knew, even though there was little useful information that he could have revealed; the bridge was ruined, his accomplices already vanished. Eyewitnesses would later say that the last time he was known to be alive was when the Matriarch and two Union Guards soldiers paid him a visit. A gunshot was heard, and the following morning it was announced that Garcia had hanged himself.

James Alonzo Garcia was buried in the Shuttlefield graveyard, beneath a tombstone that bore only his name. The bridge he built was eventually repaired, but it never bore the name of the Matriarch Luisa Hernandez, as she had intended. The locals know it as the Garcia Narrows Bridge.

They also claim that, in the twilight hours just after the sun goes down behind the Eastern Divide, you can sometimes see him walking across it, as if admiring his creation one more time.

Part 4

THOMPSON'S FERRY

"They're coming."

Lars's voice came to him as a whisper, carried by the subcutaneous implant within his left ear. Clark Thompson looked away from the windswept waters of the channel to peer up at the Eastern Divide. The limestone bluffs were slick with the rain that fell from the lead sky; he couldn't see his nephew, but he knew Lars was hiding somewhere up there, watching the entrance to the Monroe Pass, the narrow river gorge that led through the Divide. Good. If he couldn't see him, then no one else would either.

Thompson touched the side of his jaw. "On foot?"

"Skimmer. Too large to get through the pass, so they're hiking the rest of the way in."

"How many?"

"Ten . . . no, twelve. Wait a sec . . . make that fifteen." A pause, marred by a thin ripple of carrier-wave static. *"We've got a clear shot. Want us to drop 'em?"*

Fifteen Union Guard soldiers, arriving on an armored skimmer from Liberty. From their vantage point on the ridgeline, Lars and the four men with him could easily pick them off, no doubt about that. But the skimmer was doubtless equipped with a 30mm artillery gun, and the patrol was still on the other side of the Divide, well within radio range of Liberty; if Lars attacked too soon, the squad would have enough time to call for reinforcements while they turned the gun upon the ridge. Better to let them feel safe, at least until they made their way through the pass.

"Hold your fire," Thompson murmured, "but keep 'em in sight. Whatever you do, don't let 'em see you."

"Got it. Out." A thin beep as Lars disconnected.

Cold rain pattered against the wide brim of his hat and seeped into his thick beard; it pelted the waters of the East Channel, raising a thin mist that obscured the figures standing on the pier next to the anchored ferry. It seemed as if everything had been cast in monochrome hues of black and grey: the colors of early Hanael, with summer a distant memory and winter only a few weeks away.

Pulling his catskin poncho closer around himself, Thompson walked away from the town lodge, his boots crunching against sand and pebbles. The people gathered on the pier looked up as he marched down the wet planks toward them: four men and three women, with his younger nephew Garth standing nearby. Everyone looked wet and miserable, yet it wasn't discomfort that he saw in their eyes, but fear.

A tall young woman turned to him. "They're after us, aren't they?"

Thompson nodded. "There's a squad on the other side of the Divide. Guess the Matriarch doesn't want to be deprived of her dinner music."

A couple of wan smiles. This wasn't just another group of refugees from Shuttlefield, but the Coyote Wood Ensemble. Until a few days ago, they had been eight woodwind musicians, practicing their art together in peace, sometimes performing in public at the behest of the colonial governor. Then one of their group had made the mistake of composing a ribald song about Luisa Hernandez; someone had overheard the ensemble rehearsing it, with him singing the lyrics, and the following day he disappeared.

So now the remaining members were on the run, and when you're wanted by the Union Guard, there's only one place to go, and only one way to get there. Many people had come before them, yet the moment they arrived in town and told him their story, Clark knew that this time would be different.

Allegra DiSilvio shook her head within the hood of her waterlogged serape. "It's not us they want," the ensemble's leader said quietly. "It's her."

The older woman beside her didn't seem to hear. Frail and grey-haired, her thin arms crossed tightly against her patched secondhand parka, she stared at the channel with blank eyes. A bamboo flute was clutched within her left hand; it seemed to Thompson that she was holding it for comfort, a shield against a cold and threatening world.

"Sissy is . . ." Allegra hesitated, uncertain of herself. "Her son is Chris Levin, the Chief Proctor. If it weren't for her, they probably wouldn't care less, but . . ."

Thompson held up a hand. "We don't have time for this. My lookout says they're on the way. It won't take 'em long to get through the pass."

A small pile of duffel bags were bundled together on the raft next to the rotary winch. A canvas tarp had been laid across them; he stepped onto the ferry, knelt to tug at the rope that lashed them together. This was everything the group had with them when had they arrived in town early that morning, the sum total of their possessions. Stepping back onto the pier, Thompson looked at Garth. "Better get moving," he said, then pointed to the biggest man in the group. "You got a strong back?" He nodded. "Good. Then help my boy with the winch. Four arms are better than two. Everyone else, climb aboard. Stay close to the middle and don't rock the boat. Anyone who falls overboard is on their own . . . once you get going, he won't have time to stop and pick up anyone."

The passengers glanced nervously at one another, but no one objected; one by one, they stepped off the pier onto the raft, finding seats upon the wet stack of duffel bags, with the man Thompson had picked as copilot taking a position next to the upright wheel of the winch. Allegra was the next to last person aboard; she helped Sissy step onto the raft, then she paused to look back at Thompson.

"You still haven't told us what the fare is," she said.

For the last two years, Thompson had charged everyone who used his ferry. Colonial scrip was useless because no one ever went back to Liberty or Shuttlefield; you paid with whatever you brought with you that could be spared, whether it be hand tools or guns, sleeping bags or spare clothes. The barter trade of outcasts.

This time, though, Thompson shook his head. "Free ride," he said quietly. "Next time I see you, we'll work something out."

Allegra gazed back at him. "Is because we don't have anything you want," she replied, "or is it because we don't have anything you need?"

Thompson didn't answer that question. He impatiently cocked his thumb toward the raft; without another word, she climbed aboard, settling in next to Sissy Levin.

Garth was astonished. He'd never seen his uncle refuse payment. Before he could say anything, though, Thompson pulled his nephew aside, put his face next to the teenager's ear. "Whatever you see or hear," he whispered, "don't turn back. Just keep going, and don't turn back unless I tell you to."

The boy's eyes went wide. "But what if they . . . ?"

"You heard me. Rigil Kent will meet up with you on the other side. They know you're coming. Leave the raft and go with them."

"But what about you and . . . ?"

"We'll be along soon enough. Don't worry, we'll find you." Thompson clasped Garth's elbow. "We always knew it would eventually come down to this. Now get along, and don't come back unless you hear from me."

Garth's mouth trembled; there was wetness against his face that might have been tears or only rain. He knew better than to argue, though, so he nodded once, then stepped onto the raft, taking his place on the other side of the wheel. Thompson slipped the loops of the mooring lines off the pier cleats, then planted the sole of his right foot against the raft and kicked it off. Garth and the other man grabbed the wheel handle and began to turn it hand over hand.

Rainwater sluiced off the cable suspended six feet above the surface as it fed through the winch. A few seconds later, the raft was clear of the pier, slowly making its way across the channel toward the distant bluffs of the Midland Rise, half-seen through the rain and mist. The distance between New Florida and Midland was little more than two miles; with luck, the ferry would get across before the soldiers arrived.

Thompson didn't watch it go. Instead, he quickly walked down the pier, then broke into a run once he reached the beach.

He jogged up the back stairs of the lodge and pushed open the door. The main room was warm, a fire crackling within the stone hearth. It could have been lunchtime, with bowls of Molly's redfish chowder laid out across the long blackwood table that ran down the center of the room.

Yet there was no food today, only guns. On either side of the table, men and women were loading rifles they had taken from the hidden closet behind the bedroom where he and Molly slept. A few of the townspeople looked up as he came in, then they went back to fitting cartridges into the stocks and checking the sights of their scopes. No one said anything to him as he strode over to the storeroom that he'd made into his office.

As he expected, Molly was there. Calm as ever, she was selecting ceramic jars of pickled fish from the shelves, packing them into crates. "I don't know about these," she said, as her husband came in. "I mean, they're marked last April, but I opened one and it smells like it might have spoiled." She picked up a jar, held it out to him. "What do you think . . . good or bad?"

Molly. Good old Aunt Molly. She had never quite become accustomed to the LeMarean calendar, preferring to use the old Gregorian system. Yet nothing had ever spoiled while she was in charge of the community food supply, although she kept records only on strips of tape and within her own head.

Thompson took the jar from her, took a perfunctory sniff. "Okay to me. Now, look—"

"Oh, what would you know?" Molly took the jar away from him, sniffed it herself, then put it back on the shelf. "I swear, you'll eat anything. If it wasn't for me, you'd be sick as—"

"Will you just shut up a second?" Molly lifted her head, stared at him in shock; in all the years they had been married, there were very few times he'd ever told her to shut up. "The fish is fine," he continued, "We'll eat whatever you give us. Right now, I just want one thing from you. . . ."

"Clark . . ."

"Stay in here." He lowered his voice. "Bolt the door, lie down on the floor, and don't come out until I tell you to."

"Oh, for God's sake, Clark . . ."

"Honey, you're a great cook, but you can't shoot for squat, and I don't want to have to worry about you." He let out his breath. "I just told Garth to make himself scarce, and Lars can hold his own. Right now, what I need you to do is become invisible. Can you do that for me? Please?"

Molly's face betrayed no emotion, yet her hand trembled as she selected another jar from the shelf. "I'll stay here," she murmured, not looking at him. "Just be careful, all right?"

"I will. I . . ." He stopped himself. He had more to say, not the least of which was *I love you*, but the others needed him just then, so instead he gently lifted her chin and gave her a quick kiss. It was something, he realized, that he hadn't done enough lately; he felt her hand touch his arm, as if she was trying to hold him back, but he hastily withdrew from her. "Just stay out of sight," he added. "This'll be over soon enough." Then he left the storeroom, shutting the door behind him.

Thompson spent a few minutes with the militia, making sure everyone knew where they were supposed to be, what signals they would use. Only a few had implants, with the others relying on headsets, yet he warned them to keep radio communications to a bare minimum, to reduce the chances of being overheard by Guardsmen who might be scanning the same frequencies. Firepower, though, was the major concern; although everyone was armed, the seven who had semiauto carbines—Union Guard firearms, stolen or bartered over the last two years—only had one or two spare cartridges of ten rounds each, while the remaining twelve carried bolt-action rifles—crude arms bartered to them by Rigil Kent, handmade somewhere over on Midland—which carried only four rounds, plus whatever they had in their pockets. Thompson placed the ones with the carbines closer to the center of town, where they would have the minimum range and maximum efficiency, and posted the ones with the bolt-actions farther away to back them up.

"Don't waste a shot," he finished, "and don't fire until you get my signal." He paused. "And one more thing . . . let me handle the leader."

Everyone nodded, except for Lonnie Dielman. "Why not him? If you're pinned down, then . . ."

"If I'm pinned down, then take care of it. If the leader's who I think he is, though, then I want him alive." Thompson looked the younger man straight in the eye. "Just do as I say, okay?" Dielman shrugged, then nodded, and Thompson glanced at the others. "All right, then. Take your places . . . and good luck. Remember what you're fighting for."

Everyone nodded. They took a moment to shake hands with one another, knowing all too well that this might be the last time they saw each other alive, then they put on their jackets, pulled on their hats, picked up their guns, and stepped out into the rain.

Thompson was the last to leave the lodge. The rain was lightening up a little as he stepped out onto the front porch, but it was still coming down hard. From where he stood, he could see townspeople moving into position: behind the stilts supporting the blackwood cabins six feet above the ground, behind stone chimneys, behind chicken shacks and goat pens. The children had already been taken over to the other side of the channel, along with a couple of adults to shepherd them; the livestock remained where they were, if only to give the town some semblance of normality. He hoped none of them would be caught in the cross fire.

He checked his carbine, making sure that a round was chambered and the safety was off, then he opened the front door, propping it with a large geode one of the kids had given him as a First Landing Day present, and concealed the rifle behind it.

Thompson touched his jaw again. "Lars, where are they?"

"Coming through now." A pause. *"Castro's with 'em."*

Good. Just as he expected. "Stand by," he said, then he walked down the front steps and sauntered across the wet sand toward the center of town.

Company was coming. Might as well greet them.

The soldiers came out of the mist in triangular formation, fifteen men spread out across the rocky beach, marching into town with carbines in hand. Their rain-soaked fatigues were caked with mud up to the knees where they had waded across the North Bend after making their way single file through the pass; rain pattered off their helmets, and they slumped beneath the weight of their packs. A long time ago, he'd been one of them: just another grunt, sent out on yet another thankless task. Any merciful impulses he might have had, though, disappeared when he discerned the black shape among them.

Manuel Castro walked without the encumbrance of a pack; his mechanical body needed no rest or nourishment, so it wasn't necessary for him to carry a sleeping bag or food. Beneath his black cloak, his ceramic-alloy feet clicked softly against the pebbles, leaving deep impressions in the sand behind him. Although the squad surrounded him, none of the soldiers walked alongside the Savant; it might have been in deference to his position as lieutenant governor, but Thompson suspected that it was out of loathing, and not a little bit of fear.

The soldiers were uneasy; Thompson could see it in their faces as they surveyed the tiny settlement with quick, nervous glances, taking in the dark and silent cabins, the absence of motion upon the wharf where kayaks lay upended near the empty pier. In sudden hindsight, Thompson realized it might have been better to have a few townspeople visible, in order to help preserve the illusion that the soldiers' arrival was unexpected. Too late for that, he could only hope they didn't spot any of the snipers hiding beneath the cabins and on the rooftops.

The squad leader saw him, raised a hand; his men came to a halt, and he stepped forward, raising the carbine so that its barrel pointed toward the sky. "Good afternoon," he said. "I take it that you're in charge here?"

"Yes, I am." Thompson carefully kept his arms at his sides. "And you are . . . ?"

"Captain Ramon Lopez, Thirty-third Infantry, Western Hemisphere Union Guard." He hesitated. "If you say you're in charge, then you must be . . ."

"Clark Thompson, mayor of Thompson's Ferry."

Lopez raised an eyebrow. "Not Colonel Thompson? I was told you were . . ."

"Not anymore. I resigned my commission a long time ago." Long before he decided to immigrate to Coyote, in fact, bringing his wife and two adopted nephews with him. He'd tried to put the past behind him, but when they discovered that the Union was just as omnipresent as it had been on Earth, they and a handful of friends fled Shuttlefield, journeying on foot across the Eastern Divide to establish a small fishing village.

It wasn't long before others joined them, the lucky few who had managed to leave the inland colonies without being stopped by soldiers or Proctors. With fewer than forty people living there, Thompson's Ferry was more like a commune than a town. Thompson called himself mayor only when newcomers showed up. Most of them stayed just long enough to barter safe passage across the channel. They'd had a lot of passengers lately; the Matriarch was cracking down on dissidents.

"Sorry you've had to come so far, Captain," Thompson said. "In any other instance, I'd invite you and your men to stay for lunch. As it stands, I hope you won't consider me rude if I ask you to leave."

A soldier nearest the squad leader shifted from one leg to another, his left hand moving an inch closer to the trigger of his rifle. A faint smile danced at the corners of Lopez's mouth. "I appreciate your hospitality, Colonel . . . pardon me, Mr. Thompson. We don't want to cause any trouble." The smile faded. "But we believe that you've received some other visitors lately. We're here to take them home."

"Sorry, Captain, but that's not possible." Thompson pretended not to notice the restless corporal. "Again, I have to ask you to leave . . . please."

"Mr. Thompson, I don't think you understand. This isn't a . . ."

"Captain, if I may . . . ?" The Savant's voice was a modulated tonality from the grille-like mouth of his metallic skull, devoid of accent or even, Thompson imagined, a soul. "Perhaps I should explain matters to the mayor."

Lopez hesitated, then stepped aside, allowing Manuel Castro to step forward. "Mr. Thompson . . . or may I call you Clark . . . ?"

"No, you may not."

A discordant rasp, like coarse sandpaper rubbing across tinfoil; it might have been laughter. "Very well. In any case, the situation is simple. For the last two years, the Matriarch has graciously permitted your settlement to exist out here, even though it operates a ferry that regularly carries Union citizens over to Midland."

"No law against that." Thompson shrugged. "It's a new world. A lot of room here for people to come and go as they will. If some folks want to leave New Florida and set out on their own, I see no problem with that. Do you?"

"So long as they're not valuable assets to the Union, no." A softer rasp, one that might have been a sigh. "Until recently, we've allowed various . . . shall we say, undesirable individuals . . . to leave the colony, so long as they weren't necessary to our growth. Indeed, we even went so far as to construct a bridge across the channel earlier this year, which would have served much the same purpose until it was sabotaged by anticollectivist elements. . . ."

"Interesting way to describe the guy who built it." Thompson felt his throat go tight; he'd met James Alonzo Garcia, the architect of the Matriarch Hernandez Bridge, and had nothing but respect for him. "I understand he was executed."

"You have the facts wrong. He hanged himself." A moment lapsed, as if Castro was awaiting a rebuttal; when he didn't get it, he went on. "Even after the bridge was rendered impassable, we allowed your ferry to continue to siphon away those who didn't want to stay. . . ."

"Unless you stopped them first."

"Unless they were essential to New Florida's continued growth and stability . . ."

"That's not the way I've heard it. From what I've been told, Luisa's got her panties in a bunch over the bridge. Now she's looking for . . . what did you call them, anticollectivist elements? . . . under every bed. In fact, I hear you can't even sing a naughty little song about her without risking arrest."

"Oh, so you've heard about this already? Then someone who's visited here lately must have told you."

Thompson felt his face grow warm. He'd let slip more than he intended. Castro half turned away from him, raising a hand from beneath his robes to indicate the nearby pier. "A small group left Shuttlefield on foot yesterday, and we have good reason to believe they were headed here. They would have arrived either late last night or, more likely, early this morning. Musicians, mainly . . . and honestly, their departure is of no real concern to us, except that one of them is Cecelia Levin, the mother of the Chief Proctor of Shuttlefield. Mr. Levin is a close personal friend of the Matriarch. He's concerned about his mother's safety."

"If he's so concerned, then why isn't he here?"

"The Matriarch decided that this was a matter more suited for military intervention. As a former Union officer, I'm sure you understand."

Oh, indeed he did. "And you're here because . . . ?"

"As I just said, we've tolerated this settlement until now because it was harmless. Now, by your own actions, you've violated the terms of that understanding. I've come here in an attempt to . . . well, establish a better relationship."

Thompson knew what Castro was saying. Stop carrying refugees over to Midland, and the Matriarch would allow Thompson's Ferry to continue as a remote settlement. Otherwise, it would be placed under Union control. The Savant was her voice, the soldiers her fist.

"Yes, they came through here," he said. "They arrived early this morning."

"Ah. Very good. And where are they?"

"I imagine they're almost across the channel by now." Thompson couldn't help but smile. "Sorry, but you're too late."

Castro said nothing, yet his right hand made a small motion. Lopez said something beneath his breath; hearing his voice through their implants, the soldiers raised their guns ever so slightly. "Don't make this difficult," Castro said. "Contact the ferry, tell it to turn around and come back."

"And if I don't?"

"Then you'll suffer the consequences." Castro hesitated. "Colonel, there's no reason to ruin everything. Give us what we want, and we'll go away."

"Simple as that, huh?" Thompson sighed, looked down at the ground. Then, as if he was mulling it over, he reached up with his left hand to tip back his hat.

That was how the revolution began.

In years to come, historians would argue over who fired the first shot at Thompson's Ferry. Some would say that it was the Union Guard, while others would contend that it was the local militia. Culpability was the issue, yet the fact was that a misunderstanding was at the heart of the matter.

Thompson thought he'd made his signals clear to everyone. If he touched his hat with his left hand, it meant that negotiations had broken down, yet they weren't supposed to fire until they saw him reach up with his right hand and take off his hat. It was a good plan, one that allowed for a last-minute cease-fire; in retrospect, though, he realized that he hadn't counted on someone with an itchy trigger finger getting it wrong.

The first shot came from the right, from beneath the cabin where Lonnie Dielman was crouched behind the front porch stairs. The bullet went wild, striking no one; nonetheless, its effect was deadly. In the next moment, the soldiers raised their guns and locked their sights on the cabin. Lonnie never stood a chance; heat seekers ripped through the blackwood steps as if they were plaster, and Thompson caught a brief glimpse of the young man as he went down.

A half second later, the very air around him seem to explode. He threw himself to the ground as townspeople opened fire upon the soldiers. The Guardsmen, caught by surprise by gunshots from all sides, crouched on the beach and returned fire in every direction.

Lying on his stomach, stunned by what had just happened, Thompson heard a *ziiiing!* The sand a few inches from his face made a tiny implosion. That shook him out of his paralysis; he scrambled to his hands and knees, bolted toward the lodge. Within his ear he heard Lars yelling his name, but he didn't stop running until he was up the front stairs.

He'd just managed to grab his carbine when a fireball erupted a few dozen yards away. He whipped around, saw a cabin go up in flames. One of the soldiers had produced a mortar, launched an incendiary grenade through the window. He caught a glimpse of Todd Bishop on the rooftop, about leap to safety, only to be cut down before he could jump. Thompson raised his gun to his shoulder; he aimed in the general direction of the nearest Union soldier, pulled the trigger. Three shots and the Guardsman went down, slumping to the sand next to another corpse.

From somewhere behind him, he heard Molly scream. "Stay down!" Thompson shouted as he kicked the lodge door shut, then he kept firing, aiming at anyone who was wearing Union colors. Time itself seemed to expand, with seconds becoming minutes and everything collapsing into a surreal montage.

Two soldiers sprinted for the goat pen, only to be killed before they made it. One of the goats brayed as it caught a stray bullet, then toppled back on its hind legs and sprawled against a trough.

Another cabin exploded, scattering glass across the backs of two men standing on the front porch. The guardsman wielding the mortar lobbed another grenade at a third cabin. By a small miracle, it missed the target, careening between its stilts to explode harmlessly on the beach behind it. The soldier who fired it barely had time to curse before blood spurted from his neck and he fell to the ground.

Juanita Morales, who had refused to leave along with her two children, died while defending her home. She managed to take down two soldiers before a third put a bullet through her heart.

A lone Guardsman, finding himself separated from his fellows and with nowhere to run, abruptly dropped his rifle, flung up his hands. He might have been screaming for mercy, but it didn't matter, because his attempt to surrender was ignored. The back of his skull exploded and he fell backward, his hands still outstretched.

Captain Lopez, flanked by the three remaining soldiers, attempted to retreat to the safety of the Eastern Divide. One by one, they were cut down by the men standing upon the ridge high above. Lopez was the last to go; in the last moment of his life, he seemed to stare straight at Thompson, as if asking how a former Union officer could do this to another. Then a bullet caught him in the back and he keeled over facefirst.

Just as suddenly as it began, it was all over. Fourteen Union Guard soldiers lay dead within the town center, crumpled brown forms whose blood seeped into the sand, diluted by the cold rain. Through the crackling roar of the burning cabins, Thompson could hear distant reverberations, gunshots echoing off the bluffs of the Midland Rise. Within his ear, he heard Lars give a rebel yell, repeated a half second later from on top of the Eastern Divide. In town, though, everything was quiet, everything was still.

No. Not quite silent or still. A dozen yards away from where Thompson stood, Manuel Castro crawled on hands and knees across the beach. With his black cloak draped around him, he looked like a wounded slug that had emerged from the water, only to have a bag of salt dropped on it. As Thompson came closer, he heard a rasping sound, like a gear that had come loose and was grinding against metal.

The Savant had taken a bullet, he realized; he was dragging his right leg behind him, and he was unable to stand. As Thompson stopped, Castro arched his neck, peered up at him from beneath his hood.

"You planned this, didn't you?" Less a question than a statement.

"You had a chance." Thompson let out his breath, not willing to admit the truth. "You didn't take it."

"Yes, well . . . so did you." There was no pain in the Savant's voice; if there was any emotion, it was only resignation. "So what do you do propose to do now?"

Thompson didn't answer at once. Nothing would have given him any more satisfaction than to plant his gun barrel against Castro's head and squeeze the trigger, even though it wouldn't have done much good. The Savant was a cyborg, a human intelligence downloaded into a quantum comp contained within its chest, adjacent to the nuclear battery that supplied power to the body's servomotors. Castro's limbs were his weak points; even if Thompson tried to shoot him in the head, the bullets would probably ricochet. Unlike the flesh-and-blood soldiers he'd led here, the Savant was virtually immortal.

At least three of Thompson's people were dead, with no telling how many others wounded. Two cabins were ablaze, with black smoke funneling up into the grey sky, and it was only a matter of time before the others would catch fire as well. Even if no one from the squad had managed to transmit a message back to Liberty, it wouldn't be long before other Union soldiers would arrive to investigate their silence, this time in greater numbers.

His town was doomed. No option left except evacuation; load everything aboard the boats, call back the raft, and make for Midland as fast as possible. He'd known this might happen; that was why he'd told Molly to start packing up the food and Garth to remain on Midland.

His bets were covered . . . except for one detail.

* * *

The raft creaked softly, water spilling across the rough planks of its deck as it moved across the channel. The rain had stopped an hour ago; the sky had cleared above New Florida, and Uma had begun to set behind the vast wall of the Eastern Divide. Dark clouds remained above Midland, and in the waning hours of the day a rainbow had formed above the channel, a translucent arch of orange and purple that seemed to form a gateway from one world to another.

"Damn, that's beautiful." Clark Thompson stood at the front of the raft, one hand braced against crates of pickled fish. "I mean, I've lived here two years now, and I've never seen anything quite like this." He turned to look at Manuel Castro. "What do you think? Isn't that something?"

"I have no idea what you're talking about." The Savant was seated awkwardly on the raft, propped up against a barrel. His cloak had been taken away from him, and without it he looked curiously naked: a robot with a thorax like an upside-down bottle, with narrow pipelike arms tied at the wrists behind his back and spindly legs thrust out before him, the broken one at an odd angle, its knee ruined. "Do you see something?"

"The rainbow." Thompson turned to look at him. "You don't see it?"

"Sorry, no. My vision isn't sensitive enough." Castro lifted his head; multifaceted red eyes peered unblinkingly from his metallic skull. "I can see colors . . . even ultraviolet and infrared wavelengths . . . but things like sunlight shining through water vapor elude me."

"So you've never seen a rainbow?" This from Lars; he and Garth stood at the winch, turning it hand over hand. The others aboard took little interest in the conversation; their attention was upon the receding New Florida shore, watching the flames that consumed the small village they had once called home.

"Oh, I've seen rainbows." Castro didn't look back at him. "A long time ago . . . a little over eighty years, by Earth's calendar . . . I was flesh and blood, just like you. But nature wasn't as kind to my body as it's been to yours, so when I had the choice of dying as a human or surviving as a Savant, I gave up watching rainbows."

"Do you miss them?" Thompson asked.

"It seemed like a good idea at the time." Castro shrugged, an oddly human gesture. "Are we there yet?"

Thompson turned to gaze the other way. The eastern shore was still almost a mile away; the canoes and kayaks carrying Molly and the rest of the townspeople had nearly reached the Midland Rise, but it would take the slower-moving raft a little while longer to get across. "Almost. So what were you before you had yourself downloaded?"

"You'd never believe me if I told you."

"Try me. Besides, what do you have to lose now?"

Again, the queer buzz that approximated a laugh. "I was a poet."

"A poet?" Thompson looked back at him. "I don't believe you."

"Well, that makes two of us. I have a hard time believing that you were once a Union Guard officer."

Several people raised their heads. It wasn't something that Thompson kept secret. On the other hand everyone knew that he didn't like to talk about it, either. "We've all got our cross to bear," Thompson said, looking away once more. "Tell me something else . . . why did you do this?"

Castro didn't answer at once. "You know, I think I may be able to make out that rainbow. Not the same way you see it, of course . . . sort of as an atmospheric distortion. If you had my vision, you might be able to see it the same way that I do."

"Don't change the subject."

"I didn't." The Savant looked directly at him. "We see things differently, Colonel. You believe that you've just fought for your freedom. It cost many lives, and you even let the fire consume the rest of your town just to prevent it from falling into enemy hands. Nonetheless, you think you've won."

Thompson didn't reply. By then the fire had reached the lodge, its smoke rising as a thick brown plume that obscured the white bluffs behind it. Somewhere within those flames were the bodies of everyone who'd died that day, laid out upon the long table where he and the others had shared many meals together. He still felt the ache in his arms from hauling the blackwood logs he and his nephews had carried through the Monroe Pass. Sometimes freedom means giving up the things you cherish.

"But the way I see it," Castro continued, "you're only resisting the inevitable. Coyote belongs to the Union. That's a fact. You may not believe in collectivism, but it's here to stay, whether you like it or not. And so are we."

"And that's why you came here? Because of some goddamn political theory?"

"No. I came here because I want to see the human race expand into the cosmos, and because collectivism is the only social system that makes sense. What you call freedom, I call anarchy. And anarchy doesn't—"

"Can't we just get it over with?" Lars interrupted. "I'm sick of hearing him."

He and Garth let go of the wheel. The raft drifted to a stop as they stepped across the sacks and crates to stand on either side of the Savant. Castro heard them coming, but he continued to gaze at Thompson with eyes that could no longer see the colors of a rainbow but could make out the lines of a face.

"You think you've won," he went on, "because you've ambushed a Union patrol. But there are still more then two hundred soldiers where they came from, and another ship is on its way with even more. It's futile, Colonel. You're living on borrowed time and a few stolen guns. Give up now, and you may be able to get out of this with your lives."

Fists clenched at his sides, Thompson regarded the Savant with helpless anger. He didn't want to admit it, but Castro was right. They had managed to take down a squad of fourteen soldiers only because they knew they were coming. Next time, they might not be so fortunate. . . .

"You're wrong," he said quietly. "You know why? Because this is our home. . . ."

"How noble. Pathetic, but noble." Again, the eerie laugh. "I hope someone carves that on your tombstone."

"I hope so. At least I'll get a grave."

Thompson glanced at his nephews, then cocked a thumb toward the channel. Lars and Garth bent over, grasped Castro's arms from either side. They grunted as they hauled the Savant to his feet. His body was heavier than it looked, yet he didn't fight back as they pushed him to the edge of the raft. Its weight thrown off-balance, the ferry listed slightly, water sloshing across the planks.

At the last moment, Castro stalled, yet the deck was too slippery and the cords binding his wrists were too tight. Behind him, the other passengers silently watched; there was no emotion on their tired faces, save perhaps for resentment.

"Any last words?" Thompson asked. The Savant said nothing. "Write a poem about this. You'll have time." Then he nodded, and his nephews shoved him overboard.

Manuel Castro tumbled into the water with a loud splash. He sank quickly, without leaving so much as a bubble to mark his passage.

They were over the deepest point of the Eastern Channel between New Florida and Midland; his body would plummet more than a hundred feet before it came to rest upon the muddy riverbed. He couldn't drown, because he was incapable of such a death, nor would he be crushed by the pressure of all that water on top of him, yet he couldn't swim or even walk. Trapped in an immortal form, marooned in the lightless depths of an alien river, he would have plenty of time to contemplate the nature of freedom.

Thompson watched him long after he disappeared, then he picked up the black robe he'd taken from Castro. At first, he was tempted throw it overboard after him. Instead, he folded it under his arm. Someday, he promised himself, he would raise it on a pole above the ashes of the town he'd built, the day he returned to build it again.

The poet was gone, and so was the mayor. Now only the colonel remained.

"All right, let's go" he murmured. "We've got a war to fight."

Book 4

Revolution

If you are cheated out of a single dollar by your neighbor, you do not rest satisfied with knowing that you are cheated, or with saying that you are cheated, or even with petitioning him to pay you your due; but you take effectual steps at once to obtain the full due amount, and see that you are never cheated again. Action from principle, the perception and the performance of right, changes things and relations; it is essentially revolutionary, and does not consist wholly with anything which was. It not only divides states and churches, it divides families; ay, it divides the *individual,* separating the diabolical in him from the divine.

—**HENRY DAVID THOREAU**
Civil Disobedience

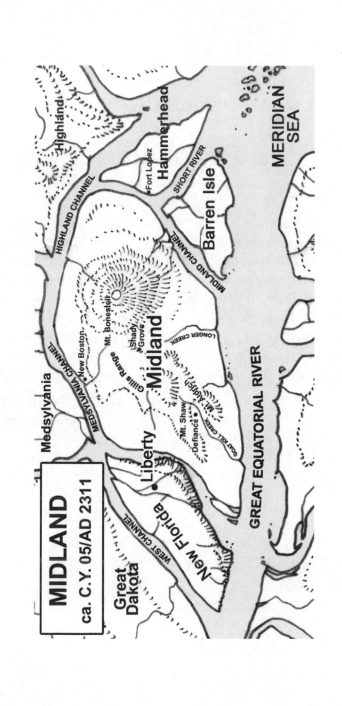

MIDLAND
ca. C.Y. 05/AD 2311

Great Dakota

Medsylvania

MEDSYLVANIA CHANNEL

WEST CHANNEL

Highland

Highland

HIGHLAND CHANNEL

New Boston

Mt. Bonestell

Gillis Range

Shady Grove

Midland

Liberty

New Florida

Mt. Shaw

Defiance

Mt. Adams

GOAT KILL CREEK

LONGER CREEK

Fort Lopez

Hammerhead

SHORT RIVER

MIDLAND CHANNEL

Barren Isle

GREAT EQUATORIAL RIVER

MERIDIAN SEA

WHSS *Spirit of Social Collectivism Carried to the Stars*

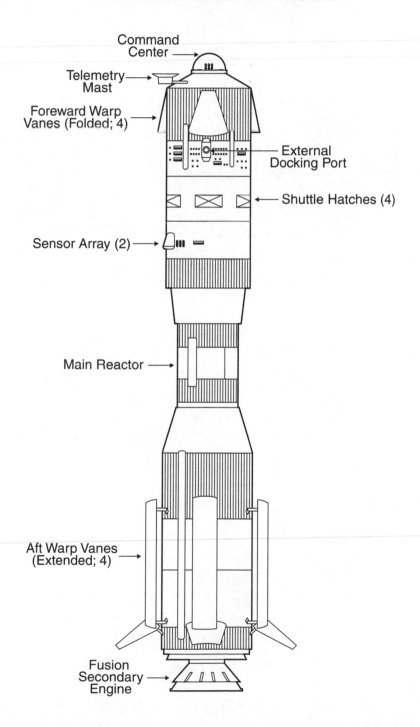

Command Center

Telemetry Mast

Foreward Warp Vanes (Folded; 4)

External Docking Port

Shuttle Hatches (4)

Sensor Array (2)

Main Reactor

Aft Warp Vanes (Extended; 4)

Fusion Secondary Engine

Part 5

INCIDENT AT GOAT KILL CREEK

A storm had passed over the valley during the night, leaving behind six inches of fresh snow. In the cool, clear light of morning, it lay thick upon the forest, an occasional gust of wind blowing tiny flakes off the branches, the bright sun causing them to scintillate like fairy dust as they drifted toward the ground. The snow muted all sound, turning the valley into a silent winter cathedral. Save for cakes of loose ice gliding along the half-frozen river that meandered between the mountains, nothing moved.

At the river's edge, a large brown form bobbed upon the cold water like a giant cork. Sunlight reflecting off glass caught Carlos's eyes. Training the binoculars upon the floating mass, his right forefinger found the autofocus; the image became sharper, losing its fuzziness. Even from a hundred yards uphill, he knew exactly what he was seeing: a Union Guard patrol skimmer, a flat-bottom hovercraft with a 30mm chain gun mounted above the glass hemisphere of its forward cockpit. The top hatch between its two fans was open; as he watched, a soldier climbed up through the hatch, looked around, then disappeared into the vehicle once more.

"Can you see 'em?" Marie whispered. She lay on the ground next to him, belly down behind the boulder that hid them from view. "How many are there?"

"Wait a minute. Still looking." The skimmer was floating next to the shore; he could hear voices, unintelligible yet distinct nonetheless. Carlos panned the binoculars toward the ramp that had been lowered from the craft, but there were too many trees in the way for him to make anyone out.

He lowered the binoculars, raised himself carefully into a kneeling position, and made a low chirping sound between his lips: *too-too-sweet, too-too-sweet*, the mating call of a grasshoarder, innocuous in the woodlands unless one knew that the small birds went into hibernation during winter. Most Guardsmen were too new to Coyote to be aware of such things.

The signal caught Barry's attention. Thirty feet to Carlos's left, he raised his head from behind the fallen trunk of a rough-bark where he and Lars were crouched. Carlos pointed to his eyes, then pointed down at the river, then traced a question mark in the air: *How many do you see?* Without hesitation, Barry raised an open hand, then added two fingers.

"Shit." Carlos settled back behind the boulders, turned to his sister. "There's seven . . . and that's just what Barry can see. No telling how many are still aboard."

"Seven? I don't think so." Frosted air drifted around Marie's mouth. "Gimme that," she said quietly, and Carlos handed the binoculars to her. She raised herself up on her elbows, took a brief look at the skimmer, then came back down again. "He's wrong. There's only six."

"How do you . . . ?"

"That's an Armadillo AC-IIb," she said, much as if she was reciting the table of elements in Bernie Cayle's science class. "Pilot, gunner, and four infantry in the back. Can't carry more than that." She caught the look in his eyes. "Sure, I'm sure. I know this stuff."

"I believe you." And it was a little scary that she did. Not so long ago she'd been a little girl playing with dolls; now her idea of fun was being able to reload a carbine in less than ten seconds with her eyes closed. That worried him; this wasn't supposed to be fun. . . .

Not a good time to reflect on such things. This was the first Union patrol anyone had ever seen in the valley. The skimmer had doubtless come upstream from the Great Equatorial River. It was a long way from home . . . and much too close to *their* home for comfort.

Another birdcall, this time from behind and to the right. He glanced back, spotted Garth crouched behind a faux birch about ten feet away, rifle in hand. Damn it, he'd told the kid to remain with the shags where they had left them farther uphill. He should have known better, though; the Thompson brothers were still new to the outfit, and wherever Lars went, Garth wasn't far behind. And neither of them was good at listening.

"Stay here," he murmured, then he crawled away from Marie, careful to keep his butt down and his rifle out of the snow as he made his way to where Barry and Lars were hiding.

"I was wrong," Barry murmured as he joined them. "There's six . . . five on the shore, one on the skimmer."

"I know. We figured that already." Carlos reached over to tap Lars's arm. "Tell your brother that when I give him an order, I want it obeyed," he said, switching to Anglo so Lars could understand him. "Got that?" Lars nodded, started to raise a hand to his jaw. "Not now! They might be on your frequency!"

"Sorry. Forgot." Red-faced, Lars lowered his hand. The Thompson brothers had subcutaneous implants that enabled them to communicate with each other. A little piece of twenty-third century tech that the kids from the twenty-first century didn't have. But the soldiers down there would have the same thing; birdcalls and hand signals might not be as efficient, but they were less likely to be intercepted.

"Think we can take 'em?" Barry asked, speaking in Anglo as well.

Good question. Five against six. They had the advantage of surprise, along with better knowledge of the terrain; he and Barry had hiked nearly every square mile of the valley ever since they moved there almost three Coyote years ago, with Marie joining them as soon as she was old enough to go out with Rigil Kent. Yet this would be the first time they'd try taking on the Union Guard, or at least in broad daylight. Before, it had always been guerrilla skirmishes, nighttime hit-and-run raids upon Liberty and Shuttlefield with darkness to hide them. This time it would be out in the open. And the chain gun on that skimmer intimidated him. . . .

"We can do it. No sweat." Lars pointed down the gentle slope; even without using the binoculars, Carlos could now make out the soldiers. Five figures, standing in a circle on the riverside. A couple of cases lay open between them; two of the men were kneeling, doing something he couldn't see. "The three of us come in on this side," he went on, "and the other two come in on the other side. Box 'em in, take 'em down. . . ."

"Let me decide the plan, okay?" But he had to admit that it was a good idea. If they came in from both sides, with any luck they might be able to catch the soldiers by surprise.

What then? Shoot them down? Carlos felt a cold knot in his stomach. As much as he despised the Union, the notion of killing six men had little appeal for him. It was different for Lars and Garth, of course; the memory of the battle at Thompson's Ferry was still fresh for them, and they had payback coming. Carlos glanced at Barry, saw the reluctance in his friend's eyes. They'd seen death a few times, too, but unlike the brothers, they weren't eager to repeat the experience.

"All right," he murmured. "You and Barry come in from the right. I'll take Garth and Marie and circle around from the left. When we're in position, I'll get Garth to com you." It was risky, but once they were closer the soldiers might get wise to any birdcalls. "One more thing," he added. "Hold your fire until I give the signal. I want to take 'em alive if we can."

"You're crazy." Lars regarded him with disbelief. "There's a half dozen guys down there. You think they're just going to . . . ?"

"I'm not kidding. We give 'em a chance to surrender first." Carlos stared him straight in the eye. "That's the way it is"

For a few long moments, the two of them gazed at one another, until Lars finally shrugged and looked away. "You're the chief," he mumbled, as if resenting the fact. "But if they start shooting . . ."

"If they start shooting, we fire back. But not until." Carlos hesitated. "That skimmer's going to be a problem, though. If the pilot gets to the gun . . ."

"Let me handle the skimmer." Barry's voice was low. "I'll circle wide, come in from the beach. If he tries anything, maybe I can pick him off first." He grinned. "And I'd love to get my hands on a skimmer, wouldn't you?"

Barry was a dead shot, and he knew how to sneak through the woods without being heard. And, Carlos had to admit, bringing home a Union Guard skimmer would be a major coup. "You got it. Are we set?" Barry gave him a thumbs-up; Lars shrugged again, his eyes on the soldiers gathered at the river's edge. "All right, then. We roll on my signal."

Carlos crawled back to the boulder, spent a few seconds explaining the plan to Marie and Garth. As he expected, Garth was just as reluctant as his brother to give the patrol a chance to surrender; he insisted upon joining Lars, until Carlos pointed out that he needed to keep them separated in order to facilitate communications between the two halves of the team.

"I'm going with Lars." Marie started crawling over to where the other two were waiting.

"Oh, no, you don't." Carlos snagged his sister by the hood of her parka; it pulled back, exposing her dark brown hair, tied into a bun behind her head. "You're sticking with me."

She angrily swatted his hand away. "If Barry's going after the skimmer, then Lars is going to need backup. Either you do it, or I will."

Marie was right; Lars couldn't handle his side alone. Carlos didn't like it very much—he was reluctant to leave his sister in a firefight—but the other reason he wanted to keep the Thompson brothers apart from each other was that they were bloodthirsty. Thompson's Ferry had been a massacre; none of the Union soldiers who'd raided the settlement had come away alive. Perhaps they had it coming, but then again . . .

"Okay. But no firing until I say so." Marie grinned, then scuttled away, keeping low to the ground. Carlos watched her go and prayed that he hadn't made a mistake.

Another exchange of *too-too-sweets*, then he and Garth began to advance down the hillside, moving single file on hands and knees, remaining behind trees and large rocks as much as possible. The deep snow muffled the sounds they made, and they were careful to avoid putting any weight upon dead branches their gloved hands found beneath the drifts. Once again, Carlos found himself impressed with how well Garth handled himself; the kid was only fifteen, but it was as if he'd been practicing this sort of thing his entire life. Perhaps he had; his uncle was a former Union Guard colonel, after all, before he'd decided to resign his commission and bring his nephews to Coyote in search of a new life.

Carlos had been Garth's age when he'd arrived here with his own family, but he'd been very much a boy then, still thinking all this was a great adventure. His childhood ended two days after the *Alabama* party set foot on New Florida, when his father and mother were killed by a boid. That was over thirteen Earth-years ago, and everything had been different since then. He doubted that Garth had much of a childhood, either. No one got to savor adolescence very long on Coyote.

The voices gradually became louder. Hearing someone laugh, he froze in place, thinking that they had been spotted. As he peered through the underbrush, though, he saw that the soldiers' backs were still turned toward him. The group was only a few dozen feet away, gathered around the two men kneeling on the riverbank. It appeared as if they were assembling some sort of instrument on a tripod. The three men standing carried rifles, but they were still hanging by their shoulder straps; the two kneeling on the ground, he noticed, weren't wearing Union parkas, but instead catskin jackets. Civilians? What were they doing with a Union Guard patrol?

Carlos glanced back to make sure that Garth was still with him, then he motioned toward a clingberry thicket at the bottom of the slope, not far from the group. Garth nodded, and Carlos began creeping closer. They could hide there for a moment, wait until Marie, Lars, and Barry were in position. Then they might be able to . . .

A shout from the skimmer. Once again believing that they'd been seen, Carlos dropped flat to the ground. Hearing footsteps against metal, he raised his eyes; the skimmer pilot was walking across the ramp, swinging a canvas bag by its strap. He was about to hop down onto shore when there was sharp *bang* like someone pushing a pin into a balloon, and the pilot suddenly twisted sideways and toppled off the gangway, falling into the shallow water below.

Damn it! Who fired? Carlos didn't have time to wonder. The men on the riverbank were already reacting to the gunshot, the soldiers reaching for their weapons, the two civilians scrambling for cover. More semiauto gunfire, again from the other side of the riverbank. One of the soldiers brought up his carbine, began firing wildly in that direction. The two civilians threw themselves to the ground, knocking over the tripod as they covered their heads with their hands.

Carlos leaped to his feet. "Hold your fire!" he yelled. "Stop shoo . . . !"

He didn't get a chance to finish before the nearest Guardsman whirled around, brought up his rifle. Carlos caught a glimpse of the black bore of the gun muzzle, and in that instant realized that he had made a mistake. The soldier was no more than thirty feet away, and he was completely exposed.

Oh, shit, I'm dead. . . .

The gunshots behind him nearly deafened him. He ducked, instinctively raising his hands to his ears, but not before he saw the soldier's parka rip apart, his helmet flying off the back of his head. Carlos barely had time to realize that Garth had saved his life; remembering his own gun, he brought it up to his shoulder, aimed at the soldier turning toward them.

No time to bother with the scope; he lined up the barrel, held his breath, and squeezed the trigger. The second soldier had just enough time to take his own shot before a bullet caught him in the gut. He doubled over like someone with a bad case of stomach cramps, then another shot from somewhere behind caught him between the shoulder blades, and he went down.

Carlos looked for another target, but there were none to be found. The remaining soldier lay facedown a few yards away, sprawled across a patch of red snow. All that could be seen of the Armadillo pilot was a pair of legs sticking up out of the water next to the skimmer's ramp. The hollow echoes of gunfire were still reverberating off the tree line on the other side of the river; the chill air, once fresh and clean, now reeked of gunpowder.

Carlos heard a rebel yell from a dozen yards away. Lars emerged from the undergrowth, his rifle held in both hands above his head. "Skragged three!" he shouted. "Score for the home team!" He did a little victory dance, looking like a soccer player who'd managed to drive a ball into the opposing team's net. "We rule!"

Sickened by what he . . . what *they* . . . had just done, infuriated by how it had happened, Carlos dropped his rifle, marched out from behind the clingberry bush. "You cold son of a bitch," he snarled, "I told you not to . . ."

Lars's face changed. Arms falling to his sides, he gazed at Carlos in confusion. "Whoa, hey, wait a second . . . I didn't shoot first. *She* did."

Carlos stopped. Unable to believe what he'd just heard, he stared at

Marie, who was coming out from behind a tree, rifle clasped in her hands. He was still taking in the smile on her face when he heard a voice behind him.

"Carlos? Carlos, man, is that you?"

One of the two civilians who had taken cover when the shooting began. He had all but forgotten them, and it was only the fact that they had hugged the ground that had saved them. Carlos looked down at the person struggling to his knees, saw a face he'd almost thought he would never see again.

"Chris?" he whispered. "Chris, what the hell are you doing here?"

GABRIEL 75/1012—WHSS *SPIRIT OF SOCIAL COLLECTIVISM CARRIED TO THE STARS*

"Shuttle from Liberty on approach, Captain. Requesting permission to dock."

Fernando Baptiste lifted his head to peer up at the ceiling of the command center. Projected against the dome was the fourth moon of 47 Ursae Majoris-B: a vast landscape of islands, some the size of small continents, separated from one another by a sinuous maze of rivers. Above the silver-blue limb of the planet, he could make out the tiny form of the shuttle carrying the governor of the New Florida colony.

"Permission granted," Baptiste told the lieutenant seated at her console a few feet away. "Inform the Matriarch that I'll meet her in the conference room on Deck 10."

She nodded, then prodded the side of her jaw as she repeated his message. Baptiste took a last glance at the section report on his lapboard, then pushed it away and carefully stood up, feeling sluggish against the pull of gravity. Nearly a week had passed since he had been revived from biostasis; during this time, the internal gravity induced by the *Spirit*'s Millis-Clement field had been gradually increased to .68g to match Coyote's surface gravity, yet he still felt sluggish, perpetually off-balance. He wasn't the only person aboard—or at least, the only baseline human—experiencing such malaise; all around him, he observed crewmen with slumped shoulders, moving as if in slow motion.

All the same, he was looking forward to setting foot on the planet below. Before he'd been picked by the Union Astronautica to command the sixth ship to 47 Ursae Majoris, he'd spent almost his entire life on the Moon or Mars, with most of his adulthood aboard one vessel or another. What would it be like to walk beneath an open sky, without having a pressurized dome above his head or be surrounded by compartment bulkheads? It would be worth spending forty-nine years in biostasis for the simple pleasure of feeling unfiltered sunlight against his face, grass beneath his feet. Would he get a skin rash if he removed his boots? Perhaps he should query the doctor if he needed another inoculation before . . .

"I'd like to join you, Captain, if you don't mind."

Baptiste looked around, saw a tall form standing beside him. Wearing a long black robe, its cowl pulled up around his head, Gregor Hull regarded him with red eyes that gleamed softly in the darkness of the command center. Once again, the Savant had come up from behind without his noticing.

"Of course," Baptiste replied. "In fact, I was about to call you." It was a lie, of course, but if the Savant knew this, there was no indication on his metallic face. "Please, come with me."

"Thank you, Captain." Hull stepped aside, allowing him to lead the way to the lift. "I'm rather hopeful that the Matriarch will clear up a mystery."

"Oh?" He waited until Hull was aboard the lift, then pushed the button for Deck 10. A slight jar, then the cab began to move downward. "I'm surprised. I would have thought that there was little in the universe that remained mysterious to your kind."

"Sarcasm doesn't suit you well, sir." As always, the Savant's voice was dull, without inflection. Except when he laughed, and fortunately that was seldom—it sounded like acoustical feedback. One more thing Baptiste disliked about Savants. Perhaps he was subconsciously bigoted against them, but the fact remained that he'd never enjoyed their company.

"My apologies. I thought I was being sincere." Another lie, and they both knew it. "What's so mysterious?"

"Shortly after we made orbit, I attempted to make contact with one of my brother Savants . . . Manuel Castro. He has been on Coyote for the past seven years. I haven't been able to hear him."

"Hear him? I don't understand."

"My kind share a symbiotic relationship." Was he imagining things, or was Hull rubbing it in, the way he phrased that? "Virtual telepathy, achieved through extralow-frequency transmissions. A sort of group mind, if you will. It's usually short-range, but we can increase the distance by tapping into long-range communications systems. I've attempted to do so, but I haven't received any response from Savant Castro."

"Have you spoken with anyone in Liberty about it?"

"I have, yes. I was informed that Savant Castro disappeared over a month ago by local reckoning . . . about three months ago Earth-time. He led a military detail to a small settlement on New Florida, to round up some colonists who had fled from Shuttlefield. Apparently there was an incident during which the soldiers were killed. When another detail was sent out to investigate, they discovered that the settlement had been torched. The remains of the soldiers were found, along with those of a few of the colonists, but there was no trace of Savant Castro."

"Which means he's dead."

The Savant shook his head; it was strange to see such a human gesture, and it reminded Baptiste that Hull wasn't a robot, appearances notwithstanding, but rather a human intelligence downloaded into a mechanical body. That made Savants perfect stewards of starships outbound to 47 Ursae Majoris; they remained awake while everyone else lay in dreamless coma within their biostasis cells, carrying on endless philosophical arguments with each other, indulging themselves in studies of things that few people would ever understand or even deem necessary. Another aspect of their existence that made them seem so remote, so disconnected from the rest of humanity . . . but then, they preferred to refer to themselves as posthuman, didn't they?

"When one of us perishes," Savant Hull continued, "it's usually by accident. In that case, our internal systems are programmed to transmit a steady signal, indicating a state of morbidity. Since I haven't received such a signal, this indicates that either Savant Castro's body has been destroyed, or he's unable to respond."

Baptiste nodded. Total destruction seemed unlikely, at least under the circumstances Hull had just mentioned. For all practical purposes, Savants were immortal, their forms designed to endure all but the harshest of conditions; the quantum comps that contained their minds were deep within their chests, protected by layers of shielding. If Castro was still alive, then what would prevent him from being able to contact Hull?

He was still mulling this over when the lift glided to a halt. The doors whisked open, and they stepped out into one of the short, narrow hallways that led to the concentric passageways circling the ship's axial center. "Perhaps the Matriarch will be able to tell us," Baptiste said as he led the Savant to the nearest intersection and turned left. "There's probably a good explanation."

"I can already think of one." Hull stepped aside to allow a crewman to pass. "Not for the disappearance of Savant Castro in particular, but for the general reason why."

The captain nodded, but said nothing. A revolt among the colonists. This had been foreseen by the Council of Savants even before the *Spirit* left Earth nearly a half century ago. Four thousand people had been sent to the 47 Ursae Majoris system since 2256, aboard the four Western Hemisphere Union starships that had followed the URSS *Alabama*, itself launched in 2070. In their endless musing, the Savants had come to the conclusion that the original *Alabama* colonists would resent the arrival of newcomers; the political system of the Western Hemisphere Union, based upon social collectivism, was radically different from that of the United Republic of America, which the crew of the *Alabama* had sought to escape when they stole their ship from Earth orbit. This was one of the reasons why Union Guard soldiers had been aboard the WHU ships sent to Coyote nearly two hundred years later. . . .

To his right, a door abruptly slid open. A sergeant major, shaven-headed and wearing a cotton jumpsuit, stepped backward out into the corridor. "And no excuses," he was saying to someone on the other side of the door. "When I get back, I want everyone ready for weapons drill. I don't care if . . ." Looking around to see Baptiste, he quickly snapped to attention, his right fist clamping against his chest. "Pardon me, sir!"

Baptiste casually returned the salute. "Carry on," he murmured. Just before the door shut, he caught sight of the room behind him: two dozen Guardsmen, wearing identical jumpsuits, sitting on bunks or standing in the narrow aisles. Throughout the *Spirit*, there were many others just like them: men and women recently revived from biostasis, sent as reinforcements for the troops already on the ground. Unlike the first four Union ships, which had carried mostly civilians as its passengers, only a few colonists were aboard the *Spirit*. His mission was primarily military in nature.

This isn't why you came here, a small voice inside him said. *This isn't what you were meant to do*. And indeed, it wasn't. Until just a few days before the *Spirit* had departed from Highgate, his mission had been to bring more colonists to Coyote. He remembered Tomas Conseco, the young boy he'd met on the maglev train a few days before launch; he and his parents were in biostasis on another level, waiting to be revived. He'd have to wait a while longer before setting foot on Coyote; first, his captain would have to quell a potential uprising, by any means necessary.

That isn't for you to decide. Again he disciplined his conscience. *You have your orders. Don't ask questions. Just carry them out*.

The conference room was located farther down the corridor. The Matriarch hadn't arrived yet; doubtless she was still undergoing decontamination procedures. Seating himself at the console at the end of the table, Baptiste spent a few minutes checking on the status of the heavy-lift landing vehicles that would ferry soldiers down to the planet. The wallscreen displayed the cavernous interior of the Bay Four; crewmen moved around a teardrop-shaped spacecraft, loading cargo through the hatch beneath its horizontal stabilizer. The *Spirit* carried three HLLVs; he wondered how and where they'd be able to land. The shuttle fields outside Liberty weren't large enough for all of them. . . .

The door opened. He looked up to see two Guardsmen step into the room. They wore winter gear and had rifles slung over their shoulders; their faces were tanned, and one had a thick beard. Union soldiers, up from the planet below; they looked like barbarians tramping through the gates. They saluted as he stood up, then assumed positions on either side of the door, making way for the woman behind them.

The Matriarch looked different from the pictures of her he'd seen: auburn hair longer, now reaching her shoulders and showing streaks of grey, her stout figure was no longer as full as it had once been. She wore the gold-trimmed blue robe of her office, yet its colors were faded; beneath it was a brown outfit of some sort of animal skin. Like her escorts, she showed signs of having spent the last several years in an untamed environment.

"Captain Baptiste?" she asked. "I'm Luisa Hernandez, governor of New Florida."

"A pleasure, Matriarch Hernandez." As Baptiste stepped forward to extend his hand, he noticed the holster on her belt. Why did she feel it was necessary to carry a weapon, or be accompanied by armed men? "I must confess, I'm surprised to see you so soon. I thought . . ."

"We'd meet once you landed?" A quick smile that quickly vanished. "I'm afraid we can't afford the luxury of time, Captain. We're in the middle of a major military operation. In fact, I've been counting on your arrival."

"I take it that you've been waiting for us." Until then, Hull had been quietly standing off to the side. The Matriarch's eyes widened a bit as she saw him; Baptiste guessed that, for an instant, she thought he was Savant Castro.

"Oh, yes." She recovered quickly, returning her attention to Baptiste. "Quite so. The fact of the matter is that we have a situation down there. With your assistance, though, we may be able to bring it to a swift conclusion."

"Really?" Baptiste pulled a chair back from the table. "Please, tell me all about it."

Matriarch Hernandez ignored the offered seat. Instead, she reached into her robe, pulled out a datafiche. "This will supply most of the background," she said, holding it out to him, "but I'll make it simple. We're engaged in a manhunt for one of the original *Alabama* colonists. He now goes by the name of Rigil Kent, but his true name is Carlos Montero."

GABRIEL 75/1038—PIONEER VALLEY

"C'mon, give us a break." Lars stood up from the hole he'd been digging for the last hour, rested his arms against the handle of the entrenching tool he'd taken off the skimmer. "We don't need to do this."

"You're right. We don't need to do this . . . but you do." Carlos didn't look up from the portable stove he'd set up a few yards away; the chunk of river ice he'd placed within the pot had melted, and he squatted next to the stove, patiently waiting for the water to boil. "If you're going to murder someone, then you're going to have to dig a grave for him."

"It's not murder if it's . . ." Marie caught the look in her brother's eye and stopped. The hole she excavated was barely deep enough for the body wrapped in a sleeping bag that lay nearby, but the ground was frozen, and she had brought up almost as much rock as soil. "Never mind," she muttered, and went back to work.

Garth had completed his task a few minutes ago. He stood next to the open grave, his hands thrust in the pockets of his parka. Another soldier lay nearby, also cocooned in a sleeping bag. "Go ahead," Carlos said. "Put him in. Then you're . . ."

"You put him in." The kid sullenly glared at him. "I'm done taking orders from . . ."

"Do as he says." Lars shoved the shovel blade back into the hard ground. "The sooner we're done, the sooner we're out of here." Carlos watched as Garth bent over, grasped the toe of the sleeping bag, and dragged it into the shallow grave. Stepping out of the hole, the kid hocked up a mouthful of saliva. For a moment it seemed as if he was ready to spit on the body, then he looked at Carlos, thought better of it, and swallowed. He picked up his entrenching tool and began to cover the corpse.

So much like David. Carlos thought. *Same attitude . . .*

That was an uncomfortable thought, and he pushed it aside. The water was boiling. Carlos picked up the pot, poured water into two metal cups he'd found in the mess kit. When Barry recovered the canvas bag the skimmer pilot had dropped in the water, they discovered that its rations included a small supply of freeze-dried coffee. Neither he nor Marie or Barry had seen instant coffee in many years . . . at least not since the last of the *Alabama*'s food supply had been used up, what seemed a lifetime ago. It was a luxury they had forgotten; no beans to grow, roast, and grind. No sense in letting it go to waste, yet Carlos couldn't help but feel another surge of guilt. The skimmer pilot had been doing nothing more offensive than fetching breakfast when Marie had shot him down.

Picking up the cups, he walked over to where the two prisoners were seated on a driftwood log. Kneeling in front of Constanza, he offered coffee to him. "Here you go," he said quietly. "Might warm you up a little."

Constanza remained silent. He stared at the ground between his boots, his arms wrapped tightly together against his chest, his hands bunched beneath his armpits. The fur-lined collar of his catskin jacket was pulled up around his face; his eyes gazed into some abyss only he could see.

"He's gone." Chris was sitting next to him, his ankles crossed, hands in the pockets of his jacket. "I've tried talking to him, but he's zeroed. Shock, I guess."

It was the first thing he'd said in nearly an hour. A sign of progress. Carlos silently offered the other cup of coffee to him. Chris hesitated, then reached up to take it from him. "Thanks. You're a real pal."

"You're welcome." Carlos walked over to the other end of the log, sat down next to him. For the moment, at least, the others ignored them. Lars, Garth, and Marie continued burial detail; Barry was aboard the skimmer, trying to figure out how to operate it. Carlos sipped the hot coffee, stared at the half-frozen waters of Goat Kill Creek. "Ready to talk?"

"What are you going to do to me if I don't? Sic your girlfriend on me?"

Carlos almost spit out a mouthful of coffee. For an instant, he felt an impulse to backhand the guy seated next to him, until he remembered just how long it had been since the last time Chris saw Marie. "That's not my girlfriend," he said. "That's my sister."

Now it was Chris's turn to sputter. He clapped a hand against his mouth as his eyes went wide in astonishment. "Holy . . . that's Marie? I didn't . . ."

"You thought she was going to remain nine forever?" Carlos shook his head. "She's eighteen, almost nineteen. Call her my girlfriend again, and we're going to have a problem." As if they didn't already.

"Sorry, man. I didn't . . ." Then Chris seemed to remember where he was. "What did you do to her? She shot our pilot down like it was a skeet shoot."

"I didn't . . ." Carlos let out his breath. He couldn't explain Marie's actions either; like Chris, he remembered when his little sister had been someone other than a sniper. Letting her join Rigil Kent had been a mistake; he saw that now. "Let's talk about something else, okay? Why are you here?"

For a moment, it seemed as if Chris was going to clam up again. He sipped coffee as he watched Marie and Lars dig graves; now that Garth had buried the third soldier, he was rummaging through the mess kit for something to eat. "I was their guide," he said, as if that explained everything. "Sort of their native sherpa."

"Don't lie." Carlos shook his head. "You've never been here before. Last time I heard, the Matriarch made you Chief Proctor of Shuttlefield. What are you doing with a Union Guard patrol in Midland?"

"Last time *I* heard, you were going by the handle of Rigil Kent." He smiled. "I looked it up, by the way. An old European name for Alpha Centauri, the closest star to Earth, besides Sol. Good name . . ."

"Don't change the subject. What are you doing here?"

Chris shrugged. "Sure, why not? Might as well tell you."

"Tell me what?"

"We're looking for you. Your little club, I mean." He gestured toward the tripod-mounted instrument, lying upended upon the ground near the bullet-pocked equipment cases. "See that? It's called a SIMS . . . schematic information mapping system. Your dad would have loved it. It's right up his alley."

"Forget about my family." Carlos felt his face growing warm; whether Chris meant to or not, he was scratching an old wound. "What does it do?"

"It's a full-suite sensory package . . . infrared, motion detection, body heat, the works. It's linked via satellite to a dozen or so like it they've been setting up all over Midland. The idea is to collect information on your people's movements. Once the data is collated, then they'll be able to predict where you're likely to be at any given time." He looked at Constanza. "It's his baby, so he might be able to explain it better. If you can get him to talk, that is."

A remote surveillance system. Carlos felt a chill that didn't come from the weather. If he and the others had been any slower coming down the hillside, then the SIMS would have picked them up as soon as they were within range. The odds would have been reversed; he might have become Chris's prisoner, and the soldiers would have been digging graves for Marie, Lars, and Garth.

Yet that was only conjecture. Reality wasn't much more kind. Goat Kill Creek led northwest into the Pioneer Valley until it reached the southern slopes of Mt. Shaw, where Defiance was located. If Chris was telling the truth, then his people were in danger of being found by the Union.

And Defiance wasn't the only settlement at risk. During the last few months, following the sabotage of the Garcia Narrows Bridge, several hundred immigrants who had been involved in its construction had managed to establish tiny villages here and there across Midland; most were scattered along the Gillis Range, with a few as far north as the Medsylvania Channel. It had become clear that the Union wasn't going to be content with New Florida; assuming control of the vast resources of Midland remained vital to its long-range plans, and the bloody events at Thompson's Ferry had demonstrated that Luisa Hernandez wouldn't tolerate any interference. The newcomers had already experienced the Matriarch's iron hand while living in the squatter camps of Shuttlefield, and they had no desire to do so again. Although Carlos had taken the name Rigil Kent for himself, it had since been adopted as the name of the resistance movement so many of them had joined.

Until recently, all they had to worry about were the Union Guard garrison on New Florida. Only a couple of days ago, another Union starship had arrived in orbit above Coyote; it could be seen from the ground at night, a bright star moving across the sky. There would be even more Guardsmen aboard that ship, more soldiers to be sent into Midland in search of Rigil Kent and his followers. The rebellion was still young, and it could easily be crushed.

Carlos glanced at the scientist seated nearby. Constanza might be persuaded to reveal where the other SIMS were located, but this was neither the time nor place. And Carlos didn't trust Chris. Even if he wasn't lying, there was something about his story that didn't quite fit. . . .

"So why are you here?" His coffee had gone lukewarm, and he made a face as he took a another sip. "Don't tell me you just wanted exercise and fresh air."

"Hey, I love the great outdoors just as much as you." Chris's expression became serious. "My mother disappeared last month. Where I come from, when people go missing, there's usually one place they go." He pointed to the ground. "You know where she is?"

"If I told you, would you help me?"

"Oh, c'mon. Get real."

"Didn't think so." Carlos stood up, tossed the rest of the coffee into the snow. "We'll take the skimmer. Your friend, too . . . he needs medical attention. I'll leave you with some rations and a compass. The East Channel's about two hundred miles from here. You should be able to find your way back."

"You wouldn't do that."

"You just said you love the great outdoors. Here's your chance to get as much of it as you want." Carlos started to walk away. "Nice to see you again. I'll tell your mom you said hi."

He was halfway to where the others were waiting when Chris called after him. "Okay, you win. What do you want me to do?"

Carlos turned around. "I want you to take a hike with me."

"A hike?" Overhearing this, Marie looked up from shoveling the last spadeful of dirt over Gondolfo's grave. "What do you . . . where are you taking him?"

"Back where we came from, of course." Before she could reply, Carlos stuck his fingers in his mouth and whistled sharply. Barry emerged from the top hatch of the Armadillo. Carlos gestured for him to come over, then looked at his sister again. "You guys take Mr. Constanza here—"

"It's Dr. Constanza," Chris said quietly. "Enrique Constanza."

"Dr. Constanza, I mean, and take the skimmer back. Chris and I will ride the shags."

"That'll take two days, at least." Lars put down his shovel. "Why can't you . . . ?"

"The skimmer only has room for six. Counting these two, we've got seven." Carlos glanced back at their two prisoners. "Kuniko should take a look at Dr. Constanza as soon as possible, so he'll go with you. Besides, we need to return the shags . . . hey, you think you can drive that thing?"

Barry had joined them by then. He shrugged. "Looks easy enough. Sort of like a maxvee, just a little different"

"I'm sure you can handle it," Carlos said. With his back turned toward Chris, he gave his friend a wink. "If we get lost, I can always call in and ask for help. Know what I mean?"

Rigil Kent avoided using satphones because they were dependent upon the *Alabama* for uplink; the Union might be able to triangulate their position by using RDF receivers to search for the point of origin. They carried short-range transceivers instead, but observed radio silence except in case of emergency. Barry understood his meaning; he gave a brief nod. "This is stupid," Marie said. "Someone can just hang on to the hatch, ride outside. We can be home in just a few—"

"Don't argue with me." Carlos dropped his voice. "Do as I say, and I won't tell anyone who fired the first shot." Marie turned red, looked away. "Just leave us with food and another pack for him. Or do you have one aboard, Chris?"

"It's in the skimmer. Of course, we could use another gun, just in case we run into any boids."

"The boids are wintering south of here. You know that." Carlos turned toward the Thompson brothers. "One more thing. Dr. Constanza is your responsibility. When I get back, I expect to find him in good health. If he has any accidents on the way . . ."

"That's not going to happen. Count on it." Barry gave Lars and Garth a dark look. "Are you sure you want to . . . ?"

"I know what I'm doing." Kneeling next to the camp stove, Carlos snuffed it out, then began to fold it. "Lars, Marie, load the SIMS and bring it with you. Barry, help Dr. Constanza aboard. Garth, pack some snow on top of those graves. I want this place to look just the way we found it."

As the others went about their tasks, Carlos shoved the collapsed stove into his backpack, then dug some rations out of the mess kit. "They follow orders well, don't they?" Chris murmured with just a trace of sarcasm.

"Sometimes." From the corner of his eye, he saw the entrenching tool Marie had dropped. It lay on the ground just a couple of feet away. For the moment, no one was paying any attention to them. Chris could easily snatch it up, bash him over the head. If he was lucky, he could then grab his rifle, shoot everyone while their backs were still turned. "When we're out here on our own," he added, "we learn to count on each other to stay alive. Know what I mean?"

Chris reached down, picked up the shovel. Carlos swiveled on his hips, watched as he folded the blade, collapsed the handle, and held it out to him. "Yeah, I know," Chris said quietly. "The only thing I don't get is why you're doing this."

"Haven't seen you in a long time." Carlos took the entrenching tool from him, shoved it into a loop on the side of his pack. "Think it's time we had a talk."

GABRIEL 75/1422—FORT LOPEZ, HAMMERHEAD

Like an immense swoop descending upon its nest, the heavy lifter came in for touchdown, its VTOL jets blasting snow away from the ring of flashing red beacons that marked the landing field. The ground crew watched as the spacecraft settled upon its tricycle landing gear; they waited until the engines cut off, then trotted over to the aft cargo hatch, while an honor guard of six soldiers took up position, three on each side of the forward crew hatch. As the hatch swung open and the gangway ramp lowered, an officer standing nearby shouted a command. The soldiers came to attention, swinging their rifles to their left shoulders and snapping their bootheels together.

It wasn't the reception Captain Baptiste had anticipated; in fact, he was quietly appalled by the formality. But he said nothing as Matriarch Hernandez led the way down the ramp, Savant Hull bringing up the rear. She pointedly ignored the honor guard as she walked past them, pulling up the cowl of her cloak. "Many apologies for not giving you a proper welcome," she murmured once they were past the soldiers. "It's the best we can do under the circumstances."

"Think nothing of it." And indeed, the absence of whatever the Matriarch considered "a proper welcome"—a military parade, perhaps, with full colors—was the least of his concerns. A cold wind whipped across the plateau, stinging his face and causing him to shiver despite the thick parka he wore. He felt light-headed—the lower atmospheric pressure, of course; he had been warned about it—but when he took a deep breath, the frigid air caused his teeth to chatter. He pulled down the bill of his cap before the wind could snatch it away. All things considered, he reflected, he would have preferred New Florida; even the name sounded warmer.

By then, the officer in charge of the honor guard had dismissed his troops and come over to join them. "Captain, Savant Hull, may I present First Lieutenant Bon Cortez," Hernandez said. "Lieutenant, Captain Fernando Baptiste, commanding officer of the *Spirit of Social Collectivism Carried to the Stars*."

"A pleasure to meet you, sir." Cortez clasped a gloved fist against his chest. "Welcome to Fort Lopez."

"Thank you, Lieutenant." Cortez was younger than Baptiste would have expected for someone in charge of a military installation; no more than twenty-five Earth-years, his beard was probably the first one he'd ever grown. "I hope you've been able to keep warm," he added, at loss for anything else to say.

Cortez smiled, relaxed just a little. "We're keeping busy, Captain. It helps a little. If you'll follow me, please, I'll show you around." As they walked away from the HLLV, two platoons of Guard infantry were marching down the ramp; Baptiste could hear the shouted commands of their squad leaders as they fell into formation next to the craft. They stamped their feet against the hard ground and hunched their shoulders against the brutal wind. Only Gregor Hull was impervious to the cold; for once, he felt envious of the Savant for his lack of mortal concerns.

"We've only been here for the last eight weeks," Cortez was saying, "just after the beginning to the month, so you'll have to pardon our lack of facilities. There hasn't been time to build permanent structures." He was speaking of the semirigid inflatable domes, each a half acre in diameter, near the landing field. "The forest is about a half mile away, and we've begun marking trees for when we get around to—"

"We felt it more important to establish a base of operations as quickly as possible," the Matriarch interrupted. "I picked the lieutenant for this job because he was instrumental in selecting the site for the bridge we constructed across the East Channel. So far, he's done a commendable job."

Baptiste noted the expression on Cortez's face; he seemed to be chewing his lower lip. "Thank you, ma'am," he said, his voice tight. "I'm glad you approve." Then he pointed to the edge of the plateau. "If you'll come this way, I'll show you why Fort Lopez is here."

"I was wondering about that," Baptiste said. "After all, if you already have a large force on New Florida, then why put a base west of Midland?"

"New Florida has been compromised, sir. Rigil Kent can sneak across the East Channel anytime they want. They've already hit Liberty twice, not to mention the job they did on the Garcia Narrows Bridge . . ." Behind them, Luisa Hernandez cleared her throat. "The Matriarch Hernandez Bridge, I mean . . ."

"We had to look elsewhere for a military base," the Matriarch said, "and Hammerhead was the most likely place." She extended a hand from beneath her cloak. "As you can see, here we enjoy a certain geographic advantage."

They had reached the edge of the plateau. Below them, a sheer granite escarpment fell away; three hundred feet down, waves crashed against jagged rocks. Fort Lopez overlooked the confluence of the Midland Channel and Short River; in the distance to the south lay Barren Isle, barely visible as small dun-colored lump. To the east, they could see the shores of Midland, with Mt. Bonestell on the far horizon. As a military surveyor, Lieutenant Cortez had done his job well. The cliff offered a natural defense against anyone who might try to cross the channel, and the island itself was a perfect place for staging military operations.

"A good choice." Baptiste admired the view. This would be a great place to build a house, were he to decide to remain on Coyote. That wasn't his intent; nonetheless, it was tempting. "But I still don't understand why it's so important to expend so much effort upon capturing a handful of malcontents."

The wind ruffled the edge of the Matriarch's cowl; she pulled it back from her face. "I thought I'd made that clear already," she said, her voice low. "Perhaps I haven't. They've attacked us again and again ever since we arrived. They've stolen firearms, destroyed spacecraft, sabotaged a bridge, ambushed soldiers, and assassinated the lieutenant governor."

"You have no proof that Savant Castro is dead." Until then, Gregor Hull had been silent. "I tend to believe that he may still be alive."

"I have no proof that he is." Luisa Hernandez shook her head. "With all due respect, Savant, you and Captain Baptiste only arrived recently. We've been dealing with this situation for just over six Earth-years. What was once a local disturbance has become a major uprising. Left unchecked, it will metastasize into a full-scale revolution. Rigil Kent . . . that is, Carlos Montero and his followers . . . have made it their mission to chase the Western Hemisphere Union off Coyote. You know as well as I that this isn't an option. . . ."

"We're aware of that, Matriarch." Baptiste paused. A gyro was lifting off the landing pad, its rotors clattering as it rose above the shuttles parked near the HLLV. He waited until the noise abated, then went on. "Have you tried to talk with the original colonists? Open a dialogue with their leaders?"

"I met with Robert Lee shortly after we arrived." She lifted her chin, almost as if daring him to challenge her. "In fact, he led a small group to the *Glorious Destiny*. . . . It was his idea to negotiate, not mine. I attempted to reach an amicable understanding, but he refused, and instead abandoned the Liberty colony and fled to Midland. Since then, their actions have been nothing but hostile."

"Which makes me wonder what you may have said that would have caused them to—"

"Captain, I refuse to stand here and listen to someone second-guess what was done six years ago. As the colonial governor, my duty is to maintain a Union presence on this world. Your duty is to back me up, by force if necessary. I say that it's necessary."

"I only wish to . . ."

"Point out the alternatives, yes. Your objections are noted." The Matriarch turned away. "Come with me now. We have work to do."

Baptiste watched as Hernandez began striding back toward camp, Savant Gregor following her. He let out a breath, looked out over the channel. Cortez remained with him. At first the younger man said nothing, then he stepped closer. "You have to forgive her, sir," he said quietly, his voice almost lost in the wind. "Ever since Savant Castro disappeared, she's been . . . well, obsessed . . . with tracking down Rigil Kent."

"So I see. . . ." And to that end, she'd laid a trap, in hopes that Montero would take the bait. "And how do you feel about it? Do you think that she may have exceeded her authority?"

Cortez stiffened, his eyes raising to meet his own. "I lost several friends at Thompson's Ferry," he replied. "Please, sir, don't speak to me of excessive authority. I owe Rigil Kent."

Then he walked away, leaving Baptiste standing by himself. Feeling cold, and in a trap of his own.

GABRIEL 75/1917—MT. ALDRICH

"This is as good a place as any." Carlos gently pulled the reins, lifting the shag's heavy head and bringing the beast to a halt. He shifted sideways on his blanket saddle, looked back at Chris. "Need a hand there?"

"No, I . . . how do you . . . ?" Chris yanked too hard; his shag bellowed in protest, and once again attempted to shake its rider off its hairy back. This time, it nearly succeeded; thrown off-balance, Chris stayed on only by grabbing two fistfuls of matted fur. The shag grunted and shook again like an enormous dog coming out of the water. Then, resigning itself to rude treatment, it obediently knelt on its elephant-like legs, giving Chris a chance to slip his feet over the side.

"A little better." Carlos suppressed a grin as the shag farted loudly. Chris staggered away from the animal, holding his nose as he massaged his aching backside. "You'll get the hang of it after a while. Once they get used to you, you hardly have to . . ."

"Yeah, yeah. Sure." Chris regarded the shags with disgust. They resembled water buffalo with dreadlocks, save for elongated snouts with upward-curved tusks like those of a wild boar. Despite their ferocious appearance, the herbivorous creatures were as docile as cows and easily trained as pack animals. "I would have rather walked."

"We'll be doing that soon enough." Climbing down from its back, Carlos took the shag's reins and, coaxing it with a click of the tongue, led it to the nearest faux birch. Once it was tied up, the beast raised its snout, peeled a strip of bark off the tree, and began munching upon it. They'd left behind the three shags Marie and the Thompson brothers had ridden, after moving their blankets and bags; since shags had an unerring sense of direction, Carlos knew they'd make their way back to their point of origin. "They don't like having riders when they're going downhill," Carlos went on as he pulled off the saddlebags, "so we'll have to lead them once we head down the mountain."

Following Carlos's example, Chris gingerly approached his own shag, took it by the reins, and tugged it over to another tree. They had spent the better part of the day climbing Mt. Aldrich, following a game trail that led around the eastern slope of the mountain. Now they were on top of a ridge a few hundred feet below the summit. Through the trees, they could make out the other side of the valley; Uma was setting behind Mt. Shaw, with Coyote's sister worlds Raven and Fox beginning to glimmer in the dark purple sky.

Carlos stood off to the side, watching Chris as he pulled a tent from one of the saddlebags and began to unroll it on the snow-covered ground. "You can help by gathering some wood," Carlos said. "The stuff on top is wet, but if you dig under it, you can find—"

"I know how to find firewood." Chris eyed the rifle that Carlos pulled off his shoulder and leaned against a boulder. "You're awfully trusting, you know that?"

Carlos shrugged as he assembled the tent poles. "What would you do? You have no idea where you are. Without me, you'd be lost." He glanced up at the sky. "Better hurry. It's going to be dark soon."

Chris hesitated, then turned and walked away. By the time Carlos had finished erecting the dome tent and had unpacked the camp stove, he reappeared with an armload of dry branches. Carlos watched as Chris kicked aside the snow, built a miniature tepee of twigs, then used a pocket lighter to set fire to some leaves he'd tucked beneath the kindling. Within minutes, a small fire was burning, bringing a little patch of warmth back to the world just as the last light of day was fading.

They ate in silence, dining on rations reheated on the camp stove. As night set in, Bear began to rise to the east; it was a clear night, and soon the stars began to come out. Carlos left Chris with the cleanup; while he was scrubbing the plates and pan with water he boiled on the stove, Carlos walked over to the tent and produced a small catskin flask from one of the saddlebags.

Chris raised an eye as Carlos uncapped the flask. "What is that stuff?"

"Bearshine." Carlos took a sip, winced, and offered the flask to him. "You remember Lew Geary, don't you? This is his stuff . . . good old-fashioned corn liquor. Try some, it's good."

"I'll pass, thanks. Stopped drinking."

"Sorry. Didn't know." Recognizing his faux pas, he capped the flask, then sat down on the saddle blanket he had spread out next to the fire. "Glad to hear it. You were in pretty sad shape there for a while."

"Yeah, well . . ." Chris picked up a branch, absently stirred the coals. "Nothing like a little family tragedy to turn you into the town drunk."

Carlos hesitated. The memories of their last days together in Liberty were still sharp. "If you want me to apologize for David again . . ."

"I'm over that." Chris shook his head. "It wasn't your fault. David brought it on himself. He did something stupid, and . . . well, he's dead, and that's it." He was quiet for a moment. "And I'm not going to blame you for Wendy, either. She had a choice between you and me, and she picked you. How is she, anyway?"

"Wendy's fine." Carlos fed another piece of wood onto the fire. "Susan's growing up fast, going to school. We've got a dozen or so kids in Defiance now, so Wendy and Kuniko have their hands full, taking care of them."

"Good." Another pause. "And my mother?"

"Doing much better, now that she's . . ." Carlos stopped, reluctant to say more.

"Now that she's away from Shuttlefield?" Chris looked up from the fire. "Go ahead, say it. 'Your mother's great, now that she doesn't have you around . . . ' "

"You know that wasn't what I was going to say." Carlos felt his temper rise. "Why are you making this hard? I'm trying to . . ."

"Make friends again?" Chris remained irritatingly calm. "Was that your idea? Take me up in the woods, have a little cookout, slip me some booze. Pretty soon I'd soften up and let bygones be bygones? C'mon, old buddy . . ."

"Stop calling me that."

"Why not? Old buddy, old friend, old pal . . . best friend from child-hood, all that." Chris smirked. "You know, even our names are alike. I was born just a couple of months before you, our dads were friends, so your father picked another name that began with a C. Chris and Carlos, Carlos and Chris. The folks thought it was cute. . . ."

"Stop it."

"Then you abandoned me. When the Union showed up, you locked my mother and me in a cabin while everyone else made a clean get-away. You know how hard that was, knowing that we were dirt so far as . . ."

"You transmitted a message to their ship, telling them where we were located." Carlos glared at him. "If anyone's guilty of betrayal, it's you, not me. And then you joined up with them, became their Chief Proctor."

"Like I had a choice? You guys weren't going to take us back. What else was I supposed to do? Live in the squatter camp along with all those poor bastards they'd conned into leaving Earth so that they'd have a source of cheap labor?"

"If you can't beat 'em, join 'em. Is that it?" Carlos shook his head. "They're going to ruin this place. Every few months, another ship ar-rives, bringing another thousand people. . . ."

"Gosh, really?" Chris rolled his eyes in mock surprise. "Why, if a thou-sand more ships arrive over the next . . . oh, say, a hundred years . . . then we'll have a million people on this planet. Why, we might even have a population explosion!"

"Given our limited resources . . ."

"Oh, c'mon" Chris chuckled as he looked askance at Carlos. "We've barely explored one tenth of this world. Even if the Union emptied all the cities and sent everyone here, we'd still have miles of elbow room."

"Is that what you want? To have this place become just like Earth, complete with its own dictatorship?" Feeling the darkness encroaching upon them, Carlos stood up, walked over to where he'd left his rifle. He brought it back to the campfire and laid it down next to him. "That's why we came here in the first place, to get away from all that. So far as I'm concerned, the Union is no better than the Republic."

"And you really think you're going to get them to pack up and go home? Dream on." Chris gestured toward the rifle. "Why'd you do that? You said yourself that I'm not going anywhere."

Carlos didn't reply. He unstopped the flask and took a sip of bearshine that burned its way down his throat. He was surprised when Chris reached out his hand. "I thought you said you stopped drinking."

"It's cold. Unless you've got some hot chocolate stashed away . . ."

"Haven't had hot chocolate since we left Earth. Be my guest." Chris accepted the flask from him, upended it, and took a slug. He gagged, coughed into his fist. "Sorry," Carlos murmured. "Should have warned you . . . it's powerful stuff."

"God!" Chris gasped, pounding his chest with his fist. "Now I remember why I don't drink anymore." Tears seeped from the corners of his eyes as he thrust the flask back toward Carlos. "So . . . why'd you get your gun? Worried I might run away?"

For a second, Carlos was tempted to tell him the truth. For better or worse, they were talking to one another for first time in years. Yet he still couldn't trust Chris, and they still had another day of travel before they reached Defiance. If they made it as far as Johnson Falls . . . "Up here at night, sometimes you hear things." He pulled the rifle a little closer. "I'd rather be safe than sorry."

"What things?" Chris unbuttoned the canteen from his belt and drank some water. "The boids stay in the lowlands and the creek cats are in hibernation. What's going to bother you up here this time of year?"

"Remember Zoltan Shirow? The First Church of Universal Transformation?"

"The freak with the bat wings?" Chris laughed. "Oh, boy, do I remember him. I heard he brought his people over here from Thompson's Ferry early last year. Good riddance . . . whatever happened to him, anyway?"

"They tried to hike over Mt. Shaw, but they got caught in a nor'wester. Everyone died up there except their guide. Ben Harlan. You might know him . . . ?" Chris shook his head. "Anyway, Ben managed to make it down the mountain. When we found him, he said that they'd killed each other. When the food ran out, they went cannibal."

Chris whistled beneath his breath. "No joke."

"No joke. After the snow melted, Ben and some other guys hiked back up, found the place where he'd last seen them. From what I hear, it was pretty gross. But when they counted the bodies, they came up two short . . . and it's hard to miss someone with wings and fangs even as a skeleton."

"So what are you saying?" Chris peered at him from across the fire. "Zoltan's still running around up here?"

Carlos was tempted to uncork the flask again. He reconsidered and left it alone. "We've had patrols in these mountains for the last year. That's how we found you guys. Every now and then, they've come back, saying that they've seen things, heard things. . . ."

"Oh, get off it. I'm too old for ghost stories." Chris stood up, arched his back. "Go ahead, keep your gun handy if you want. I'm going to get some shut-eye." He shambled over to where he'd left his pack, hauled it to the tent. "Tell me if you see Zoltan. Maybe he'd like some of that rotgut you carry around."

"I'll do that." Carlos watched as Chris crawled into the tent, shoving his pack before him. He waited while he heard him unroll his sleeping bag, then he put aside the rifle and picked up the flask once again.

He dropped another piece of wood into the fire. Sparks flickered upward into the bare branches, melded with the stars in the black sky. He was about to look down again when he spotted a single point of light, slowly moving east to west across the night.

The latest Union starship. Watching it, he felt a twinge of unease, as if someone up there was spying upon him. An irrational thought. He took a last swig of bearshine, then stood up and headed for the tent.

One more day on the trail, and then he'd be home again. He missed Wendy and Susan. He hoped that the rest of the journey would be uneventful.

GABRIEL 75/2302—FORT LOPEZ

"Captain Baptiste?" The warrant officer standing near the map wall cupped a hand against her earpiece. "Receiving orbital telemetry from the *Spirit*. They report tracking two clear signals from the ground."

"Thank you, Acosta. Put it up, please." Baptiste stood up from the chair in which he had been dozing for the last half hour, walked across the dimly lit situation room to join her. He needed to go to bed; it had been a long day, and the only thing keeping him awake was coffee. But he had been waiting all evening for his ship to fly over Midland; now that it was in position, they should be able to get a fix upon the extralow-frequency signals coming from the ground.

Giselle Acosta tapped a few keys, and a holograph formed within the map wall: a topographic map of Midland, its mountains and valleys depicted as contour lines. As Baptiste watched, two illuminated crosshatches appeared on the southeastern corner of the island, so close together that they almost merged.

"Enlarge this area," he said, pointing to the markers. Someone came

up behind him; looking around, he saw Lieutenant Cortez. "Didn't
know you were still here," Baptiste murmured. "Are you off duty?"

"Thought you might need me, sir." Cortez watched as the image expanded, becoming a broad valley surrounded on three sides by mountains. "That's the southern end of the Gillis Range . . . Mt. Shaw up here
and Mt. Aldrich down there." He pointed to a sinuous line weaving
through the center of the valley. "This river comes down between them
and empties into the Great Equatorial about a hundred miles to the
south."

Baptiste nodded. The two markers had moved farther apart now: one
on the river almost midway between the two mountains, the other near
the top of Mt. Aldrich. "They've separated," he said, then he turned to
call across the room. "Any further contact from the patrol?"

"No, sir." A corporal seated at the com station swiveled in his chair to
look at him. "Last report was at 0830 this morning."

"Looks like we may have lost someone." Cortez frowned. "But the
other two signals are still active. Should I wake the Matriarch?"

Baptiste shook his head. If they got Luisa Hernandez out of bed, she'd
only demand immediate action. But a night sortie in unknown terrain
was an invitation to disaster; their target wasn't likely to go anywhere
before morning. "Let her sleep," he replied, then patted Acosta's shoulder. "Good work. Get a lock on those coordinates and tell your relief to
keep an eye on them when *Spirit* makes its next flyover in about six
hours."

Acosta typed another command into her keyboard, and a translucent
grid appeared above the map, displaying latitude and longitude lines.
Baptiste yawned, then he looked at Cortez once more. "Get a few hours
of shut-eye, then muster two Diablo recon teams at 0500."

"Diablos?" Cortez raised an eyebrow. "Are you sure we're going to
need them, sir?"

"Rigil Kent's been pretty good at taking down light infantry. Let's see
how they handle heavy stuff." Baptiste raised a hand to stifle another
yawn as he walked away. "Four Diablos on the flight line for liftoff at six.
Tomorrow we go hunting."

"From here on, we walk the rest of the way." Carlos hopped down from his shag into the snow. "You can leave your pack," he added as he withdrew his carbine from its scabbard and pulled its strap over his shoulder. "They'll carry that . . . just not you."

Chris carefully climbed down from his mount. His shag had come to a stop on its own, and it waited patiently for him to take the reins in hand. Ever since they had resumed their journey just after sunrise, the trail had gradually led down a gentle incline, taking them off the ridge where they had spent the night until they had come to the top of a sixty-foot granite bluff. Below them, the Pioneer Valley narrowed, becoming a deep and heavily wooded canyon. On the other side, only a few miles away, they could see the lower slopes of Mt. Shaw; Goat Kill Creek lay several hundred feet below, invisible save as a slender line that meandered across the valley floor.

"Watch your step. It gets pretty steep after this." Clucking his tongue, Carlos led his shag toward a break in the trees, where the trail began to descend into the canyon. He stopped to pick up a fallen branch; breaking it over a boulder, he tossed the other half to Chris. "Here, use this. Might make it a little easier."

"Thanks." They'd spoken little that morning; too much had been said the previous evening, and neither of them felt like talking. "Y'know, I'm just curious . . . why do you call this Goat Kill Creek?"

"First spring after we moved here, we let the goats graze near it." Keeping his eyes on where he put his feet, Carlos was paying more attention to the trail than to what he was saying. "We didn't know that it floods after the snow melts. Lost a few that way. The name stuck."

"Makes sense." Chris felt the soles of his boots slide on loose gravel beneath the snow; he used the stick to balance himself. "So I guess we're not far from Defiance."

Carlos suddenly realized that he'd revealed more than he should. "Not that far," he said noncommittally. "Maybe a few . . ."

He stopped. From somewhere not far away, a new sound drew his attention. At first, he thought it was trees rattling in the wind, yet it had a different quality: artificial, more repetitive. Carlos peered at the overcast sky through the snow-laden branches, trying to figure out where the noise was coming from.

"What?" Chris asked. "You think you—"

"Hush." Carlos held up a hand. The sound was louder. It also sounded like . . .

A gyro suddenly roared overhead, passing only a few hundred feet above them. It swept over the top of Mt. Aldrich, the rattle of its blades clattering against rock and timber, shaking snow off the treetops. The shags brayed in terror; Carlos grabbed his beast's reins and fought to keep it under control as the gyro skimmed out over the valley.

What the hell? Where did that . . . ?

And it wasn't alone. He could see another gyro, cruising at low altitude up the valley several miles away. As the first aircraft banked to the left, making a sharp turn that brought it back toward them, the second slowed to a near stop, its twin nacelles canting upward into vertical position. Like a giant dragonfly, the second gyro slowly descended into the canyon, gliding back and forth as if searching for a place to touch down.

"Duck!" he yelled, but it was much too late for that. The first gyro hurtled toward them once more, this time even closer. Carlos couldn't restrain his shag any longer; in blind panic, the beast tore loose from its reins, then turned and galloped back uphill. For an instant it seemed as if the shag would trample Chris, but he let go of his own mount and threw himself out of the way. The animals nearly collided with one another as they charged up the trail.

"They're getting away!" Chris scrambled on hands and knees in an absurd attempt to grab his shag's reins. "They've got our—"

"Let 'em go!" Carlos grabbed him by the back of his jacket, hauled him beneath the nearest tree. But Chris was right; all their gear—including, he realized, his radio, along with extra cartridges for his rifle—were in packs and saddlebags lashed to the shags. Given time, they might be able to chase them down. But they were out of time, and the gyro was closing in.

It was at treetop level, its propwash causing twigs and clumps of wet snow to rain down upon them; the noise of its rotors was deafening. Raising a hand to shield his face, he caught a glimpse of the gyro's undercarriage. The craft was hovering directly above them, nacelles rotated into landing position. In another few seconds, it would come down and . . .

Yet it seemed to hesitate in midair. A couple of seconds passed, then the gyro veered away. Coughing against the snow flurry, Carlos watched the aircraft as it retreated. Gaining altitude, it glided toward the summit, searching for . . .

Of course. There was no way it could touch down there. The mountainside was much too steep, with too many trees in the way; the pilot would have to find a level spot near the top of the mountain. Unfortunately, they had passed several clearings where the gyro could safely land. Once the pilot located one of them, then he could drop into it. And Carlos had little doubt that a squad of Union Guard soldiers was aboard.

"C'mon. We're going." Carlos pulled Chris to his feet. For a second, it seemed as if he was about to resist. Carlos shoved him in the back, propelling him down the steep trail.

Their bootheels dug into snow as they half ran, half fell down the rocky slope, grabbing at saplings for support. Within minutes, Carlos lost sight of the trail. Desperately trying to spot it again, he slipped, fell back onto his butt. Swearing beneath his fogged breath, he stumbled to his feet. Chris was already a dozen yards ahead of him; as much as they needed to put distance between themselves and the ridge, he couldn't afford to lose him. He'd had suspicions before; now their survival depended upon his instincts being correct.

Carlos charged downhill until he reached the base of the bluff. A massive stone wall rose above him, shelves of granite slate forming an overhang that loomed over his head. Piles of broken talus lay at the bottom of the bluffs, where erosion had caused the bluffs to gradually disintegrate, forming ancient rockslides. From far away, he could hear a low, steady rumble, like distant drums. The trail might be gone, but Johnson Falls was only a half mile away.

Chris was struggling across the talus when Carlos caught up with him. Grabbing his shoulder, Carlos turned him around, slammed him against the cold rock wall.

"Where is it?" he demanded.

"Where's what? I don't know what you're—"

"They didn't find us by accident." Carlos yanked the rifle off his shoulder. "You're wearing some sort of tracking device. Hand it over."

Chris's mouth trembled. "Man, you're paranoid. There's no—"

"I'm not kidding." With a flick of his thumb, he disengaged the safety. He backed up a step rested the stock against his armpit, and raised the muzzle so that it was aimed straight at Chris's chest. "So help me, I'll kill you if you don't show me where it is. And I won't count to three."

Chris stared back at him, not quite believing what he'd heard. Carlos's forefinger moved within the trigger guard, and that was all that it took. "All right, all right!" Chris tore off his jacket, turned around. "It's here!"

A small plastic unit was hooked to the back of his belt. "Take it off," Carlos said, and watched as Chris fumbled at the buckle. "Who else was carrying these things?"

"We all were." His belt now unfastened, Chris reached back to pull it off from behind. "If you'd checked the guys you shot, you would have found theirs. But you buried them. . . ."

"Leaving just you and Constanza. And we separated you." Carlos took the belt from him, gave the unit a quick examination. An ELF transponder of some sort, its signal capable of being received from orbit. Probably by the Union starship he'd spotted the previous night. He yanked the unit off the belt, dropped it on the ground, and stamped on it a couple of times until it made a satisfying crunch beneath the sole of his boot. "I

figured this was some sort of setup. Finding you out here was too conve-
nient."

"Damn, you're swift." Chris's smile was fatuous, the smug look of
someone who'd played a good game and figured that he held the winning hand. "They're looking for you, genius. The famous Rigil Kent. And
now they've got you where they . . ."

The distant sound of rotors interrupted him. Looking around, Carlos
spotted the second gyro lifting off from farther down the canyon; it
looked as if it had touched down somewhere on the river, at least three
or four miles away. He couldn't see or hear the gyro that had been tracking him and Chris, but he had little doubt that it had managed to find
someplace to land farther up the mountain.

One squad coming at them from above, another from below. The
team in the canyon would be homing in on Constanza's transponder,
though, and he'd just destroyed Chris's. He had something of a head
start. So long as Marie and her guys weren't still . . .

"So what now?" Chris was almost casual about this. "Leave me?
Shoot me? Better make up your mind. I think you're going to have company soon."

"That way." Carlos gestured in the direction of Johnson Falls. "You're
coming with me."

"Sure. Why not?" Chris gave a nonchalant shrug. "Sort of figured
you'd say that." He turned, then stopped to glance back over his shoulder. "In fact, so did she."

"What's that?" Carlos didn't have to ask whom he was talking about.
"What did she say?"

"That you'd never kill me." Again, the self-assured smile. "To tell the
truth, though, that's not why I told her I'd go along with this. I just want
to be there when they bring you down."

"Sorry to disappoint you. I'm not dying today." Carlos pointed in the
direction of the falls. "Now march."

"Flight One reports Diablo Alpha is on the ground." The master sergeant seated at the carrel closest to Baptiste didn't look away from his wraparound console. "They've lost the transponder, but they've had visual contact with primary target. Closing in to intercept."

"Diablo Bravo reporting in, sir." Acosta, seated at the adjacent carrel, glanced back at him. "They have a clear fix on secondary target. It appears immobile. Moving to investigate."

"Thank you." Baptiste continued to study the map wall. Two red markers on a ridgeline below the summit of Mt. Aldrich indicated the position of Diablo Alpha. As Sergeant Cartman had just said, the crosshatch indicating the location of the ELF beacon worn by Chief Proctor Levin had disappeared shortly after he had been spotted by Flight One. The transponder worn by Enrique Constanza, though, was still active; it hadn't changed position since it had been acquired by the *Spirit* the night before, though, and that worried him.

He walked over to the Diablo Alpha carrel. "Tell them to proceed with caution," he said quietly. "This could be a trick of some sort."

"What makes you think that, Captain?" Luisa Hernandez came up from behind him, her cloak brushing softly against the cement floor. The situation room was crowded, filled with Union officers monitoring the operation. "For all we know, that might be the location of the *Alabama* party."

She had a point. Constanza's signal was coming from a point a considerable distance from the last-known whereabouts of the advance team. The loss of contact with its other four members tended to support the theory that it had been ambushed by Rigil Kent nearly fifty miles down-river; it had to be assumed that they were now dead, their transponders buried along with their bodies. If Constanza had been taken prisoner, then his captors might have taken him to a site somewhere upstream . . . perhaps even their ultimate objective, the *Alabama* party's hideaway.

Baptiste absently rubbed his chin as he watched the images being transmitted from Bravo Leader. One of the screens displayed a shot from the camera mounted on the Diablo's chest: fuzzy and monochromatic, lurching a bit with each heavy step that the team leader took, it showed a riverbank overgrown with dense brush, the river itself a silver surface reflecting the morning sun.

"Too easy," he murmured, not so much to the Matriarch as to himself.

"What did you say?" She stood next to him, her arms folded across her chest. "You think this is easy? Captain, this operation has been months in the planning. I assure you, we have the ability to . . ."

"And from what you've told me," he said quietly, "you've consistently underestimated them. You seem to believe that, simply because you have more men and more equipment, your adversary lacks resources. That's a mistake."

Her hands fell to her sides, and she glared at him with something close to contempt. Although he hadn't raised his voice, Baptiste was conscious of the fact that the room had gone quiet; all around them, officers were listening to the exchange. He wondered how many had felt the same way themselves but had been unwilling to challenge the authority of the colonial governor.

Hernandez stepped back, her eyes narrowing. "Perhaps you're correct, Captain. We should change the purpose of this operation." She turned away, walked over to the Diablo Alpha carrel. "Where are your men now?"

"Descending the ridge now, ma'am." Cartman pointed to a screen depicting the location of Diablo Alpha, a pair of asterisks slowly making their way down a close-set pattern of contour lines. Its chest camera displayed a blurred image of trees and snow-covered boulders. "They haven't made visual contact yet, but sonic patterns indicate movement about five hundred yards ahead. . . ."

"Show me the shot Flight One caught of them," she demanded. Cart-man worked his keyboard, and another screen lit to depict a jolting overhead image: two men, captured for a few brief seconds by a gyro's belly camera, peering up at them from beneath snow-covered branches. "Freeze!" She pointed to the man on the right: young, bearded, a Union carbine slung over his shoulder. "Take a good look, Captain . . . Carlos Montero, Rigil Kent himself. Tell me, do you think this is a person you'd underestimate?"

"No, ma'am, I wouldn't." It wasn't fear that Baptiste saw in Montero's face, but something else . . . a determination that, under other circum-stances, he would admire.

"Neither do I. And I've been dealing with him for much longer than you have." Hernandez prodded her lower jaw. "Patch me into Alpha and Bravo," she told Cartman. "I wish to speak with them directly."

"Matriarch," Baptiste said, "may I remind you that this is a Union Guard operation. . . ."

"And may I remind you that I'm colonial governor." She deliberately turned her back upon him. Cartman looked up and nodded, indicating that she was being heard by the two strike teams. "Diablo Alpha, Diablo Bravo, this is the Matriarch Luisa Hernandez. The mission objective has now changed. Your first priority is termination, not capture. Repeat . . . termination is now the primary objective. That is all." She prodded her jaw again, then looked at Baptiste once more. "I think that should con-vince you how seriously I regard this."

Baptiste regarded her with horror that he hoped his face wouldn't be-tray. This wasn't what he'd been led to believe they were doing. "I never doubted it," he said, carefully choosing his words, "yet you realize that your orders include the termination of two civilians . . . including your Chief Proctor."

Her face went pale, as if she suddenly realized what she'd done. There was always time to rescind the order, or at least change it. But then the coldness returned.

"Of course I know that," she said. "Just do as I say."

She walked away, and it was in that moment that Baptiste realized just how far her obsession with Rigil Kent had gone.

At first, the binoculars revealed nothing save the swaying of tree limbs in the wind. Then a shadow passed across the bottom of the bluffs, flitting across the rockslide. Almost as soon as Carlos spotted it, though, it seemed to vanish; as he continued to watch, he caught a brief glimpse of snow falling off a clingberry bush, as if knocked down by a specter following the tracks he and Chris had left behind.

"Having trouble?" Chris lay against the boulder next to him, a smirk on his face. "I imagine they're hard to spot in ghost mode."

"And I bet you're not going to tell me what that is, are you?" Carlos kept his eyes on the bluffs, hoping to spot any further movement. Yes, there it was again . . . but now there appeared to be two shadows, one just behind the other.

"Umm . . ." Chris thought about it a moment. "Okay, let me give you a hint. You're looking at them all the wrong way."

Carlos considered what he'd just said, then laid down the binoculars and picked up his rifle. Peering through the scope, he switched to infrared. Everything went dark, as if twilight had settled upon the forest. He could make out two hulking silhouettes, ill defined yet vaguely man-shaped, resembling eggs with short legs and oversize arms.

"There you go." Chris chuckled. "That's their weak point. Their suits are coated with some sort of polymer that lets them camouflage themselves, but they've never been able to mask the heat from their power systems. Go IR, and on a cold day like this, you can see 'em . . . sort of."

"You seem to know an awful lot about these things." Carlos studied the two figures slowly making their way along the bottom of the cliff. He had led Chris to a large, tooth-shaped outcropping about a hundred yards downhill from the bluff. For a few minutes, they were safe. Just enough time for him to take stock of their pursuers. "What did you call them? Diablos?"

"Diablo Mark III combat armor, uh-huh. Tactical assault gear. Some friends in the Guard told me all about them, but I've never seen one until now. Wanna let me take a look?"

Carlos ignored him as he squinted through the scope, lining up the two figures within the crosshairs. He had a clear shot, if he cared to take it. If their shielding was heavy armor, though, it was probably impervious to low-caliber ammo; shooting at them would only expose his position. "Anything else you'd care to tell me?"

"Well . . . if this is a standard hunter-killer team, then it means that the leader is probably sweeping this entire area with his sensor array. So if you think they don't know where we are, you're wrong. They're probably listening to us right now . . . if they haven't picked up the infrared beam from your scope."

Carlos felt his blood freeze. At that moment, the Diablo in front turned toward him. A cylindrical shape mounted on its right shoulder swiveled his way, as if taking aim directly at him. He ducked, pulling his rifle against his chest; an instant later, there was a faint hiss as hot flecks of superheated granite stung the right side of his face.

"Oh yeah . . . and they're armed with particle-beam lasers, too!" Chris laughed out loud. "Oh man, you are so screwed!"

Chris wiped a hand across his forehead and cheek; his glove came away with blood from a half dozen scratches. He cast a baleful look at Chris as he slid down the boulder. If they were fast enough, they might be able to get the rest of the way down the hillside before . . .

"Hey! Down here! You guys, down here!"

Carlos looked around. While his back was turned, Chris had scampered past him up the outcropping. He stood on top of the boulder, waving his arms above his head.

"I got him!" Chris yelled again, then whistled sharply and pointed toward him. "C'mon, he's here."

A dozen memories flashed through Carlos's mind as he brought up his rifle, leveled it at Chris's back. He tried not to think about all the things they'd done together when they were kids as his finger curled within the trigger guard. He took a deep breath, prayed that God would forgive him. . . .

There was a soft fizzing sound, like a white-hot rod being shoved into a pound of meat; for a half second, Carlos glimpsed a slight distortion in the air. Then Chris screamed and fell back from the boulder, clutching at his left shoulder just above the biceps. Carlos scrambled up the outcropping, grabbed Chris, and hauled him down next to him. He pulled aside his hand, looked closely: a blackened hole in his jacket, about a quarter inch in diameter. The laser had lanced through his shoulder, cauterizing the flesh and leaving an entrance wound that smelled like burned pork. Apparently the Diablo team wasn't being too particular about its targets. . . .

"Son of a bitch shot me!" Chris winced as he clasped a hand across his shoulder. "I don't believe it! He just—"

"Shut up." The falls were only a few hundred yards away, but Carlos needed to slow the Diablos down somehow, or they'd never reach them. "Stay here," he whispered, then he scrambled up the boulder again, careful to keep his head down.

A quick peek through the rifle scope showed that the two figures were still beneath the bluffs. They were heading in his direction, but their heavy armor and the loose rock beneath their feet might buy him a few seconds. Switching off the IR, Carlos peered through the scope at the top of the bluffs. There it was: an icicle formation, precariously suspended above the rockslide far below. He took careful aim, then squeezed the trigger.

Bullets split through the ice. The formation shattered, plummeted to the ground. The Diablos had no time to react before hundreds of pounds of ice cascaded down on them. The one in front escaped the worst of it, but the rear Diablo was knocked off its feet. Something within its carapace must have shorted out, because it suddenly became visible: a sand-colored golem made of ceramic alloy, its enormous arms awkwardly thrown outward as the man inside struggled to regain balance. As it toppled and fell, the team leader, now rendered tenuously visible by the ice and snow that covered its carapace, lumberously turned toward it.

Good. That might hold them for a few minutes. Carlos slid down off the boulder, wrenched Chris to his feet. "Get going! And if you do anything like that again, I swear I'll—"

"They shot me!" Holding his shoulder, Chris stared back at the Diablos. "I can't believe they . . ."

"You're expecting a medal?" Carlos shoved him. "Hurry up, or I'm leaving you behind!" He wondered why he hadn't done so already.

They plunged through the forest, dodging large rocks and fallen timber, branches whipping their faces as they raced down the hillside. Carlos felt ice within his lungs, burning him from the inside out; he coughed, wiping snow from his face with his free hand. The dull rumble of the falls grew louder, becoming a roar; through the trees, he could make out a thin white haze. Chris blindly followed him, staggering with each step he took. They needed to rest, take care of his wound, but that was out of the question. It wouldn't be long before the Diablos recovered; soon they'd be on them again, tracking them by their body-heat signatures, the sound of their breathing. If they stopped, even for a second . . .

The rumble became a deep-throated roar, and suddenly they were through the trees. A chasm opened before them: a vast gorge, several hundred feet in diameter, an enormous sinkhole deep within the mountains. Sixty feet to the right, Goat Kill Creek plunged into the gorge, a sixty-foot waterfall spilling down upon jagged rocks. Water foamed at the bottom of the falls, churned away into the valley beyond.

Chris stopped, stared into the abyss. "Oh, great," he rasped. "Just wonderful. Now where are we going to . . . ?"

"This way." Carlos turned to the right, began making his way along the edge of the gorge. If they hadn't lost the trail, it would have led them straight to the top of Johnson Falls. As it was, they'd have to bushwhack it. He could only hope that the Diablos were still behind them. . . .

From somewhere down in the valley, the distant chatter of automatic gunfire echoed off the granite well of the gorge. That would be Marie's group, engaging the other Diablo team. They must have homed in on Constanza's signal. Yet his sister had the benefit of three armed men at her side, along with a stolen skimmer. All he had was his rifle. . . .

"It's not too late. . . ." Out of breath, holding on to his shoulder, Chris collapsed against a tree. He gazed at Carlos with red-rimmed eyes. "It's not too late to give up . . . if we surrender, they might just take us prisoner . . . that's all she wants. . . ."

"You want to stay here, go ahead." Carlos searched the wooded slope above them. No doubt the Diablos were homing in upon their voices. "Give her my best regards."

At first it seemed as if Chris was going to remain behind. Then he apparently thought better of it and staggered to his feet. "Hope you know where you're going."

Carlos nodded, turned away. He did . . . but he wasn't about to let Chris know that.

They continued moving toward the falls. Without a trail to follow, Carlos had to rely on his sense of the land. Over the course of the last two years, though, he'd explored every gully and knob of this valley; the terrain was more familiar to him than the neighborhood in Huntsville where he'd spent his childhood. Somewhere farther up the hillside, he could hear faint noises; the Diablos weren't very far behind. The sound of rushing water was very loud now. Only a short way to go . . .

A sudden flash of heat against his face, and suddenly a tree branch just above his head snapped and fell, missing him by only a few inches. "Run!" he yelled, and took off, not bothering to look to see where the shot had come from.

They were sprinting headlong through the forest. Carlos couldn't see the falls anymore; the gorge was somewhere behind him. Chris was right on his heels, panting as he struggled to keep up. Another beam sliced bark off a tree a few yards to their right. The Diablo team knew where they were, but they didn't have a clear line of sight; they were firing blindly into the woods. All he and Chris could do was stay in motion, hope the trees would foul the Diablos' aim.

They were above the falls, with the creek to their left and the hillside to their right, when Carlos came upon the trail they'd lost. "This way!" he snapped, then turned to the left, his boots thudding against the soft snow on the path as he headed straight for the creek. He knew exactly where they were now; the rest of the way was clear. If they could only make it a few more yards . . .

There it was: the bridge.

Fifty feet long, a long row of rough-barked planks suspended by taut cables made of coiled tree vine, it swayed above the rushing waters of Goat Kill Creek, faintly obscured by the lingering haze of the morning fog. Two days earlier, he and his team had crossed the bridge while the first flakes of snow of the approaching storm fell upon them. Now the planks were coated with a thin glaze of ice, the ropes collecting snow; the bridge seemed frail and weather-beaten, but it was sturdy nonetheless.

Carlos sprinted past the two blackwood trees around which the support cables had been lashed. The bridge creaked as it took his weight, swayed slightly. On the way back, the shags would have waded across the shallows a little farther upstream while their riders leisurely marched across the bridge, but now the shags were gone and the bridge was his avenue of escape. Glancing back, he saw Chris right behind him. No time to savor the surprise on his face. Just a few more yards to the other side of the creek . . .

Carlos was halfway across the bridge, barely touching the frayed hand ropes as he dashed across the slick boards, when he heard someone shout his name. Looking up, he saw a figure emerge from the woods on the opposite shore, waving both arms above his head. Carlos raised a hand, started to wave back . . .

"Down!"

Carlos barely heard Chris yell before he was knocked off his feet. He went facedown; the rifle fell from his hands, clattered upon the bridge behind him. He glanced up just in time to see a thumb-sized hole appear on the walkway only a few inches away, melting the snow and causing the damp wood to sizzle.

Twisting sideways, he looked back, and for the first time he saw one of the Diablos clearly: a mechanical man, like a robot from one of the Japanese cartoons he'd watched on netv as a kid, only lacking a head. It stood at the end of the bridge, a sensor pod protruding from its massive chest peering at him like a cyclopean eye. The sausage-shaped particle-beam cannon mounted upon its right shoulder swiveled toward him. In that instant, he knew that the Diablo was locking him in its sights. The next shot wouldn't miss. . . .

"Run!" Chris shouted. "Go!" And then he brought up the rifle Carlos had dropped, opened fire on the Diablo.

Armor pinged as bullets ricocheted. The Diablo staggered, but didn't fall. Now he could see the second unit, coming down the trail just behind it . . .

"Get out of here!" Chris didn't look back at him. "Go, dammit!"

Scrambling to his knees, Carlos grabbed the hand ropes. He'd barely hauled himself to his feet when there was a hollow *shush!* above his head.

What the hell . . . ?

A half second later an explosion ripped across the place where the Diablos had been standing. He turned around to look. . . .

His feet slipped on the wet planks. Off-balance, he tried to grab the ropes, but the bridge seemed to twist beneath him, and suddenly he was no longer on it.

For a timeless moment, he was suspended in midair, a limp doll flying through space. Then there was a tremendous blow against his back, and he was underwater.

A thousand tiny knives stung his face. He involuntarily gasped, and freezing water rushed down his throat. Darkness closed upon him; fighting panic, he began to swim as hard as he could, kicking and clawing his way toward the shimmering blue light above him.

C'mon, c'mon, c'mon . . . ! You can't die here!

His head broke the surface. Coughing up water, Carlos began to thrash his way through the swift current. The undertow clutched at his ankles, threatening to yank him under once more. His thick clothing was waterlogged; it was as if the lining of his parka were filled with wet cement, his boots strapped to ten-pound weights. It was all he could do just to stay afloat.

Pain lanced through his right knee as it connected with a boulder he couldn't see. Gritting his teeth, Carlos floundered toward shore. It was still more than twenty feet away; and he could hear the roar of the falls as he was pulled toward them. Another dozen yards or so, and he would hurtle over the edge, falling into the gorge to be smashed against the rocks far below. . . .

He kicked harder, fighting to keep his head above water, trying to swim with the current instead of against it. Foot by foot, the shore came closer; he spotted a dead tree that had fallen into the creek. He managed to reach it, but when he grabbed at a branch it broke off at the root, and the rapids seized him once again and hauled him away.

The roar was deafening. Water spit at his face, blinding him. Turning his head, he saw the edge of the falls less than a dozen feet away. But his toes were touching sand, the soles of his boots sliding off rocks. If he could only grab hold of something, pull himself through those precious few inches that remained between him and dry land . . .

Another boulder rose from the waters only a foot from shore. The current swept him toward it. He wrapped his right forearm around the rock, held on with the last of his strength. He only had to reach out with his other hand, find something else to . . .

Something grasped the hood of his parka, hauled him upward. It was as if a mighty hand had reached down from the sky to tear him out of the violent water, for in the next instant he was dragged from the creek and onto firm ground.

Carlos lay facedown on the riverbank, gasping for breath as he trembled against the frigid air. So cold, so incredibly cold . . .

He saw a pair of boots, old and worn, with animal skins tightly wrapped the ankles. Someone from Defiance. Probably the same guys who'd taken out the Diablo team. "Man, I'm so glad to see you," he mumbled as he raised his head. "I thought I . . ."

The face that peered down at him was inhuman.

An elongated jaw, covered with a coarse beard, with yellowed fangs protruding from his mouth. A filthy parka beneath a soiled white robe, a pair of leathery wings rising through slits on its back. Eyes dark but brilliant, kindly yet insane.

"Zoltan?" Carlos whispered.

From somewhere nearby, voices. The gargoyle looked up, glanced in their direction. Without another word, he stood up and scuttled away, heading for the waterfall only a few feet away. He climbed onto a large boulder overlooking the gorge. His wings extended to their full length; he raised his arms to grasp their leading edges with taloned hands.

"No!" Carlos yelled.

Then the figure flung himself into the chasm.

Carlos raised himself on his hands and knees just in time to catch a glimpse of a bat-winged shape gliding across Johnson Falls. Within moments it disappeared from sight, vanishing into the shadows of the trees at the bottom of the gorge.

He was still staring after it when Chris came up behind him. Several men were behind him; Carlos couldn't tell if they were following him or chasing him, and for the moment it didn't matter. "Hey, man, you all right?" he said, laying a hand on his arm. "We thought you were dead."

"I just . . ." Carlos found himself shaking, not so much from the cold but from the face he'd just seen. Would they believe him? He wasn't sure he believed it himself. From somewhere not far away, he heard a gyro approaching. They weren't out of trouble yet. "Never mind," he murmured. "Let's just get out of here."

GABRIEL 76/0932—FORT LOPEZ

The screen showed two men on a rope bridge, one lying face-down, the other standing above him with a rifle, firing toward the camera. Then the camera zoomed past them, briefly focusing upon a couple of figures within the shadows of the trees on the other side of the creek. One of them bore something on his shoulder. Above the chatter of gunfire, they heard the squad leader's voice:

"Reinforcements spotted. Moving in to . . . oh, shit, they've got a . . . !"

A brief flash from the opposite side of the bridge. The last image was that of a small, dark shape hurtling toward the camera. Then the screen went blank.

"That's it, sir." Cartman looked up from his console. "No contact after that."

Baptiste said nothing. He didn't need another replay from Alpha Leader's external camera to know what had happened: the Diablo team had been taken out by a shoulder-launched RPG, probably one of the weapons stolen from Liberty during one of Rigil Kent's raids.

And it wasn't just Diablo Alpha that had been brought down. When Diablo Bravo had closed in upon Constanza's signal, about seven miles downstream from the falls, they found the missing patrol skimmer afloat next to the creek bank, tied to a tree. It appeared to be abandoned, but when the Diablos moved in to investigate, they came under fire by a small group of armed men lurking on the nearby hillside. Bravo could have fought them off without any problem, but it turned out that they were only a diversion; the skimmer wasn't deserted, and the men aboard knew how to operate its chain gun. All contact with Bravo team was lost less than a minute later; ten minutes after that, Alpha went off-line.

Two Diablo teams—four specially trained soldiers, equipped with state-of-the-art Union Guard combat armor—taken out by little more than guerrilla forces armed with stolen weapons. What was supposed to have been a tactical operation had become a total loss of men and equipment. Baptiste closed his eyes, rubbed his temples with his fingertips. It should have been easy. . . .

"Sir? Flight One and Flight Two are still on standby. Awaiting new orders."

Baptiste opened his eyes. Cartman patiently waited for him to tell them what to do now. The situation room had gone quiet, the officers seated at the consoles silently watching him. Two gyros remained on the scene, hovering at opposite ends of the operation zone; if the mission had been successful, they would have retrieved Alpha and Bravo, perhaps even taken aboard prisoners. That wasn't going to happen now, though, was it?

"Tell them to return to base," Baptiste murmured. "We'll . . ."

"No. Cancel that order, Sergeant."

Luisa Hernandez had been standing quietly off to one side, observing events as they unfolded. Now she walked into the light, her back erect as she approached Baptiste. "We're not through yet, Captain. There's still work to be done."

Baptiste let out his breath. "With all due respect, Matriarch, I disagree. Our ground forces . . ."

"Nullified, yes. I'm aware of that." Her face was taut, her mouth drawn into a straight line. "Nonetheless, we still have two units in the air. We can use them to our advantage." Before Baptiste could object, she pointed to the screen he had just been studying. "Sergeant, run back what we just saw." Cartman turned back to his console, tapped a few keys. Once more, the last few seconds captured by the team leader's on-board camera appeared. "Freeze it. Look at this, Captain, and tell me what's out of place here."

Baptiste examined the image. Nothing here he hadn't seen twice already. "I don't understand what you . . ."

"The bridge, Captain. Look at the bridge. For almost nine Earth-years, we've searched every square mile of Midland, both from high orbit and from low-altitude sorties. Never once have we spotted anything like this. Now, out in the middle of nowhere, we find a rope bridge. Why do you think that is?"

Before he could answer, Hernandez marched over to the map wall. "No one builds a bridge unless they mean to use it," she continued as she pointed to the last-known positions of Alpha and Bravo teams. "It can't be a coincidence that there were armed men in the area." Laying a fingertip upon the glass, she traced a circle around the upper part of the river valley. "Put it together. Their settlement must be located somewhere within range. If we act quickly enough, we may be able to find it."

Murmurs around the room as officers caught on to what she was saying. Baptiste found himself nodding in agreement. With two gyros still airborne over the valley, they might be able to backtrack the opposition's movements to their base camp. And yet . . .

"We can do this," he said, carefully choosing his words, "but I must urge you to be cautious. You may be overlooking something."

Hernandez scowled. "And that is?"

"We tried to lay a trap for them . . . but could it be that they've laid a trap for us?"

Carlos was pulling on a dry shirt when he heard voices from the mouth of the cave. Leaving the coarse tunic unbuttoned, he bent down to snatch up his rifle from where he had rested it against the wall. A few seconds later, the chopping thrum of rotors echoed through the tunnel as a gyro passed low overhead, just a few hundred feet above the gorge.

"Someone's coming." Seated near the lantern burning on the cave floor, Chris looked up. "Think it's the other Diablo team?"

Carlos didn't reply. He checked the cartridge—about eight rounds left. Not enough to hold off a determined assault. He glanced at Ted LeMare; the older man was guarding Chris, his rifle pointed at his back. Ted said nothing, but his attention was no longer on their prisoner but on the cave entrance. Chris had sworn that he wasn't carrying another homing device, and even if he was, they were far enough underground that a low-frequency radio signal wouldn't penetrate the granite around them. The gyro could simply be making another random sweep, as it had done three times already.

Chris had saved his life up on the bridge. But Carlos wasn't ready to trust him quite yet.

Jack Dreyfus was standing watch near the cave entrance. As the gyro moved away, he raised a hand to signal that the coast was clear, then disappeared from sight. More voices, this time closer. One sounded like Barry; Jack was doubtless relieved to find that his son was still alive. Carlos relaxed; he put down his gun, reached for the wool sweater lying nearby. Jack wasn't the only one to be grateful; when Henry Johnson had discovered this natural cave in the bluffs below the falls that now bore his name, he recommended that it should be stocked with spare clothes, food, and a fish-oil lantern, just in case a hunting party who'd lost their way might need them at some future time. Henry's foresight had been correct; Carlos made a mental note to buy him a drink the next time he saw him.

Light flickered off the cave walls. Jack appeared a moment later, flashlight in one hand, his other arm around Barry's shoulder. Behind them were Marie, Lars, and Garth, with Jean Swenson bringing up the rear. Marie rushed past the others, almost dropping her rifle in her haste to embrace her brother. No words were necessary; they wrapped their arms around each other, and Carlos felt his sister tremble against him. The disgust he'd felt toward her only the day before vanished; she was safe, and right then that was all that mattered.

"Welcome to the party." Ted lowered his gun, stepped away from Chris. "Got some food if anyone's hungry. Just beans, but—"

"Man, I'd eat a creek crab if . . . hey, there's the son of a bitch!" Chris had barely risen to his feet before Lars lunged across the cave to grab him by the collar of his jacket and slam him against the wall. Before anyone could stop him, he yanked a Union Guard automatic from his belt. "Man, I was hoping I'd see you again," he snarled, shoving it against Chris's face. "Payback time for you!"

"Cut it out!" Carlos got his hand on the gun, pulled it away. "No one's paying anyone back! He's with us!"

"A little late for that," Marie said quietly, as Ted hauled Lars away from Chris. "His pal's already paid up."

Carlos looked at her. "Don't tell me you . . ."

"She had no choice." Barry went to assist Garth. For the first time, Carlos saw that the kid was walking with the aid of a tree branch, his right knee wrapped in a bloodstained bandage. "Constanza was playing possum all along," he continued as he helped Garth hobble over to the thin circle of warmth cast by the lantern. "After we made it to the rendezvous point yesterday, he dropped the shell-shock act and made a grab for Garth's rifle. He got off a shot before Marie took him down."

"Enrique was an intelligence agent." Chris's face was ashen; he avoided looking at anyone. "He was a civilian scientist, sure . . . I didn't lie about that part . . . but his primary mission was this operation. I guess he wanted to make sure that the skimmer didn't fall into enemy . . . into your hands."

"We searched his body, found the tracking device." Barry helped Garth sit down, making sure that his wounded leg was set straight. "We tried to contact you, but we couldn't get through."

"My unit was switched off. The shags bolted when the gyros showed up, and that's when I lost it." Carlos nodded toward Chris. "He was wearing one, too. The whole thing was a setup. We were supposed to capture them so that the Union Guard could track us down."

"But it backfired." Ted moved away from Lars. "When Marie called in and told us what happened, Captain Lee sent Jack and me out to find you guys and Jean to look for the others. Lucky for us that we caught up with you at the bridge."

"Lucky for us that you decided to pack an RPG, too." Carlos couldn't help but grin.

Jack shrugged. "No luck to it. We figured that you might need some heavy artillery if the Union was sending a squad after you."

"We left Constanza's tracker aboard the skimmer, then hunkered down and waited for them to show up." Marie bent down to check Garth's bandage. "The skimmer's gun was what saved us. Weren't counting on having those . . . what were those things, anyway?"

"Diablos. Nasty stuff." Chris was nervous, but he appeared to realize that he wasn't going to be executed so long as he cooperated. Or perhaps there was more to it than that; Carlos noticed how he kept looking at Ted, Jack, and Jean, former *Alabama* crew members, with newfound appreciation, familiar faces he hadn't seen in years. They were far from being long-lost friends, but neither were they strangers. "It's a good thing you managed to—"

"Stop yanking me." Lars wasn't in a forgiving mood. He took his gun back from Carlos. Although he didn't aim at Chris again, neither did he return it to his belt. "If you guys hadn't screwed up, we'd all be prisoners by now. Or dead."

"And Constanza might have led them to Defiance." Barry glanced at Chris. "You had the right idea, leading him away like that."

"I had a hunch, that's all." Carlos shrugged. "It was the long way, but . . ."

"What sort of . . . ? Wait a minute, I don't get it." Now Chris was confused; he looked first at Barry, then at Carlos. "I thought you were taking me back to your camp."

Carlos knelt by the lantern. "Not the straight way, I wasn't," he said, warming his hands. "The path we took is a hunting trail. We put up the bridge late last year as an easy way of getting across the creek to Mt. Aldrich, but it's not the direct route to getting home."

"Then you knew. . . ."

"I didn't know anything." Carlos shook his head. "Like I said, I only had a suspicion. That's why I told Barry to meet us upstream from where we found you. If your friends hadn't shown up, we would have crossed the bridge, then doubled back and met up with them a few miles down the creek. If everything looked safe, then we would have taken you to Defiance."

He clasped his hands together. "Which brings us back to the here and now," he went on. "Technically speaking, you're a prisoner of war. Not only that, but you're a traitor, too."

"I told you why I did what I did. You heard what I said last night. . . ."

"That was last night. We didn't know you were setting us up." Carlos turned the lantern's wheel, feeding more fish oil to the wick to make it burn a little higher. Different campfire, but the same conversation, continued only a few hours later. "Cards on the table, buddy. Only way either of us is going to get out of this is to deal straight."

From somewhere outside, they could hear the Union gyros prowling back and forth across the gorge as they searched for Rigil Kent. "We both have something to win," Carlos went on, "and we both have something to lose. You want to see your mother again . . . and believe me, she wants to see you, too. We've got an injured soldier, and no one wants to wait here until Hernandez sends in another Diablo team. And I think you know by now that she considers you expendable."

Chris slowly nodded. Everyone was watching him. "We want to go home," Carlos continued. "Some of these guys would just as soon shoot you, but I'm willing to give you a second chance."

"I . . ." Chris hesitated. "Why would you do that?"

"Oh, for the love of . . ." Lars turned away in disgust. "Don't trust him. He's a friggin' boid in the bush."

"Shut up and gimme your radio." Carlos held out his hand, staring at Lars until he surrendered his unit. "A long time ago we were friends. We grew up together. Then I made a mistake, then you made a mistake, then . . ." He shook his head. "Maybe it's time we got past all that. Do you want to go home, Chris?"

For a moment, there was no one else in the cave. Just the two of them, guys who'd played army with toy guns, told each other dirty jokes, shared secrets about teachers and girls. They had gone to the stars together, watched their fathers die, gone on a misguided adventure and survived only to become distant from one another, and finally enemies. Yet Carlos knew that, even if Chris said no, he'd never kill him. He'd had that chance once already that morning and hadn't taken it. For better or worse, he was still his friend.

"Yeah." Chris's voice was very quiet. "I'd like that."

Carlos nodded. "Okay. We can do that . . . but first you've got to prove yourself."

Chris watched as Carlos unfolded the radio antenna. "What do you want me to do?"

"You've been a traitor before." Carlos extended the unit to him. "Now I want you to be a traitor again."

"Have they spotted him yet?" Baptiste approached Cartman; who was now monitoring communications from Flight One.

"No, sir. He's still . . ." The sergeant stopped, cupped a hand against his ear. "Just a moment. They've got movement on the river, not far from the falls."

"Pull up the forward camera." Baptiste watched as the middle screen of the carrel lit to display an image from the gyro's nose camera. He could see what its pilot was seeing: an airborne view of the gorge, the falls in the background, the creek directly below. The image tilted slightly to the right as the aircraft swung around. "Give me the audio feed, too," he added. "I want to hear what they're saying."

"Where's Flight Two?" Luisa Hernandez had come up to stand beside him. "They should be close by."

"Just saw something down there. Close to the creek bank, about seventy feet from the falls." The voice of Flight One's pilot was laced with static, yet discernible. *"Closing in . . ."*

"Flight Two coming in to cover Flight One, ma'am." Without waiting to be told, Acosta tapped at her keyboard. The screen above her board showed an image from the Flight Two's nose camera, nearly the same as Flight One's, except from a higher altitude. The other gyro was visible in the foreground, about two hundred feet below. "Do you want audio feed?"

"Negative." Baptiste spoke before the Matriarch could respond; he caught the sour look on her face, but chose to ignore it. He didn't want to be distracted by cross talk between the pilots. "Monitor their channel and tell me if something important comes up," he told Acosta, then returned his attention to the screen in front of him. "Patch me into Flight One," he said, touching his jaw. "Flight One, this is Gold Ops. What do you have?"

The image steadied, became horizontal; the falls were no longer visible, and they could only see the rushing waters of the creek. *"Gold Ops, we thought we saw something move down there. Could be our man. Coming down to check it out."*

"We copy, Flight One." Baptiste continued to stare at the screen. "Get ready for pickup, but keep a sharp eye out. We don't know what's down there. Over."

"Suspicious, aren't you?" During all this, Gregor Hull had glided up behind him; now he stood between him and the Matriarch, a black-robed specter, aloof yet omnipresent. "You don't trust our man anymore?"

Baptiste gnawed his lower lip, refrained from making a comment. No, he did not. Ten minutes ago, Flight One had received a radio message on a coded frequency from Chief Proctor Levin. Everyone else involved in the operation had been lost so far, and Levin's tracer had failed almost two and a half hours ago. Suddenly, Levin had made contact, claiming that he'd escaped from his captors and requesting rescue, with pickup in the gorge below the falls.

Baptiste shot a glance at the Matriarch from the corner of his eye. Her face remained stoical, registering no emotion. The moment the Diablo teams had hit the ground, she'd written off Levin as expendable; he'd been little more than bait for Rigil Kent, not worth saving if he got in the way. Now that he was known to be alive, she wanted him back. All well and good. The mission had been a failure; they might be able to salvage something from it yet.

Nonetheless, before Diablo Alpha had been brought down, the team leader's camera had captured two men on the bridge. The camera had moved away before their blurred features could be discerned. One of them had opened fire upon the hunter-killer team just moments before it was wiped out.

He could have been Carlos Montero. That was what the Matriarch believed. Yet he might have been someone else . . .

"Visual acquisition." The pilot's fuzzed voice jerked him from his reverie. *"We got someone, Gold Ops. Two down, dead ahead . . ."*

Baptiste rested his hands upon the back of Cartman's chair, leaned close to study the screen. Yes, there he was: a small figure, standing on a boulder near the creek's edge, waving both hands above his head. The camera zoomed in, caught a face: a young man, in his late twenties, with long blond hair and a short beard.

"That's him." The Matriarch smiled. "Flight One, go down and take him aboard."

"I don't think that's . . ."

"We need him," she said, barely glancing his way. "He's been in close contact with Rigil Kent. He may know something we . . ."

"Gold Ops! We're . . . !"

A sharp bang, followed by a high-pitched screech. In the same instant, the screen went dark. "Flight One down!" Acosta shouted. "Flight One is down!"

Hernandez's mouth dropped open. "What? I . . . what did you . . . ?"

Baptiste shoved her aside, bolted toward the next carrel. Acosta stared at her screen, watching in openmouthed horror as a flaming mass plummeted into the creek, rotors still spinning as it disintegrated against the rocks. "It just . . . sir, it just . . ."

"Get them out of there!" Baptiste yelled. The warrant officer was in shock, unable to perform her duty; he shoved her aside, stabbed at the console. "Flight Two, this is Gold Ops! Get out of there! Return to base at—"

"No!" The Matriarch rushed forward, tried to pull Baptiste away from the console "He's down there! Rigil Kent is down there! We've almost got . . . !"

Baptiste turned around, shoved her away with both hands. Staggering back, she tripped over the feet of the sergeant. She would have fallen to the floor if one of bodyguards hadn't been there to catch her. "Hold her!" Baptiste yelled, snapping his finger at the Guardsman. "Detain the Matriarch! That's an order!"

The soldier hesitated, caught in a moment of uncertainty about whose authority was greater. Baptiste was a Union Astronautica senior officer, though, while Hernandez was a civilian, so his duty was clear. He gently grasped Hernandez's arm, murmured something to her. For a moment it seemed as if she would resist, then she surrendered.

"We copy, Gold Ops. Returning to base." Baptiste looked at the screen again, saw the gorge disappear as the gyro peeled away. The pilot was probably grateful to receive the order to withdraw. Someone down there had an RPG; the next heat seeker would have his name on it.

"You're out of line, Captain." Hernandez glowered at him, still held back by the Guardsman. "I can have you placed under arrest for this."

"No, ma'am, you can't." Before Baptiste could respond, Savant Hull stepped forward. "This is a military operation, and Captain Baptiste is the commanding officer. In this instance, his authority supersedes yours."

She stared first at him, then at Baptiste. "You can't . . ."

"It's done." Baptiste let out his breath. "This mission is over. I'm not going to put anyone else at risk just so that—"

"Matriarch?" Acosta looked over at her. "Flight Two says they're receiving another ground transmission. The person sending it says he wants to talk to you . . . personally."

For a second, no one said anything. "Put it on so that we can all hear," Baptiste said quietly. "And tell Flight Two to remain on station."

A few moments passed while the orders were carried out. Then the fuzzed tones of a low-frequency radio signal filled the situation room, and they heard a young man's voice:

"Matriarch Hernandez, do you hear me?"

Acosta nodded, indicating that she was patched into the comlink. The Matriarch prodded her jaw. "I hear you, Chief . . . Chris, I mean. Good to know you're alive and well."

"Yeah, I'm still here." A short, rancorous laugh. *"How nice of you to be concerned, considering that one of your men put a hole in me. Know what a laser feels like when it's going through your shoulder? Hurts like hell, lemme tell you."*

"I'm sure it was a mistake." The left corner of the Matriarch's mouth twitched upward. "We tried to pick you up, but we came under enemy fire. If you'll tell us where you are, we can make another attempt."

A low hiss from behind Baptiste. From the corner of his eye, he saw Cortez standing nearby. Like everyone else in the room, he was silently listening to this exchange. The Matriarch's calm self-assurance had returned; she cast a smug look at Baptiste. This wasn't over yet. She'd get her man back, then they'd hunt down Rigil Kent.

"No, I don't think so, but thanks anyway. Before I go though, a friend of mine would like to talk to you."

The Matriarch's eyes widened. She was about to reply when another voice came over. *"Matriarch Hernandez, this is Rigil Kent. . . ."*

Murmurs swept through the room; Baptiste heard someone mutter something obscene. Acosta reached to her console, trying to get a lock on the source of the signal. *"I'm going to make this quick,"* the voice continued. *"You've succeeded in getting a lot of your people killed today, I'm sorry for that, but you picked the fight, not us. We appreciate one thing, though . . . convincing Chris that he was on the wrong side. He's back with us now. Thanks for that, at least."*

Hernandez's face had gone pale. "You . . . you're holding him prisoner," she stammered. "I demand that you . . . that you release him immediately before we . . ."

"You're in no position to demand anything, Matriarch. Now go away. This is our home, and you're not wanted here."

The transmission ceased suddenly, as if someone at the other end had flipped a switch. Baptiste looked down at Acosta, and she shook her head; she'd failed to pinpoint its source. "Tell Flight Two to return to base," he murmured, then he turned to speak to the Matriarch.

Luisa Hernandez was no longer listening. Without another word, she turned her back on him and walked away. No one dared to speak or even look at her as she strode through the operations center, followed a few steps behind by her reluctant bodyguard. The Guardsman stationed at the exit saluted as she marched past him; his stiff gesture went unacknowledged. Winter sunlight briefly streamed through the door, followed by a cold draft before it slammed shut again.

It had been a bad morning for the colonial governor of Coyote.

GABRIEL 76/1803—DEFIANCE, MIDLAND

Twilight came as a gradual lengthening of shadows upon the snow-covered ground, cast by Uma as it sank behind the summit of Mt. Shaw. A cool wind drifted through the blackwoods, curling the woodsmoke that rose from fieldstone ovens sheltered by the forest canopy, causing bamboo chimes to rattle and clank gently in random melody. As darkness closed upon the village, fish-oil lamps flickered to life within tree house windows. Dogs barked as they helped their masters herd goats and sheep into their pens; within work sheds on the ground, glassblowers and potters extinguished their kilns, put away their tools. The evening air was filled with the aroma of cooking food; here and there were the creaking of rope ladders, the muted buzz of conversation, an occasional laugh. The day was done; Defiance was settling down for the night.

"I can see why they never found you." Chris walked alongside Carlos as they strolled along a path leading through the center of town. All around them, small wood-frame cabins were suspended within the boughs of enormous trees, with rope ladders that led to floor hatches and porches dangling to the ground below. "A hundred people here . . ."

"A hundred and fifty-two. Like you said, we've been having a population explosion lately." Chris glanced at him, and he shrugged. "We've had a few more babies, and we've picked up some people from your side of the river."

"All these people in one place, and the Union never figured out where you were." Chris winced as he shook his head. He'd spent the better part of the afternoon in the clinic, letting Dr. Okada tend to his shoulder

wound, yet every move he made hurt a little. "But the farms, the graz-
ing land. How did you . . . ?

"See all those poles over there?" Carlos pointed toward a broad
meadow near the edge of the forest. "That's where we hang camouflage
nets. From above, it looks like just another empty field. Can't tell we've
got crops there unless you approach them from the ground." He had already shown him the water tanks, the grain sheds, the privies and communal bathhouses, all concealed by the blackwoods surrounding them.
"We're careful about how we do things," he added. "There's some rules
you're going to have to learn."

"Like what?"

As he spoke, a figure came toward them: Ron Schmidt, who long ago
had worn the uniform of the United Republic Service. Now he wore a
catskin serape over his patched URS parka, a carbine slung on its strap
from his shoulder. "Ten minutes," he murmured. Carlos raised a hand
and he went on, pausing to shine a flashlight beam upon a couple of
children playing on a catwalk between two tree houses.

"That's one of 'em," Carlos said. "No one outdoors after sundown except the night watch. Keeps down on thermal emissions . . . especially
important during winter. The chimneys have caps on them, and all the
windows have shutters. In ten minutes, it'll be dark as hell around here.
Unless you know where to look, you'd never know there was someone
living here."

"You've got it all figured out."

Carlos shook his head. "No, not really. We've been lucky so far. The
Union hasn't found us because they didn't know where to look. But
now they know we're somewhere in this valley, so they're going to
come searching for us. I don't think trees and camouflage nets are going
to hide us much longer."

"And you're going to blame me, right?"

"Uh-uh." Carlos stopped, turned toward him. He couldn't see Chris's
face, but he could hear the accusation in his voice. "So far as I'm concerned, our bills are paid. You're going to have to work things out with
everyone else, but . . ."

He stopped. They weren't friends again; there were still many things that had to be settled between them. On the other hand, neither were they enemies anymore. They would just have to see how things would come out, one day at a time. "When push came to shove, you did the right thing," he finished. "That'll get around."

"Yeah, well, maybe." Chris didn't seem convinced. "I've been away a while. I'm going to have to . . ."

From a tree house not far away, someone played a bamboo flute. An old tune, "Soldier's Pay," dating back to nineteenth-century America. A few seconds later, a second flute joined in, a little more hesitantly, as if the second person was still learning the melody.

Chris listened, turning his head to focus upon the music. "Is that her?" he asked quietly.

"That's her. She's been getting better. Allegra's been a great help."

"I thought she'd be. That's why I encouraged her to look after my mom." Chris started to walk toward the tree house, then stopped. "Look, there's one thing I've got to know."

"Sure." Carlos shoved his hands in his pockets. "What is it?"

"When you found me, you had a feeling that this was all a setup, but you didn't shoot me. Then you found out for sure that it was a trap, and you didn't shoot me. And then I tried to give you away to the guys who were chasing us, and still you didn't shoot me."

"Yeah? And . . . ?"

Neither of them said anything for a few moments. "Nothing," Chris said at last. "Just checking."

"Go on home," Carlos said quietly. "I think your mother's calling you."

An old line, remembered from a shared childhood, long ago and far away. Chris laughed softly, understanding something that didn't need to be said, then turned to walk toward the light gleaming through the cracks of a shuttered tree house window.

Carlos watched him go. It was late, and he was tired. His wife and child were waiting for him. He turned around, began making his way through the night. For the moment, at least, all was well. Now it was time to go home.

Part 6

SHADY GROVE
(from the memoirs of Wendy Gunther)

The revolution against the Western Hemisphere Union occupation of Coyote was the turning point of our lives. We'd come to the new world to escape one form of tyranny, only to have another take its place; we tried to run away, but found that doing so was little more than a temporary solution. Sooner or later, we had to stand and fight.

No one wanted a war, but we got one anyway. Yet there are worse things than war. I discovered that in the winter of c.y. 06, when the Union Guard attacked Defiance.

They appeared shortly after sunrise on the morning of Anael, Barchiel 29. Bill Boone was just ending his shift on overnight watch when he spotted two aircraft coming in over Mt. Aldrich from the east. He ran to the bell post and sounded the alarm, but it was early and most of us were still in bed, so only a few people managed to grab their guns before the gyros touched down in a farm field about three hundred yards from town.

Carlos and I were awakened by the bell, but we thought it was only another drill until the shooting began. He threw on his clothes, pulled his rifle off its hooks, and was down the ladder before I was even dressed. We'd discussed what we would do if something like this happened, so my duty was clear; I yanked Susan out of her bed, shoved her beneath it, then pulled off the mattress and stuffed it in after her to catch any stray bullets that might come our way. She screamed like hell—little girls don't like rough treatment, least of all before breakfast—and I tried to calm her as best I could, but by then I knew we were in trouble.

I was supposed to stay in the tree house and protect Susan, but that's not what happened. This may sound negligent, but when your home is under attack, you've got a choice: either bolt the door and hide, or pick up a gun and go out to face the enemy. I'd long since made up my mind, without telling Carlos, that if the Union ever attacked Defiance, I wasn't going to play the role of defenseless female. When I was a kid back on Earth, I had the benefit of paramilitary training in Republic youth hostels; if anything, I was a better shot than my husband. So I told Susie to stay put and that Mama would be back soon, then I took down my own rifle, jammed in a cartridge, opened the floor hatch and jumped, not bothering to use the ladder.

I like to think I was brave. Perhaps, but I was also stupid. I was wearing nothing more than a thin nightshirt and a pair of drawstring pants, and in my haste I'd forgotten to pull on moccasins or a jacket; when my bare feet hit the ground, they sank into three inches of snow. If I wasn't fully awake by then, that did the trick. I hardly noticed, though, because all around me were my neighbors, coming down rope ladders and running across catwalks from one blackwood tree to another. An ice-fog lay thick above fields where only last autumn corn had grown high beneath camouflage nets; I couldn't see Carlos, but from the mist I could hear the popcorn sound of guns in full-auto mode, interspersed with the more distant noise of enemy fire.

The snow numbed my feet as a chill wind ripped through my clothes. I was useless as far as leading any sort of cavalry charge, so I headed for the nearest dry spot I could find, a well about a dozen yards away. The low stone wall that surrounded it had been swept clear of snow; I jumped on top, taking cover behind the wooden yoke supporting the bucket.

It was an absurd moment—Wendy Gunther, wife of the legendary Rigil Kent, crouched in her pajamas on top of a well—but there wasn't much else I could do. Leaving the cabin was a bad move; I had realized that by then. Yet there I was, all the same, so I held my rifle against my chest and waited for something to come close enough for me to shoot.

But the Union wasn't fighting fair that day. A sudden boom from out in the fields, then a high-pitched whistle as something hurtled through the air. I barely had time to realize what it was before a tree house only a few dozen feet away exploded. Wood flew in all directions; I instinctively ducked, falling off the wall just in time to avoid having my skull fractured by a broken post that went sailing past my head.

"They've brought in a missile carrier!" someone yelled, and I raised my head to peer over the wall. I couldn't see anything save for vague forms firing into the fog, yet somewhere out there was a Union Guard skimmer. Doubtless it had come up Goat Kill Creek in a coordinated attack with the gyros. Another shriek, then a patch of ground about sixty feet away went up in a fireball. Men were thrown in all directions, hitting the ground as if they were little more than broken toys.

It's easy to talk about courage when you're sitting at the table, sharing a bottle of sourgrass ale with your husband; it's something else again when you find yourself the target of an armored hovercraft loaded with enough rockets to take out a small town. Hiding behind the well, I covered my ears, closed my eyes, tried to wish it all away. It was a bad dream, nothing but a bad dream. In a minute, I'd wake up to find out that I was still in bed, with Carlos curled up against me and Susan asleep on the other side of the room. Yet I couldn't ignore the evidence of my senses: the cold, the smoky odor of burning wood, the gunfire. This was no nightmare. My town was under attack. If we didn't do something, then we were all going to die. . . .

"Get some rifles up here!" All around me, voices. "Don't fall back!" "Find some water, put out that fire!" "C'mon, dammit, *move!*"

No, I thought, *you can't do this. Go back to the cabin. It's warm and dry and safe up there. Susan needs her mother. You're not supposed to be here. . . .*

"Fan out! Don't let 'em get through!"

Another rocket ripped into the settlement. Another tree house went up in flames. For a terrifying moment I thought it was my own, until I looked back and saw that, no, it wasn't mine, but the Gearys'. But it could have been my home, and Susan could have been . . .

"Where's the kids? Someone get the kids out of here!"

In that instant, something came over me. It wasn't bravery, or courage, or honor, or any of those things. Fear, yes, but also pure rage, plain and simple. Someone out there wanted to kill me, but worse than that, they wanted to kill my little girl, too.

And I just went berserk.

Before I fully realized what I was doing, I was on my feet, charging out from the tree house village, racing into the fields with my rifle in my hands. The cold meant little to me now, the fact that I was barefoot even less. Nothing mattered save the cauldron of hate that boiled within me, a white-hot furnace that melted away all considerations for my own safety. This was my home, everyone and everything I loved and held dear. I couldn't—I *wouldn't*—let that be taken away.

Through the fog, I spotted a figure—little more than a silhouette, but obviously a Union soldier. I went down on one knee, braced the rifle stock against my right shoulder. *Line up the target in the crosshairs. Take a deep breath. Hold it. Fire.* The rifle kicked against my shoulder. Three sharp cracks, and the half-seen Guardsman sagged in upon himself, toppled to the ground. I leaped to my feet again, continued to run forward. . . .

"Wendy!" From somewhere behind me, Carlos. "What are you . . . ?"

To my left, another soldier, this one closer than the first. I could see his uniform clearly, along with the face beneath his helmet. He gaped at me in astonishment, as if not believing what he was seeing, then his gun started to turn my way. No time to take careful aim; I sprayed bullets in his direction until he grabbed at the right side of his chest and pitched sideways. He squirmed on the ground, blood bubbling upward from a punctured lung, as I walked over to him. He was trying to raise a hand toward me, as if to beg for mercy, when I fired again. One shot, and his brains were blown across the snow. No mercy.

My friends and neighbors were running past me. I was about to join them when a heavy force slammed into my back, knocking me face-down to the ground. Snow stung my eyes, blinding me for a moment, as the rifle fell from my hands, landing a few feet away. For a second I thought I'd been hit. . . .

"What do you think you're doing?" Carlos was kneeling on top of me, pinning my body to the ground. "Stay down!"

I was trying to crawl out from under him when I heard engines. Rubbing snow from my eyes, I saw the colony's captured Union skimmer roar past, Clark Thompson standing behind the 30mm chain gun mounted above its bubble canopy. He turned the gun on a line of advancing soldiers and mowed them down, then the skimmer—doubtless piloted by Barry Dreyfus, who had liberated the craft only a month earlier during the Goat Kill Creek incident—roared away into the mists.

Carlos removed his knee from my back. "I thought I told you to . . ."

"Get off me!" I impatiently shoved him aside, scrambled to retrieve my rifle. "You want me to fight or what?"

Carlos started to argue, then thought better of it. "Just stick close," he said as he yanked me to my feet. "You don't want to get lost in this."

I wasn't about to object. The soldiers were among us, and it was hand-to-hand combat within a white veil. I caught a glimpse of Paul Dwyer, blood streaming down one side of his face, as he buried a machete within the chest of a soldier. Ron Schmidt and Vonda Cayle ran past us, firing at anything that moved. Ben Harlan and Molly Thompson and Klon Newall: all newcomers to Defiance, yet nonetheless just as determined to defend the settlement as if they'd been with us from the beginning. Ron Schmidt, one of the URS soldiers who'd tried to retake the *Alabama* when it was being hijacked, shot someone, then fell as someone else shot him.

A few feet away, Ellery Balis knelt to the ground, a stolen Union Guard RPG resting upon his right shoulder. As a gyro lifted off a hundred yards away, Ellery trained his weapon on the aircraft. He squeezed the trigger and a shell lanced through the fog. The gyro's port nacelle exploded; the aircraft careened sharply to one side, lost altitude, plummeted back into the mists, and went up as an orange-red blossom. Ellery pumped his fist once, then stood up, tucked the RPG beneath his arm, and ran away.

"Let them handle this." Carlos pulled at me, trying to lead me to safety. "You're only in the way."

"No!" I tore myself loose. "I want to see!" In hindsight, I must have sounded like a petulant child, being told that she couldn't stay to watch the gory part of a flix. And perhaps I was; I'd never been in battle before, and there was a certain terrible fascination to all this. And I'd killed two men myself; now I wanted more.

There were no other soldiers in sight. I could still hear gunfire within the fog, but it was less frequent. Somewhere out there, I heard the chatter of dueling chain guns, like two mad pianists trying to top one another in a lethal symphony. The missile carrier hadn't fired any more rockets, which meant that its crew must be engaging Thompson's skimmer. Another gyro lifted off; I could see wounded Guardsman within its open aft hatch, staring down at us. Ellery fired another grenade at it, but it missed and the gyro peeled away.

And then, all of a sudden, an eerie calm descended upon the field. No more shots. No more explosions. It was if God had come down to silence the guns. Now I could only hear the groans of the wounded, the cries of the dying. The sun had risen above the mountains, its warmth burning away the fog, revealing bodies strewn over the ground. Some still twitching, others perfectly still.

Finally, I felt the cold, and with it, a strange delirium. Leaning against Carlos, I turned away, began to lurch back toward town. It was over. We were safe. No one could touch us. We'd fought back and won. But I felt no jubilation, no rejoicing. Only sickness.

A body lay on the ground before us, lying in a patch of blood-drenched snow. For a second I thought it was a Guardsman, then I came close enough to recognize the face . . .

Tom Shapiro. The former first officer of the *Alabama*, the first man to set foot on Coyote. His chest had been ripped apart, his sightless eyes dully reflecting the cold light of the rising sun.

I stared at him for a few moments, then I tore myself away from Carlos, staggered a few feet, collapsed to my knees and threw up.

We lost Tom that morning . . . and twelve others, too, including Michael Geissal, Tony Lucchesi, and Ron Schmidt. The latter three were blueshirts, members of our local militia: the first to fight, and the first to die. Their lives weren't meaninglessly sacrificed, though; the bodies of fifteen Union Guard soldiers were also found, and no telling how many of their wounded had been airlifted out by the gyro that Ellery failed to take down.

Over twenty of our people were wounded as well—some critically, including Henry Johnson, who took bullets in the gut and his left knee and came close to bleeding to death before Kuniko got to him, and Jean Swenson, who suffered massive internal injuries and severe burns across most of her body when one of the tree houses collapsed on top of her. As soon as the battle was over, we set up a tent as a temporary hospital—Kuniko's infirmary simply wasn't large enough—and started drafting people as blood donors.

Shortly after Defiance was established as a new colony, Kuniko started breaking me in as her assistant. Most of the *Alabama* crew members had first-aid training, but Dr. Okada was the only one among us who had gone to med school. So when I wasn't doling out pills and delivering babies, I was also learning how to perform minor surgery.

If I had been Kuniko's student before the firefight, that day I received my final exam. Until then, the most I'd done was assist her in an emergency appendectomy; after the Union attack I found myself removing bullets, tying off veins, stitching wounds, performing transfusions, and trying like hell not to lose either my wits or my stomach. By noon my arms were drenched with blood up to the elbows; we didn't have enough instruments to exchange them after each operation, so it was all that we could do to have them sterilized in boiling water before we went to work on the next patient. Don't ask about nanites, cloned tissue grafts, or any of that stuff; we didn't have them. This was combat surgery at its most brutal, as primitive as anything since the early twentieth century. We didn't have enough drugs to go around, so we reserved general anesthesia for those who needed it the most, administered local sedatives to the others, and offered bite-blocks and jolts of bearshine to those strong enough to take it.

Not everyone made it. We did our best for Jean, and she toughed it out as long as she could, but shortly after midday she lapsed into a coma and two hours later she passed away. I pulled a sheet over her face and said a silent prayer for her; a few moments to dry my tears, then I went out to tell her husband that she was gone. That was the hardest thing I'd ever done; Ellery probably saved a lot of lives when he shot down one of the gyros, but in the end he'd not been able to save his own wife.

Someone once said that liberty is paid for with the blood of patriots. If so, then the bill was paid in full, for we saw a lot of blood that day.

Sometime around twilight, I finally left the tent and began trudging home, making my way along a quiet path that led through the trees. For a few minutes, I was alone, which was what I needed. I was exhausted, heartsick, and miserable. I'd seen enough violence and death to last a lifetime. The next morning we'd have to bury thirteen of our friends. Up on the high meadows outside of town, their graves were being dug in the frozen ground with pickaxes, along with those for all the soldiers who'd been killed. My husband and daughter were waiting for me; I wanted to take them in my arms, tell them how much I loved them, then collapse in my bed and sleep for a year. It was early evening, yet it felt like midnight.

"Wendy? Got a few minutes?"

I looked around, saw Robert Lee coming toward me. From the Town Council meeting, I assumed; while I was in the tent, Vonda came in to tell me that it was being convened in an emergency session. I was a Council member—the youngest, in fact—but there was no way I could attend. Vonda told me that she'd explain my absence, and someone would tell me later what happened.

"Yeah, sure." The last thing I wanted to do just then was talk to anyone. But this was town business, and it couldn't be avoided. "How did the meeting go?"

"Maybe I should wait till later. You look like you need a rest."

Someone had delivered hot coffee to the tent, but I hadn't eaten all day, and my eyes were heavy-lidded. I was about to agree when I raised my face to look at him. Robert E. Lee wasn't just the mayor; he was also captain of the *Alabama*, our leader from the very beginning. Over the course of the past few years, his dark hair had become streaked with silver, his beard white as ivory. We'd often remarked on how much he'd come to resemble his famous ancestor, sometimes even jokingly referring to him as General Lee, yet at that moment the similarity wasn't just superficial. There was a darkness within his eyes that I'd never seen before; he looked like a man who'd just fought a bloody battle and was aware that he'd have to fight again all too soon. You don't say *sorry, try me again tomorrow* to someone like him.

"No, go on. Let's have it now." I looked around, spotted the well behind which I'd taken cover an impossible amount of time ago. Strange that I would find myself there again; I sat down on the wall, bunching the hood of my parka around my neck.

Robert took a seat beside me. "First off," he began, "I want to tell you what a fine job you've done today. We would have lost more people if it hadn't been for you and Kuniko."

He was trying to say the right things, but only a couple of hours ago I'd pronounced Jean Swenson dead. Doctors might get used to the fact that they occasionally lose patients, but I barely qualified as a paramedic. Jean's death made me sick to my soul, and I wasn't ready to handle any well-meaning words of gratitude.

"Thanks," I mumbled, and there was an uncomfortable silence. Not far away, the ruins of the Geary house smoldered upon the ground. The tree in which it had been built was still standing; blackwoods are as tough as they are large, and it takes a lot to destroy them. If only human flesh were as resilient . . .

"So what happened at the meeting?" I asked again, trying to change the subject.

Robert straightened his back, gave me the full rundown. Two houses were destroyed by enemy fire. The Geary and Sullivan families were moving in with friends until new homes could be built for them, but the Construction Committee informed the Council that it was unlikely that new tree houses could be erected within the next two months—i.e., the end of Machidiel, the last month of winter. A grain silo had also been destroyed; like the cabins, it could be rebuilt, but one-third of the autumn harvest saved for the feeding of livestock had been lost. The Farm Committee had been instructed to put the goats and chickens on half rations and look toward culling their numbers by slaughtering the older animals. That in turn, meant a reduction of food; we could only hope that we'd be able to hold out until we could plant new crops next spring.

Finger-pointing was inevitable. Some of the Council members were inclined to blame Rigil Kent—that is, Carlos and his brigade—for bringing the Union down upon us, yet Robert refused to hear any of it. He pointed out that the Union had been looking for Defiance for over two Coyote years now, and, despite all our precautions, it was only a matter of time before they managed to locate our position. Luisa Hernandez would have ordered a raid even if there hadn't been a resistance movement, he said, and in fact we should be thankful that Rigil Kent had captured a patrol skimmer last month; otherwise, we probably wouldn't have been able to beat off the attack.

There was one bright point. Lew Geary had inspected the missile carrier—hearing that, I had to wonder; though his house had been destroyed, the man was still capable of examining the machine that did it—and determined that it could be salvaged. Even though its cockpit was riddled with bullet holes and one of its engines had been shot up, its launchers still worked, with eight rockets remaining in their magazines. Lew already had his people working on it, and they hoped that the skimmer could be restored to operating condition. To defend the town if—or, more likely, when—the Union returned.

And that was the question. When would they attack again? And what could we do about it?

"This isn't over. Not by a long shot." Robert idly tapped at the ground with a stick he'd picked up. "They know where we are. Sooner or later they'll try again."

"We need to fortify the town."

"We discussed that. Sandbag emplacements, tiger traps. And now that we've got enough guns to go around, everyone is going to be armed." He shrugged. "But I've got a feeling that they were just testing our defenses. Seeing how much we could take."

"You don't think they were serious?"

"Oh, they were serious, all right . . . to a certain extent." He turned his head to gaze across the field where only a few hours earlier we'd fought for our lives. "But we know that they've received several hundred troops from the ship that arrived last month, along with heavy equipment like that missile carrier. So why didn't they throw everything at us at once?"

"They were taking a poke at us. Seeing what we're made of." I remembered the bullies I used to have to deal with when I was in the youth hostel. The dumb ones came straight at you with their fists; if you could take them down the first time, then they'd leave you alone, knowing that you'd fight back and it wasn't worth getting a bloody nose. The guys you really had to watch out for, though, were the ones who prodded and needled you, seeing how much you could take, observing your weaknesses. Only then would they attack—late at night, when you weren't ready for a pillowcase over your head and sawed-off baseball bat to your stomach. "I think I understand."

"I thought you would." Robert nodded appreciatively; he knew my life story. "Then you know our situation. Even if we arm everyone in town, we're still on the defensive. That isn't where you want to be if you have any hope of winning. Sooner or later, we're going to have to take the fight to them."

I raised an eyebrow. "You've got a plan?"

"Sort of." His voice became quiet. "Nothing I've told anyone yet . . . or at least, no one who's still with us. Tom knew, but . . ."

Robert stopped, looked away. Before his hand came up to rub his face, I saw tears in his eyes. As long as I'd known Captain Lee, this was one of the few times I glimpsed even a trace of deep emotion. Perhaps Dana, his mate and the *Alabama*'s former chief engineer, saw a side to him that we didn't. To most of us Robert was intensely private, even enigmatic. Tom Shapiro had not only been one of his senior officers, but also a close friend. Losing him hit closer to home than he was willing to admit.

"I've got an idea, yes," he said, looking back at me again with dry eyes. "If it's going to work, though, I've got to know that we've got little to lose. As it is now, there's too much in our way."

"What are you saying?"

He let out his breath. "We've got to do something about the kids."

As soon as he spoke, I knew he was right. I'd charged into battle, barefoot and with little more than a rifle to defend myself, only because I was afraid for Susan. If Carlos and I had been killed today, then our daughter would have been left an orphan, just as both he and I had been left without parents the first few days after the *Alabama* reached Coyote.

Susan had been the first child born on the new world, but now there were nine other children in Defiance. Among them was Tom's son, Donald, born only a few months later; his wife Kim was not only a widow now but also a single mother. I'd tried my best to protect my daughter, but taking out a couple of soldiers doesn't count for much when a missile carrier is lobbing rockets at your home. And the neighborhood bully likes it when you've got one hand tied behind your back.

"You want to get them out of here?" I asked, and he nodded. "Got any suggestions?"

"In fact, I do," Robert said. And then he told me all about it.

I went home and slept for a few hours. Night had fallen by the time I woke up, and Carlos and Susan already had made dinner. Carlos warmed up some of the leftover stew; while I ate at the table, he took Susie to bed and read her a story. We'd been making our way through *The Chronicles of Prince Rupurt*—a generation of Coyote children were growing up with Leslie Gillis's fantasy—yet I noticed that he skipped the scene where Rupurt fights the skeleton army. Susie had been very quiet all evening; she was ten years old by Gregorian reckoning, so she was very much aware that several of her parents' friends had lost their lives that day, and she didn't need to be frightened any more than she already was. When story time was over, I gave her a good night kiss while Carlos turned the lamps down, then we put on our coats and slipped out onto the porch to have a talk.

We could see lights glowing in tree house windows, hear muted conversations, and yet the paths and crosswalks were empty. There was a certain stillness I'd never seen before, as if Defiance was an injured animal, licking its wounds as it curled in upon itself. Not far away, we could see Lew and Carrie picking through the ruins of their home, their flashlight beams roaming across the wreckage as they searched for any belongings they might be able to salvage. From somewhere nearby, there was the sound of two flutes: Allegra DiSilvio and her companion Sissy Levin, playing "Amazing Grace" in duet as night closed in on town.

Carlos unfolded a couple of camp chairs and set them up on the narrow porch, and we kept our voices low so as not to wake Susan. I told him about what Robert and I had discussed a few hours earlier, how he thought it was wise to send the children away in case there was another attack. I wasn't surprised when Carlos told me that Robert had already broached the subject with him as well.

"I think it's a good idea. If Susan had been killed, it would have been . . ." His voice trailed off, and he looked at me sharply. "That's why you went out there, wasn't it? You were trying to protect her."

"I know. That wasn't part of the agreement." I looked away. "It was either that, or . . ."

"I understand. It was just that . . ." He shook his head. "Look, when Rigil Kent has gone out, I've never had to worry about you and Susie, because I knew you were safe back here. But when I saw you today, I couldn't do what I had to do, because I had to look out after you as well."

"I'm sorry. I didn't mean to—"

"Let me finish." He held up a hand. "I realize all that. You did what you thought had to be done. But you know, and I know, that the next time this happens . . . and there probably will be a next time . . . we can't afford to worry about mothers and children being caught in the cross fire. If we have to . . ."

"You're not listening to me. You think I'm against the idea. Not at all. Not in the slightest. Robert's right. I think it's time to get the kids out of here."

"You do?" He peered at me through the darkness. "How much has he told you? I mean, about where we'd go . . . ?"

"He mentioned a new settlement up north along the Gillis Range. Shady Grove, near Mt. Bonestell. The Union doesn't know about it yet, so . . ." Suddenly, I realized what he'd just said. "What do you mean, 'we'? He asked if I'd be interested in taking the children up there, and I told him I would, but he said nothing about . . ."

"Robert's playing both ends against the middle. Typical politician." Carlos chuckled, then became serious again. "No one expects you to go off into the wilderness all by yourself. It's almost eight hundred miles to Shady Grove. He asked me to go with you, and I told him that I would."

"But . . ." This caught me by surprise. "What about everything else? Like, defending the town?"

"We've got plenty of people here for that. They don't need my help." He hesitated. "There's more to this than you know," he added. "I need to talk to some people up there."

I was about to ask about that before I remembered something Robert had said earlier: *Sooner or later, we're going to have to take the fight to them.* For the past two years, Rigil Kent had been waging guerrilla warfare against the Union. Occasional raids on Liberty and Shuttlefield to steal weapons and destroy shuttles, the sabotage of the Garcia Narrows Bridge . . . hit-and-run tactics, without any clear purpose except to encourage hope that the Union would surrender New Florida and leave those who'd fled to Midland alone.

For a while, it seemed as if our side was winning. Then the Union Guard raid on Thompson's Ferry ended in the settlement's destruction and the loss of many lives. Shortly afterward, the Union had established a military base on Hammerhead and an attempt was made to capture Carlos. Though the mission was unsuccessful, they managed to figure out where Defiance was located. Since then, reports had come in about Union attacks upon settlements along the Gillis Range: Forest Camp, on the Midland side of East Channel, was assaulted, and New Boston, near the Medsylvania Channel, had been hit as well. Shady Grove was one of the few towns that had remained untouched.

A few weeks ago, though, our satphone link to the new colonies had been severed, indicating that someone had boarded the *Alabama*, still in high orbit above Coyote, and pulled the plug on the transceiver. So now all contact with the other towns was either done by shortwave radio—itself a risky business, since those transmissions could be monitored from space and triangulated to their source—or through word of mouth, which was more reliable but much slower.

Carlos had assumed the name Rigil Kent in order to protect his identity if any of his small group of resistance fighters was ever captured. There weren't many to begin with—Carlos, Barry, Ted LeMare, and a few others—but as their numbers expanded to include second-wave immigrants who'd fled from New Florida, his alias came to be attached to the group as a whole, and Carlos found himself in the role of a military leader. Warlord of Coyote . . . almost sounded like a twentieth-century fantasy novel. Didn't seem so funny now.

"Robert told me you've got something planned," I said quietly. "What is it?"

Carlos didn't respond for a few moments. I knew that silence: he was wrestling between a choice of how much he wanted to tell me and revealing no more than I needed to know. "We're working on something," he said at last. "It's pretty big, and there's going to be a lot of people involved. But more than that . . ." He shrugged. "Sorry. Can't talk about it."

Of course, there were good reasons why he couldn't take me into his confidence. Nonetheless, we'd journeyed down the Great Equatorial River together, split up, patched things together again, had a child, gotten married . . . a lot of water under the bridge, and it stung that he couldn't trust me. "Yeah, okay, sure . . ."

He caught the hurt in my voice. "I'm sorry, but we're still pulling things together. That's one of the reasons why I'm making the trip with you. It's not just to help you watch out for the kids. It's also because I have to . . ."

"Talk to some people. I understand." A new thought occurred to me. "But if Shady Grove's that far away, why don't we just take the *Plymouth*?"

The *Plymouth* was the remaining shuttle from the *Alabama*; its sister ship, the *Mayflower*, had been left behind in Liberty, after we'd cannibalized it for every usable component. For the last three years it had remained grounded, concealed beneath camouflage covers in a field about a mile from town. Now and then Robert, Dana, and Tom had gone out there to clean it up, reactivate its major systems, and test-fire its engines, yet it hadn't moved an inch since it was used to evacuate most of the *Alabama* party and our belongings from Liberty. It was still flightworthy, though; if you wanted to transport nine children and several adults across eight hundred miles, that was the quickest way to do it.

Carlos shook his head. "We're not using *Plymouth*. We'd get there quicker, but . . ." He hesitated. "We'd just as soon not remind the Union that we've got a spacecraft. If they remember it at all, better to let them assume that it's rusting away somewhere."

Ah-ha! But I didn't say anything. "So we're riding shags? Or are they classified as well?"

He chuckled, patting my knee. "Yeah, we'll have the shags. As many as we need. I know Susie thinks they stink, but . . ."

"She'll get used to it. The other children will love it." I took his hand. "So it's you, me, the kids . . . and who else?"

"Don't know yet. Haven't thought that far ahead. Maybe Chris . . . ?" He caught the look in my eye—I still had personal problems with his oldest friend—and quickly shook his head. "Chris should stay back, help hold down the fort."

"Barry's good with children. Maybe Klon, too." The kids loved Uncle Klon; he made a great Santa Claus, and his pad was filled with old fantasy stories he'd brought with him from Earth.

"They'll need both of them back here. Barry's my second-in-command while I'm gone, and Klon has to help build the fortifications. It's going to be hard for us to spare many people for this. Besides, we've only got room for four adults." He paused. "I was thinking about asking Ben. He's got this sort of backcountry experience."

"If he'll do it." It had been nearly a year since Ben Harlan had attempted to lead the members of the Church of Universal Transformation across Mt. Shaw. He still didn't like talking about what had happened up there; he'd lost someone whom he cared about. But Carlos was right; Ben knew what the Gillis Range was like in the dead of winter, and he got along well with kids. "I'll ask him," I said. "Maybe he'll sign on." I thought about it for a moment. "Kim should go, too. She'll want to look out after Donald."

"We can't risk sending Kim. She knows how to . . ." He stopped himself, but I knew what he was going to say. Kim Newell had been the *Plymouth*'s copilot; with Tom gone, she was needed to fly the shuttle, for whatever they intended to do with it. "I think we should take Marie."

Something within me went cold. "I know she's your sister, but . . ."

"She's good with a gun. And the kids like her. . . ."

"Hell they do. Susie hates her."

"Marie's going. I've already told her so." Before I could object, he stood up, headed for the door. "It's late. Time to go to bed."

* * *

The caravan left Defiance two days later.

We were supposed to leave shortly after daybreak, but it wasn't until midmorning that we were able to mount up. There were a lot of teary farewells as mothers and fathers hugged their children, made sure that they had their hats and gloves, promised them that they wouldn't be gone very long. A couple of kids refused to let go of their parents and had to be gently prised away; others wept or threw tantrums when they were told that they couldn't take their dogs or cats because we wouldn't be able to feed them. I had a lot of private discussions with their folks; each one needed to tell me about their child's personal needs, and I had to assure them that they wouldn't be neglected.

I'd half expected Ben Harlan to refuse to join us, so it came as a surprise that he didn't. He still walked with a limp from having lost two toes to frostbite during his ordeal on Mt. Shaw, and he warned me that he couldn't do any serious hiking, but when I told him that we'd ride most of the way, he was willing to undertake the task. He liked the children, and besides, he'd lately graduated from herding goats to minding the shags. And, although he didn't say so, I think he privately needed to confront the mountains again, if only to exorcise the memories of what had happened to him the year before.

The saddest moment came when Kim Newell said good-bye to Donald. They'd been through a lot in the last forty-eight hours; first Tom's burial, now this. She would have preferred to go with us, but she also knew that she was needed there, so she clung to her son until we were ready to saddle up. When I looked back, she had her head against Robert's shoulder, weeping as if she'd never see her son again.

We had five shags: four to carry adults and children, and one to haul all the food and camping equipment. Susan and the four other older children—none of whom was more than ten Earth-years, with Susie the eldest—were able to sit upon saddles along with the adults, although we made sure that they were secured with harnesses so they couldn't fall off. The four youngest children were little more than toddlers; for them, we'd fashioned papoose bags that were slung over the sides of each animal.

We gave names to the two groups, taken from the Prince Rupurt stories—the older kids were called Scouts, the younger children Dauphins—while the grown-ups were referred to as High Riders. The arrangement worked out well; at any one time, each shag carried a High Rider, one or two Scouts, and one Dauphin. Susan was designated Chief Scout for as long she chose to serve. I whispered in her ear that, at some point, she might have to share that title, to which she agreed, albeit reluctantly.

The shags were well suited for the trip; their coarse fur was warm, their elephantine legs tramped through the snow as if it were nothing more than soap flakes. The children were still upset, so again we tried to make the best of it by giving the Scouts the privilege of naming the shags. After much discussion, they settled upon Achmed, Zizzywump, Sally, Old Fart, and George the Magnificent. Go figure; it helped cheer them up a bit.

We made good time; by early afternoon of the first day, we reached Johnson Falls, where Marie and I dismounted to lead the children across the rope bridge over Goat Kill Creek while Carlos and Ben took the shags through the shallows upstream. We gave the shags a few minutes to shake off the icy water—which the kids loved, since it reminded them of big, grunting dogs—then we climbed aboard again and continued making our way on the trail leading us up the northern side of Mt. Aldrich.

I knew the kids pretty well because Kuniko and I had seen them troop through the infirmary at one time or another with the usual childhood bruises, fevers, and earaches. Susan, Donald, Lewis, Genevieve, and Rachel were the Scouts; Lilli, Alec, Ed, and Jack were the Dauphins. Every one of them had their own personalities, with which I was familiar, and before long the High Riders were known to them as well. Carlos was our undisputed leader—whatever he said, that was the rule—and they looked up to him with reverence. I was Dr. Gunther, the surrogate mother who made sure their caps were on tight and their harnesses weren't too loose. Ben was the easygoing chum who told jokes, tended to the shags, and made sure that we'd stop whenever anyone needed to pee.

But Marie . . . they didn't know quite what to make of Marie. As a teenager, she was the youngest of the High Riders, and the children immediately realized that she wasn't that much older than they. Yet she remained aloof from them: sitting stolidly upon her saddle, rifle never leaving her hands, eyes constantly searching the mountainside as if expecting Guardsmen to emerge from the woods at any moment. Donald rode with her until we reached Johnson Falls; after we crossed the bridge, though, he insisted upon riding with me, and almost threw a fit until Susan, in her role as Chief Scout, volunteered to take his place.

It wasn't just Marie's inability to warm up to children that made me wish we'd left her behind. She hadn't been very much younger than Susan was now when the *Alabama* reached Coyote; since then, a certain hardness had entered the eyes of the little girl who'd once splashed around in Sand Creek and giggled whenever she saw Carlos and I sneak a kiss. Over the course of the last couple of years, she'd changed into a person whom I barely recognized—cold, tough, cynical, and on one notable occasion even bloodthirsty. Only a month ago, she'd shot an unarmed Union soldier in cold blood, and smiled about it as if he'd been nothing more than a swamper caught prowling through the garbage.

Marie was scary, and she made the children nervous, yet Carlos insisted that we bring her. "I don't want to leave her here," he'd said when we argued about it the day before our departure. "Lars and Garth are a bad influence, and I'd like to get her away from them for a while. And since I'm putting Barry in charge of the outfit while I'm gone, I don't want the three of them getting together to pull something behind his back."

It was difficult to argue with that. The Thompson brothers were stone killers, no question about it; Carlos had recruited them to join Rigil Kent shortly after they moved to Defiance along with their uncle and aunt, on account of the fact that they'd fought the Union Guard before. It wasn't until much later that he realized just how merciless they could be. Marie had lately been spending a lot of time with Lars, and not just to trade tips on how to keep their rifles clean. That worried him, too, even though he tried not to pry into his sister's personal business. Lars and Garth might not be able to conspire against Barry, but if they had Marie on their side . . .

So there were good reasons why Carlos would want to keep his sister close to him. Besides, she was good with a gun, and we'd be on the trail for four weeks. It was still winter, so the boids were in their migratory grounds on the southern coast of Midland, but there was no telling what else we might run into out there in the wilderness.

All the same, though, I privately vowed to keep a close eye on my sister-in-law. We might be kin, but I didn't want to leave her alone with the children for very long.

Fortunately, the journey to Shady Grove was largely without incident.

We spent two days climbing Mt. Aldrich and coming back down the other side. In terms of geography, that was the hardest part, because there was no clear pass over the mountain and we had to spend a cold and windy night on a ridge below the summit. But we set up the tents so that we were all together, and after dinner that night Ben began telling the kids about Prince Rupurt, a story they'd never heard. It wasn't something Leslie Gillis had written. Indeed, Ben would later tell me that he'd been making it up as he went along. But the children were fascinated all the same, and that night he ended with a cliffhanger that made them want to hear more. "Tomorrow night," he said, "and only if you're good." Then we put out the lights and went to sleep.

And that pretty much set the pattern of our days for the next two weeks. Shortly after sunrise the High Riders would get up, stir the ashes of the campfire and get a fire going again, then start making breakfast while we woke the children. A bite to eat, then the Scouts would disassemble the tents and help the Dauphins into their papooses, while we reloaded everything on the shags so we could start making our way north along the southeast side of the Gillis Range. Once we descended from the mountains, the forest occasionally gave way to lowland marshes, which were still frozen over, so the shags had little trouble going through the swampy areas. On good days, we'd make fifty miles or more; at our worst, when we'd encounter a ravine that we'd have to skirt, only about forty. But, aside from the occasional snow squall or having to stop to retrieve something valuable that someone dropped, we made good time.

It wasn't always easy. The children got homesick, and it passed like a virus among them, with a lot of crying jags, until they finally got over it. Lewis and Donald got into a nasty fistfight one evening over whose turn it was to wash the dishes, and days went by before Genevieve would talk to Rachel again after a feud over something about which I never learned. Lilli got diarrhea, and Ed and Alec came down with colds, so I had to tend to them. Jack demanded that he become a Scout—and indeed, he was the oldest and largest of the Dauphins—so after considerable discussion we decided to make him a Scout Apprentice, with all due privileges: now he had to wash dishes and help the older kids forage for firewood. Two days of that, and he wanted to be a Dauphin once more. Yet every night, all their differences were put aside as they curled up against each other and waited for Ben to continue the further adventures of Prince Rupurt. I think Ben spent most of his time trying to figure out how he'd get Rupurt and his friends out of the latest peril he'd put them in the previous night.

We had other ways of having fun. Every few days, we'd choose a new Chief Scout. Carlos taught the Scouts how to make a fire with damp wood, how to determine location from the position of the sun and stars, how to guide a shag with little more than a slight tug of their reins, while I showed the Dauphins how to make snow angels and tie square knots. One night, we sat up late to watch a rare convergence of Coyote's sister moons Dog, Hawk, and Eagle against Bear's ring-plane.

And every day, our destination grew a little closer. Mt. Bonestell was the highest point on the Gillis Range, and also the second-tallest volcano on Coyote, exceeded only by Mt. Pesek on the western side of Hammerhead. Like Mt. Eggleton and Mt. Hardy in the southern hemisphere, it had been named after a twentieth-century astronomical artist—Henry Johnson's idea—yet even though Pesek was the largest, Bonestell was impressive in its own right. An enormous cone rising twenty-six thousand feet above sea level, its flat-topped summit was beyond the reach of any climber unaided by oxygen. Frequently shrouded by high clouds, it was awesome to behold on a clear day. We had compasses and maps to guide us, but even if we'd lost them, we would have been able to find our way to Shady Grove simply by hiking toward Mt. Bonestell.

On the eleventh day, shortly after we'd stopped for lunch, we heard the low clatter of rotors. Looking up, we spotted a pair of tiny specks moving across the sky, coming from the west. Not taking any chances, Carlos quickly moved the caravan beneath a couple of blackwoods, and there we waited while two gyros cruised high overhead, heading due west. Until then, the Union had been the least of our worries. This small incident reminded us that our journey wasn't a camping trip, as we had managed to pretend, but something far more serious.

Three days after we saw the gyros, we were about sixty miles from Shady Grove. We'd entered the broad mountain valley between the Gillis Range and Mt. Bonestell, where Longer Creek flowed south from the highlands. The marshes behind us, once again we were surrounded by dense forest, yet we'd located a trail leading north to the settlement. Barring any problems, we'd reach our destination in a couple of days. Ben was carrying the radio, and, once we were within range, Carlos planned to get in touch with the settlement and tell them we were coming.

Late that afternoon, as Uma was beginning to set behind the mountains, we came upon a small clearing that looked suitable. By then the Scouts and Dauphins had become accustomed to their roles. While the High Riders unloaded our equipment from George the Magnificent, the Dauphins helped unroll the tents, and the Scouts went into the woods to scrounge for firewood. The kids liked sharing the responsibilities; the older ones had made it a game to see who could find the best dry wood, and the toddlers had learned how to use branches to sweep away snow to make room for the tents. So we had the tents set up, and Lewis and I were breaking up kindling for the fire, when we heard a girlish scream from the woods.

At first, I didn't think much of it. We'd become used to this sort of thing; someone finds a dead swamper decaying under the leaves, or a kid takes a snowball and shoves it down the back of another kid's parka. Easy to ignore. But then I heard the scream again, and this time it had a note of pure terror. The others heard it, too, because Carlos and Marie dropped the rain tarps they were setting up and Ben scrambled out of the tent where he'd been taking a siesta. I told Ben to stay back with the Dauphins, then Carlos and Marie grabbed their rifles and we bolted for the woods.

We were only about fifty yards from camp when Genevieve came running toward us. Clingberries covered her arms and legs where she'd charged through the undergrowth, and there was a thin streak of blood across her nose from when a low branch had whipped against her face, but it was the look in her eyes that I noticed first: absolute horror, as if she'd just seen something that scared her half to death. She ran past Marie and Carlos and barreled straight into my arms as I knelt to stop her.

"I saw . . . I saw . . . I saw . . . !"

"Easy, easy. It's all right. Everything's okay." I stroked her hair as she buried her face against my parka. Never before had I felt a child tremble so much. "You're safe. You're fine. . . ."

"What did you see?" Marie was standing nearby, her rifle half-raised. "C'mon, kid, spill it."

"Marie . . ." Carlos shot her a look, then crouched down next to us. "We're here," he said, laying a hand on Genevieve's shoulder. "Nothing's going to get you, I promise. Now what did you . . . ?"

"A . . . a . . . a m-man. A l-l-little man."

I stared at her. "You saw a man?"

"Uh-huh. A li-little man." Genevieve snuffled, raised her face. Tears diluted the blood from her cut; she started to wipe them away, but I caught her hand, not wanting the scratch to get infected. "B-but not like a real man. L-like a . . . a monkey. A monkey, with fur and everything."

A little man, or a monkey. Which was more implausible? The nearest human settlement was over sixty miles away, nor were there any monkeys, or simians of any kind, on Coyote. Genevieve must have learned the word from tutorial discs, because it was beyond the range of her experience.

"Probably a creek cat." Disgusted, Marie lowered her gun, started to turn away. "Hell . . ."

"Go see what you can find." Carlos nodded in the direction from which Genevieve had come. "If you spot anything . . ." He hesitated. "Don't shoot. Just come back, that's all."

Marie looked at him askance. "You can't be . . ."

"Just do it, all right?" By then we could hear the other Scouts crashing through the underbrush toward us; they'd heard Genevieve's screams and were rushing over to investigate. Marie gave her brother a skeptical look, then walked away. Carlos watched her go, then turned to Genevieve again. "You saw a little man," he said quietly, looking her straight in the eye. "What did he do? Did he say anything?"

"N-n-no. H-h-he was just standing behind a t-t-tree, w-watching me." She was calming down a little, beginning to pick clingberries off her parka. "And . . . and then he started for me, and th-then I . . ."

"You ran away?" I asked.

"Uh-huh." She looked up at me again. "Did I do something wrong?"

"Not at all, sweetie. Not at all." I took her in my arms again, but she was through crying by then. When her friends showed up a few moments later, Genevieve told them all about what she'd seen.

Marie returned a while later with nothing to report, and that was it for the evening. We discussed the incident over dinner, and although Genevieve stuck to her story, the other kids either disbelieved her, or else believed her but decided that this was just another story like the ones Ben had been telling them all along. When you're very young, the line between fact and fantasy is thin; this was a good ghost story, and it helped us get them in bed a little earlier than usual.

Carlos and I didn't get a chance to talk that night. Even if we had, though, I don't think he would have told me everything he knew. Yet just before we tucked away the kids, he told Ben that he'd take the overnight watch, and quietly cautioned us to keep our guns where we could find them in the dark.

He knew something we didn't. But he wasn't letting on.

Two days later, late in the afternoon, we reached Shady Grove.

The town was smaller than Defiance by at least half, and looked little like it: a nine-foot stockade wall of blackwood timbers surrounding a half dozen longhouses, thatch-roofed barracks providing shelter for ten people, each arranged around a small commons where a well had been dug. Just outside the stockade were barns and corrals for livestock, tool-sheds and grain silos; not far away was a broad plastic dome, apparently a greenhouse. The front gate was open, and we could see woodsmoke rising from behind the walls. Nonetheless I had the impression we were approaching a fortress. It should have been comforting, but it wasn't.

A watchtower rose on stilts from the center of town; as we came within sight, a sentry called down to someone below. We'd barely reached the gate when several dozen men and women rushed out to greet us. The residents of Shady Grove might have been strangers, yet they had received our radio message, and they treated us as if we were long-lost relatives they hadn't seen in years. They clapped us on the back, shook our hands, introduced themselves so fast that I was barely able to remember their names. Several men helped us unload the shags before they were led to a nearby corral, then we trooped inside the stockade and went straight to the main lodge, where we discovered that they had already prepared dinner for us.

Shady Grove had been in existence for a little less than four months. Its population was just over fifty—all adults, although a few women were obviously expecting children soon—but in that short time they had done well by themselves. Life in Shuttlefield and Forest Camp had taught them how to make do with what little they'd managed to bring with them when they'd escaped. The greenhouse we'd seen earlier was carefully stitched together from transparent plastic tarps and heated by a wood furnace; in this way they managed to grow crops even in the dead of winter. The longhouses had been built with energy conservation in mind; internal partitions allowed for privacy while allowing heat from woodstoves to circulate through the rafters, and the cracks between the log walls were stuffed with cloverweed as insulation. One of the long-houses served as the main lodge; long tables ran down half of its length, and it was there that everyone had breakfast and dinner. No one was starving; no one was sick. Everyone there worked hard to survive, sure, but that was the way it was in Defiance, too.

It seemed as if everything was perfect. We'd crossed eight hundred miles of wilderness to find a settlement inhabited by friendly people who'd welcomed our arrival. There was a storage space in the back of

the lodge that could be cleared out to make room for the children; a few
more bunk beds would have to be built, but that wasn't much of a problem. And they had enough food to go around, so long as no one minded
shag stew on occasion. Although the residents also used shags as pack
animals, they weren't disinclined toward slaughtering the old and weak.
I decided to keep my mouth shut about the practice. People in Defiance
had come to revere shags as more than livestock and seldom had we
eaten one, and only then in desperation.

The mayor of Shady Grove was Frederic LaRoux. A geologist by training, he'd been a member of the expedition that Chris Levin had led up
the East Channel to pick out a site for the Garcia Narrows Bridge. Following the sabotage of the bridge, he and the others had fled Forest
Camp, making their way across the mountains to establish Shady Grove
on the other side of the Gillis Range. Carlos had met him back then, but
only briefly, and over dinner they came to know each other a little better. When the tables had been cleared, and Carlos broke out one of the
jugs of bearshine he'd brought with us, the discussion became more serious.

"I appreciate the necessity of what you've done," Fred said, speaking
in Anglo, "and why you had to do it. But Rigil . . . Carlos, I mean . . ."

"Don't worry about it. You can call me Rigil." Carlos grinned as he
poured a shot of bearshine for LaRoux. His mastery of the newer form of
English had become better since Chris had taught him the nuances.
"Most people in the new settlements know me only by that name. I'm
used to it by now."

"As well you should. You've become something of a legend, you
know." Fred settled back in his chair, idly swishing the liquor around in
a ceramic mug. "Rigil Kent, scourge of the Union, leader of the revolution." He raised an eyebrow. "When we first met, you were younger
than I expected. But now that I see that you have a wife and child . . .
this explains much."

"Just trying to protect them, that's all." Carlos glanced in my direction.
Ben had escorted the children to bed, and everyone else was either cleaning up or doing other odd jobs. For the moment, it was only the three of
us. "I hope this isn't an inconvenience. We're asking a lot of you."

"Under any other circumstances, no, it wouldn't be." Fred shook his head. "Either the Union doesn't know we're here—rather unlikely, since we're out in the open—or our town is so small and remote that they don't consider us much of a threat. It's also possible that they've seen our stockade and figured that we'd be a hard target to take down."

"They used a missile carrier against us," I said, speaking up for the first time. "Your walls wouldn't stop something like that."

Carlos cast me a look; but LaRoux just nodded. "She's right. We couldn't fight them off if they came at us the way they came at you. But we've kept our heads low, haven't caused any trouble. Maybe that's the reason."

"Maybe for now, but not very much longer." Carlos bent forward. "Sooner or later, they're going to—"

"Why is this inconvenient?" Yes, I was trying to change the subject. Carlos was looking for recruits, but my top priority was the safety of the children. "Is there something we should know about?"

Fred took a drink, made a face as the corn liquor scorched his throat, then rested his mug on the table and tapped his fingers against it. "There's an irony in all this," he said, very quietly, "because I was thinking about sending someone down south to ask if we could take refuge in your town."

Carlos stared at him. "But you just said—"

"I know, I know. But this isn't about the Union." He let out his breath. "Tell me something . . . while you were coming up here, did you feel any tremors? Did the ground shake at all?"

Carlos and I looked at each other. "No . . . no, we didn't," he said, and I shook my head.

"Good. Glad to hear it." Fred took another sip. "Twice since we've been here, we've experienced small tremors. Nothing major, just enough to break a few things and knock down part of the stockade. All the same, I think we made a serious mistake by settling here."

"Earthquakes?" I nearly said *Coyote-quakes*, but that would have sounded silly.

"No. Worse than that." He hesitated. "We don't have any seismographs, and right now I'd give an arm and a leg for a decent tiltometer, but it's my professional opinion that Bonestell is coming out of a dormant period."

"The volcano?" I leaned across the table to look him straight in the eye. "We thought it was, y'know, dead. Inactive. Whatever."

"Not a chance. Oh, Mt. Pesek is probably extinct. It's a shield volcano, very old, maybe one of the reasons why Coyote has a breathable atmosphere in the first place. Ditto for Mt. Eggleton down south. But I have little doubt that Bonestell is coming out of dormancy, and that it's only a matter of time before it blows."

"How long?" Carlos asked.

"Can't say. Even if I had the right instruments, I couldn't tell you that. Predicting volcano eruptions has always been an inexact science at best. But I wouldn't bet against its happening sometime in the next year. If and when that happens, the last place I want to be is here." He glanced over his shoulder to make sure he wasn't being overheard, then lowered his voice. "We're happy to take care of your children, but pretty soon we're going to have to abandon the town and head south ourselves. Maybe you ought to keep that in mind."

While we were mulling it over, he drained the rest of his mug. "But that's not all," he said as he reached across the table for the jug. "There's something else . . . we're not alone out here."

"What do you mean?" Carlos kept his voice neutral, but there was something in his face that told me he was hiding something.

Fred started to pick up the jug, then reconsidered and put it down again. "The last couple of months, some of our people have seen things in the woods. Sometimes they look like . . . well, I know this sounds silly, but they look like monkeys." He glanced first at me, then at Carlos. "I know how this sounds, but it's not cabin fever. We've had things turn up missing, stuff that was left outside overnight. Anything small enough to be taken away."

Carlos remained quiet, absently running a fingertip around the rim of his mug. "One of the girls saw something like that yesterday," I said.

"She did?" Fred nodded grimly as he let out his breath. "You know, I'm almost glad to hear you say that. I didn't want to mention it to you, because . . . I dunno . . . maybe you'd think we'd gone around the bend. But if you've seen these things, too . . ."

"Keep the children in the stockade," Carlos said abruptly. "Don't let them go out, not under any circumstances." He knocked back a slug of bearshine, then looked at me. "He's right. This was a mistake. We should have never come here."

"What?" I couldn't believe what he was saying. "You're . . . I mean . . . you're telling me we—"

"Fred, we appreciate your hospitality. You've been very kind, and we won't forget this. But I think we should take the kids and head back as soon as we can." He pushed back his chair and stood up. "If you want to send anyone with us, we can make room for them. It may not be safe here much longer." He hesitated, then added, "With the volcano being active and all, I mean."

Fred was just as astonished by Carlos's reaction as I was. "Sure. Whatever you say. I can ask around, see if anyone wants to—"

"It's been a long ride to get here. Let's talk more about this tomorrow." Carlos stepped away from the table. "I'm going to go check on the kids, make sure they're tucked away. See you in the morning. Good night."

I caught up with him just before he opened the door leading to the back of the lodge. "What aren't you telling me?" I whispered, grabbing his arm and pulling him aside. "You know something."

Carlos didn't reply. For the first time since we'd been married, he avoided looking at me. "It's important," he said at last. "I've kept it from everyone for a long time now. Maybe I should I have talked about it earlier, but"—he glanced back at the dining room, where Fred was still seated at the table, gazing at us in puzzlement—"this isn't the time or place," he added softly. "Ask me again tomorrow."

"If it's that important . . ."

"It is." Now he looked me straight in the eye. "But it'll keep until the morning. Will you trust me till then?"

I was tired. He was tired. It wasn't a good time to carry on a long conversation. "All right," I said, letting go of his arm. "Sure. But tomorrow . . ."

"Of course." Carlos forced a smile, then bent down to give me a kiss. "I love you," he murmured. "Now let's make sure the kids are in bed."

When morning came, I awoke to find Shady Grove already up and around. The smell of hot coffee and cooked food permeated the log walls; chickens cackled and roosters crowed as they were fed, and men and women murmured to one another while they walked past the shuttered windows of our longhouse. Carlos turned over and wrapped himself against me. I opened my eyes to see Ben scratching at himself; in the bunk above him, Marie tried to burrow beneath her blankets.

It was a cold winter morning, and it had been many days since any of us had slept in a bed with a roof over our heads. One of the women had told me that the community bathhouse had warm water. The tank was solar-heated, and so long as we didn't pump too much we could get a decent shower. So I prised myself loose from Carlos, put on my clothes, and headed for the bathhouse. The others could sleep a little while longer; I just wanted to feel clean again.

The sun was up, rising over the southwestern flanks of Mt. Bonestell. No clouds in the sky; with luck, maybe we'd get through the day without any more snow. Through the open gate of the stockade, I could see townspeople heading out to do the morning chores. No one in Shady Grove slept late, and neither did the children. The Scouts were playing tag in the commons while the Dauphins built a snowman nearby. I spotted Susan talking to an adult, and for a moment I considered going over to introduce her, but decided to let her make friends by herself. She might like it here . . . if Carlos allowed her and the other children to stay, that is.

The bathhouse had two stalls, marked MEN and WOMEN, with a dividing wall between them. It was small, with unfinished faux birch floors and walls, but there was a small stack of shag-fur towels on the table and a bar of lavender soap in an aluminum can nailed to the wall beneath the showerhead. I took off my clothes and hung them up on the door, then shivered against the cold as I worked the pump handle until I received a thin cascade of water. Not much better than lukewarm, but still a luxury I hadn't enjoyed in two weeks; I stood beneath the shower and felt the sweat and grime of eight hundred miles wash off me.

Carlos couldn't be serious about taking the children back. Yes, it was possible that Mt. Bonestell might erupt, but LaRoux hedged his bets about when it might occur. Even if an eruption was imminent, surely they'd have enough advance warning to evacuate the town and head south. But that wasn't what bothered my mate; it was the sightings of these so-called monkeys. Clearly he knew something about them, and he had admitted as much. If only he'd tell me . . .

From somewhere nearby, I heard a dinner bell begin to ring. Time for breakfast. I rinsed my hair, then turned the spigot to shut off the water and reached for a towel. Even if Carlos insisted on leaving, there was no sense in rushing home. I was in no hurry to hit the trail again, and the kids would only fret. If we stayed a couple of days, he might come to his senses. I loved him dearly, but sometimes he took things much too seriously. . . .

Feeling much more civilized, I made my way across the compound to the lodge. The children had already gone in, leaving behind a half-finished snowman, and only a couple of townspeople were in sight. The gate remained open. There was no one on duty in the watchtower; the sentry was climbing down the ladder, heading in to get some chow. I noticed all these things, but paid no attention to any of them. My hair was wet, and my stomach was rumbling; the only thing that mattered was getting in from the cold and putting some food in my belly.

The dining hall was filled to capacity: men and women crowded next to one another on the benches, passing bowls of kasha and plates of fresh-baked corn bread down the line. The kids were scattered here and there across the room; they were probably sick of seeing each other, because only a few of the Dauphins sat together. The older ones had joined adults who'd taken them under their wing; to see the townspeople already adopting the Defiance children as if they were their own reinforced my belief that we'd done the right thing by bringing them there.

I found Carlos, Marie, and Ben sitting with Fred LaRoux at the far end of the middle table. "See you've found the bathhouse," LaRoux said, grinning, as Carlos and Barry moved to make room for me. "Enjoy yourself?"

"Very much, thank you." I could have dried my hair a little better, though, for it hung in damp snarls around my face. "Wish I could do that every day."

He shrugged. "Three times a week is all we get, or at least until we get around to building more facilities. No shortage of well water. We've got a pretty deep aquifer, but putting in sewer pipes is murder." He glanced at Ben. "Did y'all have the same problems?"

"Sort of." He took a bowl of wheat porridge that was handed to him, passed it to Carlos. "Piping wasn't a problem so much as heating the water. We've kept everything under the trees, so there was no way we could use passive solar systems. We're still taking cold baths."

I smiled at that. Ben hadn't been around when we'd put in the water pipes, yet he knew enough about them to be able to discuss them. "Did Susan like her shower?" Carlos asked, dipping his spoon into his bowl to stir the kasha. "Hope so . . . the kids are beginning to reek."

"She didn't come with me." I looked at him in puzzlement. "Last time I saw her, she was outside, talking to someone."

"She must have come in with them, then." Carlos put down the spoon, raised his head to peer across the room. "Susan!" he called out, and a woman seated about a dozen feet away looked toward him. He ignored her, called again: "Susie! Susie Gunther!"

No response. I searched the room with my eyes, called for her myself. No Susan.

Rachel was the nearest Scout, and one of Susan's closest friends. I got up and went over to her. "Have you seen Susan?" I asked.

Always fastidious, Rachel took a moment to chew and swallow the corn bread in her mouth. "She went out," she said nonchalantly, as if that explained everything.

"Out? Out where?"

"Out the gate."

I turned toward Carlos, but he was already pulling on his coat and heading for the door. I tried to tell myself that it was probably nothing. Susan had taken it upon herself to see to the shags; she was particularly concerned about Old Fart, who had begun to show his advanced age. Just a small matter; we'd find her in five minutes, after which she'd receive a scolding from Mama and Papa and a long time-out in the long-house while her friends got to play.

But she wasn't at the corral, nor was she visiting the greenhouse nor any of the outlying sheds. We didn't find her feeding the chickens, and she wasn't playing hide-and-seek under the floor beams of the long-houses. Within a half hour, almost everyone in town had joined the hunt; breakfast was forgotten as people who barely knew her name searched for her in every conceivable place.

The adult with whom I had seen her talking told Carlos that she'd expressed interest in Longer Creek; he'd told her that it flowed down from the hills north of town, and that it was where they did most of their fishing. He hadn't seen her since then. So Carlos, Marie, and I walked around behind the stockade, and sure enough, there were her footprints in the snow, leading in the direction of the narrow river and the woods that surrounded it.

We started to follow them, still calling her name, but we'd just entered the woods when Marie suddenly stopped. "Oh, hell," she muttered, staring down at the ground, "look at this."

There were Susan's footprints, barely six inches in length, continuing through the ice-crusted powder. But now, on either side of her, were several other sets of tracks; bipedal and four-toed, less than four inches long, with deep heel marks and sharp indentations at the end of each toe.

"Oh, my God." Carefully stepping around them, Carlos followed Susan's footprints a little farther. "Oh, dear God, no . . ."

Then I saw what he was seeing. The alien tracks emerged from the woods on either side of Susan's; they surrounded hers, and there was a deep impression in the snow where she had fallen down. Her footprints emerged from the scuffle, becoming deeper as if she'd tried to run away. In her panic she'd headed in the wrong direction, away from the stockade and toward the forest.

"They caught her here." Marie pointed to another place where she'd fallen down. "There must have been two . . . no, three, maybe four . . ."

"Oh, God." Carlos was fixated on the tracks. "They wouldn't do this. It's not their way. They only want *things*. . . ."

"What the hell are you talking about?" I lost my patience. No, not just my patience; my mind, too. I grabbed Carlos's shoulders, turned him around to face me. "What haven't you told me? Who are they?"

In that instant, I saw something in his eyes I hadn't seen in years. Fear, as terrible as any man could have, yet not of death, but of the unknown. He pulled himself loose from me, turned to his sister. "Marie, go back and get the guns. Tell Ben to stay back and take care of the kids, but you get the guns and round up a few more people, then come after us."

"Why don't you go back yourself and . . ."

"They're fast. Believe me, they're already way ahead of us. If we follow them now, we may be able to catch up to them. But if we go back to town, they'll have that much more of a head start. And Ben can't keep up with us, not with that bad foot of his." He pointed back the way we'd come. "Now move . . . and get back here quick as you can."

Marie hesitated, then turned and began to sprint back toward town. "C'mon," Carlos said, taking my arm. "We don't have much time." He glanced at me, saw the look on my face, and nodded. "I'll try to explain as we go along."

Three and a half years ago, by the LeMarean calendar, Carlos had taken off by himself to explore the Great Equatorial River. I've told my part of that story before; how he'd left me, Barry, Chris, and Kuniko behind after our attempt to explore the river had failed. I was carrying Susan then, so I couldn't go with him—not that I particularly wanted to; Carlos and I weren't on good terms at that point in our relationship—and so for nearly three months he was on his own, not returning to Liberty until I was going into labor.

I thought I'd learned everything about that *hegira*—his term for his "spiritual journey"—but I was wrong. There was one thing he'd kept secret, not only from me, but also from everyone else.

He'd paddled his canoe along the southern coast of Midland, seeing our future homeland as no other human had ever seen it before, until he reached its southeast point. Following a brief conversation via satphone with me and Chris—and I hate to admit it, but we weren't very kind to him—he decided to keep going west, raising his sails to cross the

Midland Channel to a small island south of Hammerhead. At first, it seemed as if the island was little more than sand and brush, yet on his first night there he discovered that it was far from deserted.

"I thought they were just animals." As he spoke we were hiking uphill, following the tracks as we made our way through dense forest toward the lower slopes of Mt. Bonestell. "Like raccoons or maybe overgrown pack rats, but then I found something that made me realize that they were intelligent. There was this tiny knife—"

"What?" Despite the urgency of the moment, I stopped. "You're saying you found intelligent life on Coyote?"

He looked back at me. "Uh-huh. That's what I'm saying. Now c'mon." Still talking, he continued up the trail. "Intelligent, but very primitive . . . sort of like little Cro-Magnon men. They knew how to make tools, how to build fires, erect structures from the sand. Even something of a language, although damned if I could understand it." He chuckled to himself. "And, man, were they a pain in the ass. I spent nearly a week on the island, and it was all I could do to keep them from stealing everything I had. I called them sandthieves after a while. But they were pretty peaceful. Just as curious about me as I was about them."

"And you didn't tell anyone about them?" If the circumstances had been different, I would have had a hard time believing him.

"No, I didn't. I . . . oh, no. Look at this."

We'd come to Longer Creek. It wasn't very wide at that point, its surface frozen over, but that wasn't what distracted him, Susan's footprints stopped abruptly on its bank. Carlos bent over, picked up something from the ground, turned around, and held it out to me.

"Oh, God!" I whispered, putting my hand to my mouth. It was Susan's cap, the one Sharon had woven from shag fur and given to her for First Landing Day last summer. "Is she . . . ?"

Carlos knelt, inspected the smaller tracks within powdery snow on top of the ice that lay across the shallow creek. "No. She's still with them. They just picked her up to carry her across. She probably tried to fight, and that's how her cap got knocked off." He took a few tentative steps out on the ice; it groaned a bit, but remained solid. "We can make it across," he said, offering his hand. "Let's go."

We carefully walked across the creek, trying to avoid soft spots in the ice; when we were on the far side, the tracks continued, Susan's among them. I could see Mt. Bonestell clearly through the trees, looming above us as a massive, snowcapped dome. "Go on," I said. "Give me the rest of it."

"Not much more to tell." Carlos shrugged as he continued to lead the way. "They're intelligent, no question about it. But I was pretty cynical about everyone I'd left behind, and I didn't want all these people descending upon them, the way European explorers did to the Native Americans, so I kept it to myself. Even named the place Barren Isle so that no one would think anything important was there. And I haven't told anyone until now." He looked back at me. "You're the first."

"But if they're peaceful—"

"I *thought* they were peaceful." He stopped, bent over to clasp his knees and catch his breath. "But these aren't the same sandthieves. The ones I found over there didn't know how to swim or build boats, so they couldn't have come over here. And if everyone says they're the size of monkeys, then this bunch must belong to a different species, or tribe, or"—he shook his head—"whatever. The ones I met weren't that large. But they must be just as intelligent, and if they've taken Susan . . ."

"Let's go." I didn't need to hear any more; I pushed past him, taking the lead. My daughter had been abducted by these creatures. I didn't care how peaceful their relatives on Barren Isle might be; I wanted her back.

The slope quickly became steeper, the snow more thick, yet urgency pumped adrenaline into my blood, making me forget the cold in my lungs and the ache in my muscles. More than once I was tempted to stop for a moment, take a break, but then I'd look down at the ground to see Susan's small footprints surrounded on either side by those of the sandthieves, and my steps would quicken. That, and the realization that we *had* to be catching up to them. Carlos said the sandthieves were fast, and doubtless they were strong enough to scurry up a mountainside without breathing hard. Yet they had a human child among them; even if they were forcing her to run, her very presence would slow them down. And twice already Susan had tried to escape; if they were half as intelligent as Carlos said, then they'd realize the need to keep a close eye on her, and that would slow them down even more.

So we couldn't be far behind. And as it turned out, we weren't.

So intent were we upon following the tracks, we didn't look up to notice that the mountainside had changed, until I raised my eyes and saw a massive bluff looming before us. At first I thought it was another limestone formation, like those prevalent throughout Midland, yet as we came closer, I saw that it was dark grey rock. Much later, talking it over with Fred LaRoux, I'd learn that this was ignimbrite, volcanic ash left behind by ancient eruptions that had been compacted over time to form a substance much like concrete. Sometimes called tuff, it had often used on Earth as construction material. In parts of China, houses were built of bricks carved from ignimbrite quarries, but in northern Italy the opposite approach had been taken, with homes and shops being excavated within tuff deposits.

That's what we were seeing now. The vast rock wall rose above us, and within that wall were dozens of doors and windows, resembling natural caves, until I realized that their shapes were much more regular, their distance from one another obviously deliberate. The trees around the wall had all been cut down; here and there along the wall I spotted small wooden platforms jutting out from above-ground doorways to form terraces. Rough fabric, like woven grass, covered some of the windows as curtains, while smoke from fires burning somewhere inside seeped through chimney holes here and there.

It looked somewhat like an ancient Pueblo cliff dwelling, yet that wasn't my first impression. What I saw was a fortress, hostile and impregnable, somehow obscene. And from behind all those doors and windows, eyes that studied us as we emerged from the woods.

Carlos stopped. "That's far enough," he said quietly, almost a whisper. "They know we're here." He nodded in the direction of the nearest window. "See? It's hard to sneak up on them. Probably heard us coming a long time ago."

I caught a brief glimpse of a tiny face—coarse black fur surrounding overlarge eyes and a retracted snout—before it disappeared. Here and there, I spotted small figures within doors and windows, vanishing as soon I looked directly at them. We were watching them, but they'd been watching us for much longer.

And not just watching. The air was still and quiet, scarcely a breeze moving through the trees behind us. Now I could hear a new sound: a rapid cheeping and chittering, punctuated now and then by thin whistles and hoots, animalistic yet definitely forming some sort of pattern. They were talking to one another.

"Oh, crap," I murmured. "What do we do now?"

"Stay calm." Carlos pointed to the tracks we'd been following. They led away from us, straight toward a doorway at ground level. "She's somewhere in there. They must have just taken her inside."

So what do we do now? Charge into an alien habitat in search of our daughter? Fat chance. From the looks of it, the cliff dwelling could have been honeycombed with dozens of passageways, all of which so small that we'd have to bend double just to get through the largest of them. We were unarmed, and Carlos had already discovered that these creatures were capable of making knives. A small cut from a tiny flint blade might not mean much, but a hundred such cuts just like it would kill you just the same. Negotiation? Sure, sounds good to me. What's the word for hello? So I did what any mother would do.

"Susan!" I shouted. "Susan, can you hear me?"

I stopped, listened. Silence, save for the cheeps and chirps of the cliff dwellers. I raised my hands to my mouth. "Susan? Sweetie-pie, do you hear me?"

"Susan!" Carlos yelled as loud as he could. "Susan, we're out here! Answer us, please!"

We shouted and screamed and called her name again and again, then we'd stop and wait, and still we heard nothing. In the meantime, the sandthieves were becoming a little braver. Apparently realizing that we weren't about to storm their habitat, they ventured to the windows and stood in the doors, cheeping madly at one another until it almost sounded as if they were mocking us. And maybe they were; one of them, a little larger than the others and wearing what looked like a serape, stood on an upper parapet and jumped up and down, hooting in glee. Frustrated, I picked up a stick and wound back to hurl it at him.

"No!" Carlos snatched the stick from my hands. "It'll only excite them. Trust me, I've tried that already."

"Trust you?" I turned upon him. "Why didn't you trust *me*? If you'd only told me . . . if you'd just been honest . . ."

"I didn't know . . . I didn't think they—"

"Mama!"

The sound of Susan's voice stopped us. For a moment, we couldn't tell where it was coming from, except that it was in the direction of the cliff dwelling.

"Susan!" I shouted. "Baby, where are you?" I could see nothing in the windows except sandthieves; yet they'd suddenly gone silent, and even the big one on the parapet was now longer prancing. "Susan? Can you—?"

"Here! I'm up here!"

I raised my eyes to peer at the top of the bluff, and there was Susan, a small figure standing alone at the edge of a wooden platform. My heart froze when I saw her. She was nearly sixty feet above the ground. Two or three more steps, and she'd fall over.

"Stay there!" Carlos yelled. "I'm coming to get you!" I couldn't see how he could, yet he was determined to try anyway. He'd taken no more than a few steps, though, when another voice came to us from above:

"Stay where you are!"

Looking up again, I saw a human figure standing next to Susan. No, not quite human; with great wings like those of a bat rising from his back and fangs within an elongated jaw, he resembled a gargoyle. Although I'd never laid eyes upon him before, I immediately knew who he was. And so did Carlos.

"Zoltan," he whispered.

*   *   *

Zoltan Shirow. The Reverend Zoltan Shirow, if you cared to call him that. Founder of the Church of Universal Transformation, the religious cult that had followed him to Coyote. They'd worshiped him as a prophet, believing that he held the key to human destiny, yet the truth of the matter was that he was a madman, and the only destiny to which he'd led them was death.

The last person to see Zoltan alive was Ben Harlan. From what he'd told me and the other members of the Defiance Town Council, he'd fled for his life when it became apparent that Zoltan intended to kill him on Mt. Shaw. He later led an expedition to the camp just below the summit, where they confirmed that the group had resorted to cannibalism. Zoltan's own remains were never found, and the body count had come up short by two. Since then there had been reports, delivered occasionally by hunters who'd ventured into the Gillis Range, of a bat-winged figure lurking within the woods, sometimes with a woman beside him.

No one had ever given much credence to these claims, least of all me. Yet there was Zoltan, alive and well, standing next to my little girl. Even from the distance, I could tell Susan was badly frightened; she didn't want to be anywhere near him, yet she was all too aware that she was standing close to the edge of the platform.

"Don't you dare . . ." My voice was a dry croak; I had to clear my throat. "Don't you dare hurt her!" I shouted. "Bring her down from there!"

Carlos glanced back at me. "Wendy, don't provoke him. He's—"

"I have no intention of hurting her." Although Zoltan scarcely raised his voice, we could hear him clearly. The sandthieves were all quiet now, and I noticed that most had fallen to their knees. "In fact, if you want her back, then I'm happy to oblige."

Before Susan could react, he bent forward and swept her up in his arms. And then, holding her tightly against his chest, he stepped off the platform.

I think I screamed. I must have, because I heard the sound echoing off the cliff. Yet, as the two of them plummeted toward us, Zoltan's wings unfurled, spreading out to their maximum span, catching the air and braking their descent as if he was wearing a parachute. Zoltan couldn't fly—his wings, grafted onto his body long ago on Earth, didn't have the muscle structure necessary for that—but apparently he'd learned how to use them to glide short distances in Coyote's lesser gravity.

Nonetheless, it was a long fall, and he was burdened with Susan's extra weight. He hit the ground hard, taking the impact on bent knees, his breath whuffing from his lungs. He managed to hold on to Susan the whole time, though, and as soon as they were down, she wiggled out of his arms and dashed toward us. Carlos knelt and caught her; she wrapped her arms around him, sobbing and refusing to let go as he murmured into her ear.

From the cliff dwellings, the sandthieves leaped up and down, chattering and squawking to one another, out of their minds from what they'd just seen. I couldn't blame them; I was pretty much out of my own mind, although for different reasons. "What the . . . ? Who the hell do you think you are?" I demanded, ignoring both husband and daughter—in fact, forgetting everything else—as I marched toward him. "What do you think you're doing, pulling something like—"

"Quiet!" Zoltan raised a hand as he slowly stood erect. He winced as he did so—no doubt he'd pulled muscles in his thighs and calves—yet he maintained the unholy charisma that had allowed him to gather more than two dozen disciples to his side and lead them across time and space to an unknown world. "I've done as you've asked, in the quickest way possible. Aren't thou grateful for the miracle you've witnessed?"

He turned to Carlos. "And you . . . you, I know. Once already I've saved your life. Now I've saved that of your daughter. Have you no gratitude in your heart?"

"What's he talking about?" I looked at Carlos. "When did he . . ."

"I'll tell you later." Carlos shot me a sidewise look—*not now*—as he stood up, still holding Susan in his arms. "I remember. You didn't give me a chance to thank you before, but . . . well, thanks. And thank you for letting her go."

Obviously, there was more to all this than I knew. I'd have to get the whole story from Carlos at another time; as before, he'd been keeping secrets from me. Just then, though, I was more concerned with the present. "Why did you take her?" I said, looking at Zoltan again. "She's just a little girl. She means no harm to you."

"Exactly. She's just a little girl." Zoltan smiled, revealing the tips of his fangs. Not very comforting. "The *chirreep* . . . that's what they call themselves . . . had never seen a human child before you came here. Adults, yes, but never a kid."

"You know their language?"

"Only a little. They actually have to show something to you and tell you what it's called before you know what it means. So when they told me that a group of small outsiders . . . *kreepah-shee*, their word for you . . . had appeared in the valley, I tried to get them to explain what they meant." An apologetic shrug. "So they found one and brought her to me. They didn't know she was a child . . . just an immature *kreepah-shee*."

Now I understood. As Carlos had told me, the sandthieves—the *chirreep*—were an alien race, very primitive, that had only recently felt the hand of man. Zoltan had asked an innocent question, and they'd done their best to oblige him: take one, bring it back, and show it to him. By their nature, they were used to stealing things, so why stop at a child?

"So what are you to them?" Carlos handed Susan over to me, being careful never to turn his back on him. "Their leader? I mean, either you found them, or they found you, but obviously they respect you."

"Can't you tell?" I nodded toward the *chirreep*; they were still silent, their heads lowered into supplication. "He's not their leader . . . he's their god."

"Thank you for recognizing that." Zoltan's wings rippled slightly as he stood a little straighter. "Many years ago, when I received divine inspiration to come to this world, I believed the Almighty wanted me to lead the human race to a higher plane. Since then, I've come to realize that I misunderstood His message. Man is a flawed creature, beyond redemption. I learned that when my followers . . . all but one, whom I saved as my consort . . . perished because of their inadequacies, and the one whom we'd trusted as our guide betrayed us. He paid for his sins. Cast out, he died alone, and now his soul suffers in—"

"You mean Ben Harlan?" Carlos shook his head. "Alive and well. He told us all about—"

"Be quiet!" His wings stretched out once more, and the *chirreep* quailed in alarm, squeaking among themselves at this outburst. "I won't tolerate blasphemy in my house!"

"Sorry," I said. "I apologize for my husband." If Zoltan wanted to believe that Ben had been his own personal Judas, then let him. We might have found Susan, yet we were still on dangerous ground. "Please, go on, Reverend Shirow. I'd like to hear more about—"

"I no longer acknowledge that name. It belongs to the man I once was, before the final station of my transformation. I am now *Sareech* . . . the messiah, the one who has come from the stars." He beckoned to the *chirreep* behind him. "These are now my people, the ones I was truly meant to lead. Unspoiled, innocent, without original sin. Man is lost, but they . . . they are my flock. And they are under my protection."

If Zoltan hadn't been insane before, he certainly was now. When he'd come to Coyote, he'd been satisfied with merely being a prophet. With his original followers gone, having stumbled upon a primitive species willing to worship him, he'd elevated himself to godhood. And indeed, there was no one else who could challenge that claim. He was the only human on Coyote who looked the way he did . . . and the *chirreep* didn't know any better.

"I understand this," Carlos said. "Believe me, I do. I found some sand . . . *chirreep*, I mean . . . several years ago, on an island south of here."

"You have?" Zoltan peered closely at him. "The *chirreep-ka*? Their cave drawings tell of another tribe across the waters, lost many years ago, but I didn't . . . they didn't . . . know they still existed."

Some god. He didn't even know about another group of sandthieves only a thousand or so miles away. "They're there, all right," Carlos went on, "but I didn't let anyone know about them. I wanted to protect them, keep their existence a secret. And I won't tell anyone about your *chirreep* if you'll just . . ."

"It scarcely matters, does it?" Zoltan looked at Susan, huddled in my arms. "When she was taken, you came after her, and in doing so you found this . . . and I have no doubt that others will follow you. Perhaps this is part of my destiny. To save them from you and your kind."

For a moment, he'd almost sounded human again. "Then we can go?" I asked. "We can . . ."

"Leave. No one will harm you." He smiled, once again exposing his fangs. "Besides, it makes very little difference what you may say or do. *Corah* will soon speak again, as it did many years ago. It once changed all life on this world, and soon it will do so again."

"*Corah?*"

He pointed toward the summit of Mt. Bonestell. "*Corah.* The destroyer." When he looked at us again, his eyes promised fire. "Now go. Make peace with yourselves, if you can. The end of the world is near."

Then he turned and began to walk back toward the cliff dwellings. Seeing that their god was returning to them, the *chirreep* broke their silence; once again, they began to twitter and chirp amongst themselves, bounding in and out of the doors and windows of their city. It wasn't hard to figure out what they were saying. All hail mighty *Sareech*, our lord and savior. He confronts the *kreepah-shee* and sends them packing. *Sareech* is our man. . . .

"Let's go," Carlos murmured. "I don't want to give him a chance to change his mind." He took Susan from my arms. "C'mon, Scout. Piggyback ride down the mountain."

Susan nodded, but didn't smile or say anything as her father swung her up on his shoulders. She'd lost a bit of her innocence that day, although it would be many years before I knew just how much. But for the moment, we had our daughter back, and that was all that mattered. . . .

Just before I turned away, I caught a glimpse of something moving on the parapet where we'd first seen Zoltan and Susan. Looking up, I spotted a lone figure: a woman, wearing a frayed and dirty white robe, its cowl raised above her head. Thin and terribly frail, she leaned heavily against a walking stick, like someone who was ill; she peered down at us, and in the brief instant that our eyes met, I felt a sense of longing, as if she was silently begging us not to go.

Zoltan had mentioned having a consort, someone whom he'd claimed to have saved. And Ben had told us that he'd left someone behind. I struggled to remember her name. . . .

"Greer?"

I didn't speak very loudly, yet Zoltan must have heard me, for he turned and looked back at me. There was a flash of anger in his eyes, and again I realized just how vulnerable we still were. Carlos must have heard me, too, because he stopped at the edge of the clearing. "What's that, honey? You say something?"

"I just saw . . ." But when I looked up again, the figure had vanished from the parapet. Like the ghost of a dead woman, seen only for a moment in the half-light of winter's day. "Never mind," I murmured. "Let's just get out of here."

So we took Susan and made our way back down Mt. Bonestell, saying little to each other as we followed our own footprints through the forest. About halfway back, we met up with Marie; she was leading a group of men from Shady Grove, all of them armed with carbines, ready and eager to take on whatever we might have found. It took a lot of double talk, yet we managed to convince them that a posse wasn't needed. Some strange aboriginals had taken off with our girl, but they'd abandoned her after a while, and we'd found her on the mountain. More a nuisance than anything else. We just wanted to go home.

We didn't tell Ben about finding Zoltan, nor did I tell him about having seen Greer. Ben had suffered enough already; he was already half-convinced that Zoltan was dead and that the woman he'd once loved had joined him. Why rip open an old wound? At best, the knowledge that they were both still alive would have broken his heart all over again; at worst, it might have prompted him to go charging up the mountain, in the vain hope that he might be able to save her. But if that was indeed Greer, then she was beyond hope of redemption; she'd become the consort of an insane god, and there was nothing that could be done for her.

So we swore Susan to silence and kept this knowledge to ourselves. That evening, though, after everyone had gone to bed, Carlos and I met once more with Fred LaRoux. In the quiet of the main lodge, with a fire in the hearth and drinks in hand, we came clean, telling him everything that we knew, while insisting that the *chirreep* posed no direct threat to Shady Grove. He was disturbed to learn that Zoltan Shirow was still alive. His first impulse was to send some of his people up the mountain to find him, but Carlos and I managed to make him realize that doing so would probably cause more harm than good. So long as Shady Grove kept the gates locked at night, Zoltan and his *chirreep* would probably leave them alone so long as they left him alone.

We remained in Shady Grove for a few more days, then we loaded the Scouts and Dauphins aboard the shags and began to make the long journey back to Defiance. This time, though, we didn't make the trip alone. Nearly two dozen men and women came with us, those willing and able to take up the fight against the Union. They were only the first; through the remaining months of winter, word would spread to other camps and settlements scattered across the Gillis Range, until an army was assembled for a final assault on Liberty, the colony we'd been forced to abandon so long ago.

In the end, Zoltan Shirow—*Sareech*, the mad god—was right all along. War wasn't the worst thing, and even *Corah* wouldn't have the last word. We'd seen the shape and form of spiritual slavery; only the apocalypse itself would bring salvation.

Part 7

LIBERATION DAY

Darkness lay heavy upon the north shore; sunrise was still a half hour away, and the stars had yet to disappear from the night sky. Bear hung low above the western horizon, its ring-plane rising above the channel. The winter snow had melted a few weeks earlier, and a cool breeze stirred the tall grasses of the marshlands surrounding the inlet of North Creek; the grasshoarders were still asleep in their nests, though, and the boids had yet to begin to hunt. A new day was coming to this part of Coyote as it always had, in peaceful serenity, heretofore untouched by the hand of man.

Now there were new sounds: murmured voices, wooden paddles faintly bumping against canoe gunnels. From time to time, thin beams of light moved across black waters, briefly exploring the shoreline before disappearing once more. Tiny wavelets lapped against the sandy beach, forced ahead by low shapes that glided quietly toward shore.

As the lead canoe approached the inlet, the figure hunched in its bow stroked in reverse, gently slowing his craft. The keel softly crunched against sand, and he briefly thrust the paddle downward to test the depth. Then, carefully balancing himself upon the gunnels, he stood up and stepped over the side, his boots splashing through calf-deep water.

Pulling a light from his jacket pocket, Carlos aimed it toward the channel and flashed three times. A moment passed, then from the darkness there was a rapid succession of flashes in response. Putting the light away, he took a moment to look around. He was almost home. And this time, he was bringing a few friends with him. . . .

"I could use a hand here." Chris had climbed out and was wading ashore. "Unless you're too busy admiring the view, of course."

"Sorry." Carlos turned to help him haul the canoe ashore. "Never seen this part of the island before."

"Who has?" Chris bent down to loosen the ropes of the tarp covering their gear. "But you look like you're posing for a picture. Like Washington crossing the . . . y'know, whatever."

"Hey, if you've got a camera . . ."

"Left it behind, George. Maybe next time."

The rest of the flotilla was approaching the shore: canoes, pirogues, a couple of keelboats, more than three dozen boats in all. The thin light cast by masked lamps illuminated shadowed figures as they climbed overboard to pull their craft onto dry land. They moved quickly, wasting as little time as possible; with sunrise fast approaching, they'd have to hurry to make camp before daybreak.

Over the course of the last nine days, eighty-six men and women, from settlements all across Midland, had navigated the Medsylvania Channel from their departure point at New Boston. They'd traveled under the cover of darkness, sleeping during the day under camouflage nets so as not to be spotted by low-flying aircraft. Two nights ago, Red Company crossed the confluence of the East Channel, where the Medsylvania Channel became the West Channel, until they reached the northeastern tip of New Florida. From there, North Creek flowed south to Sand Creek, which in turn led straight to Liberty. Carlos noticed that they all kept their voices low, as if they were expecting a Union Guard patrol somewhere nearby. Liberty was a long way from there, yet no one was taking any chances.

Hearing someone coming up behind him, he looked around to see his sister walking toward him. "Spotted a small blackwood grove about fifty yards that way," Marie said quietly. "I think we can make camp there."

"Very good. Take as much equipment as we need, leave everything else here." Carlos turned to two men standing nearby. "You and you . . . pull out the nets and start covering the boats. I want everything under wraps before the sun comes up."

"Got it, Rigil," one of them said. More than half of Red Company still referred to him as Rigil Kent, the alias he'd chosen for himself long ago, even though they now knew his real name. *Just as well,* he thought. *If this fails, that'll be probably be the name they carve into my tombstone.*

That was an uncomfortable notion, so he sought to avoid it. "You got the satphone?" he asked Chris.

Chris had just unloaded their packs. He glanced at his watch, then gazed up at the night sky. "Little early for that, don't you think? *Alabama* isn't due over for another hour or so. We don't even know if they . . ."

"You're right. Just skittish, that's all." He hesitated. "Wish I knew where the other guys are."

Chris bent over one of the packs, loosened its flap, and dug inside until he found the satphone. "Relax," he said softly as he handed it to Carlos. "You've done as much as you can. It's up to them now."

Carlos nodded. A hundred and seventy miles southeast of their position, Blue Company would be paddling across the East Channel, making landfall at the Garcia Narrows. A couple of thousand miles away, White Company was hiding somewhere along the eastern coast of Midland, watching the bluffs of Hammerhead across the Midland Channel. And meanwhile, out in space . . .

"If you're going to pitch this one . . ." Chris began.

Carlos glanced at him, not knowing at first what he was talking about, until he realized that he'd been holding the satphone for a long time. Chris was remembering the day, long ago, when Carlos had unwisely thrown a satphone into Sand Creek. "If I did, would you . . ."

"Hey, what's that?" Chris pointed past him. "Look over there."

Carlos turned around. For a moment, he didn't see what his friend had spotted, then he saw it: an orange-red radiance low upon the eastern horizon, faintly illuminating the undersides of morning clouds. For a moment, he thought they'd miscalculated the time before local sunrise. But dawn wasn't due for at least another half hour, and, although the glow flickered faintly, it didn't subside as heat lightning would. Whatever it was, it was coming from Midland.

And suddenly, he realized what he was seeing.

"Oh, God," he whispered. "Not now. Please, not now . . ."

"Range three hundred yards and closing." Kim Newell barely looked up from her controls; her gaze was locked on the computer screens, her left hand steady upon the yoke as she gently fired a quick burst from the forward RCRs. "On course for rendezvous. Stand by for docking maneuver."

"Roger that." Robert Lee instinctively reached up to tap his headset mike before he remembered that there was no reason to activate the ship-to-ship radio. Indeed, there was little for him to do at that point; Kim was in the left seat, and she knew the *Plymouth* much better than he did. All he was doing was riding shotgun.

So he gazed up through the canopy and watched as the *Alabama* steadily moved closer. It didn't look the same as the last time he'd seen her—over four and a quarter years ago by the LeMarean calendar, he reminded himself, or nearly thirteen years by Gregorian reckoning. Five hundred feet in length, the starship filled the cockpit windows; five of the seven crew modules that had once formed a ring around its forward section were missing—they'd been jettisoned shortly after *Alabama* had arrived—and the shuttle cradles along its central boom were empty. The aft navigation beacon had burned out, leaving the engine section in the dark, and long-term exposure to solar radiation and micrometeorites had warped and pitted some of the hull plates. The ship had survived a 230-year voyage from Earth, yet it was meant to travel between the stars, not linger in high orbit. After so many years of being subjected to the effects of space weather, the giant vessel was slowly falling apart, like a sailing ship left to rot at the wharf.

All the same, though, it was good to see the old lady again. As Kim coaxed the *Plymouth* closer, Lee felt his throat grow tight. It had been a long while since he'd considered himself to be a starship captain. Now, at least for a brief time, he would be the commanding officer of the URSS *Alabama* once more.

He felt a hand upon his shoulder. "A little worse for wear," Dana Monroe murmured, floating next to him in the narrow cockpit, "but she's still there." She gazed up at the ship. "Glad you made the trip?"

"Yeah. Sure." Lee took his mate's hand, gave it a squeeze. "Ready to play chief engineer again?"

She gave him a hard look. "*Play* chief engineer? Sir, that is an insult."

"Sorry. Didn't mean to question your professional—"

"Oh, cut it out." She leaned forward to give him a kiss on the cheek. "But if it's play you've got in mind," she whispered in his ear, "if we get a chance maybe we can see if there's still a bunk where we can—"

"Range fifty feet and closing." Kim nudged the thruster bar again. "Six . . . five . . . four . . . three . . . ." There was a sudden jar as *Plymouth*'s dorsal hatch mated with *Alabama*'s docking collar. "Rendezvous complete, Captain."

The maneuver caused Dana to bump the back of her head against the canopy. She muttered an obscenity beneath her breath, but Kim didn't notice; she let out her breath, then reached forward to shut down the engines. Lee gazed at her with admiration. Kim claimed that flying a shuttle was like riding a bicycle, but they both knew that operating a spacecraft was far more complex than that; considering how long it had been since she'd last piloted *Plymouth*, her performance had been outstanding. True, she had been rehearsing this mission for the past two months, borrowing time from her farm chores to perform flight simulations in the cockpit, yet the fact remained that *Plymouth* hadn't moved an inch since it had been covered with camouflage nets. In that time, Kim had been more concerned with raising a little boy with her husband. And now that Tom Shapiro was gone . . . but it wasn't the time to mourn for lost friends.

"Thank you, Lieutenant." Ever since they'd lifted off from Defiance six hours before, they had subconsciously reverted to their former

United Republic Service ranks. Old habits die hard, even after so many years. "How's the airlock pressure?"

Kim looked up to check a gauge. "Equalized. We're okay to pop the hatch."

Lee unbuckled his harness and pushed himself out of his seat. Kim followed him. Dana had already left the cockpit, floating back to the passenger compartment to undo the ceiling hatch. She pulled it open, then moved aside, allowing him captain's privilege of being the first person aboard.

Lee squirmed up the narrow manhole and found the zebra-stripped panel that covered the controls for the inner hatch. Flipping it open, he pushed a couple of buttons. The airlock hissed slightly as it irised open, revealing darkness beyond. Deck H5 was pitch-black save for a couple of small red diodes on a wall panel on the opposite side of the ready room. The air was cold, with a faintly musty odor. With the heat turned down, the ship was colder than he'd expected; he was glad he was wearing a catskin jacket and trousers rather than his old URS jumpsuit.

He unclipped a penlight from his belt, then glided over to the wall panel. Recessed lights within the low ceiling flickered to life, revealing the narrow compartment. Everything looked much the same as he'd left it, down to the empty hardsuits stowed in their apertures and the fungal growth they'd discovered on the consoles shortly after they'd awoken from biostasis.

Dana followed him, but Kim hovered within the airlock. "Look, you guys don't need me," she said. "Maybe I ought to stay back, keep the boat warm."

She was clearly unsettled by the silence, nor could Lee blame her. It felt strange to be back here again. "Suit yourself. See you in a few."

'Thanks, Captain. And . . . the docking cradle?"

"I'll take care of it topside." *Plymouth* was mated to *Alabama* only by its docking collar; until they entered the bridge and reactivated the AI, Kim would be unable to remote-operate the cradle that secured the shuttle to the ship. A minor safety precaution, but best not to leave anything to chance. "We'll be back soon. Don't go away."

"Not without you. Good luck." Kim retreated to the shuttle, careful to close the inner hatch behind her. Lee watched her go, then he and Dana pushed themselves over to the central access shaft leading up through the ship's core.

The darkened shaft echoed softly as they floated upward, its tunnel walls reverberating with the sound of their hands grasping the ladder rungs. Lee was tempted to make a brief tour of his ship, yet there was no reason to do so; with most of the crew modules missing, there was little to be seen, save the hibernation modules and the engineering and life-support compartments farther up the hub. He briefly considered climbing up to the ring corridor on Deck H1, where Leslie Gillis—poor Les, condemned to a solitary existence for thirty-five years—had painted a vast mural across its walls. Sometime in the future, he'd have to visit the ship again, perhaps even dismantle the bulkheads and have them shipped home so that Gillis's artwork could be preserved for future generations. But now wasn't the time.

Lee stopped at Deck H4, undogged the hatch, and pushed it open. The command compartment was cold and dark, with only a few muted lights gleaming from beneath brittle, fungus-covered plastic covers that shrouded the consoles and instrument panels. The rectangular portholes remained shuttered; the chill air held a faint scent of dust and mildew. Something on the far side of the compartment moved; when he aimed his penlight at it, he spotted a maintenance 'bot scuttling away upon spidery legs.

"Like a haunted house," Dana said softly. "Only we're the ghosts."

She'd felt it, too. "Let's make this a little less spooky." Lee turned to a wall panel next to the hatch, found the switch that illuminated the compartment. "All right, we're in. Let's go to work."

Dana went straight for the com station. She pulled aside the cover and shoved it beneath the console, then tapped a few instructions into the keyboard. "Just as I figured," she murmured, studying the screen. "Main antenna's been disabled. Won't track incoming signals."

Of course. The Union had figured out that the resistance movement was using satphones to keep in touch with one another. Once the Union knocked out *Alabama*'s ground-to-space relay system, then the guerrillas were unable to communicate across long distances, even though Rigil

Kent had already stopped using satphones for fear of revealing their whereabouts. "Can you fix it?"

"No sweat. I'll reboot the AI, then I'll have you enter your code prefix. Once that's done, I can realign the antenna. With any luck, we'll have the satphone back in thirty minutes, tops." She glanced over her shoulder at him. "Take a break. I'll call when I need you."

"Thank you, Chief." Lee pushed himself over to his chair. It had been many years since the last time he'd sat there; the soft leather was cracked and worn, and creaked softly as he settled into it. He had to search for the belt straps that held him in place, and another minute passed before he remembered how to open the lapboard. How strange. He could skin a creek cat, milk a goat, chop down a faux birch, make a fire with damp wood . . . yet now his hands wavered above the keypad, uncertain of what to do next.

He sighed, shook his head. *Come on, Lee, get on with it. There are people down there depending on you.*

He took a moment to lock down the *Plymouth*. And then, almost as if of its own accord, his right hand sought out the controls that operated the window shutters. Dana was still at the com station keyboard, awakening the ship's computer from its long slumber; he had a couple of minutes to kill, and it had been many years since he'd enjoyed the pleasure of looking down upon a world from space. As the shutters slowly rose, he unfastened his belt again, then guided himself hand over hand along the ceiling rails until he reached the nearest porthole.

From an altitude of 450 miles, Coyote lay before him as a vast blue-green plane that curved away at either end, its clear skies flecked here and there with tiny clouds. 47 Ursae Majoris had risen from behind the planet; Lee winced and held up his hand, then the glass polarized, blocking the worst of the glare. *Alabama* was passing over the daylight terminator; looking down, he could see the first rays of dawn, just touching the east coast of New Florida.

With any luck, Red Company and Blue Company would already be in position. Once he and Dana reactivated *Alabama*'s communications system, the two teams, along with White Company, would be able to talk to one another via satphone, coordinating their movements without fear of

having their transmissions intercepted by the Union Guard. At that point, the operation would enter its second phase. But until then, he could steal a few moments to . . .

Something caught his eye: a brownish red cloud hovering just below the horizon. *Alabama* had crossed the East Channel and was above the western side of Midland; now they were above the Gillis Range, he could see that the cloud lay above the subcontinent's eastern half. At first he thought it might be a storm front, yet there had been no indication of foul weather when *Plymouth* had lifted off. The closest edge of the formation seemed to taper downward; like the funnel of an enormous tornado, it rose from the high country past Longer Creek, where . . .

"No," he murmured. "This can't be happening."

"Robert?"

Lee didn't respond. He'd heard his wife, but only faintly, as if from a thousand feet away. It wasn't until she'd pushed herself across the command deck and gently touched his arm that he pointed down at the massive fumarole below them. It took a few moments for her to realize what she was looking at; when she did, he heard her gasp.

"Oh, lord . . . that's Mt. Bonestell isn't it?"

"Uh-huh." He took a deep breath. "Hurry up with the com system. We've got a problem."

0551—MT. BONESTELL, MIDLAND

When the world came to an end, when the apocalypse finally arrived, it was with all the fury and thunder foretold by the biblical scriptures Sareech had read long ago.

First the ground shook, an earthquake that rippled the mountainside

as if Satan himself had suddenly flexed his arms somewhere in the caverns of Hell. He could hear trees snapping as if they were little more than dry twigs, the vast forest crashing down upon itself in waves of percussion that steadily moved toward him, and through it all was the odor of sulfur, heavy and poisonous, as the morning sun disappeared behind a thick, black pillar of smoke that ascended upward into the heavens, blocking out the dawn, eradicating all warmth, all light, all hope.

The *chireep* were in full panic. For many days, they had felt the tremors, smelled noxious odors rising from the flanks of *Corah*, the mountain upon which they had built their city. Some had fled—the unfaithful, those who were more afraid of *Corah* than Sareech's holy wrath—but most remained behind, believing that their god-from-the-sky would save them. Now they swarmed through the tunnels of the cliff dwellings even as the walls began to cave in, burying alive the young and elderly; they huddled together on parapets, crying out to him in words that he barely understood:

Save us, Sareech! *Rescue us! The destroyer has awakened! Use your powers to send* Corah *away! We call upon you, please stop this!*

This was the moment for which Sareech knew he'd been destined. Many years ago, far beyond the stars, he'd been Zoltan Shirow. He had been born a human, had lived his early life in that mortal shell, understanding nothing of the cosmos until the Holy Transformation had occurred. Not recognizing his own divinity, believing himself to be a mere prophet, he'd traveled to this world with his followers, only to discover that, as humans, they were inherently sinful, damned beyond hope of redemption.

One by one, his congregation had perished in the mountains. Only one among them he managed to save, after they consumed the bodies of the others in order to stay alive. Greer stood beside him; her body had become frail to the point that she was unable to walk without the aid of a stick, and her blue-green eyes had grown dark and haunted, her hair grey and matted. It had been a long time since he'd last heard her speak, yet she was still his consort even though she was no longer able to share communion with him.

Nonetheless, she was a holdover from his past. The *chireep* were his

true people. They'd found him, worshiped him as a god, and, in their doing so, Zoltan had discovered his destiny. He was not a prophet, but far more. He was Sareech, capable of taming the Destroyer.

So now, as the ground quaked and ancient forests tumbled and the air itself became foul, Sareech stood his ground. Standing on top of a wooden platform high above the cliff dwellings, he raised his arms, let his batlike wings unfold to their farthest extremity.

"I am Sareech!" he shouted. "I am God!"

As he spoke, a hideous black curtain rumbled down the mountainside, a wall of superheated ash that ignited the undergrowth, setting bushes and fallen trees ablaze. Even the bravest of the *chireep* were running away; chirping madly, they scrambled downhill in one last, desperate effort to escape. Two of his followers clutched at his legs, their oversize eyes insane with terror, their claws digging into his calves and knees, no longer even praying for salvation, merely hoping that death would be swift.

Only his consort remained unmoved. Beneath the cowl of her ragged white robe, she stared at him, ignoring the ash descending upon them. Her eyes challenged him, daring him to justify his claim to divinity.

At last it was the time. It was within his power to perform a miracle; it was the moment when he would conquer the elements. Opening his hands, Sareech reached forth, calling upon the black mass hurtling toward him to part on either side, just as Moses had once willed the Red Sea to open wide and allow the escape of the Children of Israel.

"I am Sareech! I am—"

"Go to hell," she said.

Then a wall of ash struck them with the force of a hurricane. He had one last glimpse of his consort—her head lowered, her eyes shut, her tattered robe catching fire—before she was swept away like an angel in flames.

In the next instant he was pitched off the parapet, hurled toward the ground far below. As hot ash filled his lungs, roasting him from the inside out, and his skin was flayed and his wings were ripped from his back, he had one last thought, as if a solemn and merciless voice had finally spoken to him.

You are not God.

Barry Dreyfus blew into his cupped hands, then stamped his feet on the skimmer's forward deck. The sun had come up only a short while earlier, but it didn't make the morning feel any warmer; a chill breeze blew across the channel, kicking up small whitecaps on the dark blue waters. He craved a cup of hot coffee, but was unwilling to venture below to brew a pot on the camp stove they'd brought with them. It was his turn to stand overnight watch while the others slept; so close to enemy territory, he didn't dare leave his post.

The missile carrier lay at anchor within a small lagoon, concealed by the willowlike fronds of parasol trees he and his father had cut shortly after they'd arrived the night before. It had taken over a week for White Company to make the journey down Goat Kill Creek from Defiance to the Great Equatorial River, then east along Midland's southern coast until they reached the confluence of the Midland Channel, then northwest up Midland's east coast until they reached the most narrow point of the channel, directly across from Hammerhead. Although the captured Union Guard hovercraft was capable of thirty knots, they had traveled only in darkness, weighing anchor just offshore during daytime. There had been one close brush, five days earlier, when a Union gyro had flown over them when they'd stopped near Longer Creek. Fortunately, the aircraft didn't spot them, and since then they had seen no other patrols.

He tried not to think about how cold and tired he was. His shift had ended ten minutes ago, but he was reluctant to wake up anyone. His father, Paul Dwyer, Ted LeMare . . . they were curled up in the hovercraft's tiny cabin, and needed all the rest they could get. Twenty miles away, across the broad delta north of Barren Isle that marked the confluence of Midland Channel and Short River, lay Hammerhead, and high upon its rugged granite bluffs was Fort Lopez.

Barry could barely make out Hammerhead at that distance, yet during the night he'd seen the lights of Fort Lopez, watched gyros taking off occasionally. If all went according to plan, in the morning they would attempt to take the Union Guard stronghold out of commission by launching the skimmer's rockets against its landing field. With any luck, they might be able to destroy the fort's gyros and military shuttles. Fort Lopez was unassailable by ground force, but it was vulnerable to its own weapons. All White Company had to do was maneuver the missile carrier within striking range, and the balance of power on Coyote would shift. Red Company and Blue Company would do the rest.

If all went according to plan, that is. Barry didn't want to think about how many things could go wrong. . . .

Hearing the cabin hatch creak open, he looked around to see his father climb up the short ladder. Jack Dreyfus peered at his son through bleary eyes. "Why didn't you wake me up?"

"I'm okay." Barry shrugged, gave the old man a grin. "If you want to sleep longer . . ."

"Stop it. You sound like your mother." Jack stepped onto the deck, then arched his back and yawned. "I could kill the jackass who designed these things. No room for a man to get any sleep. And with Paul snoring all night . . ."

"Yeah, uh-huh." Barry had heard the same complaints every morning for the last week. His father never stopped thinking like an engineer. He and Paul Dwyer had restored the skimmer to operating condition after it was shot to pieces during the Battle of Defiance; considering their limited resources, they had done a superlative job. Jack was a perfectionist, though; nothing anyone else ever did was good enough for him. "Did you make some coffee?"

"Ted's up. He's working on it now." Jack stretched his arms, then turned his back to him. "I need to take a—hey, what the hell is that?"

Barry turned to look in the direction his father was gazing. Until then, his attention had been focused upon Hammerhead; he hadn't looked to

the west, toward Midland. At first he saw only the lagoon—nothing unusual there—but then his eyes moved upward, and he saw a thick blanket moving across the sky. Clouds that looked like black cotton boiled
across the heavens; deep within them, he could see flashes of lightning.

"Storm coming in," he said. "We're about to get hit."

"Uh-uh. That's no storm." And indeed, the clouds were darker than
any Barry had ever seen, either on Earth or on Coyote. They resembled
smoke from an burning oil refinery, or maybe a coal mine that had been
set ablaze. And they were moving *fast*. "That's so weird," Jack added, absently rubbing the stubble of his new beard. "It's almost like . . ."

Feet rang against the cabin ladder, then Ted appeared within the open
hatch. "*Alabama* just called in. They say . . ." Then he glanced up at the
darkening sky. "Oh, hell . . ."

Jack turned toward him. "What's going on?"

"Mt. Bonestell just blew." Ted's eyes were fixed upon the menacing
clouds. "And it's coming our way."

0656—DEFIANCE, MIDLAND

The eruption couldn't be seen from the colony—Mt. Bonestell lay
over the horizon, and the closer mountains of the Gillis Range blocked the
plume from sight—yet the townspeople had been awakened by tremors
so violent that tree houses had creaked ominously in the swaying blackwoods and the bell in the center of town had rung several times. Thinking
about it later, Wendy Gunther realized that they should have anticipated
something like this, for the animals had been acting strange for the last
couple of days: chickens stopped laying eggs, goats refused to give milk,
dogs barked for no reason, and shags had restlessly paced around their

corral. But no one had been that observant, and the livestock and pets didn't have the capacity to tell their masters what was upsetting them.

It wasn't until she received the priority message from the *Alabama* that Wendy discovered that this was no mere earthquake, but something far more serious. As acting mayor in Robert Lee's absence, the colony's precious satellite transceiver had been placed in her care; she'd left it switched on, awaiting word that the *Plymouth* had reached the ship and that orbital communications had been restored. She was still picking up broken crockery and trying to calm Susan when the unit beeped for the first time in several years.

Lee's transmission didn't last very long, but Wendy managed to save the photo images he sent down before the ship passed over the horizon. Suddenly, shattered plates and a child were the least of her concerns. Once she copied the images into her pad, she put on her parka and boots, then shinnied down the rope ladder from her tree house and ran off to gather the members of the Town Council who'd remained in Defiance . . . and one more person, a recent arrival who knew much about such things.

So now Fred LaRoux was seated in front of the comp set up in the Council office, studying a succession of high-orbit images captured by *Alabama*'s onboard cameras. Save for the occasional whispered comment—"oh, boy," "uh-oh," "that's not good"—the geologist remained quiet until he ran through the series twice, sometimes backing up to zoom in on one frame or another, while the Council members sat or stood around him, murmuring to each other as they gazed at the awesome views of Mt. Bonestell as seen from space.

Wendy finally lost patience. "So what's going on?" she asked, leaning across the table so that Fred couldn't ignore her any longer. "Are we in trouble?"

He sighed. "Good news first, or bad?" He didn't wait for her response. "Good news is that the prevailing winds are pushing the plume to the east, not the west. So we're not directly in the line of the ashfall . . . it's moving away from us, toward the Midland Channel."

"White Company's over there." Henry Johnson leaned heavily upon his walking stick, taking the weight off his wounded knee. "Is this going to affect their mission?"

Fred nodded. "When that ash comes down, it's going to clog up their hovercraft fans . . ."

"But it's just ash. I don't see how—"

"This is rock ash, not wood ash. With an eruption of this severity—and believe me, this is severe—they're going to get several feet of what amounts to powdered stone. They'll be dead in the water if they don't get out of there quick as they can." He glanced at Wendy. "Better fire a message to them as soon as you can, warn them what's about to happen."

Wendy nodded, even though she knew it was hopeless. It would be another two hours before *Alabama* came within transmission range once more; until then, she'd be unable to bounce a signal to White Company. Just then, though, that was the least of their problems. "You said that's the good news. So what's the bad news?"

"Lava?" Kuniko Okada had been watching the comp screen with the same horrified fascination as the others.

Fred shook his head. "If this was a Hawaiian-type eruption, then we'd expect lava flows, yes, and even then I wouldn't be worried. Oh, maybe I'd be concerned, if my people hadn't come down here. . . ."

Fred had been the mayor of Shady Grove, a small settlement in a lowland valley beneath Mt. Bonestell, eight hundred miles northeast of Defiance. Six weeks earlier, fearing an eruption, he'd evacuated the town's sixty residents and brought them down the Gillis Range to Defiance. Since then, many of them had joined the Rigil Kent brigade; they were among the members of Red Company and Blue Company, poised for a final assault upon New Florida.

"But lava isn't a problem here," he continued, pointing to dark grey plume captured by *Alabama*'s cameras. "See that? Instead of liquefied rock, what we're seeing here is vaporized lava, coming up from a magma chamber beneath the planet's crust, along with a lot of superheated gases."

"Then . . . so what?" Vonda Cayle stood behind Wendy, nonchalant about the whole thing. "If it's just smoke, then I don't know what we're supposed to be worrying about."

"You don't understand." Fred rubbed his eyelids between his fingertips. "Look, this is a major Plinean eruption. No, not just an eruption, an explosion. What probably happened is that a bubble of magma, under very high pressure, gradually rose through the planet's crust until it reached the surface, at which point it simply blew up." He clicked to another view of the volcano, one made from nearly directly overhead. "It's hard to tell, but I think it's a safe bet that the force of the explosion was roughly equivalent to that of a nuke. Probably took out the top of the mountain. That's what we felt down here."

Fred expanded the screen so that the plume appeared in close-up. "So that's not just smoke . . . that's ash, millions of tons of it. The heavier particles stay close to the ground and roll downhill in what we call a pyroclastic flow. Think of a tidal wave, but instead of water you've got ash, rock, even boulders, moving more than a hundred miles an hour, reaching temperatures as high as three hundred degrees. Anything in its path is either crushed or incinerated."

Wendy stared at the screen. Although most of the plume extended to the east, she noticed that smaller pyroclastic flows extended in all directions, including southwest toward Shady Grove. "Good thing you got your people out of there."

"Yeah, well, I had a feeling something like this was going to happen when we started feeling tremors a few months ago." Fred hesitated. "But your friend Zoltan . . . if he didn't leave—"

"Don't call him my friend." When she and Carlos had encountered Zoltan Shirow a couple of months ago, his madness had become complete; he believed himself to be a god, with the sandthieves—the *chirreep*, he called them—worshiping him as such. She doubted that Zoltan had survived, but she couldn't help but feel remorse for the primitive creatures who had probably lost their lives. And she'd also briefly seen one of his original followers.

She must have died, too. Glad that I didn't tell Ben about her. Wendy repressed a shudder, forced her thoughts back on track. "Mt. Bonestell is a long way from here. We shouldn't have to worry about that."

"You're right. The effects of pyroclastic flows will be localized . . . say, only about thirty or forty miles from the caldera. But that's not the worst of it." Fred clicked to another view of the eruption: this one farther east, showing the plume as it moved toward the eastern side of Midland. "The wind will carry the lighter particles across the rest of the island, all the way to the Midland Channel, then to Hammerhead, Highland, even beyond. So you're going to see significant amounts of ash—up to two or three inches—falling across a broad area. Fortunately, we don't have any settlements out that way. . . ."

"But Fort Lopez is going to get hit, won't it?" Henry smiled. "A little good news there."

"Well, yeah, it's pretty dangerous to fly aircraft through a volcanic plume. Ash will muck up rotors and jet intakes. But even if their gyros are grounded, they might be able to launch their shuttles, so long as they only use rocket boosters and don't overload them."

"White Company could be in trouble, though. The skimmer . . ."

"Uh-huh. If they're in the path of the ashfall, then the skimmer's turbofans will be knocked out. Better hope they're smart enough to get out of there. But that's a minor detail. Look here."

Fred pulled up another image. This one showed Mt. Bonestell from a greater distance, as the *Alabama* passed over the Great Equatorial River south of Vulcan. The mountain itself was nearly invisible, but the plume could be easily seen as an enormous pillar rising high into the heavens, the sun catching its hazy outer reaches and tinting them luscious shades of orange and red. *A funeral pyre for a god*, Wendy thought, involuntarily recalling her earlier thoughts about Zoltan.

"Here's the problem," Fred went on. "The plume doesn't contain only ash, but also a mixture of gaseous compounds. Carbon dioxide, carbon monoxide, sulfur dioxide, chlorine, argon, fluorine, the works. They're going to hit the upper atmosphere forty or fifty miles up and be caught by the jet stream, and pretty soon they're going to spread across the entire planet. Even if this was a minor eruption, we might have something to worry about, but like I said, this isn't a hiccup."

"What are you getting at?" Again, Wendy found herself becoming impatient. "You say we're in trouble?"

"Wait a minute, all right?" Fred gave her a stern look. "We haven't been here long enough for us to study the geological history of this planet. All we can do is look at what's happened on Earth in the past and make an educated guess. That having been said . . ."

He let out his breath. "Look, about seventy-four thousand years ago,

Mt. Toba in Sumatra underwent an eruption that put up to four hundred thousand megatons of dust and gas into the atmosphere. It caused the average global temperature to drop by somewhere between three and five degrees centigrade, with the temperature in certain regions dropping as much as fifteen degrees over the course of six years. Global cooling caused hard freezes that killed off all tropical vegetation and knocked out at least fifty percent of the forests. No doubt quite a few animal species went extinct as a result."

"Oh, God . . ." Kuniko held a hand to her face.

"That's the worst-case scenario. Doesn't mean that it'll happen here. But"—Fred held up a hand—"when Mt. Laki in Iceland erupted in the late 1700's, it dumped about two thousand megatons of aerosols into the upper atmosphere and dropped the average temperature in the northern hemisphere by one percent. The same thing happened again when Mt. Tambora blew in the early 1800's, and also with the eruption of Krakatau later the same century. Global cooling leading to short summers, loss of vegetation, shorter growing season . . ."

"And you think this could happen here," Wendy said.

"That could very well be the case, yes. The only question is the magnitude of the eruption. I don't have much to go by, but with any luck this isn't a Toba event. If it is, we're sunk, because the volcanic winter could last at least two Coyote years, and we'll all die. And even if it's only on the scale of a Laki or a Tambora event, then we're still in trouble."

Wendy understood. This was only the earliest part of spring on Coyote; the weather was still cool, but in a few weeks the rainy season would begin. Once that was over, the time would come to plant the first of several crops that would sustain them not only for the rest of the year, but also for the long winter months that lay ahead. But if their livestock starved, if they had no grain stockpiled, if next winter came around and there was insufficient food to keep everyone fed . . .

"I think I see what you mean," she said softly. "Bad time for a revolution, isn't it?"

Fred nodded. "Uh-huh. Better hope it's not too late for peace talks."

As he gazed up at the ceiling of the command center, Fernando Baptiste came to the realization that he had no words for what he was seeing. During his long career as an officer of the Union Astronautica, he'd witnessed many impressive sights: the first light of dawn upon the summit of Olympus Mons, the transit of Galilean moons across the face of Jupiter, liquid methane raining down from the clouds of Titan. Yet none of these was as beautiful, nor as terrifying, as what was now displayed upon the dome of the bridge: a volcano of an alien world in full eruption, great clouds of pumice billowing forth to cover half a subcontinent.

Beautiful, yes . . . but also ominous. Coyote might be largely uninhabited; nonetheless, there were thousands of people down there. Baptiste didn't need an extensive background in planetary science to know that an eruption of this magnitude would have severe consequences. Yet he was helpless to do anything about it that would matter. How could one contend with forces of such awesome power?

"Captain?" The officer on duty at the com station turned to him. "Receiving transmission from Fort Lopez. The base commandant is online."

"Put him through, please." Baptiste touched a button on his armrest that elevated a flatscreen; a moment later, Bon Cortez's bearded face appeared. "Good morning, Lieutenant. I take it this isn't a social call."

"I only wish it were, sir. I expect you already know what's happened."

"I do indeed." Less than an hour ago a yeoman had knocked on the door of his quarters, awakening him with an urgent request to report to the bridge. Since then the *Spirit* had completed an orbit of Coyote; now that the ship was once again above the planet's daylight side, he'd been able to view the eruption with his own eyes. "How's your situation?"

"It's not getting any better, sir, if that's what you're asking." Static fuzzed his voice; the screen wavered slightly, losing focus. *"We're beginning to receive ash from the volcano . . . not much, at least so far, but it's bound to get worse. We've also noticed a marked decrease in visibility."* He glanced to one side, murmuring to someone off-screen, then looked back again. *"We've got a camera outside. If you'd like to see . . ."*

"Yes, please." The com officer had been listening to the conversation, and didn't need to be told what the captain wanted. A broad window opened on a section of the ceiling. Across the command center, crewmen stopped what they were doing to gaze up at the dome so that they could see what the men at Fort Lopez were seeing.

It was as if a vast black curtain was slowly being drawn across the sky, quickly moving across the Midland Channel toward Hammerhead. In the foreground, Guardsmen stared up at the advancing cloud formation, while flecks of what looked like pink snow flashed past the camera; ash was already accumulating on the windshields of the gyros parked on the landing field nearby. It was still early morning on Hammerhead, yet it seemed as if a premature twilight was descending upon the island. And when it did . . .

"Lieutenant, I recommend that you move the gyros," Baptiste said. "They may not be able to fly under these conditions."

Cortez's face was still on his screen, yet his image was breaking up. Same thing with the outside shot; lines raced across the view of the landing field. The ash cloud was causing electromagnetic interference. *"Sir? What did you say about the gyros? I don't understand—"*

"Get them out of there. Do you copy?"

"Yes, sir. But where do we . . . ?"

His voice crackled, became incoherent. Baptiste could barely see him, and the outside view was almost lost as well. The cloud had moved between Hammerhead and the *Spirit*, he realized, and was interfering with the uplink.

"Get them airborne!" he snapped. "I don't care where, just move 'em!"

Cortez responded with something that sounded like an affirmative, then the screen went dark. Looking up at the dome, Baptiste caught one last glimpse of the landing field—the gyros were still on the ground, and it seemed as if a blizzard was descending upon them—and then even that image was lost.

"Loss of signal, sir," the com officer said.

"Do what you can to get it back." Baptiste settled back in his chair. "We can't afford to lose contact."

With luck, Cortez might have enough time to get some of the gyros in the air before they were all grounded. Yet even if he did, where would they go? Not to the west; Midland already lay beneath the cloud. Maybe north or south, toward Barren Isle or Highland, for what little good that would do; the aircraft would consume half their fuel just getting out from under the plume. And there were not even names for the wilderness areas that lay west beyond Vulcan, let alone reliable maps.

Once again, he realized the futility of the war. So much effort had been put into fighting the Midland colonies that further exploration of this world had been neglected. Baptiste forced himself to calm down. Perhaps it wouldn't matter. Rigil Kent had been inactive for the last couple of months. It had been a long, tough winter, and the raids the Union had made upon Defiance and the other colonies had probably sapped their strength. This eruption would doubtless affect them as well, cause them to retrench even more.

If so, why did he have the disquieting feeling that he was wrong?

0834—NORTH CREEK, NEW FLORIDA

Carlos gazed at the tiny screen of his pad. The unit was hardwired to his satphone; he could view the images of Mt. Bonestell that had been relayed from orbit. "I see what you're talking about," he said. "This changes everything, doesn't it?"

"I'm afraid it does." Lee's voice from the pad's speaker was tinny yet distinct. The skies above New Florida remained clear, and with *Alabama* once again directly overhead, the satphone's parabolic antenna had no trouble achieving an uplink. *"I don't want to abort, but I'm ready to do so if you think we should."*

Carlos glanced at Chris and Marie. They were sitting cross-legged across from him, beneath the shade of one of the blackwoods where Red Company had pitched camp. Everyone else dozed within their tents, save for a couple of men standing guard near the boats, which had either been pulled ashore or, in the case of the keelboats, covered with camouflage nets. Chris didn't say anything as he idly plucked at the grass, but Marie shook her head.

"I'd like to hear more," he said. "Any word from White Company?"

"We're still trying to make contact with them. The ash cloud's causing radio interference. Defiance tells us that the skimmer's engines would be clogged by ash, though, so we must assume that they're out of the picture. But their gyros probably won't be able lift off either. If that's the case, Fort Lopez is already out of commission . . . at least, that's what they think."

Carlos nodded. Once White Company knocked out the landing fields on Hammerhead, Red Company would move in on Liberty from the north and Blue Company would take Shuttlefield from the east. The three attacks were scheduled to occur simultaneously at 0600 the next morning; taking out the Union Guard's air superiority was vital to the operation's success. The ashfall might have done so already, but still . . .

"Sounds a little iffy, Captain. Are we sure Hammerhead is down?"

A short pause. *"We don't know for sure . . ."* Lee replied after a moment. *"We haven't seen anything take off from Hammerhead, but that doesn't mean they didn't launch their gyros before the cloud moved over them. They're probably just as confused as we are, so . . ."*

"I see." Carlos absently kneaded his hands together. It had taken months to put this operation together, and now that they were so close to achieving their objective, nature had thrown a monkey wrench into the works. *Damn! If it had only erupted a couple of days later . . .*

"I say we go ahead." Chris lifted his head. "We've got everyone in place. If we abort now, we might not get another chance for a long time."

"He's right," Marie said. "We've come a long way already. . . ."

"Then we'll just go back the same way," Carlos said. "That's not the issue."

"Hell it ain't." Chris looked him straight in the eye. "C'mon, man, how much has it taken for us to get this far? Until now, they've had us by the short hairs. Now we've got them. You want to duck out now just because of bad weather?"

Carlos started to object, but stopped short. No one had been drafted; everyone there had volunteered because they wanted to be free, to live their lives without fear of Union Guard troops raiding their villages, not to work as forced labor upon projects created by the Matriarch for the further industrial development of this world. Their own lives were at risk, but also in the balance were those of countless individuals—not only in the present, but for years to come. The future of Coyote itself rested upon the decisions he'd make that morning, that moment.

He took a deep breath. "Sir," he said, "I've decided . . . we've decided . . . to proceed."

A short silence, just long enough for him to wonder whether they had debated too long and *Alabama* had already passed beyond range. But then he heard Lee's voice once more: *"Glad to hear it. I think you're doing the right thing. And for your information, Blue Company concurs."*

Carlos smiled. Of course, Lee would have been in contact with Clark Thompson. Blue Company was holding position on the Eastern Divide, waiting to march up the Swamp Road from Bridgeton to Shuttlefield. "Thank you, sir. Glad to know that Blue is with us."

"So am I." Again, a short pause. *"There's something else . . . I think we should consider advancing the timetable."*

The suggestion took him almost as much by surprise as learning that Mt. Bonestell had erupted. "By how much?" he asked. And more importantly, he wondered without asking, why?

"Let me ask. How long do you think would it take for your team to reach Liberty?"

Carlos snapped his fingers, pointed to the rolled-up map they'd been using to lead the flotilla. Chris quickly laid it out across the ground, placing stones on its corners to keep it flat. Carlos gave it a brief study; from where they were now, they would have to travel about thirty miles southwest down North Creek until they reached the point where Sand Creek branched off, then another twenty-five miles to Liberty. Fifty-five miles. Yet they would be traveling downstream all the way, and with the water running high because the snowmelt farther north, they shouldn't have trouble with shoals or sandbars.

"If we start out this evening—" he began.

"I'm thinking much earlier than that. What if you left now?"

"Is he crazy?" Marie whispered. "We can't . . ."

Carlos shot her a look. "If we leave now, we could get there"—he made a quick mental calculation—"sometime tonight, shortly after sundown."

"Sure," Chris murmured. "And we'd get there too tired to fight."

Carlos quickly nodded as he held up a hand. "Captain, my people have been rowing all night. If we spend the next twelve hours or so on the river, they'll be half-dead by the time we reached Liberty."

Not only that, he suddenly realized, but they'd also be moving in broad daylight. If anyone aboard the Union starship above Coyote were to focus their telescopes down upon New Florida, then they'd be able to see Red Company heading their way. The advantage of surprise would be lost.

"I realize what I'm asking you to do." Lee said. *"Clark Thompson voiced the same concerns, and he has the same problem."* Carlos glanced at the map again. He was right; Blue Company would have to travel by foot for almost forty miles before they reached the southern end of Sand Creek, then cross the river and hike another dozen or so miles until they reached Shuttlefield. *"There's a good reason for this. I've got an idea, one that may save a lot of lives. If it's going to work, though, I'm going to need to have Red and Blue teams within striking range of the colonies by the end of the day."*

"So what's your plan?"

He didn't hear anything for a couple of seconds. *"I can't tell you that right now."* Lee said at last, *"so I'm just going to ask you to trust me. Can you do that?"*

A leap of faith. That was what Lee was asking him to make. Chris had his face in his hands, and Marie was slowly shaking her head, yet Carlos found himself remembering the past. Two hundred and forty-five years ago, when they were only children, their fathers had made a similar leap of faith when they'd joined the conspiracy to hijack the *Alabama* and take it to 47 Ursae Majoris. And three and a half Coyote years ago, after the first Union ship had unexpectedly arrived, Lee had trusted him to lead the original colonists from New Florida into the Midland wilderness. Once again, it came down to a matter of trust. And again the future was at stake.

"Yes, sir," he said, "I can."

"I won't keep you then. You've got a lot to do. We're remaining aboard Alabama, so you'll be able to reach us again in another couple of hours. But do so only if you have to."

Back to radio silence. "I understand, sir."

"Thank you. Good luck. Crimson Tide over and out . . ."

"Good luck to you, too. Red Company out." He signed off, then disconnected the satphone from his pad.

Marie regarded him with disbelief. "Wow, that was easy, wasn't it? And he didn't even thank us. . . ."

"He's grateful. Believe me." Carlos folded the satphone's antenna, then stood up. "You heard him. We're on a new schedule. Go wake up the others, tell them to break camp and load up. We're shipping out."

His sister started to say something else, but one look at his face told her that it wasn't the right time. Heaving an expansive sigh, she stood up and marched away. Chris slowly stretched his arms. "I think I'd mind a lot less if I knew the reason why."

"He knows what he's doing. And like you said, we may not get another chance." Carlos forced a smile. "Look at it this way. If everything works out, then you get to see Luisa again a little earlier than you expected."

"Now that you put it that way . . ." Chris heaved himself to his feet, then walked away, clapping his hands as he whistled sharply. "Okay, people, wake up! Time to ride!"

"Crimson Tide to White Company. Please respond, over." Lee listened for a moment, but heard nothing through his headset but carrier-wave static. "White Company, this is Crimson Tide. Do you copy? Over."

"Give up, Robert. We're not getting anywhere." Dana pointed to one of the screens above the com panel. "Transmitter's working fine, and we've got a good fix on where they should be. We just can't break through all that—"

"I know, I know." One more try, just for the hell of it. "*Alabama* . . . I mean, Crimson Tide to White Company. If you copy, boost your gain. Repeat, boost your gain and respond. Over." He counted to ten, then finally surrendered to the inevitable. "Feels almost like they can hear us, but . . ."

"If they did, we would have known by now." She unfastened her seat belt, then floated out of her chair and pulled herself along the ceiling rail until she was next to him. "I'm sure they're fine," she added, putting a hand on his shoulder. "They just can't talk to us, that's all."

Lee absently took her hand as he gazed out the porthole. Once again, *Alabama*'s equatorial orbit was taking it over the Midland Channel. Indeed, they were passing directly over Hammerhead, yet the only way they had of knowing that was the ground track displayed on the nav station's flatscreens. The terrain itself was rendered invisible beneath the volcanic plume that covered everything between Mt. Bonestell and Mt. Pesek. Even from this distance, they could see the tiny sparks of St. Elmo's fire that roiled within the thick clouds. Short-range radios on the ground might be able to penetrate the electromagnetic interference, but from space . . .

"I guess . . . I hope you're right." If Fred LaRoux was correct, then White Company was immobilized. If that was the case, they could still clear enough ash from the skimmer's fans for them to restart the engines and retreat back down the channel. If worse came to worst, they could always abandon the missile carrier and make their way on foot across Midland until they reached Defiance.

Nonetheless, White Company's mission was a key part of the operation. Even if Fort Lopez's gyros were grounded, there was no guarantee that military shuttles couldn't be launched. And with several hundred Guardsmen garrisoned on Hammerhead, the Union still had the ability to repel Red Company and Blue Company as they moved in on New Florida.

Lee shut his eyes. Five hundred years ago, his ancestor must have faced these same choices. Yet even at Gettysburg, all General Lee had lost was a battle; the Confederacy might have perished, but America itself survived. The stakes for which he was fighting were far higher: freedom not just for a country, but for an entire world. And what he intended to do was something his great-grandfather would have never imagined. . . .

"Robert? Robert, are you . . ."

"I'm fine. Just thinking, that's all." He opened his eyes, gave her a tired smile. "Better get to work. We've got a lot to do before the next orbit."

"Sure." Dana released his hand, but she lingered by his side. "You didn't tell Carlos what you mean to do. Or Clark either."

He shook his head. "They might be caught. If so, I don't want to risk either of them telling . . ."

"You know them better than that."

He couldn't fool her, and he should have known better than to try. "It's better that they don't know," he said quietly. "If anything goes wrong . . ."

"Then let's make sure we don't screw up." Dana grasped the handrail, started to pull herself away. "So what do you want me to do first? Take the helm, or . . ."

"I'll handle navigation. You go prime the main engine." He checked his watch. "Another hour and forty-five minutes before we're in range of Liberty. Move fast." He started to unbuckle his seat belt, then he snapped his fingers. "And we'd better tell—"

"Kim. I know. She's going to love this." Dana grinned at him. "Y'know, I bet she thinks we've been fooling around up here."

"Believe me, I wish we were."

1146—LIBERTY, NEW FLORIDA

Almost noon, and the town was going about its daily routine. A pair of shags led by a drover pulled a cart loaded with manure down Main Street, their hooves splashing through muddy potholes as they headed for the farm fields outside town. A couple of women walked past on the plank sidewalk, carefully avoiding eye contact with a handful of off-duty Guardsmen lounging on a bench outside their barracks. Across the road, someone washed the front windows of his cabin. Just another day, much like any other day in early spring.

Nonetheless, as she watched all this from the front steps of the community hall, the Matriarch Luisa Hernandez had a certain sense of foreboding. With her bodyguard standing nearby, she should have felt safe, and yet she found herself gazing up at the sky. It remained clear, the bright midday sun promising a warm afternoon, but she'd seen the images of Midland relayed from the *Spirit*, listened to Captain Baptiste's report of the eruption. Mt. Bonestell was a long way from there, the winds were carrying the plume from its eruption away from New Florida.

On the other hand, contact with Hammerhead had been lost earlier that morning. Apparently the ash cloud was interfering with the satellite relay. She told herself that it was little more than an aberration. A temporary inconvenience, nothing to be worried about; her people were already working to reestablish communications with Fort Lopez through other means. But still . . .

In the three and a half years—almost eleven Earth-years; had it really been that long?—since she'd arrived on Coyote, nothing had gone the way she'd expected. It should have been a straightforward task: assume control of the colony established by the *Alabama*, institute a collectivist system of government, put the second wave of settlers to work at developing local resources, and ultimately transform this world into a new Earth. She'd anticipated difficulties, of course—this was a frontier; there were bound to be hardships—but nothing that she and the Guard shouldn't have been able to handle.

Yet it hadn't gone that way. The original colonists had not only refused to cooperate, but had also gone so far as to flee to Midland, leaving behind little more than a collection of log cabins stripped to the bare walls. The more recent settlers, those either selected by lottery or able to bribe their way aboard Union starships, had gradually turned against her; Shuttlefield had become a ghetto, and those who'd left before she barred emigration had joined forces with the resistance movement on Midland. Her effort to build a bridge across the East Channel had ended in disaster when its own architect had collaborated with Rigil Kent in its sabotage. And although she'd established a military base on Hammerhead and given the Guard the task of seeking out the *Alabama* party's hidden settlement, the recent raid upon Defiance had been repelled, at the cost of many lives and some irreplaceable equipment.

So, after all these long seasons, she found herself in control not of a world, as she had dreamed, but instead of little more than an island. And only marginal control, at that; she'd shifted most of the Guard to Hammerhead, leaving behind only a small garrison to defend New Florida. It was a risky move, yet she was convinced that the key to victory was taking an offensive stance; rooting out the Rigil Kent movement had become her top priority.

In a few short weeks, she'd take the battle to them. The locations of the major settlements on Midland had been determined by Union patrols. Although the Defiance raid had been unsuccessful, it had helped her gauge its defensive capability. There were over four hundred

Guardsmen on Hammerhead, along with gyros, armed skimmers, and military shuttles. Once the rainy season had come and gone and the creeks resumed their normal levels, she'd issue orders to attack. There would be no quarter asked and none given; by the end of spring, Coyote would belong to her.

But now . . .

A volcano erupts, and suddenly her forces on Hammerhead are rendered incommunicado. Luisa wrapped her arms around herself, drawing her cape a little closer despite the warmth of the day, and stared stubbornly at the calm blue sky. A minor setback, that was all. A slight delay in her plans. She'd faced defeat before, and had survived. This, too, would pass. . . .

The door behind her swung open. "Matriarch . . ." an electronic voice began.

"I hope you're going to tell me you've reached Fort Lopez," she said, not bothering to look around.

Heavy footsteps upon the wooden boards, then a tall figure cloaked in black moved beside her. "We have indeed, ma'am, but there's something else you should—"

"Fort Lopez. Tell me what you've learned."

Luisa couldn't help being impatient with Gregor Hull; he reminded her too strongly of his predecessor. Manuel Castro had accompanied her aboard the *Glorious Destiny*, and he had served as the colony's lieutenant governor. No, more than that; when he'd disappeared the previous autumn during the raid upon Thompson's Ferry—although his body was never found, she was certain that he was dead—she had lost her closest confidante. As another posthuman, Savant Hull was physically identical to Savant Castro. Although he'd assumed Manny's role, he could never replace him. Indeed, his very presence was an insult to Castro's memory.

The Savant hesitated. "As you wish," he said after a moment. "Satellite communications with the base are still impossible, but one gyro managed to escape."

"Only one?" Luisa looked at him sharply. "What about the others?"

"Two more lifted off. One attempted to fly through the ash cloud, but it lost power and crashed in the Midland Channel. The other reported engine trouble and was forced to turn back. It was able to land safely, and none of its crew were—"

"Get on with it."

"The third got away, but only because its pilot broke formation. It touched down on the southeastern coast of Midland, where its pilot was able to uplink with the *Spirit* while maintaining shortwave radio contact with Fort Lopez."

The Matriarch let out her breath. One gyro out of twenty. If only the ground crews had acted more quickly on Baptiste's orders . . . "I can imagine the rest. Lieutenant Cortez has grounded the rest of the squadron."

"Yes, ma'am, he has. He doesn't wish to risk losing any more aircraft. There are already four inches of ash on the landing field. . . ."

"No excuse."

"Matriarch, this isn't snow. This is volcanic ash. It doesn't melt. Two military shuttles are being prepared to lift troops and equipment to a safe location, but it may take some time before they're flightworthy. Even then, it won't be safe for them to carry more than half their usual payload, because—"

"I understand." Luisa disliked being lectured, and the Savant sounded as if he was speaking to a child. "Tell them to do the best they can, but I want Fort Lopez to be ready to resume operations as soon as possible. Is there anything else?"

"Yes, ma'am. Robert Lee wishes to speak to you."

For a few seconds, the Matriarch didn't comprehend what Savant Hull had just said. She watched the man across the road cleaning his cabin windows, admiring the diligence he exercised, soaping and rinsing every single pane. From somewhere not far away, she heard children playing softball in a field that hadn't yet been planted with the first spring crops. And suddenly, for only the second time in all these years, the man who had eluded her for so long wanted to parley with her.

"Now?" she asked. "Is he . . . I mean, do you have him online now?"

"Yes, Matriarch. His transmission is being received via satphone. I'm patched into our system, and I can relay it to you. If you wish me to provide translation—"

"That won't be necessary. Put him through."

As a pastime, she'd studied English during the last few years; she partially blamed her lack of understanding the older form of Anglo for her inability to negotiate with Lee when she'd first met him. She sat down on the steps, then raised her right hand to push aside her hair and prod her jaw, activating the subcutaneous implant beneath her skin. Savant Hull knew how to open the private channel to her; a few moments passed while he established linkage between her, him, and Liberty's satellite transceiver. There was a double beep within her inner ear, then a faint hiss.

"Captain Lee?" she asked.

"*Matriarch Hernandez.*" The voice was faint, yet unmistakable. "*You've kept me waiting.*"

"My apologies, Captain. I didn't realize . . ." Luisa stopped herself. She was the one in charge here, not him. "You have something you wish to discuss?"

"*Yes, I do. I assume you've already learned about the eruption of Mt. Bonestell.*"

"I've been informed, yes." She glanced up at Savant Hull. "Quite an event. I trust none of your people are in immediate danger."

"*At least for the time being, no. Thank you for your concern.*" A brief pause. "*It's come to my attention that this may have long-term consequences, ones of which you may not be aware. I've been reliably informed that the—*"

"Captain, would you hold a moment, please?" She prodded her implant, breaking the connection, then turned to Hull. "You say you're receiving this as a satellite transmission?"

"Yes, ma'am. Obviously he's been able to restore *Alabama*'s orbital communications system."

Which meant that, if Lee wasn't in Defiance, then he was probably aboard the *Alabama*. That wasn't a surprise; although the original colonists had left behind one of their shuttles when they had fled Liberty, they had taken the other. Yet why would Lee have returned to his ship? Something was odd. . . .

No time to worry about that now. She reopened the channel. "Sorry to keep you waiting. One of my aides wanted to speak with me."

"*They're probably wondering how I'm able to contact you. The truth is, I'm*" *aboard the* Alabama. *We came up here to restore our com network, so that our settlements could talk to one another again."*

His admission was unexpected and caught her by surprise. "I appreciate your candor, Captain. I regret having to isolate your settlements, but the terrorist actions of Rigil Kent made it necessary for us to take such measures."

Another pause. *"Matriarch Hernandez, we can debate the reasons for our conflict another time. This isn't why I've contacted you. You just expressed appreciation for my truthfulness. Are you willing to accept that I may tell you the truth about other issues?"*

"I'm listening."

"I've been told by one of my people—Dr. Frederic LaRoux, you may know him—that Mt. Bonestell poses a grave threat to everyone on this planet. It's releasing acidic gases into the upper atmosphere that will cause the average global temperature to drop by as much as five degrees centigrade. This will probably— no, very likely—result in climate changes that will drastically affect crop production over the course of the coming year."

The Matriarch smiled as she heard this. "I'm out in front of the community hall. The sky is clear and the temperature is very pleasant. Mt. Bonestell is on your side of the world. If it erupts, that's your problem."

"Don't fool yourself, Matriarch. It's your problem, too. You may not be able to see the effects now, or tomorrow, or even next week, but it'll affect you as well. Much the same thing happened on Earth in the past, and our people have little doubt that it's about to happen here, too. If we lose the summer crops, then we'll suffer drastic food shortages, and you should know by now how much we depend upon agriculture to carry us through the winter months."

She frowned. He had a point, whether she liked it or not. Despite her best efforts to increase crop production, New Florida depended upon six months of warm weather in order to grow enough food to stock the warehouses during the long, harsh months of Coyote's winter. The swampers knew how to hibernate within ball plants, but humans didn't have that option. "Assuming that your people are correct," she asked, "what do you suggest we do about it?"

"Matriarch, your people and mine have been fighting for over three years. As I

said, the reasons are beside the point." Lee paused. *"I think the time has come for us to seek a truce. We can't afford to engage in war while we're trying to stay alive."*

Luisa felt her pulse quicken. She stood up, walked down the steps, Savant Hull and her bodyguard following close behind. "You're willing to surrender?"

"No. Not a surrender. Armistice. A cessation of hostilities."

She clasped a hand over her mouth. After all this, the man was suggesting peace talks! She didn't know whether to laugh out loud or scream with victory. "I think"—she took a deep breath, hoped that she wasn't betraying her emotions—"I think we should discuss this further. What do you suggest?"

For an instant, she thought she heard another voice in the background, as if someone else aboard the *Alabama* was arguing with him. Then Lee returned. *"I'm prepared to meet with you in Liberty, face-to-face, provided I can come under flag of truce. Are you willing to do that?"*

"Certainly. Of course." This was getting better all the time; she found herself dancing from one foot to another. "Your shuttle will bring you here?"

"Yes. We can arrive at"—a few seconds passed—*"1900 hours, by your time. We'll touch down in the landing field just outside Liberty."*

The center of Shuttlefield. Perfect. "Very good, Captain Lee. I look forward to seeing you again."

"Same here, Matriarch. I hope our talks will be fruitful. Alabama *out."*

She heard a buzz within her ear, signaling that the satphone link had been broken. Luisa heaved a deep sigh. "I got him," she said quietly, unable to keep the smile from her face. "I finally got him."

"If you say so." As always, the Savant registered no emotion. "But don't you think—"

"I think very well, thank you." She turned away, allowing her bodyguard to open the front door of the community hall for her. In only a few hours, her enemy would walk into her hands, voluntarily and of his own free will. "Come now. We need to prepare for his arrival."

He must be desperate. All the better. The negotiations would be very short, and entirely on her terms.

Lee switched off, then slowly let out his breath as he settled back in his chair. For a few moments he gazed out the window, watching Midland as it passed below once more. *Alabama* was in its third orbit since they had come aboard; the titanic column of ash rising from Mt. Bonestell was clearly visible, and, if anything, it had become larger since the last time he'd seen it. He hoped that Fred LaRoux was overstating the consequences of the eruption, but he didn't think so; already the thin gauze of the upper atmosphere above the limb of the planet had subtly changed color from light blue to reddish brown.

"You know what she's going to do, don't you?" Dana floated upside down above the engineering station, consulting a pad she'd clipped to a panel while she carefully entered a new program into the keypad. "She thinks you're going to give up, and when she finds out you're not, she's going to take you hostage."

"That thought occurred to me, yes." He tapped his headset mike. "Kim, how's it going down there?"

"*I've got reentry plotted,*" she replied, "*but if we're going to touch down by 1900, we're going to have to depart by 1300 at the latest. Sorry to rush you, but we've got a tight window.*"

"Understood." Lee glanced over Dana; she briefly nodded and gave him a thumbs-up. "Shovel some more coal into the engines, we'll be there as soon as we can." He clicked off, then unbuckled the seat belt and pushed himself toward the engineering station. "I have no doubt whatsoever that she'll try to take full advantage of the situation. She's the kind of person who sees everything in terms of power."

"And you think you can deal with someone like that." Not a question, but a statement.

"I think so." He grasped a ceiling rail to brake himself. "I was once married to someone who thought that way."

Dana glanced away from the comp screen. "Sorry," she murmured, embarrassed by what she'd said. "I forgot."

"Don't worry about it." It had been many years—almost 245, in fact—since the last time any of them had seen Elise Rochelle Lee, the daughter of a United Republic of America senator, once his wife before . . . Lee shook his head. He seldom thought of Elise anymore, and when he did his memories were bitter. "Let's just say that I've had practice, and leave it at that."

Dana said nothing, but her eyes expressed sympathy before she returned to her work. Lee watched as she tapped a few more keys, double-checked what was on the screen against the datapad's display, then loaded the program into the AI. "All right, we're golden. Main engine's back online and I've preset the ignition sequence for 1930 on the nose. All we have to do now is set the trajectory and engage the autopilot."

"I've already worked out the trajectory." Lee reached for the pad. "Want me to insert the final numbers?"

"Let me handle it. I've got 'em in my head. Excuse me. . . ." Dana unclipped the pad, then performed a graceful somersault that sent her in the direction of the helm station. "If you want to do something, you can disengage the command lock-out on the autopilot. I know your code, but it'll save me a minute. Oh, and yeah, Kim might appreciate it if you opened the cradle."

"Got it." Lee returned to his chair. Not bothering to seat himself again, he pulled up the lapboard while hovering overhead, then typed in the six-digit string that would allow Dana to enter a new course into the navigation subsystem. Once that was done, he pushed the buttons that would reopen the shuttle cradle and let *Plymouth* undock from the ship.

The instruments made their discordant music of random beeps and boops, and for a moment it almost seemed as if the ship was alive again. Lee let his gaze roam across the command center. He had trouble remembering Elise's face, but it was all too easy for him to recall when this place had been filled with his crew, shouting orders to one another in those last minutes before *Alabama* launched from Earth orbit. Now it was just him and his chief engineer, preparing their ship for one last journey. . . .

"Done and done." Dana turned away from the helm, pulled herself along the rails toward him. "We're on the clock now. Better get below before Kim throws a fit."

"Yeah. Sure." Lee started to reach down, intending to close the porthole shutters, then realized that it was pointless. He withdrew his hand . . . then, on impulse, he hit the switch anyway.

"Why did you do that?" Dana watched the shutters slowly descend upon the windows, blocking out the sunlight and casting the compartment into darkness once more. "It doesn't matter."

"Yes, it does." It was hard to explain, but he felt like it was the right thing to do. Like offering a blindfold to a man being marched before a firing squad. He turned toward the hatch. "Come on," he said, feeling a dryness in his throat, "let's go before I change my mind."

1301—WHSS *Spirit of Social Collectivism Carried to the Stars*

"There it is," Baptiste said. "Increase magnification, please."

He watched as the image displayed on the ceiling changed. What had once been a tiny sliver of reflected light almost lost among the stars suddenly became a recognizable shape: the *Alabama*, picked up by the *Spirit*'s navigation telescope.

The other ship was nearly two thousand miles away, gliding just above the limb of the planet. Over the last few months, his crew had be-

come used to spotting the derelict every now and then; its equatorial orbit was higher than the *Spirit*'s, though, and on a slightly different plane,
and so the vessel would disappear beyond the horizon after each brief
encounter. Only once had anyone gone aboard the *Alabama*, and then
just to disable its communication system. Baptiste always meant to pay it
a visit, if only out of curiosity—after all, it was an historic artifact—but
he had never found the time nor the opportunity, and after a while its
presence faded to the back of his mind.

Once again it occupied his full attention. As he watched, a tiny
wedge-shaped form detached itself from its midsection. A brief flare of
light, then it slowly fell away from the ship, beginning a long descent toward the planet below.

"That must be the shuttle," the com officer said unnecessarily. "I should
be able to locate its radio frequency, sir. Do you wish me to hail it?"

"Negative." The last thing Baptiste wanted its crew to know was that
it was being observed. "Reopen the channel to Liberty, please." He
waited until he heard the double beep within his ear, then prodded his
jaw. "You're correct, Matriarch. There was someone aboard the *Alabama*."

"*Was, or is?*"

"Was. Past tense. We just saw a shuttle depart." He peered more
closely at the *Alabama*. No light within its portholes. "From what I can
tell, its docking cradles are empty. I doubt there's anyone aboard."

"*I see.*" A brief pause. "*All the same. I'd like to be certain. Can you send
someone over there to check?*"

"Just a moment." Baptiste glanced at the navigator. She tapped a couple of keys, then pointed at her screen. He punched up her console display on his private screen, quickly studied the orbital tracks of both
ships. "I can do so, but it'll take some time for a skiff to make rendezvous. Six hours at least, and only if we launch at once."

"*Please do so, Captain. At the very least, I'd like to have their satphone capability taken down again.*"

"Yes, ma'am." He didn't like Luisa Hernandez very much; she was arrogant, her methods crude and imperialistic, and once already they'd
crossed swords. Although he was in charge of military operations, she

was the colonial governor, and in certain matters her authority super-
seded his. It was her original order to deny orbital communications to
the resistance movement, and in that regard she had the final say. "I'll
send a team over right away. If that's all—"

"It isn't, I want you to come down here and join me."

Several people looked up as she said this. They were patched in to
their conversation, as normal for space-to-ground communications. It
was no secret among the crew that the captain detested the Matriarch,
and that he'd returned to the ship, on the pretext of maintaining command discipline in order to avoid having personal contact with her. Baptiste deliberately turned his back on them. "Do you think that's
necessary, ma'am?"

*"Captain, may I remind you that Robert Lee is aboard that shuttle, and that
he himself has requested this meeting? If he's planning to surrender—"*

"You said earlier that he requested an armistice."

*"Only a choice of words. This situation obviously poses a threat that he can't
handle. Or perhaps he's been considering this for a while, and just sees this as a
way out. Either way, he wants to bring hostilities to an end. As commander of
Union Guard operations, your presence here is crucial."*

Baptiste bit his lower lip. She had him there. In breaking off her operation nearly three months earlier to capture Rigil Kent, he'd asserted his
rank as the most senior Union Astronautica officer on Coyote. The role of
being a commander of an occupational force wasn't comfortable for him,
though, and since then he'd been happy to let the Matriarch do as she
would with the Union Guard reinforcements he'd brought from Earth.

He knew he couldn't wash his hands of the matter any longer. And,
he had to admit to himself, he was curious as to why Lee would make
such a sudden gesture toward peace. And the timing . . . there was
something odd about the timing. . . .

"Yes, Matriarch. I'll be there as soon as possible."

"Very good, Captain. I'm looking forward to—"

"Thank you, Matriarch. *Spirit* out." He impatiently cut the comlink,
then stood up from his chair. "Prepare a shuttle for me, please," he said,
turning to the senior watch officer standing nearby, "and tell the pilot I
want a fast descent to Liberty." With luck, he might be able to beat Lee's

shuttle to the ground. "And detail an inspection crew to the *Alabama*," he added as he headed for the lift. "Tell them to burn extra fuel if they have to, but I want them aboard as soon as possible."

The watch officer was already issuing orders as the lift doors closed behind Baptiste. His hand wavered in front of the panel as he briefly considered stopping by his cabin to exchange his duty fatigues for a black dress uniform. If this was a disarmament conference, then perhaps he should be suitably attired for the occasion.

Then he thought better of it, and pushed the button for the shuttle deck. Doing so would only waste time. Besides, he was reluctant to do anything that might make the Matriarch look good.

And he doubted that Robert Lee would care very much about his appearance.

1521—Sand Creek, New Florida

Sand Creek split off from North Creek at the tip of a broad peninsula, where it took its own course to the southeast, passing grassy savannas dotted by isolated groves of faux birch and blackwood. One after another, the flotilla turned to the left, the keelboats and pirogues trimming their sails to catch the late-afternoon wind, the canoes keeping to the center of the narrow river in order to ride the current. The water level remained high, so no one ran aground on the narrow sandbars that lay submerged beneath the surface.

Peering back over his shoulder, Carlos watched as the last of the boats made the turn, making sure that no one continued down North Creek by accident. He and Chris had switched places a few hours ago; now he sat in the stern, the better to keep track of everyone. They had long since given

338 Allen M. Steele

up trying to remain in the lead. The pirogues and keelboats had the advantage of speed, and it made little sense to try to outrace them, so they contented themselves with remaining near the rear of the flotilla; once they got closer to Liberty, he and Chris would paddle back to the front.

For a while, though, the current was pulling them along. Carlos laid his paddle across the gunnels, giving his arms a moment to rest. His back ached and his biceps felt like coils of lead cable; arching his spine, he felt vertebrae gently crack, and he shook his arms in an effort to loosen his muscles. Never before in his life had he pushed himself so hard. Even when he'd made his solo journey down the Great Equatorial River, he hadn't attempted to travel such a long distance in so short a time. And he didn't want to think about how far they still had to go.

"Got some water?" Chris was hunched in the bow seat. Like Carlos, he'd pulled off his shirt once the day had become warm; the sun had reddened his shoulders, and sweat plastered his hair against the back of his neck. He was just as tired, yet he continued to plunge the blade of his paddle into the brown water, mindless of the fact that Carlos had stopped paddling.

"No problem." Carlos reached forward, pulled aside his jacket to find the catskin flash. It was little more than a quarter full, and although he was tempted to take a drink himself, he tossed it forward. "Take a breather. Let the river do the work."

"I hear you." Chris pulled up his paddle, then reached back to find the flask. Unstopping it, he tilted back his head and upended the flask, letting some of the water fall across his face. Carlos said nothing; they could always beg some more drinking water from one of the larger boats. "What a job, man. What a job."

"Just a few more miles to go. We're halfway there. It'll soon be over."

That was a half lie, and they both knew it. They had passed the halfway point shortly before they entered Sand Creek, but more than a few miles lay between them and Liberty. They had made good time, and the current was with them, but the journey was far from over. Soon enough, they'd have to put down paddles, pick up their guns, and face dozens of Union Guard soldiers who'd had little more to do all day than clean their weapons.

Whatever Lee was planning, Carlos hoped it was the right thing, because Red Company was going to arrive dead on its feet. *Alabama* would be passing over again soon; he was tempted to pick up the satphone and bounce a signal to Blue Company, just to see how it was doing, but he and Clark Thompson had agreed to maintain radio silence unless absolutely necessary until the two teams were within sight of their respective targets.

"Yeah, well, the sooner, the—" Chris's voice abruptly dropped to a whisper. "Hey, look over there."

Carlos raised his head, peered toward the riverbank to their right. At first he didn't see anything—sourgrass as high as his chest, spider bush snarled along the edge of the water, a few trees in the background—then something moved, and he saw a boid looking straight at him.

No—not just one boid, but two . . . three . . . four. A hunting pack. Though dun-colored feathers rendered them nearly invisible against the tall grass that surrounded them, their enormous parrotlike beaks were easily discernible. Four avians, the smallest his own height, their murderous gazes locked upon them. They stood together on the creek bank, less than a dozen yards away. Carlos knew that the shallows wouldn't stop them from attacking, not with prey so close at hand.

It had been years since the last time he'd seen a boid at such close range; they didn't like the high country of Midland and had learned to avoid human settlements. Years ago one of these creatures had killed his parents, and another had come close to killing him as well; its skull used to hang from the wall of his tree house, until Susan complained that it gave her nightmares and Wendy had made him take it down.

Keeping his eye on them, Carlos slowly bent forward, searching for his rifle. Yet the boids remained where they were. They stood still, silently watching as the canoe drifted past. It wasn't until Chris picked up his paddle and carefully moved them farther away from shore that Carlos relaxed. Looking back over his shoulder, he saw the boids disappear back into the tall grass.

"I'll be damned," he murmured. "They didn't attack." He looked at Chris. "That close, and they didn't attack."

"No, they didn't. And you know why?" He grinned. "They're scared of us."

All at once, the exhaustion left him. There was no more doubt, no more need for rest. Taking a deep breath, he picked up his paddle once more.

"We're going to win," Carlos said very quietly, more to himself than to Chris. "We're going to win this thing."

1859—SHUTTLEFIELD, NEW FLORIDA

Plymouth came out of the setting sun, making a low, sweeping turn to the west that shed the rest of its velocity. In the last few seconds before it descended upon the landing field, Lee caught a brief glimpse of the shantytown that surrounded the place where this same craft—once named the *Jesse Helms* before Tom Shapiro had rechristened it—had made the first landing upon Coyote.

Good grief, he thought, his eyes widening as he gazed upon the sprawl of shacks, hovels, and tents. *They've actually got people living here?* Then the jets kicked up dust around the cockpit and the wheels touched down, and Kim reached forward to pull back the throttles and kill the engines.

"All right, we're here," she murmured. "What do you want me to do now?"

"Stay put." Lee unfastened his seat harness. "Raise the gangway after I'm gone and shut the hatch . . . just in case."

"Right. Just in case. Captain . . ."

"Open the belly hatch and lower the ramp, please." He avoided looking at her as he stood up. "If it doesn't work out . . . well, you'll know if it doesn't. Get off the ground and head back to Defiance." She started to object. "Don't argue with me. You have your orders."

"Aye, sir." She reached to the center console and toggled a few switches; there was a thump beneath the deck as the hatch opened and the gangway began to descend. "Good luck," she added. "I hope everything works out."

"Thanks. So do I." Lee pulled on his jacket, then left the cockpit. As he expected, Dana was waiting for him in the passenger compartment; she'd already opened the inner hatch, and a cool breeze was drifting in. She was putting on her serape, but he shook his head. "Sorry, no. You're staying here with—"

"Like hell. Where you go, I—"

"No, you're not." He planted his hands on her shoulders, backed her into the nearest seat. "Look, you said it yourself . . . there's a good chance I could be taken hostage. If they get me, that's fine, but if they get both of us, then they can use you to make me do whatever they want. You're not going to be able to help me very much, so you're staying here."

Tears listened at the corners of her eyes. "Damn it, Robert," she said softly, "do you have to be so . . . so logical all the time?"

He smiled down at her. "Sorry. Can't help myself." He leaned down to kiss her; she wrapped her arms around his neck, and for a few moments they held each other. "Now go forward and keep Kim company," he said as he released her and stood up. "And close the hatch after I'm gone."

"Yeah. Sure." She hesitated. "Robert, I—"

"Me, too." And then he turned and, ducking his head slightly, headed down the gangway.

Twilight was settling upon the landing field, the evening wind picking up as Bear began to rise to the east. A large crowd of Shuttlefield residents, kept at a distance by a ring of armed Guardsmen, had gathered around the *Plymouth*; he heard his name being murmured in tones of astonishment as he marched down the ramp, and even the two soldiers waiting to meet him regarded him with awe. Here was Robert Lee, the commanding officer of the *Alabama*, a figure of history and legend long before they were born. Lee couldn't help but smile; he probably would have the same reaction if Christopher Columbus suddenly landed in a spaceship.

Enough of this. He turned to the nearest Guardsman. "I'm here to meet with Matriarch Hernandez," he said, speaking in the pidgin Anglo he'd managed to pick up over the past few years. "Can you take me to her, please?"

"I . . . I . . ." The soldier was speechless, and for a moment Lee thought he'd drop his gun and ask for an autograph. "Yes, of course, but we . . . I mean . . ."

"Captain Lee?" From behind the two Guardsmen, another figure stepped forward. Wearing a dark blue jumpsuit that bore the insignia of the Union Astronautica, he carried an air of authority and obviously was unimpressed with fame. "Permit me to introduce myself," he said, addressing him in flawless English as he extended his hand. "I'm Captain Fernando Baptiste, commanding officer of the *Spirit of Social Collectivism Carried to the Stars.*"

The captain of the starship that had brought the Union Guard reinforcements to Fort Lopez. "Pleased to meet you, Captain Baptiste," he said, formally shaking his hand, "but I had rather expected the Matriarch to be here herself."

"My apologies, Captain. She's waiting for you in Liberty, at the community hall. I was sent to escort you to—"

They were interrupted by the sound of the gangway being retracted. Lee turned to watch the ramp fold against the *Plymouth*'s underside. "You're a prudent man, Captain," Baptiste said quietly, as the belly hatch slammed shut. "It might not have occurred to me to take such precautions."

Lee said nothing as he studied Baptiste from the corner of his eye. He wore the uniform of the enemy, yet Lee sensed no malice in the man; indeed, he had the strong feeling that he was in the presence of a kindred soul. An adversary, perhaps, but possibly a reluctant one. He noted the satphone clipped to Baptiste's belt, and a new thought occurred to him.

"I've learned to be careful," he said. "Especially when dealing with the Matriarch."

"Yes . . . of course." Turning aside, Baptiste beckoned in the direction of Liberty. "If you'll follow me, please?"

They set out on foot, marching side by side along the long, muddy road that led from the edge of Shuttlefield across fallow farm fields toward Liberty. Despite the Guardsmen who formed a protective ring around them, the crowd continued to follow them, peering through the soldiers, occasionally shouting Lee's name. At one point his left foot found a pothole in the road; he tripped, started to fall forward, only to find Baptiste reaching out to catch him.

Lee regained his balance, but this small incident told him that, at least for a few minutes, his safety was assured. The Matriarch might have plans for him, but Baptiste meant him no harm. The reception he'd received so far was cordial, but that could easily change. Yet if there was a possibility, however remote it might be, that he might be sympathetic to his cause . . .

The last light of day was waning, and the first stars were appearing in the night sky. He turned his head to peer toward the west, searching the heavens for one particular point of light that should be rising there. "Looking for your ship?" Baptiste stopped, allowing Lee to do so as well. "I think it should be coming over around now."

"Yes, it should." There were low clouds in the western skies, obscuring his view. He glanced at his watch. Fifteen minutes . . . "Captain Baptiste," he murmured, deliberately keeping his voice low, "have you been able to reach your people on Hammerhead?"

He nodded meaningfully toward Baptiste's satphone. "That way, no," Baptiste replied, speaking quietly as well. The soldiers, distracted by the crowd around them, weren't paying too much attention to the two men. "Too much atmospheric interference. But we've been able to communicate with them via short-range radio." He peered at Lee through the gloom. "Why do you ask?"

Lee hesitated. It was an enormous gamble, and he was all too aware that he was putting many lives at risk, his own included. But if it paid off . . .

"Listen to me," he whispered. "We don't have much time. . . ."

Once again, the starship was dark and silent, its passageways deserted, its compartments cold and lightless. The only movement aboard were those of the maintenance 'bots as they patrolled the corridors and cabins, making minor repairs here and there, making sure that the vessel remained clean.

In the ring corridor on Deck H1, a 'bot stopped to vacuum a clump of dust it had found beneath a hand-painted mural: a young man, leading a procession of figures across a hilltop, a giant ringed planet looming in the background. It had just completed this minor chore when the floor trembled ever so slightly beneath the adhesive soles of its six legs. Registering the disturbance, the 'bot sent an electronic query to its mother system. A fraction of a second later, the AI instructed the machine to return to its niche; the ship was about to engage in a major course maneuver. The 'bot quickly scurried away, its diodes briefly illuminating a work of art that no one would ever see again.

Three hundred yards from the *Alabama*, a skiff from the *Spirit* was closing in upon the ship when the ship's reaction-control rockets suddenly flared. As the pilot watched, its bow pitched downward until it was pointed at the planet far below. He barely had time to report his observation before *Alabama*'s secondary thrusters ignited, and the giant vessel began to move away from him.

Grabbing his yoke, the skiff pilot fired his RCRs to take his tiny craft to a safe distance. His precaution was wise, for few seconds later *Alabama*'s main engine came to life, its white-hot flare silently lancing out in space.

Through his cockpit window, he watched in awe as the mammoth spacecraft began to fall toward Coyote.

With its main engine burning at full thrust, it took only a few minutes for *Alabama* to reach the troposphere. The ship wasn't designed to land upon a planet, yet the deorbit maneuver its captain had programmed into its autopilot guaranteed that it would take a long, shallow dive through the planet's atmosphere. And even though *Alabama* wasn't streamlined, it was still over five hundred feet long, with a dry weight of nearly forty thousand tons.

Even as the massive cone of its Bussard ramscoop disintegrated, bow shock formed an orange-red corona around its spherical fuel tank, until the intense heat of atmospheric friction ignited the last remaining fuel. In the last few seconds, the 'bots shut down for good before the explosion ripped apart the forward decks, and Leslie Gillis' mural of Prince Rupurt was lost for all time.

Yet the *Alabama* survived, if only for a little while longer. Just long enough for it to complete one final mission.

1932—LIBERTY, NEW FLORIDA

Robert Lee found Luisa Hernandez waiting for him within the community hall, the place he and the others who'd built it with their bare hands had once called the grange hall. He was pleased to see that the mural of the *Alabama* that graced one its walls hadn't been taken down; long benches ran down the length of the floor, and the wood-burning stove that they'd installed to heat the room had been removed, but otherwise it was much the way he'd left it.

The hall was vacant, except for several soldiers positioned near the windows. The Matriarch stood near the middle of the room, another Union Guard soldier close behind her, a Savant standing nearby. As Lee entered, a Guardsmen stepped in front of him; with no preamble or apologies, he quickly patted Lee down, searching for any hidden weapons. Lee submitted to the search, taking the moment to size up the woman standing before him.

She'd aged quite a bit since the last time he'd seen her; her hair had grown longer, and it was thin and tinged with grey. The lines of her face had become sharper, her stout figure less fulsome. Even so, Lee reflected, there had seldom been any days in which she'd had to skip a meal or nights in which she'd slept in the cold. Others might have starved while she tried to sustain a cocoon of comfort around herself, but no one survives Coyote without feeling the hardships of the frontier.

The soldier completed his task, turned to the Matriarch, and nodded. "Captain Lee," she said, as if none of this had happened. "Good to see you again."

"Matriarch." Behind him, he heard the front doors close, shutting out the crowd that had followed him from the landing field. Only Baptiste had accompanied him inside, and he stood off to one side, his hands behind his back. "You're well, I take it."

"It's been a long winter." An offhand shrug beneath her robe; the same one she'd worn the first time they had met, Lee observed, yet noticeably faded, patched in several places with swamper hide. "Care to sit?" she asked, gesturing to the nearest table; as her hand rose, he caught a glimpse of the pistol holstered beneath her robe. "Perhaps some coffee?"

"No, thank you." Lee remained standing. "Matriarch, about the eruption . . ."

"Yes, of course." Still maintaining a pose of amicability, she took a seat, crossing her legs and folding her arms across her chest. "You're concerned about the long-term effects, and nor can I blame you. Defiance and the other settlements on Midland will undoubtedly suffer quite a bit from it."

"No question about it, but so will you. New Florida's distance from

Mt. Bonestell matters little. This may be the last warm day we'll experience for quite a while. And you know as well as I do how much we depend upon regular crop rotations to keep everyone fed."

"Oh, come now." She gave him a condescending smirk. "I doubt it'll be as serious as you believe. And even if it is, we're not entirely at the mercy of nature. Greenhouses can be built, hydroponics can be implemented."

"I agree. If we act now, the worst of this can be mitigated. But we can only do so if we're not having to fight each other at the same time. The first thing we must do is bring an end to this conflict."

"Absolutely. No question about it." She was having a hard time keeping a straight face. "I'm more than willing to negotiate terms of surrender."

Lee nodded. "Thank you. I'm pleased to hear this. Our first condition is that the Union Guard must lay down its weapons at once, and—"

"Captain! I must . . . come now, be serious! We're discussing your surrender, not mine!" Even as she laughed at his expense, Lee watched Baptiste move closer to the Savant. Behind her back, there was a whispered consultation. He tried to remain calm, even though he knew what was being said.

"I'm quite serious," he continued. "Your forces must surrender at once, beginning with giving up their firearms. If they do so, I promise that no harm will come to any of them, and they'll be treated fairly by—"

"Enough." The smile faded from her face as she raised an indulgent hand. "Captain Lee, you've got a good sense of humor, but the joke's gone far enough. Rigil Kent has inflicted some damage upon us, I'll grant you that, yet the fact remains that your people are outnumbered by at least ten to one. Not only that, but we have more weapons at our disposal than—"

"No, ma'am," Lee said, "you don't. Or at least not for very much longer." And then he turned to Baptiste. "Captain . . . ?"

Hearing his name, he looked away from his private discussion with the Savant. "Matriarch," he said, "a few minutes ago Captain Lee advised me to order the emergency evacuation of all personnel from Fort Lopez. I've done so, but I'm not sure if there's been enough time to—"

"You've . . . *what?*" Standing up, Hernandez turned to stare at him. "What are you . . . ?"

At that instant, from somewhere not far away, they heard the distant sound of gunfire.

For a few seconds, everyone in the room froze, then one of the soldiers rushed to the door. He flung it open, and now they could hear small-arms fire from not far away, along with shouts from the crowd outside. The Matriarch's bodyguard immediately moved to protect her, while Baptiste sought cover behind a table.

Only the Savant and Lee remained where they were. The posthuman was almost placid, his only visible reaction a slight lowering of his head within his hood, as if he was listening to distant voices no one else could hear. Then his metallic face turned toward Lee, his ruby eyes seeking his own.

"Very good, sir," he said. "Very well played."

1947—MIDLAND CHANNEL

"Hey, you see that?"

Hearing his father's voice from the bow, Barry Dreyfus looked up from his work. For the past hour or so, he and Ted had been clearing ash from the intake ducts of the skimmer's turbofans. It was the second time they'd done so; even after they'd left the lagoon and retreated down the channel, ash had continued to fall upon them, clogging the intakes and threatening to overheat the engines, forcing Paul Dwyer to shut them down before they burned out.

Pathetic. Instead of taking out Fort Lopez, they were limping home in a crippled skimmer, their mission a failure. Oh, perhaps the gyros were grounded, yet a few minutes ago they'd spotted a shuttle lifting off from Hammerhead, swiftly rising until it pierced the heavy clouds that shrouded the night sky. At least three more were still on the ground; if the Union could launch one, then they'd soon be able to launch the others. If that happened, the Union would be able to dispatch reinforcements to New Florida.

Then Barry raised his eyes, and these thoughts were forgotten. Even though the sun had long since gone down, to the west he could see a faint glow within the clouds: a thin halo of light, quickly moving to the east, growing brighter by the moment. At first he thought it might be the shuttle returning to base, but that didn't make any sense. Why would . . . ?

"Holy . . . !" Ted yelled, and in that instant a miniature comet broke through the overcast, a white-hot fireball that painted the underside of the clouds in shades of scarlet and burnt orange as it streaked across the dark heavens. Thinking that it was headed their way, Barry instinctively ducked, until he realized that it was falling toward . . .

"Get down!"

Jack Dreyfus's voice was lost in the sound of the sky being ripped open, and then the fist of an angry god came down upon Hammerhead. Barry threw up his hands, yet even with his eyes shut he could see the retinal afterimage of the nuclear blast seared across his plane of vision.

The roar sent him to his knees. He put his head down, feeling the deck rock beneath him. When he opened his eyes again, the first thing he saw was the concussion rippling across the channel, a series of sustained thunderclaps that sent up tiny waves across the dark waters. Then he raised his head, and stared in shock at the distant granite bluff. Where Fort Lopez once stood, there was now a fire-drenched mushroom shape rising high into the sky.

"What was . . . ?" His voice was a dry croak, without any expression save bewildered astonishment. "What did . . . I don't . . ."

"I'm not sure." Ted's eyes were wide as his own. "But I've got a feeling that was something very precious."

The first shots were already fading in the distance when the advance team reached the boat dock. Jumping from his canoe onto the dock, Carlos crouched low, brought up his rifle, quickly scanning the area through its infrared sights. As before, no soldiers were visible; the dock and the nearby boathouse were deserted.

He reached down to offer Chris a hand, but he was already clambering out of the stern, gun in hand. No time to tie up; they let the canoe drift away as they dashed toward the boathouse. Behind them, more canoes were approaching the dock: the strike force to retake Liberty.

The boathouse was the same one where he and Chris had built the canoes they'd used to explore the Great Equatorial River. Carlos didn't give himself a chance to reflect upon that irony as they flattened behind its log walls, taking a moment to assess their situation while they waited for the others to catch up. To the south, they could hear scattered gunfire coming from the direction of Shuttlefield.

"That's Blue Company," Chris whispered. "Clark's guys shouldn't have much trouble. A few Guardsmen, some Proctors . . . they'll go down easy enough."

Carlos nodded. He was more concerned about what was happening north of Liberty. They had left the rest of Red Company a half mile upstream, to invade the colony from the opposite direction. With luck, simultaneous incursions from north and south would divert the Union Guard's attention from the creek, giving his team a chance to infiltrate the town center just a few hundred feet away.

"You ready to do this?" The hours they'd spent on the river had left him feeling light-headed; he reached down to massage a cramp in his leg.

"We've got a choice?" Chris glanced back at him. "I mean, if you want to take a nap, go ahead, we'll—"

"Never mind." Hearing movement behind them, he looked back and saw shadowed forms advancing toward them, the weathered boards creaking beneath their boots, Bear's pale blue glow lending a soft luminescence to their faces. Marie was the first to join them, her carbine clasped against her chest. She caught his eye, nodded once. They were all there. Time to move in.

Carlos raised his hand, silently pointed to either side of the shack, then leveled his palm and lowered it: *Half of you go this way, the other half go that way, and stay low.* No one had to ask what he meant, or who was going where; they'd rehearsed this phase of the operation many times over the past month, and everyone had memorized Chris's hand-drawn maps of the colony. While a half dozen Rigil Kent members fell in behind Chris, Marie, and five others followed Carlos.

A narrow dirt path led them through brush and tall grass until they came up from behind the community hall. By then they could hear gunfire coming from the north as well; Red Company had apparently engaged the Union Guard. Between the grange and the nearest cabin, he spotted Guardsmen emerging from their barracks across Main Street, running toward both Shuttlefield and the north side of Liberty.

The battle for New Florida had begun. Although he was tempted to join the fight, Carlos focused upon his principal task. Raising his hand, he brought his people to a halt, then crouched low and peered through the sourgrass. Light glowed within the windows of the community hall; apparently someone was inside. Good. The Matriarch might have taken cover within; since his group's primary objective was capturing her, that left Chris's team clear to achieve their task of taking down the Union Guard barracks.

The clatter of gyro rotors. Carlos looked around, saw aircraft lights rising from Shuttlefield. There was a thin streak of fire from the ground, and a half second later the gyro exploded. As it plummeted to the ground, he heard distant voices raised in victory. The gunfire resumed, only more sparsely. Blue Company had taken out a gyro; now the people of Shuttlefield were joining the fight as well, rebelling against the Guardsmen and Proctors who'd been their overlords for so long,

Staying as low as possible, Carlos moved his people closer to the hall. They were less than forty feet from the entrance when a pair of soldiers came around the front of the building. Although people were fighting on either side of them, they were sticking close to the hall. Someone important was inside; he had little doubt who it was.

Carlos turned around, only to find Marie crouched next to him. He pointed toward the soldiers, and she nodded; she knew what to do. Raising herself up on one knee, she propped her rifle against her shoulder, took careful aim at the Guardsmen. One shot, and one of them went down; the other barely noticed that his comrade had been hit before the next shot took him down as well. Carlos tried not to notice the grin on his sister's face. It had to be done, and she was an incredible sharpshooter; despite that, he felt horror at the pleasure she took from killing people. When this was over . . .

Worry about that later. Carlos jumped up, tore out of the high grass, raced toward the front steps of the hall. He was less than a dozen feet away when the door slammed open and another soldier emerged onto the porch. Seeing Carlos, he whipped up his rifle and fired. Bullets zinged past Carlos's left ear even as he crouched, aimed, fired. The Guardsman fell, his body keeping the door ajar.

Bolting up the stairs, Carlos dashed inside with his rifle raised. The light dazzled him, causing him to blink, and the warmth of the room was suffocating after the cool of the evening, yet now he saw several figures standing only a few feet away.

A Savant, cloaked in black, standing silently in the background. A Union Astronautica officer half-hidden behind an overturned table. A middle-aged woman in a frayed purple robe, her right hand outstretched, holding a pistol on . . .

"Don't shoot!" Lee snapped.

Carlos's expression, so determined just an instant before, changed to one of bewilderment. It was obvious that Lee was the last person he expected to see there. Yet his rifle remained fixed upon the Matriarch, his index finger poised on the trigger.

"What . . . how did you . . . ?" Carlos began. Behind him, several other members of Rigil Kent were rushing into the hall. Seeing Lee, they came to a stop, yet no one lowered their weapons.

"I'll tell you later." Lee carefully kept his voice even. "Right now, I want you and everyone else to just calm down." That wouldn't be easy—outside the building, they could hear the sounds of gunfire—but the last thing he wanted was to have the negotiations end in a shoot-out. He looked past Carlos to the two men standing closest to the door. "Go out and stand watch. Make sure no one comes in."

They hesitated. "Do it," Carlos said, and they reluctantly went back the way they had come, leaving the door open. "Captain—"

"Not now." Lee returned his attention to Luisa Hernandez. Her pistol, which she had produced the moment her bodyguard had dashed outside, was still aimed straight at him. At that range, she'd couldn't miss. "I believe we were discussing terms of surrender."

"You had this planned all along." Her voice trembled with barely suppressed rage. "Under flag of truce, you came here to negotiate peace, knowing that your people were preparing to attack—"

"I didn't plan to be here until just a few hours ago. Carlos wasn't aware of what I was doing, were you, Carlos?" The younger man shook his head, but she ignored him. "There's still a way to resolve this peacefully, Matriarch. There's no reason why more of your people should die . . . and believe me, your troops are outnumbered."

The left corner of her mouth flickered in a sardonic smile. "For now," she said, her gun still leveled upon him, "but not much longer. Oh, you may be able to take control, but I can have reinforcements from Fort Lopez here within an hour."

Lee looked over at Baptiste. He had risen from behind the table he'd kicked over, and he stood silently nearby, a witness to the endgame. "Captain . . . ?"

"Matriarch"—he cleared his throat—"Ma'am, it's my sad duty to report that Fort Lopez has been destroyed. Captain Lee informed me of this just before we arrived."

Her eyes widened. "How . . . you can't know this! Why would you trust his word—"

"It's true." For the first time, Savant Hull spoke up. "While you've been . . . um, engaged in negotiations . . . I accessed the *Spirit*. Sixteen minutes ago, a force as yet unknown struck Hammerhead, obliterating our base there—"

"That force was the *Alabama*," Lee interrupted. "Before I left, I preset its guidance system for a deorbit trajectory that would bring it down on Fort Lopez. I gambled that, even if most of the forward section disintegrated during atmospheric entry, the engine's fusion reactor would survive long enough to reach the ground."

"He didn't do it without fair warning." Baptiste stepped around the table. "After he arrived here, he informed me of what he'd done. That gave me a chance to contact Fort Lopez and order an emergency evacuation of all troops. I did so before we—"

"Thank you, Captain. Well done." Hernandez looked at Hull again. "And were the troops evacuated?"

"One shuttle was able to lift off before the base was destroyed. From what I've been able to gather, it carried eighty-eight survivors. They're now en route to the *Spirit*."

Lee winced as he heard this. He glanced at Baptiste. "My apologies, Captain. I'd hoped you might be able to rescue more."

"I'm sure you did," Hernandez said coldly. "Captain Baptiste, make contact with the shuttle, tell it to change course. It's to land here, with the objective of—"

"No, ma'am. I refuse."

She gaped at him in astonishment. "What did you say?"

Baptiste assumed a formal military position: feet spread apart, hands locked together behind his back, back rigid and chin uplifted. "It's my judgment," he continued, staring straight ahead, "that the objectives of this mission . . . that is, to establish a self-sustaining colony upon this world . . . have been neglected by a personal desire for—"

"Get those soldiers on the ground!"

"It's over, Matriarch." Lee spoke softly, yet his quiet voice carried more force than her outraged shout. "Captain Baptiste knows the truth, and I suspect the Savant does as well. You can't conquer a place whose people don't want to be conquered. The most you can do is occupy it for a short time. Ancient Rome learned this, and so did Nazi Germany and the United Republic . . . those who want to be free will remain free, at any cost, even their own lives."

All this time, Hernandez had held the pistol upon him. Suddenly she seemed to shrink in upon herself, like a woman who had once worn pride as her armor and suddenly found it replaced by mere flesh. The pistol wavered, shook within her grasp; Lee found himself remembering the last time he'd stared down a gun barrel, many years ago aboard the *Alabama*.

"What is it that you want?" she asked, almost in a whisper.

"Removal of all Union Guard troops from Coyote. Relinquishment of all territorial claims by the Western Hemisphere Union. Return of the *Spirit* to Earth, along with anyone who wishes to go back . . ."

"Of course." Her hand dropped, as if tired of holding the gun for so long. Her eyes were dull, registering hopeless defeat. "It's all yours. You win."

Lee fell silent. All the years of exile, all the years of revolution, had come to this moment: a quiet surrender, in a place he'd once helped build. His namesake had surrendered inside a courthouse in Appomattox, with his defeated troops gathered just outside; this evening, with the last few shots of battle dying off in the distance, his own war was drawing to a close.

Turning away from the Matriarch, he found Carlos waiting nearby. To his relief, the younger man had lowered his rifle. That was a good start. "Tell your people to cease—"

"Robert!"

Gunshots from behind him, then something slammed into his back: three bullets that punched through his spine, his lungs, his heart. His mind barely had time to register the pain before his muscles lost control and he pitched forward, his hands grasping at the unexpected wetness at his chest. He hit the floor facefirst, barely able to think, unable to move.

Everything came to him as a hollow roar of sensation—gunshots, voices, hands grasping at him. He fell over on his back, saw Carlos staring down at him even as his vision began to form a lightless tunnel. He heard something pounding, at first with loud persistence, and then much more slowly. Carlos was saying something to him—*Captain, can you hear me?*—but he could barely comprehend the meaning of the words.

Beneath the pain there was a warm inviting pillow. He felt himself falling into it. Yet there was one last thing he had to say before he rested . . .

He spoke, hoping that Carlos heard him. Then darkness closed in upon him.

2614—Shuttlefield, New Florida

Within the stark glare of the Union shuttle's landing lights, a long row of bodies lay upon the ground, each wrapped in a black plastic bag. A pair of Guardsmen picked up their fallen comrades one at a time, and carried them up the ramp, where other soldiers secured them to the deck with cargo nets. Twenty-two bodies in all, including that of the Matriarch; Carlos couldn't tell which was hers, and he was reluctant to ask.

"I'm sorry it had to end like this," he said quietly, careful not to raise his voice lest it break the silence. "I know that sounds awful, but if there could have been any other way . . ."

"You don't have to apologize." Baptiste stood next to him, watching the dead being taken away. The night was cold, and his hands were shoved in the pockets of the military-issue parka someone had given him. "In fact, I prefer that you didn't. These men died in the line of duty. It's not for you to say whether it was right or wrong."

Carlos didn't know what to say to this. He'd killed one of the men himself; the fact that he'd done so to liberate his home mattered very little at that moment. Sometime the next day, he'd have to bury some of his own: twelve Rigil Kent members, along with seven colonists from Shuttlefield and Liberty who'd given up their lives in the name of freedom.

And one more, whose death weighed upon him most of all.

"But you're right." Baptiste looked down at the ground. "There could . . . there should have been another way. This world belongs to you, and we had no right to take it from you." He looked up at Carlos. "If there's anyone who owes an apology . . ."

"Thank you, but . . . maybe you're right. Anything you'd say now would only be an insult."

Baptiste said nothing, but simply nodded before turning his face away. Within the ring of armed men surrounding the landing field, Carlos watched Union Guard soldiers marching aboard other shuttles. With their guns taken away, they represented the defeated remnant of the force that had once held New Florida. Among them were several dozen civilians: a handful of Union loyalists, but mainly those colonists who'd simply decided that they'd had enough of Coyote. More would join them before the last shuttle lifted off early the next morning, yet Baptiste had assured him that the *Spirit* had enough biostasis cells to accommodate everyone who wanted to return to Earth.

"Are there going to be more?" Carlos asked. "I mean, will the Union send more ships out here?"

"I don't know." Baptiste shrugged. "My ship was the last one in the fleet . . . and believe me, they were expensive to build. But that was almost fifty years ago, and I don't know what's happened since then. For all I know, there could be more on the way . . . or none at all."

"But Savant Hull will be awake during the journey, right?" Carlos had seen him board the shuttle just a few minutes ago. Baptiste nodded. "Then tell him to send a message to any ships they see coming this way. Tell them that . . ."

He took a deep breath. "Tell them that this is our home. We want freedom, and we'll fight to keep it that way. Tell them, Captain."

Baptiste didn't respond. Once more, his eyes returned to the bodies of the fallen Guardsmen. "I believe you," he said at last, his voice low, "and I'll pass the word along, but tell me one thing."

"Yes?"

"What are you going to do now?" Baptiste turned to look him in the eye. "You've won your freedom. So what are you going to do with it?"

Carlos met his gaze without blinking. "We'll do what we've always done best. We'll survive."

For a long while, the two men regarded one another in silence. Then Baptiste offered his hand, and Carlos took it. "Good luck to you," Baptiste said. "I hope you find what you're looking for."

Then he turned away, joining the procession of men, both living and dead, going aboard the shuttle that would take them back to the *Spirit* and, eventually, back to Earth. In the days to come, Carlos would regret never having thanked him for the choice he'd made, or for failing to realize that his last words echoed something that had been said to Lee a long time ago.

After Baptiste disappeared within the craft, Carlos watched the last few Union Guard soldiers march up the ramp. It slowly rose upward, then the hatch closed behind it. He stepped back as the ascent jets whined to life. A ragged cheer rose from the crowd as the shuttle slowly lifted off, and a few people fired their guns into the air. All he felt was exhaustion, as if the weight of a world had settled upon his shoulders.

Coyote was free. Yet Robert Lee's last words haunted him, echoing through his mind: *It's yours . . . it's yours . . . it's yours . . .*

Part 8

HOME OF THE BRAVE

The monster rose from the East Channel on a clear and sunny afternoon in late summer, a day so warm and fresh that it was as if the world had not skipped a season and a retrograde spring had finally come. The monster wasn't aware of these changes; for ten months he had known only the darkness and cold of the silent depths that had been his prison. At long last he'd had finally escaped, and now he emerged to see the sky again.

The creature that shambled out of the water was human-shaped and had a human mind, yet he wasn't human. His ceramic-alloy body, once a burnished shade of chrome silver, was now dull and corroded; weeds clung to the creaking joints of his skeletal limbs, and dark mud caked the clawlike feet that sank deep into the coarse gravel of the river shore. His right leg, broken last autumn by gunfire at close range, had been braced with a piece of sunken wood, lashed against it with lengths of tightly coiled weed; even then, he was only able to stand upright with the assistance of a waterlogged tree branch he'd fashioned into a makeshift crutch. Within his skull-like head, only his right eye emitted a ruby glow; his left one had been shattered when he'd attempted to scale an underwater cliff, only to become half-blind when he slid back down and his face struck a sharp rock.

Ten months in the channel. Ten months by the Coyote calendar; by Gregorian reckoning, that was two and a half years. That's how long it had taken for him to find a way out of his watery tomb. A hundred feet down, there had been only the most wan light from far above. Trapped within a narrow canyon, he'd crawled along its belly through silt and sludge, dragging his broken leg behind him as he struggled through muck and the decaying carcasses of dead fish, until he finally discovered a slope he was able to climb. And even then, more than seventy feet separated him from the surface. It had been a long hike across the river bottom until he reached the shallows, and yet he'd done it. He had no choice but to survive; death was a gift he couldn't give himself.

For a long while he stood upon the rocky beach, water drooling off his body, held upright only by the length of wood that he'd come to think of as his best friend. Sunlight registered feebly upon his remaining eye; lacking stereoscopic vision, everything seemed flat and one-dimensional.

Turning around, for the first time he saw where he was. The massive limestone bluffs of the Eastern Divide towered above him; a half mile away, an immense wooden bridge rose above the channel, connecting New Florida to the distant shores of Midland. He remembered the bridge; he'd watched it being built, witnessed the act of sabotage that caused its midlength spans to come crashing down. Now the bridge had been repaired; indeed, he could dimly make out forms moving along its roadway.

Seeing the bridge intact again, he felt a surge of joy. In his absence, the Matriarch had persevered. Once he returned to Liberty, she'd make sure that the ones who'd dare attempt to murder a Savant were brought to justice. She would not let their crimes go . . .

"Over here! It's over here!"

Hearing a child's voice shouting somewhere behind him, he looked around, saw a couple of small figures running toward him: two boys, carrying fishing rods. Lurching the rest of the way out of the water, he raised his free hand. One of the boys stopped, his face expressing fear. The other one slowed down but continued forward, more curious than afraid.

"Who are you?" the boy demanded.

"S-s-s-sa . . ." Covered with sand, his vocodor made only a harsh noise; the boy stared at him quizzically until he adjusted the pitch and volume, tried again. "S-s-savant Manuel Castro. I—"

"What happened to you?" The boy stared at his broken leg. "You look like crap!"

He was unaccustomed to such impudence, especially from one so young; nonetheless, it was good to see another face, hear another voice. "I was captured by members of the resistance. They took me prisoner, then threw me off a raft several miles upstream. They tried to kill me, but as you see—"

A stone struck the side of his head.

Castro felt no pain, yet his vision blurred for a half instant. Looking around, he saw the other boy pulling his arm back to hurl another rock at him. "A Savant! Tomas, get away! It's a Savant!"

"Stop that!" he shouted. "Under authority of the Matriarch, I order you to!"

"You know the Matriarch?" Tomas peered at him.

"Of course, the Matriarch Hernandez!" The other boy threw his rock, but it missed him, splashing into the water behind him. "Stop this! And tell me who you are!"

"I'm Tomas Conseco, and I'm taking you prisoner." Then Tomas kicked the crutch out from beneath his leg.

Castro toppled to the ground, and the boys attacked him. He wrapped his left arm across his face to shield his remaining eye, as for several long minutes they kicked him and pelted him with stones and gravel. When they finally got tired of their sport, the boys grabbed him by the arms and began dragging him across the beach. He was impressed by their strength; only hatred could lend so much muscle to those so young. For a moment, he thought they were going to pitch him back into the channel—which would have been a blessing—but instead they hauled him toward the bridge. Yet the worst indignity came when Tomas opened the fly of his trousers and, with hideous glee, urinated upon him.

It was at that point when the Savant Manuel Castro, former lieutenant governor of New Florida, realized that many things had changed while he'd been away.

On the eve of First Landing Day, Liberty was busy preparing itself for the festivities.

As he strode through town, Carlos saw townspeople suspending pennants between woodframe houses, stringing lights above their windows. Out front of the grange hall, vendors and craftspeople were setting up tents; the early arrivals had already put out their wares upon benches and tables: handmade clothing, catskin boots and gloves, cookware and cutlery, labor-saving devices for the frontier home both complex and simple, hand-carved children's toys. Shags carrying visitors from the Midland colonies shambled down Main Street, with Proctors directing them to stables where the beasts could be kept while their owners found temporary lodging either with friends or in one of the boardinghouses in Shuttlefield.

And everywhere Carlos looked, the new flag of the Coyote Federation rose from poles or hung from porches; it had even been painted across the faux birch walls of some of the houses that had recently been built along the side streets. Despite his dark mood, this gave him a certain sense of satisfaction. During all the public meetings he'd chaired as mayor, not even the long debates over the exact wording of the various articles of the Liberty Compact had raised as much ire as the ones pertaining to the flag's design, and it wasn't until Vonda Cayle presented her compromise—the Ursae Majoris constellation, transposed upon three horizontal bars of red, white, and blue—that all sides were satisfied. Now that the "Big Dipper" had been formally adopted, everyone took pride in it; at least it wasn't as scary as the one proposed by the Forest Camp delegation, which featured a snarling coyote above the slogan "Don't Mess With Me!"

The long, cold summer of '06 was almost over, and everyone was ready for a party, yet that wasn't what occupied his mind just then. Ignoring the bunting and decorations, giving only passing nods and hand-waves to citizens who called his name, he headed for the windowless log cabin at the end of the street. First Landing Day could wait; before he could join the celebration, there was some family business that needed to be settled.

The Chief Proctor was waiting for him outside. "She's in there," Chris said, then held up a hand as Carlos marched toward the door. "Look, wait a minute—"

"Wait for what?" Carlos started to walk around him, but Chris stepped in his way. "How many times have your guys brought her in? Two? Three?"

"It's the fourth . . . but it's more serious than that." Chris dropped his voice. "This time she's put someone in the infirmary."

Carlos stopped, stared at him. It wasn't the first time Marie had been taken into custody by the blueshirts; on three occasions his sister had been charged with public drunkenness, and the last time she'd also faced charges of assault and battery stemming from a brawl in which she'd been involved. "What happened?"

"Lars was with her," Chris said quietly. "They picked a fight with some guys from Forest Camp. About what, I don't know, but Lars threw the first punch."

"So it was just a fight."

"It got worse. Witnesses say she broke a bottle and slashed someone's face with it. Wendy just called, told me that she's had to put ten stitches just below the right eye." Chris paused. "Sorry, man, but that's assault with a deadly weapon. I can't look the other way this time."

Carlos nodded. The first two incidents, he'd asked Chris to do nothing more than lock her up for the night. The third time, he used his position as mayor to persuade the magistrates to be lenient with her; grudgingly, they had only sentenced her to house arrest and four weeks of public service, the minimum penalty under Colony Law.

"All right. I understand." Chris was right; this time, she'd gone too far. Carlos ran a hand through his hair as he forced himself to calm down. "Is Lars with her?" Chris nodded. "Let me talk to them, please."

Like other buildings erected during the first year of the colony's existence, the stockade had recently been expanded. The original log cabin—where, ironically enough, Chris himself had been interred on several occasions before he'd straightened himself out—now served as his office; the new part was built of fieldstone and cement and served as the county jail. Unlocking a solid blackwood door, Chris led Carlos down a narrow corridor of stone cells fronted with iron bars; at the end of the corridor, he found his sister.

"Heard you coming a mile away." Marie lay on her back upon a small bunk, one arm cast across her forehead. "You should keep your voice down," she added, pointing to the tiny window above her. "I could hear you through there."

"If your ears are that good, then you know what we were talking about."

"I only said I heard your voice. Didn't say I know what you said." Marie sighed. "Okay, all right. I'm sorry. Won't do it again, I promise. Now would you get my shoes back? My feet are cold."

"Mine too." In the cell across from hers, Lars Thompson sat on his bunk, holding a blood-soaked tissue to his nose. "Hell, you think I'm going to kill myself just because I pounded some lumberjack?"

"Looks like that lumberjack got in a few pounds of his own," Carlos said, and Lars glowered at him with mutual disdain. He'd never liked Lars, not even when he'd been a member of Rigil Kent, and especially not since he'd become his sister's boyfriend. Lars had been in trouble before, too, yet his uncle was Clark Thompson, the leader of Blue Company during the Battle of New Florida, now a member of the Colonial Council. Like Marie, he'd also benefited from family influence.

"I understand you started it." Carlos folded his arms as he leaned against the bars of his cell. "Want to tell me why?"

Lars said nothing. "He was sticking up for the corps," Marie said, lacing her hands together behind her head. "This guy claimed that, if it hadn't been for Bob Lee—"

"Robert Lee." Carlos hated it when people called the captain by a nickname he'd detested when he was alive. Especially those who knew better.

"Whatever . . . if it hadn't been for him, there was no way we'd have taken down the Union. That we were outnumbered, outgunned . . ."

"And he was right," Carlos said. Lars started to object, but he stared him down. "Go on. You were saying . . . ?"

"So one thing came to another, and . . . aw, c'mon! Where was he when we crossed the East Channel? I asked him, and he said he was taking care of his wife and kid!"

"We asked for volunteers, not conscripts." She began to argue, but he raised his hand. "So you two decided to defend the honor of Rigil Kent. Is that it?"

"Hell, yeah!" Lars stood up, advanced toward the bars. Carlos could see the dried blood on the front of his shirt; how much of it was his own, and how much was someone else's, there was no way of knowing. "And what would you have done?"

"Oh, I don't know." Carlos shrugged. "Asked if he had a picture of his family? Offered him a drink? Proposed a toast to Captain Lee?" He ignored Lars, looked straight at Marie. "Anything but open his face with a broken bottle. I understand Wendy had to put some stitches in him. I wonder how he's going to explain that to his wife and kid the next time he sees them. He's just lucky he'll be able to see 'em at all."

"I wasn't trying to hurt him." Her voice became very small. "Just give him a scratch."

A sarcastic retort hovered on his lips. Instead, he regarded her for a few moments, once again wondering what had happened to his sister. He'd discussed this with Dr. Okada, in her capacity as chief physician; although psychology wasn't her specialty, it was her opinion that Marie was afflicted with some sort of personality disorder. She'd come of age waging guerrilla warfare. When she should have been engaging in the usual rites of puberty, instead she'd been learning how to shoot people with a high-powered rifle. Indeed, she'd even taken pleasure in her task; even if she wasn't sociopathic, her lack of remorse put her close to the edge.

Or maybe it was just that she and Lars didn't know what do with themselves now that the revolution was over. The remaining members of the Union Guard had long since left; the Coyote Federation was at peace. Everyone else had put down their guns and picked up hammers and nails. Even Lars's younger brother, Garth, who'd been bloodthirsty in his own right, had helped build the greenhouses that helped keep everyone alive. But perhaps there were bound to be a few who weren't ready to stop fighting, if only because that's all they'd ever learned how to do.

Nonetheless, he couldn't tolerate this behavior any longer. "I don't know what I'm going to do with you," he said, "but if you think you can just let this pass, you're—"

His com unit chirped just then. As much as he wanted to ignore it, he plucked it from his belt, held it to his ear. "Mayor's office," he said, trying to ignore Lars's sniggering.

"Carlos, it's Jaime from AirMed." That would be Jaime Hodge, a gyro pilot with Liberty's medical airlift team. *"We've just picked up someone from Bridgeton and we're flying him in. Touching down in Shuttlefield in ten minutes."*

Carlos let out his breath. He turned away from Marie's cell. "Jaime, can this wait? I'm in the middle of—"

"You may want to get over there. It's Manuel Castro . . . we've found him."

Carlos's hand trembled on the phone; he tightened his grip to keep from dropping it. The last person in the world he'd ever expected to turn up again . . .

"I understand," he said quietly. "Don't let anyone else know about this."

"Sure. He's in pretty bad shape. We've already called ahead to the infirmary, and they're sending down the ambulance to meet us."

"I'll meet you there." Carlos clicked off, then turned to Chris. "Something's come up. Keep 'em here until their arraignment. I'll inform the magistrates that we need to—"

"Carlos!" Marie jumped off the bed, rushed to the bars. "I'm your sister! You can't—"

"Sorry, kid, but you and your boyfriend have crossed the line." He reluctantly gazed back at her. "Nothing I can do."

"You're the mayor! You can . . . come back here!"

But he was already walking away, trying not to hear her voice as it rose to become an angry shriek that followed him down the cellblock. Even after he shut the door, he still heard the obscenities she shouted at him.

Manuel Castro lay motionless upon an examination table in the Shuttlefield infirmary's emergency room, his robotic form incongruous in a place meant for flesh-and-blood humans. Nonetheless, Wendy had propped a pillow beneath his head and draped a sheet over his body; Carlos found her with the Savant, her hands in the pockets of her smock.

"A couple of kids from Bridgeton found him near the bridge," she said. "Apparently he'd just dragged himself out the channel. They were beating on him when some adults spotted them. They got them to stop, then called AirMed."

"A couple of kids?" Carlos found that hard to believe.

"Well, he was in pretty sad shape to start with, being underwater for so long." She shrugged. "And since it sounds like they were recent immigrants, they had it in for the first Savant they'd seen since the revolution. I got the name of one of them. Tomas Conseco, from the *Spirit* . . ."

"Never mind." No point in trying to press charges; he wouldn't have been able to make them stick. Everyone had a grudge against the Union, even the children. "How's he doing?" Carlos peered at Castro. The Savant hadn't moved since he'd arrived. "Has he said anything?"

"Not since we got him here." Wendy gently pulled aside the sheet. "Right leg is broken . . . he'd tied a splint around it to stand upright . . . and the left eye is shattered. We should be able to fix the leg, but the eye may be irreplaceable." She shook her head. "What am I saying? This is beyond me. He needs a mechanic, not a doctor."

"All the same, I'm pleased to see you again, Wendy." Castro's voice, a modulated purr from his mouth grille, startled them; Wendy dropped the sheet, automatically stepped away. "You *are* Wendy Gunther, aren't you? It's been many years since the last time I saw you."

"Yes . . . yes, it is." She stammered a bit, trying to regain her composure. Carlos wondered why he'd remained quiet. Probably to assess the situation. "I'm surprised you recognize me."

"You've grown quite a bit, yet your voice is still much the same." Castro's own voice sounded reedy; the vocoder had been damaged during the months he'd spent underwater. He turned his head slightly, fixing his remaining eye upon Carlos. "But you, I don't recognize. Who may you be?"

"Carlos Montero, the mayor of—"

"Oh, my . . . Rigil Kent himself." A buzz from the grille that might have been laughter. "You don't know how long I've waited to meet you, Mr. Montero. The Matriarch was quite obsessed with finding you. And now you've become . . . what did you say you were the mayor of?"

"Liberty. And also Shuttlefield, since that's now part of Lee County."

"Lee County. And you're now its leader . . . elected, I take it." Carlos nodded. "Then it's reasonable to assume that Robert Lee is no longer with us?"

"No, he isn't. He—" Carlos stopped himself. "You've been gone a long time, Savant Castro. Things are quite a bit different now."

"So I take it. You know, when I was lieutenant governor, I sincerely doubt that a child would have dared to relieve himself upon me." Again, the odd buzz. "I take it that Luisa Hernandez is no longer the colonial governor and that there has been . . . shall we say, a change of government?"

"That's correct." No point in telling him, at least for the time being, that the Matriarch was dead as well. He'd learn these things in due course. "We never expected to see you again. You were reported lost in action during the Battle of Thompson's Ferry."

"Lost in action. That's one way of putting it, I suppose. And who said so, may I ask?"

"Umm . . ." Carlos had to search his memory. "Clark Thompson. He and his nephews said that they attempted to capture you, but that you fled from the scene. After that, you were never seen again."

"Thompson said that, did he?" The Savant turned his head to gaze up at the ceiling. "A slight embellishment of the truth. I guess he didn't want to admit to throwing me off his raft in the middle of the channel. You know, it took nearly three weeks for the ropes he'd used to tie my hands behind my back to loosen enough for me to free my hands? This may be a mechanical body, Carlos—or should I call you Rigil?—but three weeks is a long time to lie on your back in a hundred feet of water."

Carlos felt his face grow warm. Glancing at Wendy, he saw the look of horror in her eyes. "He never told us that," he said quietly. "He just said that you . . . ran away."

"Every war has its share of atrocities, Mayor Montero, and the victors always have the liberty of revising history. Why should this conflict be any different?" The Savant turned his head slightly, gazing at the white-washed blackwood walls, the rows of faux birch cabinets containing surgical instruments. "A lovely hospital, Dr. Gunther. I had a chance to look at it while your people were bringing me in. New, isn't it?"

"Built last summer. Savant Castro—"

"Please, call me Manny. I asked you to do so when we met aboard the *Glorious Destiny*." He paused. "Orifiel, Gabriel 17, C.Y. 03. And today is Camael, Uriel 46, C.Y. 06. My internal chronometer has remained functional, and my long-term memory is perfect. It's one of the few things that helped keep me sane."

Carlos nodded. He had to remember that, despite all appearances, there was a human mind within that mechanical body. Something that Clark Thompson and his boys had conveniently forgotten. "Savant Castro—Manny—a lot of things have changed. The Western Hemisphere Union is no longer in control of New Florida. In fact, the last Union starship departed almost five and a half months ago, along with the rest of the Guard. Since then, Coyote has experienced severe climate changes because of a volcano eruption on Midland. We managed to survive, but only because we built greenhouses to—"

"This is all fascinating, Mr. Mayor, and I'm sure I'll enjoy learning the rest of it in due time. But just now, one thing alone interests me."

Castro pushed aside the sheet, then used his arms to raise himself upright. Turning himself around, he allowed Wendy to help him sit up on the examination table. If not for his damaged leg, he could have walked away at any time.

"As you say," he continued, "ten months have passed. I went into the East Channel the lieutenant governor of a colony and came out a cripple at the mercy of a pair of brats. If the Union is no longer here, then I'm clearly both out of time and out of place. So the only question that matters: What are you going to do with me?"

Wendy said nothing. Carlos shook his head. "I can't tell you," he said at last. "The truth is, I don't know."

A hollow boom from somewhere in the fields just outside town, then a tiny rocket shot up into the night sky, its vapor trail forming an arc that carried it high above the rooftops of Liberty. A couple of seconds later it exploded, creating a red fire-blossom that flung sparks across the pale blue orb of Bear.

The crowds gathered in the streets applauded and shouted in delight, then watched as another skyrocket launched behind the first one. Carlos tried to remember the last time he'd seen fireworks; when he did, the memory came with a sharp pang of regret. July 4, 2070, the summer evening he and his family had been taken into custody by the Prefects. His last night on Earth, a lifetime ago . . .

"Aren't you enjoying this?" Wendy sat next to him on the porch of their house. Not far away, Susan played in the backyard with a few of her friends. First Landing Day wasn't until the next day, but the organizing committee had decided to schedule the fireworks a night early. The day itself would be marked by the crafts fair, a baseball game, a shag race, a concert by the Coyote Wind Ensemble, and, at the end of the day, the big dinner at the grange hall. Just like Independence Day back on Earth, only this time without mass arrests of dissident intellectuals.

"Who says I'm not?" Carlos reached for the jug of ale on the table between them, poured some more into his mug. "I think it's really pretty."

"Then why the frown?" Wendy took the jug from him, poured another drink for herself. "You're thinking about Marie, aren't you?"

Actually, he wasn't . . . or at least not at that moment. Oddly enough, he realized that his thoughts had been more upon Manuel Castro, about what he'd said earlier that afternoon. Marie and Lars would doubtless receive a stiff sentence for what they'd done today: at least six months in the stockade, plus hard time working on public service projects: road construction, laying sewage pipes, digging drainage ditches, the lousy jobs that no one wanted to do. Not that it would matter much to either of them, at least in the long run. Ever since the Union Guard had been ousted and Chris had overhauled the Proctors, crime had become infrequent enough that townspeople remembered who the perpetrators were and what they'd done. There were people in Liberty whom everyone remembered being bullies and thugs from the days of the squatter camps, and—almost universally—they were distrusted and disliked. So even after Marie and Lars served their sentence, they'd return to the community as ostracized members . . . and Carlos foresaw that such treatment would just make them even more bitter than they'd been before.

Even so, there was always a chance that they'd eventually be accepted again, just as he'd been many years ago after he returned from his time alone on the Great Equatorial River. On the other hand, Manny Castro would never be a part of the community. He couldn't change what he was, and as such he was a living reminder to everyone of the Union occupation of Coyote. The tents and shacks of Shuttlefield were gone, replaced by rows of wood-frame houses built during the course of the spring and summer, but no one who once lived there was likely to forget that Savant Castro had once served as the Matriarch's right-hand man.

They'd done well these past few months; indeed, even better than anyone had expected. Two days after the last Union shuttle lifted off and the bodies of the dead—including Captain Lee—had been laid to rest, an ad hoc committee convened at the grange hall to formulate survival plans for the colonies on New Florida and Midland. Everyone knew that time was of the essence; the eruption of Mt. Bonestell meant that Coyote's northern hemisphere would experience cold temperatures for at least four to six months, with a resultant loss of crops. So the first priority was building greenhouses; with available timber on New Florida at a premium, it was decided that the Garcia Narrows Bridge had to be repaired as soon as possible. Once that was done . . .

Carlos watched as another skyrocket bloomed above town. Everything had fallen into place after that. The bridge was quickly repaired, enabling teams of loggers to journey across the East Channel to the dense rain forests of Midland; blackwood, rough-bark, and faux birch were felled and hauled by shags to the lumberyards of Forest Camp and Bridgeton, where they were milled into wood planks for the construction of enormous greenhouses and solar-heated sheds for the livestock. Now that the war was over, there was no shortage of colonists to assist in any crash program; for weeks on end, the air had been filled with the sounds of nails being hammered into wood as structures half the size of football fields rose up in the place once occupied by squatter camps.

The towns of Defiance and New Boston received lumber in exchange for sending men to join the labor force. Although the provisional government extended an open invitation to the Midland settlers to return to New Florida, many preferred to stay where they were. Only Shady Grove, the small town that once existed beneath the shadow of Mt. Bonestell, remained abandoned, buried beneath volcanic ash.

Even as the greenhouses were rising and the surplus lumber was being used for the construction of new homes, the Coyote Federation was being formed, and just as foul-smelling communal outhouses were being leveled to make way for sewage pipes and septic systems, social collectivism was replaced by democracy, with individual rights guaranteed by the statutes of the Liberty Compact.

It was a long, hard summer, with some days in Muriel so cold that snow had fallen from leaden skies and ice had formed along the creek banks. Yet no one froze to death in a tent; everyone had to tighten their belts a little, but no one starved. Although there were quite a few complaints, no one loaded their guns and marched on the grange hall, where the newly elected mayor of Liberty spent every waking hour struggling to figure out how to keep several thousand people alive.

At long last, the skies had begun to clear, the days had become warm again. It wouldn't last long—a brief Indian summer before the autumn equinox only a few weeks away—but they would survive another winter. And, indeed, perhaps even come out better than they had been before.

Another skyrocket; the crowds yelled in response. Carlos was blind to it all, though, and deaf to the thunderclaps and shouting. "Excuse me," he said, standing up from his rocker. "Just need to stretch my legs."

"Sure." Wendy watched as he walked down off the porch, ignoring the children playing tag nearby. She'd become accustomed to his long silences. "Take your time."

How far they'd come. Clean streets; no more trash along the sides of the road. Warm houses; the original log cabins still stood, yet he and Wendy were among the few who still lived in them. A long row of wind turbines just outside Shuttlefield providing electrical power to everyone. A new infirmary, with free medical treatment guaranteed for all. A schoolhouse was going up soon. And yet . . .

It's yours. . . .

Once again, Robert Lee's last words came back to haunt him. He might have taken Lee's place, yet he could never fill the long shadow he'd left behind. He'd picked up the torch, but what good was it if he couldn't use it to shed light?

Oh, his people would survive, all right. And now that the clouds had parted, there was hope of a short growing season before another long winter came upon them. But it wasn't enough just to survive, was it? If their existence upon this world—indeed, their reasons for coming to Coyote in the first place—were to mean something, then it had to be for something more than keeping a roof over their heads and food in their bellies. Even the most brutal dictatorship can guarantee that; freedom had to stand for something more.

Meanwhile, his own sister sat in a jail cell across from her lover, two malcontents with nothing else to do with their time than to pick fights. What did freedom mean to them? And there was Manuel Castro, once thought to be dead, now returned to life, only to find himself alone in a world in which he had no place. What good was freedom to him?

A long time ago, Carlos had sought freedom. A canoe, a rifle, a cook pot, a tent . . . that was all he'd needed. Three months alone on the Great Equatorial River, and he'd managed to get as far as the Meridian Archipelago. To this day, no one else had explored Coyote as much as he had; the war had prevented it. And there was an entire world out there. . . .

From somewhere close by, his ears picked up a musical sound: a lilting melody, carried by a dozen flutes in harmony. Allegra DiSilvio, rehearsing her ensemble for the concert. Chris's mother would be playing with them; under Allegra's tutelage, Sissy had become an accomplished musician, and to see her today one would never believe that she'd once been a hermit living on the outskirts of Shuttlefield. Indeed, lately she'd been spending a lot of time with Ben Harlan. It only made sense; both had suffered the loss of loved ones since they'd come to Coyote, and both had seen the darker side of the human soul. And just last month, much to Carlos's surprise, Allegra had moved in with Chris. She was nearly old enough to be his mother, but apparently the age difference meant little to either of them. Chris had been the first person on Coyote to show her any kindness, after all, and on this world, such tenderness went a long way.

So Chris had taken his mother's best friend as his lover, while Sissy herself had found someone to replace his father. It was a strange relationship, but . . . Carlos smiled at the thought. New families appearing to replace ones that had been lost. On the frontier, the heart finds its own way.

The music faltered, stopped for a few moments, then started again. "Soldier's Joy," an ancient song from the American Civil War. Captain Lee's ancestor had probably marched his troops into combat with this tune, hundreds of years ago. Back when America had been a frontier, just as Coyote was now.

Inspiration stopped him in his tracks. A crazy idea, possibly irresponsible . . .

But perhaps, just perhaps . . .

Clark Thompson met him outside the vehicle shed, down by Sand Creek near the boathouse. Dark circles beneath his eyes testified that he hadn't slept well last night; Carlos had little doubt that he'd stayed up late, discussing the Mayor's proposal with his wife and younger nephew.

"They're waiting inside," Carlos said as Thompson approached. "Chris brought them down from the stockade just a few minutes ago. I haven't said anything to them about this yet." He hesitated. "It's your call, y'know. You can always call it off."

"I know that." Thompson was not only Lars's legal guardian, but also a member of the Colonial Council. He could veto this with just one word. "Before I tell you what I've decided, let me ask you one thing. Do you really think this is the right thing to do?"

Carlos didn't answer at once. Instead, he gazed at the first amber light of dawn, just beginning to break in the east. He remembered when he'd set out on his own, in a small canoe he'd built with his own hands, on a long journey that would eventually take him nearly halfway around the world. That morning had been almost exactly like this one.

"I can't . . . I don't know." He owed Clark an honest answer. "If you are asking me if I think this is wise, then I have to ask if you think it's wiser to let them sit in the stockade till next spring."

"At least then they'd be safe. We'd know where they were."

"Perhaps, but I don't believe that'll solve anything. They'll just come out more hardened than before, and we'll just have the same problem again. This way, maybe they'll grow up a little . . . and we might learn something as well."

Thompson nodded, "That's sort of what I've been thinking, too. Of course, it's a hell of a risk."

"They're used to taking risks. Maybe that's the problem. They've lived on the edge so long they can't cope with peace and quiet. And it's not like we're asking them to do something they haven't—"

"It is, but"—Thompson looked down at the ground, shuffled his feet a bit—"y'know, I can't but wonder if this isn't partly my fault. I made that boy grow up tough. Hell, I made him shove Castro over the side of that raft. I didn't know he'd, y'know, turn out this way."

Carlos bit his lip. He thought of how things could have been different with his sister. Marie should have never been allowed to carry a gun; she was too damn young. "None of us knew. We were caught in something we didn't know how to control. We got what we wanted, and now we're paying the price."

"Yeah, well . . ." Thompson shrugged. "And you say the magistrates approve?"

"I spoke with them last night, after I dropped by to talk to you and Molly. They said that if you gave your approval, then this was acceptable to them as well."

Thompson said nothing for a few moments. At last he looked up. "Very well, Mr. Mayor, I say yes."

Carlos let out his breath. "Thank you, sir. Do you want to come in with me while I . . . ?"

He firmly shook his head. "No. I don't want Lars trying to talk his way out through me. And maybe it's just as well if I turn my back on him."

There was a trace of tears in the older man's eyes. Carlos realized that the decision must be tougher on him that he cared to admit. "I understand," he said quietly. "I'll let you know how it turns out."

Thompson nodded, then, without another word, turned and walked away, heading back to his place. Carlos watched him go, then he opened the door and walked in.

The vehicle shed had been built by the Carpenters' Guild during the Union occupation; a large, barnlike structure, it contained most of the ground vehicles left behind by the Guard. Skimmers of various makes and sizes, a couple of hover bikes, the disassembled fuselage of a gyro that had been cannibalized for spare parts. Someone had switched on the lights; near the front of the room, Lars and Marie sat on a couple of crates, with Chris and another Proctor standing guard nearby, stun guns inside open holsters on their belts.

"Stand up," Carlos said, shutting the door behind him. "We've got something to talk about."

"Not till we've had breakfast." Marie glared at him like a petulant child and didn't move from where she was sitting. "You're supposed to feed us, y'know."

"Was that my uncle out there? I thought I heard him." Lars lifted his head, raised his voice. "Hey! Uncle Clark! Come in here and tell this fascist to get us some food!"

"Your uncle doesn't want to speak to you." Carlos kept his voice even. "To tell the truth, he's turned his back on you." He looked straight at Marie. "And I'm about to do the same."

Her mouth fell open. "What are you—"

"Shut up."

"Aw, c'mon. We haven't eaten since—"

"I said, *shut up!*"

His shout rang from the sides of the craft parked around them. Marie visibly flinched, and the smirk disappeared from Lars's face. "This isn't a breakfast meeting," Carlos went on, stepping a littler closer. "No coffee and biscuits for you two, and no one leaves this building until we're done. And I thought I told you to get to your feet . . . so do it, now!"

Marie stood up, her legs shaking. When Lars didn't move, Carlos glanced at Chris. The Chief Proctor stepped forward, pulling his stun gun from his belt. Seeing this from the corner of his eye, Lars hastily rose from the crate, yet he wasn't done giving him lip. "Class act, Mr. Mayor.

Out-of-the-way place, no one around to watch, the maggies nowhere in sight. And two blueshirts to do the dirty work." He glanced at Marie. "I told you the power's gone to his head."

Marie wasn't nearly so brave. "Carlos," she murmured, her mouth trembling with newfound fear, "I'm your sister. You can't let them do this. It's not right."

For an instant, he saw once more the little girl who used to bug him to read her bedtime stories when their father was too busy with his work. But she was an adult now—twenty years old—and very close to becoming someone he'd never recognize again. He had to do this, for her own sake.

"Whatever you think I'm going to do, you're wrong." Carlos lowered his voice. "No one's going to touch you. You're going to walk out of here without a scratch. Which is more than I can say for the poor guy you attacked yesterday."

"Well, when we see the maggies—" Lars started.

"You're not seeing the magistrates. There's not going to be a court date for you—or at least not unless you insist. But I've met with them already, and I've been told that, if they find you guilty, you'll spend the next six months in the stockade." He peered more closely at him. "Six months Coyote-time, and Chris here will make sure you and Marie are assigned to cells as far apart as possible. The only time you'll see the sun is when they let you out to clean septic tanks and dig ditches, and in the middle of winter that can be a real bitch."

"You'd do that, wouldn't you?" Marie's eyes were cold.

"You bet. I'll see to it personally that your time is as hard as I can make it." He looked at Chris. "You with me on this?"

"Oh, yeah." Chris gave them his most callous grin. "I've got a lot of lousy jobs for y'all to handle. And it's funny how often I forget to turn the lights off or change the sheets."

"On the other hand," Carlos went on, "there's always an alternative. Something a couple of hardcases like you are well suited for."

He sauntered past them to a Union Guard patrol skimmer parked nearby. "You've seen this kind of machine before. Marie, I remember that you once identified it for me . . . an Armadillo AC-IIb. Just like the one we captured on Goat Kill Creek."

"Uh-huh. Even got a chance to operate it." She gave the skimmer a passing glance. "Let me guess. You want us to clean it."

"No, I want you to take it."

She stared at him. "You want us to . . . what?"

"You heard me. I want you and Lars to take it." Carlos slapped his hand on its armored hull. "Drive it out of here. Leave, go away. Go exploring. We'll equip you with one month's rations, two rifles and ammo, a medkit, sleeping bags, tents, lamps . . . whatever you need to survive. Even a satphone so you can report in. The Union left a comsat network in orbit, so you'll be able to keep in touch."

"I don't . . . I don't . . ." Marie shook her head in confusion. "I mean . . ."

"What's the catch?" Lars regarded the skimmer with astonishment. "I mean, you can't just be . . . y'know, cutting us loose like this without some strings attached."

"Oh, there's strings attached all right." Leaning against the skimmer, Carlos held up a finger. "First, you can't stay on New Florida or head for Midland. If you're seen by any of our scouting parties, or try to enter any of the settlements, then you'll be arrested and sent back here. For the next six months. After that, you're free to return."

"But if you're only giving us one month of rations—"

"Then I guess you'll have live off the land. But you two spent time in Rigil Kent . . . you know how to hunt and fish." Carlos held up another finger. "Second, once every forty-eight hours, you use the radio to report to me personally. Tell me where you are . . . and, more importantly, what you've seen. I don't care if it's nothing but swamp or grassland or another hill, I want to know what you've found out there."

"You want us to just"—Maria waved a hand in some imagined direction—"go exploring. Wander around. Look for stuff."

"That's right. In the five years we've been here, no one has yet crossed the West Channel to see what's on Great Dakota, or gone north to check out Medsylvania, or seen the Northern River. The war's kept us too busy. So you're going to be our scouts. Do that for the next six months, and you can consider your sentences commuted as time served for the benefit of the Coyote Federation."

"Uh-huh. Just the two of us." Lars gave Marie a lascivious grin. "Oh, I think we can go along with . . ."

"No. Not just the two of you. I think you need the mature guidance of a responsible adult." Stepping away from the skimmer, Carlos turned toward the rear of the shed. "Manny? If you'd join us, please?"

The Savant detached himself from beneath the shadows of the skimmer behind which he'd been hiding. He limped slightly upon his left leg, restored to near-complete motor function by a couple of machinists, and he remained blind in one eye, yet his body had been cleaned up, and once again he wore the black robe that had been taken from him by Clark Thompson.

"It'd be my pleasure." His left eye gleamed as he turned his head toward Lars. "I believe we've already met. Thank you for such a delightful swim. I thoroughly enjoyed it."

"Uh-uh!" Lars backed away. "No way I'm going with this . . . this—"

"Yes, you are," Carlos said. "Not only that, but I expect you to treat him with all due respect, because if he doesn't come back with you—"

"I assure you, Mr. Mayor, I intend to survive this trip." Castro hobbled toward Lars, extended a claw from beneath his robe. "We have much to talk about, Mr. Thompson. Or may I call you Lars? My friends call me Manny."

Marie turned to Carlos. "You're not giving us a choice, are you?"

"Sure I am." Carlos touched her shoulder. "Come here."

He led her away from the others, shaking his head at the nearby blueshirt when he tried to follow them. "This is how you're going to grow up," he murmured once they were alone. "You're getting freedom, and all the responsibility that comes with it. It's the same choice our parents had when they decided to come here. It's the choice I had many years ago. And now it's your turn."

"I . . . I don't . . . !" The corners of her eyes glistened. "I don't know what to do. I don't know where to go."

"Nobody does," he said softly. "We just have to make it up as we go along." He gave her a hug, kissed her gently on the cheek. "It's your world now. Go find it . . . and come back safe."

And then, before he could give himself a chance to reconsider, he re-

leased her. Turning his back on his sister, Carlos walked away, not looking back until after he'd shut the door behind him.

Morning had come upon Liberty, cool and quiet, with a warm breeze
drifting in from the south. Roosters crowed within pens, answered by
the barking of dogs, the nagging of billy goats. He could smell breakfast
being prepared within a thousand kitchens, hear the faint sounds of
townspeople rising to do their chores. Another day upon Coyote had begun.

Tucking his hands in his pockets, Carlos Montero began walking back
toward town. Ready to see what awaited him today, in the land of the
free, the home of the brave.

COYOTE CALENDAR

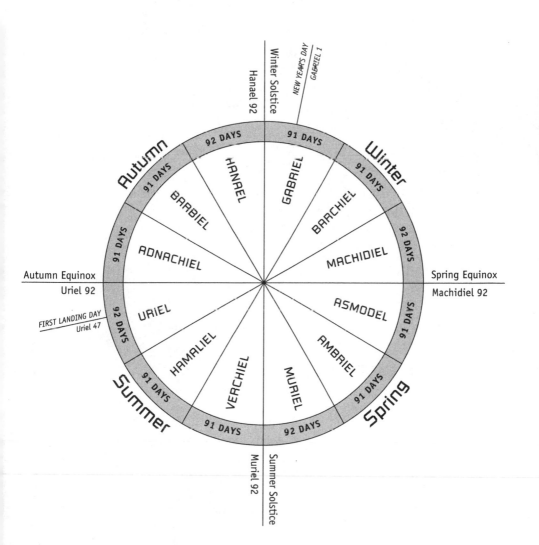

ACKNOWLEDGMENTS

The author wishes to express his gratitude to his editor, Ginjer Buchanan, and his literary agent, Martha Millard; to Gardner Dozois and Sheila Williams, for publishing an early version of this novel as a series of stories in *Asimov's Science Fiction*; to Judith Klien-Dial, Ron Miller, and Horace "Ace" Marchant, for their support and advice; and to his wife, Linda Steele, for keeping him sane during another journey into the wilderness.

October 2001–April 2003
Whately, Massachusetts

SOURCES

(Author's note: For additional citations,
consult the Sources page of *Coyote*.)

Berry, Adrian. *The Giant Leap: Mankind Heads for the Stars*. New York: Tor
Books, 2000.

Fisher, Richard V., Grant Heiken, and Jeffrey B. Hulen. *Volcanoes: Crucibles of
Change*. Princeton University Press, 1997.

Harris, John. *Wonderwoman and Superman: The Ethics of Human Biotechnology*.
Oxford University Press, 1992.

Macauley, David. *Building Big*. Boston: Houghton Mifflin Company, 2000.

Rampino, Michael R. "Supereruptions as a Threat to Civilisations on Earth-
Like Planets." *Icarus*, 156: 562–569 (2002).

Slater, Lauren. "Dr. Daedalus." *Harper's Magazine*, July 2001.